THE PATRIOT

By Pearl S. Buck

THE PATRIOT

THIS PROUD HEART

FIGHTING ANGEL

THE EXILE

A HOUSE DIVIDED

THE MOTHER

THE FIRST WIFE AND OTHER STORIES

SONS

THE GOOD EARTH

EAST WIND: WEST WIND

*

ALL MEN ARE BROTHERS
[SHUI HU CHUAN]
TRANSLATED FROM THE CHINESE

THE PATRIOT

by *Pearl S. Buck*

THE JOHN DAY COMPANY

New York

PART ONE

I

THERE lived in the city of Shanghai in the fifteenth year of the Chinese Republic and in the western year nineteen hundred and twenty-six, a rich banker whose surname was Wu, who had two sons. His family for several generations had been wealthy, and for at least three had been known in the life of the city, although in differing ways. Mr. Wu held the family's present position because he was the head of the Great China Bank, which had branches all through central and southern China. He had as a young man gone abroad to Japan and to Europe to visit banks, and upon his return he had at once begun to build the bank which later became so powerful in the new republic.

But his father, old General Wu, had nothing to do with banks except, as a military man, to look at them hopefully in times of the war in which nevertheless he never fought. General Wu, in his youth during the late Manchu dynasty, had been sent abroad, not by his parents, who were indeed filled with terror at the idea so that his mother wept and refused food until he was allowed, by special imperial decree, to delay his going long enough to give her a grandson. Only when a red and crying child, now Mr. Wu the banker, was placed in her old arms immediately after his birth, did she allow General Wu, then an impetuous and handsome lad of eighteen, to go abroad. He was sent with several other young men, by the Emperor, during the brief years when it seemed that the dynasty would reform its old and obsolete army.

But the reforms were never made. All the world knows that the strong and powerful Empress Dowager overruled her weak son, and put down his reforms, and General Wu found himself without money after less than two years in Berlin. His father sent him enough to come home, and it was at that time that the young officer perceived the importance of banks. Bankers, he decided, were the men who ruled nations, not emperors or kings, and he made up his mind forthwith that his two-year-old son should become a banker.

And he was able to do as he had decided. Before his ship reached the docks of Shanghai, his old father had died, and his mother, unable to linger after, killed herself by swallowing her jade and gold rings. General Wu, therefore, found himself at the head of the Wu family, since he was the only son, and its huge fortunes were his, as well as the ancestral houses and lands, which were not in Shanghai but far away in the inner province of Hunan.

The money was stored in curious places. Old Mr. Wu, deceased, had never understood or trusted banks. He looked upon them as a purely foreign scheme for extortion. His large sums of cash were therefore in the shape of silver shoes, which he kept in boxes under his own roof. General Wu's first act was to deposit all these silver shoes in the vaults of various banks. His next was to use many of them in the building of a great square brick house in the French section of Shanghai, which was then the fashionable place to live. He hired a young French architect to build the house, and also to have it furnished. When it stood completed he moved his family into it, though it looked like a wealthy house in Paris and was not in the least Chinese. When his wife complained of its discomforts, such for instance as the thick carpets which meant that nothing could be dropped upon the floors, he reminded her that thousands of women in foreign countries had to put up with such discomforts. Thereafter he paid no attention to her. He lived in the house peacefully enough for forty years, while his eldest son grew up and became a banker and his other sons were born and grew up and went their ways. His daughters he never included in the number of his children, although he performed his duty and married them to well-to-do men, and having done his duty, ceased to think of them further. His eldest son continued to live with him and his aging wife in the large French house, and at the proper time was married to a well-educated young Shanghai lady, and by her he had his two sons, I-ko and I-wan.

Old General Wu was perfectly satisfied when these two grandsons were born. He had lived a peaceful life and had never been in a war nor seen a battle. But he was called General because the Emperor, long dead, had sent him to a German military school, and also because of his great wealth. Moreover, he possessed several uniforms, which he had ordered a Shanghai tailor to copy for him from the uniforms of an English general, an American admiral, and a French marshal when these officers visited Shanghai at various times and inspected the troops of their countries stationed there. Old General Wu was a handsome figure in any one of the uniforms, though the one he wore most often was a combination of them made after his own design, with an added touch of the Russian cossack. He did not, of course, wear these uniforms at home. There he wore soft old robes of heavy brocaded silks and satins and on his feet velvet shoes. But the uniforms hung in his closet and were brushed by a manservant at every change of season, when also all his medals, some of which he had bought and some of which had been presented to him by different persons who wanted money, were polished and put away again.

In this house I-ko and I-wan grew to young manhood with

fair happiness, their chief trouble being only in the difference of their two natures. For I-wan had always been the favorite with the whole household, grandparents, parents, and servants. I-ko, the elder, was a pouting child, easily spoiled, who turned, it seemed naturally, to mischief and malice. But I-wan was cheerful and tender, and the same indulgence which had been so ruinous to I-ko seemed not to hurt him at all. He had reached his eighteenth year and had got into only one difficulty, which he had never had to explain to his grandparents and parents because they knew nothing about it. He had been arrested and put in jail. It is true that he remained there only one night. As soon as it became known whose son he was, the head jailer himself rushed into his cell, the sweat pouring down his face.

"Sir, forgive me for being a fool," he cried to I-wan, who was sitting on three bricks piled one on top of the other in a corner of a crowded and filthy cell. "But why didn't you tell me, sir, that your father is Mr. Wu, the banker, and your grandfather the old General?"

"If I deserve to go to jail, I deserve to go to jail," I-wan replied with majesty.

He was the only one among the prisoners who wore a silk robe, and the ends were draggled with filth. A young man who was in the cell with him had asked him scornfully, "Why don't you tuck up your wonderful robe?" He was a rough-looking young man in a government-school uniform of cheap blue cotton. I-wan himself went to a private school kept by missionaries for the sons of rich men. There they wore no uniforms, but always silk robes.

"Because I have better ones," I-wan had replied.

It was at this moment that the jailer came in. When he heard what I-wan said, his face fell into still more alarm.

"Don't be angry with me, young lord!" he begged. "Why, your

father could have me thrown out of this pleasant jail if he liked! I am a poor man. Come out and I will hire a horse carriage and have you returned to your father unharmed. And when you reach home, plead for me, young sir, I beg you!"

I-wan would have liked to refuse proudly. But he was only eighteen and he was tired and hungry, and the cell was foul. His cellmates, moreover, were a sullen and dirty-looking group of men of different sorts and ages, and of them all only the young student in the uniform seemed good. He rose, therefore, but with dignity, and went out.

But as the frightened jailer was about to lock the iron gate again I-wan paused.

"Wait!" he commanded. "Let that student come out, also."

"That I cannot," the jailer said. "He is a revolutionist."

"So am I," I-wan declared.

It was true that he had been arrested in the foreign school as a revolutionist. Soldiers had come in and searched them as they searched all students anywhere they found them. I-wan had been walking alone and as it happened reading a book then very popular among all the students and written by a German named Karl Marx. Since he had always done as he liked, he made no secret of it when the soldiers demanded what he was reading.

"Karl Marx," he said, scornfully, for what did soldiers know?

But to his amazement they had at once arrested him and dragged him to prison and thrown him into the cell, where he had raged all night long, at first aloud, until the other prisoners had snarled at him to be quiet so they could sleep.

"The son of the great banker Wu could never be a revolutionist," the jailer now declared.

But I-wan stamped his foot.

"I will certainly see that you lose your job!" he shouted.

The little jailer turned a paler yellow.

II

"But how shall I explain?" he wailed.

"Say I commanded it," I-wan said. "Say that I personally am responsible."

While this was going on the young man came and stood at the door, his square strong face unmoved, but his eyes brilliant and watchful.

"Oh heaven!" the jailer wailed. "Oh mercy!"

But I-wan snatched the keys from his hand and himself opened the gate while the jailer moaned and pulled his own hair.

"You can say you know nothing about it," I-wan said, and held the door with his body and his foot only wide enough for the young man, who came out at once and stood waiting. Then I-wan locked the gate again and gave the key back to the jailer, and he touched the young man on the arm and they walked away together, while behind them the dirty and cowed faces of the prisoners pressed against the bars.

The two young men did not speak until they had climbed into the old horse carriage which the jailer called.

"I hope, sir," he begged of I-wan, "that you will remember my plight if I am asked—"

"Let me know," I-wan said curtly, and gave the horse driver the number of his father's house.

They were already in the carriage, but at this the young man turned to him.

"You must know I cannot go there."

"Why not?" I-wan asked.

"I am really a revolutionist," the young man declared, smiling curiously.

"Are you?" I-wan asked. "But I have always wanted to find one."

"There are plenty of us in the university," the young man said lightly. And then before I-wan could stop him, he had leaped

12

from the low slowly-moving carriage. "My name," he said quickly, "is Liu En-lan, and I thank you for freedom." He ran then into the crowd before I-wan could lay hold upon him, but he turned once, smiled a wide bright smile, and was gone. There was nothing for I-wan to do but to go home.

When he entered the house he found he had not even been missed. Often he came in late when he went to the theater, which was his usual amusement place since he was especially fond of plays about the heroes of ancient times, such as one found in stories of good robbers, who robbed the rich and gave to the poor. Two or three times a week he went to these plays and came home near dawn and opened the door with his own key.

And in this house everyone slept late. Day after day he rose and ate his breakfast alone and went to school, having seen no one except servants. Now he went upstairs to his own room. It was exactly as it had always been. He went to the bed and tossed it as though he had slept in it. Then he took off his clothes, bathed himself and put on over his white silk undergarments a plain robe of blue silk. He had scarcely done this before there was a cough at the door, it opened, and his mother's bondmaid, Peony, came in with tea as she did every morning.

"I am late," she said hurriedly when she saw him already dressed. "I overslept myself."

"It doesn't matter," he replied. "I am not going any more to that foreign school."

"What now?" she asked, surprised, setting down the tray.

"I am going to the public university," he announced.

"But that school!" she cried. "Anybody can go to it!"

"Therefore I can go," he declared.

"Your father won't let you," Peony retorted, "nor your grand-father."

"Then I won't eat," I-wan said with energy.

13

"Which means," she said mischievously, "I must carry food in here under my coat as I have before when you wanted something. Shame, I-wan! It's I-ko's trick!"

They both laughed.

But that was how I-wan came to go to the National University, and how he came to know the revolutionists and to become one of them. For, surely enough, as soon as he stopped eating, his mother flew to his father and his grandmother assailed his grandfather, and within fewer than four days he was wearing a uniform exactly like the one Liu En-lan wore, except that his mother insisted that it be made of the best English broadcloth and cut by his grandfather's tailor. On this I-wan yielded, since after all it was but a small compromise and it gave his parents and grandparents some feeling of satisfaction in their authority. "At least," they said, examining the new uniform when he put it on, "it is very becoming to him."

"Come here," his grandmother cried, "let me feel your cheeks!"

And still for compromise he bent and let her feel his cheeks with her dry old hands.

"Little meat dumpling!" she murmured.

And he endured this, too, because, after all, he had what he really wanted.

Two years later, in this fifteenth year of the republic, I-wan, without anyone of his family dreaming such a thing could be, had become one of those revolutionists whose secret groups met in every school in China. He lived two wholly separate lives, his old life as the younger son in a rich house, and this other life as a passionate young man among other such young men, dreaming of overthrowing the new republic and setting up a still newer one, since they were as rebellious against the republic as their fathers had been against the throne. Neither life had anything to do with the other. None of his schoolmates had even seen the big square house where he lived, until one day in early autumn, he stopped on his way from school at a sweet-shop near his home. When he came out again someone passed him and called his name. It was Peng Liu, one of the band of revolutionists, and the only one he did not like, though Peng Liu was of no importance. He was the son of a small shopkeeper in the city, a small mean-looking fellow with narrow eyes and a loose mouth through which he perpetually breathed with a foul breath. No one liked him, though these things, after all, he could not help.

"I-wan!" Peng Liu called. "Where are you going?"

"Home," I-wan replied, and wished he had thought of a lie, because now Peng Liu sauntered along with him and there was nothing to do with him until they reached the big house. He made up his mind, however, that he would not ask Peng Liu to come in. Peng Liu would never understand why, though a revolutionist, he lived in this house, and he would not like him the better for seeing its luxuries. Besides, why was Peng Liu here at all? His home was far away in the Chinese part of the city. Had Peng Liu purposely followed him?

He stopped at the gate and shifted his school books. He looked about him quickly and then he glanced at the windows of the house to see if I-ko might be there watching him. He did not want I-ko to see Peng Liu. He would immediately suspect Peng Liu's poor garments and meager, sickly face. But there was no one at the windows, and there were few people loitering in the hot sunshine of an early September afternoon in Shanghai. So he said in a low clear voice, "Until tomorrow, comrade!"

"Until tomorrow," Peng Liu said quickly.

"Coward!" I-wan thought with scorn. "He is afraid to say comrade even when no one is near."

But Peng Liu lingered. "Is this where you live?" he asked

15

with wonder. He looked up at the huge square brick house with columned porticos.

"I can't help it," I-wan said. "My grandfather built it and my father lives with him, and naturally as yet I live with my father."

"It's a fine foreign house," Peng Liu said.

But I-wan despised the humility in his voice. He thought, "Peng Liu would like to come in, but I won't ask him. Besides, I-ko would despise him."

"Good-by," he repeated aloud.

"Good-by," Peng Liu replied.

I-wan turned away sharply and ran up the marble steps and let himself quietly into the house. But he could not be quiet enough for his grandmother when she was not drowsy with opium. And because she loved him so well she tried every day not to be drowsy when he came home from school.

He was late today because of a secret meeting and because after it he had been hungry and stopped at the sweet-shop and that was why her voice was impatient when she called, "I-wan, come here! Where have you been?"

At that moment Peony came out of his grandmother's room and took his books and his hat. She framed her soft red lips into voiceless words.

"She is very cross!"

He shrugged and frowned.

"Coming, Grandmother!" he answered. "Has I-ko come home?" he asked Peony. He waited until he saw her shake her head, and then went into his grandmother's room.

Every day since he was six years old and starting school he had to come straight to his grandmother as soon as he reached home, and every day he hated it more. He was sullen whenever he thought of it, that this old woman was waiting for him and that he must come to her. In their secret meetings when they talked of throwing off family bondage, he had sprung to his feet and shouted, "Until we are free of our families we can never accomplish anything!" He was thinking of his own family, but especially of his grandmother.

"Here I am, Grandmother," he said sulkily.

But she never noticed his sulkiness. She was sitting on the edge of the big, square couch. The lamp and pipe were ready for her use. She had only been waiting for him.

"Come here," she said. So he went a little nearer. "Come here, so I can feel you," she insisted.

He had to go near her, though this was what he hated most. She put out her thin long-nailed hand and took his hand in both of hers.

"Your palms are wet!" she exclaimed.

"It is very hot outside," he said.

"You've been hurrying," she scolded. "How often have I told you never to hurry? It destroys the life force."

"I like to walk quickly," he declared.

"It is not what you like," she said. "You have to consider the family. You are my grandson."

No, this was what he hated most of all, this sense that to her he was valuable only because he was her grandson, a person to carry on her family.

"I must sometimes do what I like," he said sullenly.

She gripped his wrist suddenly between her thumb and forefinger.

"You are always doing what you like," she said loudly. "You think of no one but yourself—it is this generation! I-ko is the same. He has not come near me all day."

Then immediately she was afraid she had made him angry,

17

so she reached for her comfit box with one hand, still clinging to him with the other, and gave him a candied date.

He would have liked to refuse it, but when he saw it, he felt hungry against his will. He was always hungry! So he took it, frowning, and ate it.

"There," she said, laughing. "I don't give these dates to anyone but you." She began caressing his arm under his sleeve. "They are good for the blood—no one gets them but you and me. Although—" she raised her voice a little so that Peony waiting in the hall might hear, "I know that miserable girl slave steals them when I am asleep!"

"I, Mistress?" Peony's silvery tranquil voice answered through the open door. "Never, Mistress!"

"Yes, she does," the old woman said to him. "She steals everything she can, that girl. We've had her eleven years but she has no gratitude. She was only seven when we bought her and she was already a thief."

He did not answer. He was not going to defend Peony and have his grandmother accuse him of wickedness. He had made that mistake before. He pulled his hand away.

"Grandmother, I have a whole English paper to write before tomorrow," he said.

"Ah, yes," she said quickly, "you mustn't sit up too late."

"Good night, Grandmother," he said, bowing.

"No, not good night," she said coaxingly. "Come in again before you sleep."

"But you'll be lying stupid under that stuff," he said rudely.

"No," she said eagerly, "no, tell me when you are coming and I will be awake for you."

"I can't," he replied. "How can I say when I shall be finished with all those books?"

She sighed. Then her eyes fell on the opium pipe and she wavered.

"Well, that is true," she murmured. She waited an instant. "Peony!" she called.

"Coming," Peony answered.

She came into the room on quiet silk-shod feet and helped the old lady to lie down and began to prepare the lamp. I-wan had not gone.

"I put your books on your table," she said to him.

The old lady's eyes were already shut.

"You ought to be ashamed of yourself!" I-wan whispered. "Pandering to her like that!"

Peony opened her black apricot-shaped eyes widely.

"I have to do what I'm told!" she said. He frowned and shook his head and marched to the door. Then he glanced back. She was stirring the sticky stuff with a tiny silver spoon. But she was not looking at it. She was waiting mischievously for him, and when she caught his glance she stuck her red tongue far out of her mouth. He slammed the door on the sight.

But there was no shutting out that sweet sick smell of opium. Upstairs in his own room he threw his windows wide but it was still no use. The evening air was windless and the smell hung through the house, faint yet penetrating. All his life he had smelled it and hated it. In an old Chinese house courtyard walls would have cut it off, perhaps, but up through these vast halls and piled stairways the ancient odor of opium crept like a miasma. It was the essence of everything I-wan hated, that stealing lethargic fragrance that in its very sweetness held something of the stink of death. The house was saturated with it. It clung in the silk hangings on the walls and in the red cushions on the chairs and couches. I-wan, pulling silk stuffed quilts about him at night in bed smelled, or imagined he did, that reek.

For that reason, he had told himself, he wanted his room bare, as bare as En-lan's little dormitory cubicle in the university. He made Peony take down the heavy damask curtains which the French decorator, years before he was born, had draped across the windows. Every window in the house had them except now these two in his rooms. Without them the windows stretched tall and stark, and the light fell into his room like a blast of noise. Peony was always complaining about the hideousness of his room. She was always trying to soften this hard light. Today when he came in he saw at once she had been doing it again. In the window she had put a blue vase, and in that a branch of rosy-flowered oleander. For a moment he thought, "What have I to do with flowers? I'll take them away."

But he did not go beyond thinking. He did not want to hurt Peony's feelings because she was the only one in this house to whom he could talk at all. And he had not made up his mind whether or not he would tell even her everything— that is, that he had joined finally that secret revolutionary band and that some day soon he must renounce all else. When he thought of renouncing this house and this life, his heart swelled and shrank too. Still, it was the only way to save the country—to cut off all this old dead life—the life of capitalism!

Yes, I-ko was dead, too, as dead as his grandmother, even though he was a young man. He was dead because he cared for nothing except himself and his own pleasures. Because of his position as the son of the president of a great modern bank, he had an easy place near his father. I-wan himself did not know of all that I-ko did. But he knew enough to know that he would never be like I-ko if he could help it.

Now he took off his dark blue school uniform and put on a long robe of soft gray-green silk. This was because his grandfather disliked to see him at home in the rough school uniform.

"When you come into my presence," he had directed I-wan, "appear in your natural garb."

"When I renounce them all," I-wan thought to himself as he fastened the small buttons of twisted silk, "I will never wear anything but the uniform." For of course in that life of revolution to which he would go, this robe would be absurd. To clamber over rocks, to march long miles among country villages, to preach on the streets to the people and tell them they ought to revolt against the rich and those who oppressed them—one could not wear a silk gown for such things. He must even change his name. No one would believe in the son of a rich Shanghai banker—

He heard a little cough and suddenly Peony put her head in at the door.

"Your grandfather asks why you delay, and your parents command you to come at once," she announced.

"I'm coming," he said shortly.

Her voice changed. She came into the room and went straight toward the window.

"Did you see the oleander?" she asked softly.

"Yes," he said.

Now he was taking off his leather shoes and putting on black velvet slippers. If his grandfather heard him clacking on the floors in his school shoes he would simply have to turn around again and come back and change.

"Aren't they beautiful with the light shining through them?" Peony asked.

He looked up. For the first time in his life he suddenly saw Peony not as Peony, the bondmaid with whom he had played and quarreled as long as he could remember. She was a pretty girl standing by those flowers. If he did not know she was only Peony, he would say she was a pretty girl.

"I didn't look at them," he said. And without a word he went out. Why did he now notice how Peony looked? He remembered when Peony was a small yellow-faced mite who never seemed to grow at all.

"Certainly she costs us nothing in food," his mother always said. . . . No one could say Peony was yellow, now. She would never be tall, but she was not yellow.

He crossed the great square upstairs hall and he stood before a heavy walnut door opposite his own and coughed.

"Come in," his grandfather called.

So he went in.

It was impossible to despise his grandfather as he did his grandmother. His grandfather knew many things, though, being old, he forgot much. But he would allow greater knowledge to no one. Even though I-wan perceived the absurdity of this in an old man, he continued to be a little afraid of his grandfather. When anybody said the foreigners did thus, his grandfather could always say whether they really did or not. When anyone asked him to tell something about the foreign countries, he always said, "I was in all the western countries, and each is different from the others and all are different from us —that is the chief thing."

If pressed further he would tell of strange things he had seen. At first, fifty years ago, these things seemed stranger than they did now. A train, for instance, fifty years ago was like nothing so much as a dragon. To people listening he said, "Imagine a dragon roaring across the country, smoke pouring from its nostrils—" Now of course there were plenty of trains. Everybody in Shanghai had seen trains. The old man could say no more about them. But he maintained his dignity.

"Sit down," his grandfather said. "What have you studied today?"

I-wan sat on the edge of his chair and began. "Sir, I studied today history, geography, English, and mathematics."

"No military science?" his grandfather asked sharply.

"Tomorrow is science, sir," I-wan answered.

"Military science—military science is the thing," his grandfather said. "Now when I was in Germany I saw troops passing in review, and I received certain definite ideas. That is why I hired a German tutor for you last summer."

I-wan sat staring at his grandfather without seeing or hearing him. He had trained himself to do this by much experience. Germany fifty years ago—what had it to do with him? He sat thinking and not thinking, his eyes following his grandfather's thin yellow hand as it moved up and down in his white straggling beard. If he should tell Peony tonight when she came to make up his bed that he was a revolutionist—but if he told her that some day he must renounce them all, that he could never come home again, of course Peony would not see him again, either. Then she would cry. Perhaps he would not tell anybody—just not come home any more when the day of revolution broke. In the secret meeting today Liu En-lan had said, "Next spring—"

"Now you may go," his grandfather said kindly. "You listen well and I have great plans for you, I-wan."

I-wan rose, bowed, and turned. At the door he bowed again. He seldom spoke in his grandfather's room unless he must answer a question. He was always glad to get away, too. The room was full of old books and too much furniture. It was musty and unaired and smelled of an old man. His grandfather did not open the windows often. In the daytime he declared it was cooler to keep them shut and at night he feared the moist air. I-wan shut the door behind him.

"This house is full of smells," he thought. Even Peony had a smell. She used a jasmine scent. It was too sweet and he had told her so, but she loved it and would not give it up.

"The trouble is with you," she always insisted. "Your nose is too keen to smell. What other people like, you dislike. You make a point of it." She said such things in her pretty voice. The words were sharp but they sounded soft. . . .

Now he must go to his parents, and then he would be free. He knocked at another door and entered at once without waiting. Here were the two huge rooms which he knew best of all, because as a baby he had learned to walk on this smooth parquetry floor covered with heavy Chinese rugs. He knew every ornament, from the vases in the carved blackwood cabinet, which he was never allowed to touch, to the ivory balls and elephants with which he could always play as much as he liked. He still liked sometimes to take the big hollow ivory filigree ball into his hands and turn it and try to separate with his eye the seventeen different ivory balls within, each separate and turning.

His mother was sitting by the window embroidering, and his father was at a huge blackwood desk at one end of the room. He was still in the foreign dress he wore at the bank and he looked up as I-wan came in.

"Ah, you've seen your grandparents," he said. "I am only just come home—I must change." But he did not move. "Has your brother come in?" he asked.

"No, Father," I-wan answered.

Madame Wu looked up from her satin with her soft doubting face and put out her hand to her son.

24

"Come here," she said in English. She spoke English well and was proud of it. In her youth her father had kept an elderly English lady for years as her governess. "You look tired, I-wan."

"I am tired," he answered in English. He liked speaking English. He could leave off the long courteous phrases he had to use in Chinese. In English one could not sensibly say, "Your honorable—" and "I, the humble one—" Still his mother was very Chinese sometimes. She had certain superstitions which did not at all suit her pure English accent. All his little boyhood he went with a silver lock and chain about his neck to lock his life in. He used to pull at it in secret, but he could not break it. The silversmith had welded the last link fast around his neck.

"You are so late," his mother said.

"We had a meeting after school," he replied.

"What are these meetings?" his father asked in Chinese.

"Political meetings," I-wan answered, still in English.

"Don't get yourself entangled," his father said. Now he spoke in English, too, as he did only when he wanted to be sure the servants could not understand. He spoke English fluently but badly, confusing his l's and r's and n's, as he did in French and German also. "Young students can do nothing to change those in control. But those in control can cut off your heads."

"I-wan!" his mother cried. "Promise me—"

His father went on without heeding her.

"The government is not going to hear any nonsense from boys and girls," he said warmly. "Besides, none of you understands all that is involved in running a country. You are full of criticisms and rebellions. But what do you understand of money and banking, of foreign loans, for instance?"

"Why do we need foreign loans?" I-wan burst out. They

25

had been talking about foreign loans this afternoon in the meeting and En-lan had got up and in the quietest way had offered his life to their cause, as a protest. Until that moment they had not understood the importance and danger of the new million-dollar loan from Japan, for which the surety was to be a certain great iron mine in the north.

"This latest loan from abroad," En-lan had said, "is not given freely any more than any other loan. There are certain privileges that go to the foreign nation that lends us money. The students have protested to the government officials but they pay no attention to us. With your permission, I will conceal a pistol in my sleeve and shoot the Minister of Finance as he goes home for dinner with his new concubine."

No one spoke. They were all staring at him. And he drew back his lips in a snarl, and between his shining white teeth he hissed, "His new concubine cost him ten thousand dollars! Only Ministers of Finance can keep buying new concubines!"

It was the first time one of their group had offered his life to kill an enemy. It had been done often enough elsewhere so that well-known men were doubling their bodyguards, especially since a student had broken into the office of the Minister of Foreign Affairs. That was after the twenty-one demands that Japan had made. . . . They broke into excited talk. But then it was decided that En-lan could not be spared yet—too much was to come.

Nevertheless what he had offered to do had made the hour intense for their cause.

"Why do we need foreign loans?" his father repeated. "Because every country in reconstruction needs foreign loans."

He was a large man with a handsome flat-cheeked face, and he prided himself on being a modern man. Among his friends

26

were many foreigners of all nations, but chiefly Japanese. Mr. Wu was one of those Chinese who believed in close friendship with Japan. "Asia for the Asians," he liked to quote, after the Japanese Minister of Foreign Affairs had first used these words in a speech before the League of Nations.

"You cannot understand," he now said to his son kindly, "because you are at the idealistic age. I also at twenty had certain ideals. I was a secret follower of the Young Emperor and his reforms. Most young men were. I daresay you also follow some such cult with your fellows."

"I-ko never was like this," his mother murmured.

"I-wan is more like me," his father said sharply.

I-wan sat down. He did not answer his parents. Long ago he had learned that trick. It was at once filial in respect and by it he told nothing. His mother had taken up her embroidery again, and his father his pen. He did not care what his father said, he told himself, and yet—his father could so easily prick something in him with a few words, and make him feel small and young. As if the revolutionists now could be compared to whatever those young men had been under the weak Emperor! His father was busy and rich and successful now, though he had been a spoiled child, coaxed and coddled as I-ko had been when for so long he was the only son. The old servants still in the house were full of stories about his willfullness as a child. But somehow his father had not been made weak by spoiling. Instead he only continued to be opinionated and domineering and to do as he liked. I-wan knew that sometimes his parents quarreled bitterly, but he did not know about what. His mother had been a rich man's only daughter and there were few women so well educated as she had been in her youth. But still she obeyed her husband, even though they quarreled. Everyone obeyed him, even his parents, although he made a show of yielding to them, since that was suitable.

"May I go now, Father?" I-wan asked.

"In a moment," his father replied.

So he sat waiting, but rebellion grew hot in him.

"My father," he thought, "has nothing to say to me, but he keeps me waiting to show that he can. He never wants to give me permission at once to go away. He wants to show his power over me." His lips curled a little. When he renounced them all—

"Have you any plans?" his father asked suddenly in Chinese.

I-wan looked up. His father had put down his pen.

"I have been thinking for some time we ought to plan your future," he said. "Your mother, too, has plans."

"Twenty," his mother said. "You are a man."

I-wan felt himself turn scarlet. His father went on, kindly, observing his son.

"Let your mind rest," he said. "We shall not force you or your brother in anything. We have not betrothed you and shall not. Long ago we talked of it, and we decided to leave you and I-ko free to choose your own wives."

"Thank you, sir," I-wan murmured.

Of course he knew they had done this. I-ko loitered in his room sometimes at night, talking of girls he knew whom he might marry if he liked. He could never decide which of these girls he wanted to marry, and sometimes he ended by laughing at himself.

"There is still no law against more than one wife," he would say, "though the women are growing so independent they want you to promise you won't marry anybody else! How can a man promise that?"

Nevertheless, although he had always taken his freedom for

granted, for the first time now I-wan felt gratitude toward his parents. Plenty of his schoolmates were already betrothed because their parents compelled them. That also was one of the things they were to fight for—the freedom of choice in marriage. The girls, especially, were excited for this. They said over and over at the meetings, "We must have the right to marry whom we like, or not marry at all, even, if we do not wish to do so."

"Of course," everybody had agreed.

Sometimes when two or three young men were alone together they discussed this determination of the girls. They agreed still that the girls were right. Nevertheless, they asked themselves, what would happen if women began to refuse to be married? It would be very embarrassing to a man to ask a young woman to marry him and have her refuse.

Once En-lan had grinned at I-wan. "Calm yourself," he said. "Do you remember the girl who spoke loudest and longest for freedom?"

He did. She was a pretty, fiery girl from the southern province of Fukien. En-lan put his hand in his pocket and pulled out a letter and handed it to him. It was a passionate love letter, signed with her name. I-wan was amazed and secretly a little envious. "Shall you marry her?" he asked En-lan. En-lan shook his head. "Why should I marry when as a revolutionist any day I may be dead?" he asked. "Besides, she does not ask for marriage."

It was true. The girl had written, "Only bid me come to you and I will come. We are free."

I-wan handed the letter back to En-lan and he put it in his pocket.

"Besides," he said again, "my parents have a wife for me at home. That is why I never go home."

29

"A wife!" I-wan had cried. He was always finding out something new about this En-lan, whom he had rescued out of jail. . . .

"But it is time we decided the direction of your education," his father went on. "Naturally, I hope to take you into the bank with me, as I did your elder brother."

I-wan did not answer. He would never go into the bank. How they would all hate him if he helped to make those foreign loans! He could not bear the thought of their hatred. He knew very well that upon the black list the revolutionists kept his father's name was written down, among others of influence and wealth. He thought for a moment with passionate envy of En-lan. En-lan was a peasant's son and proud of it.

"My father is a common man," En-lan was fond of saying. "My mother cannot read or write." En-lan was hard toward all who were rich. He would never understand why, though I-wan also despised capitalists, he still secretly loved his father in spite of all his rebelliousness toward him. En-lan would say in his quiet definite way, "If it were I, I would say, since he is a capitalist and an enemy he cannot be my father. . . ."

"I shall not hurry you or force you," his father was saying kindly. "You are my son. But when you know what you want, tell me."

He nodded and I-wan rose. As had so often happened before, his irritation was gone. His father's show of authority had ended in such kindness.

"Thank you, Father," I-wan murmured.

"Where are you going?" his mother asked.

"To my room to study," he replied.

She nodded, content to know he would be in the house, and he went out and closed the door after him. Later they would meet downstairs at the great table in the dining room to eat a dinner

30

that would have been a feast to En-lan. But it was what they had every day.

Nevertheless, thinking of it he grew a little hungry. He would, he decided, see what was in the comfit box that Peony kept filled on his table. And the teapot would be hot in its padded case. He hastened to his room, feeling free and his own for a while. He liked the hour he had alone before dinner. He talked of study, but he never studied until after dinner. Then he hurried away, muttering that he must study, that he had so much to do. Sometimes indeed he did study, though sometimes he went straight out to the theater.

But tonight he must study. He had a long composition to write in English. It was his secret wish to excel En-lan in writing. But he never could. En-lan had a strange power of writing. Strive as he would, I-wan could never win such praise from the elderly English lady who taught them as was given to En-lan. Tonight, he thought, he would try harder than ever. Almost more than the teacher's praise, he wanted En-lan to think well of him. And then, instead of idling, he sat down at the table and drew out his writing book. He would begin now to do his best.

He was getting very sleepy. He looked at his clock. It was nearly midnight and he had only just finished his English composition. He read it over and thought well of it, though of course it would come back dotted with red marks. Miss Maitland would correct it in many unforeseen places. But it was good. He had chosen as his subject the story of Sun Yat-sen, and he had told it well. He had decided pleasurably to read it again, when he heard a soft movement about his bed. But he did not look up. It was only Peony unrolling the quilts and bringing in hot tea to set beside his bed. Then he felt her

31

standing beside him, and he felt what he had felt before, her hand on his shoulder and her cheek against his hair. Suddenly he remembered how she had looked standing against the oleanders in the late afternoon. He moved away from her, growling at her, "How long will you use that disgusting perfume?"

"Forever," she said pertly, "and forever—because I like it. Don't study any more! You must be finished. It is time you went to bed."

"You know nothing about what I have to do," he said.

"If you are not yet finished, then you are stupid," she retorted. She touched his cheek with her soft and scented palm. "And I know you are not stupid," she said.

He felt his heart beat suddenly once, twice, and he was disturbed. For years they had been playmates. He knew, and she knew, too, that she was a bondmaid and allowed in the house to be more than that only because they were all fond of her and had petted her, especially since his sisters died. But indeed between the two of them there had been something like being brother and sister. They never spoke of her being a bondmaid. He did not think of it because he was so used to her and she did not speak of it. But for the last few months something else was beginning between them, something he wanted and hated. It was this way she had of putting her hand on his shoulder and her cheek on his hair. Some night he would stretch out his own arm and put it around her, though he did not want to do it. He had never done it, but he had thought of it, and he was ashamed. If he had not belonged to the band he would have done it, perhaps.

Besides, he did not want to be like I-ko. I-ko was forever teasing Peony, touching her cheek and seizing her hand and putting his arm about her. Whenever he did this, Peony flung herself away from him. Once she had scratched him, four long

32

scratches down both his cheeks, so that for several days he could not go out because everyone knows that when a man has four long parallel scratches down both his cheeks, a woman's two hands have done it. There was trouble in the house because of it. Madame Wu spoke alone to Peony, and his father spoke to I-ko. And Peony came into I-wan's room and cried and said, "I hate your brother I-ko! He has always been wicked."

I-wan did not ask how I-ko was wicked. He did not want to know. He had felt a faint prickling in his spine and he had said solemnly, "I will never be wicked to you, Peony."

She had sobbed awhile, and sighed, and then she looked up at him and smiled.

"You don't know how to be wicked," she had said. . . .

So now he was ashamed when he felt pleased at her touch on him, and he drew away from her.

"You don't like me any more now that you are grown up," she murmured.

"Yes, I do," he said loudly, "exactly as I always have."

"I'm so lonely," she whispered.

He rose, slamming his composition book shut.

"You go away," he said. "I don't want you here any more when I am going to bed, Peony."

He made his voice surly because he was afraid of her. He was afraid she would cry or be angry with him because she had always helped him get ready for bed and then had drawn the bed curtains and put out the light.

"Open the windows," he had always commanded her.

In summer she obeyed, but in winter she begged him, "Not tonight—it's so cold."

"If you don't open them, I'll get up myself after you are gone," he called out of the quilts.

So she had to open them, summer and winter. . . . He turned

33

his back to her now so he need not see her face when it was hurt. But he heard her laugh, and he turned around quickly. She was not hurt at all. She was smiling, her eyes teasing, her voice gay.

"You are too big," she said, "you are a man now—so you don't want me here any more, little I-wan! A big grown man!"

He rushed at her and pushed her to the door and she clung to his hands, laughing and laughing. He pushed her out of the door at last, though her soft hands clung to his like something sticky. There, he had her off! He pulled the door sharply shut and turned the key. Then he stood and listened. There was not a sound. He put his hand to the key to turn it back and see if she were there. Then he drew away. Of course she was there, teasing him, waiting in silence. He would not open the door. He turned and walked loudly across the floor and began to undress himself. When he was washed and ready for bed he went to the window and noisily threw it wide. If she were there, she would hear that. He had an inner wave of desire to go and look to see if she were there. But if she were she would come in. And he was afraid of her if she came in. He had vowed himself to his country. Besides, he would not be like I-ko.

He sprang into bed and drew the curtains, and he smelled again that faint sweet odor of the opium. He hated it instantly, and in his hatred he forgot Peony. He would not, he thought, drifting away into sleep at last, have to endure it forever.

The band was meeting in the English classroom. It was the safest room because the university always gave the foreign teachers the poorest rooms in a small old building at a distant corner of the campus. It was a two-story building and there was only one stairway. It was Peng Liu's duty to loiter at the

34

head of the stairs as though he were waiting for someone. But in reality he was guarding the stair. He was good at being a spy. His little eyes saw everything and he could pretend stupidity and ignorance so naturally that anyone would be deceived. If anyone came up, he would call out a loud greeting, and the others would hear it through the open transom of the door of the English room, which was opposite, and immediately they would scatter through two other doors into other classrooms, where they would be studying in little groups and couples and alone. But so far no one had ever come up the stairs, even though they had been meeting now for nearly two years and had become part of many others like themselves in the National Brotherhood of Patriots. That was what they called themselves since the government announced that all communists would be shot. They were not communists, therefore, but patriots.

"They can scarcely shoot patriots," En-lan had said, grinning his wide peasant grin. "When the revolution comes, everything will be different. We shall then kill everybody else."

In this room I-wan knew them all, and yet really he knew none of them, except En-lan. That is, he knew every one of these twenty-three faces, nine of them girls, and he knew their names. But except for Peng Liu and En-lan, whether they were rich or poor, or who they were, he could not tell. They had not known each other until they had begun to gather here in this room. When I-wan had first come there were only eleven, and only two of them girls. Where these others had come from he did not know, except that when a new one entered it was the rule that he stand up and announce himself and then someone among those already known would stand up also and vouch for him that he was not a spy.

It was through En-lan that he had come here. When he came

35

to this university he found En-lan at once, and En-lan had told him of the brotherhood, and had vouched for him. I-wan was grateful and he asked him afterwards, "How can you vouch for me when you do not know more about me than my father's name?"

"I do know you," En-lan had replied. "I know what you did for me."

"You don't care whose son I am?" I-wan had asked.

"What does it matter whose son you are?" En-lan had answered. "I know you are the sort of fellow who ought to be with us."

And yet, although none of these twenty-three persons was among I-wan's old friends, nor were any of them like those sons of the rich who had been his schoolmates once, he felt when he came into this room that here were those to whom he belonged. Whether they knew who he was or not, he did not care. He even preferred that they did not know. He felt ashamed before them that he was the son of the banker Wu, who was one of the richest men in Shanghai. When I-wan saw a small hole torn in his uniform or a button gone, he let it be, so that he could look as poor as any of them and he purposely tumbled his smooth black hair so that it would look more like En-lan's dry tough hair, browned by the dusty winds and the sun of the northern deserts.

It seemed to him that here alone in his world was life, eager and good. In his home no one thought of anyone else outside the family. Each person did what he liked for himself, his only other regard being the family. No one looked to see what was happening to people outside. I-wan had not either, until he found the book by Karl Marx which had sent him to prison. And yet he could never be sorry he had been in prison, because that was where he had found En-lan. . . .

"Why were you in prison?" he had asked En-lan when they had come to know each other. He knew by now a curious thing about En-lan. When there was something he wished known he wrote it down instead of talking about it. He talked slowly and hunted for words, but he wrote easily and with plenty of words. So now, as often, he did not at once answer I-wan.

Then he said, "I will write it down."

A few days later he handed I-wan some sheets of paper torn out of his English composition book.

"Read it in your own room," he told I-wan, "and then burn it up."

I-wan, alone that very night in his room, read these pages, and this is what En-lan wrote:

"I-wan:

"When you came into the prison I had already been there seventy-three days, and it was as though I had been there for ten years in that cell. If I pressed my face against the bars of the small window, I could just see a triangle of sky above the prison wall—nothing more. It was not a large bit of sky. It seemed to me about the size of the three-cornered piece of black cloth which my mother always wore tied over her head to keep the dust of the deserts out of her hair. I have already told you my village is in the far north, and the bitter winds from the Gobi sweep down laden with yellow sand. Some day, the old men have always said, the village will be covered with sand, and people will be buried, their flesh drying without decay in the intense dryness of the sand and the wind.

"Standing thus, my face pressed against the prison bars, staring at my bit of sky, I gave up hope. It came to me at last, a few days before your coming, that perhaps I would never

37

lie dry and clean in death in the sands of my village. No, my body might fall in the prison yard, full of bullets, and I would be thrown into the warm soft rich earth of this half-foreign southern city. And in my village they would never know what had become of me or why I did not come home any more.

"The village has always been too far for me to go home at New Year or at any time except in summer. And even in summer I walk a good deal of the way, because train fare, even in the coolie cars where there are no seats, is more than I could pay. But in those years before my parents married me to the woman I shall never see, I always felt I must go home because I had so much to tell them. Everybody in the village, every one of the twenty-six families, is kin to me, and everybody has given what he was able to pay my school bills. If there was no money, the women of the family made me shoes or socks or a coat.

"I would not for anything have told them that after a few months I did not wear these things, because the smart students of the modern city laughed at me. I did not mind this so much because I laughed, too. I could see I looked funny in the long, too loose robes of blue cotton and in the clumsy northern shoes. For of course I knew the women had said to each other, 'We had better cut them plenty big. He might grow taller, and with all the good food in the south he will certainly be fatter.' So they cut them far too large for me, since I grew neither taller nor fatter. But I could not bear the laughter for their sakes.

"So I found a pawnshop where ricksha pullers and poor men stopped to buy clothing, and because my things were made of such stout home-woven stuffs and so strongly sewed, I sold easily and the pawnshop keeper gave me a fair price. With this I bought myself the blue cotton uniforms, such as many of the students wore who liked to be patriotic. I wore one when I went to prison.

38

"You asked me, I-wan, how I came to be in prison. It is a simple story. One day soldiers came into our English classroom and they shouted my name. I was reading a poem by an English poet. I could not understand it very well, but I felt through the dimness of foreign words that there was beauty. It began, 'I wandered lonely as a cloud—'

"I had been studying English for three years. At home in the village they all crowded around me in the summer evenings and begged me, 'Speak some English for us to hear!' So I would say slowly and clearly, 'My name is Liu En-lan. How do you do. I am very well, thank you.' Everyone listened in silence, and when I stopped they burst into laughter and they laughed until tears ran down their cheeks. 'It sounds like hens cackling,' they said. 'Now tell us what it means.' And they listened again while I told them, admiring me for all I knew.

"And my old uncle, Liu Ih, the oldest man in the village, always nodded his head and sucked his pipe and said, 'I knew we made no mistake when we let him go to school. No one from this village has ever gone to school, but times are changed. He will bring honor to us all. He will get a fine government job with all this English and pay us all back—with interest.' 'Yes, I will,' I always promised. I gazed around at their faces, and I loved them greatly as they looked at me, their eyes innocent and wistful in their lined dark faces. At their feet stood little children, staring at me in wonder and in silence, to whom I knew I was a hero. When I was graduated with honors, I would get the fine job and do everything for them. I would hire a good teacher and all the children should go to school. . . .

"So that morning I had been reading through the foreign words toward that beauty, 'I wandered lonely as a cloud.' . . . Miss Maitland was saying slowly, 'This is a poem by a great English poet, whose name was Wordsworth.'

39

"At this moment something struck the door and we all looked toward it. It was a flimsy door, and it burst open at once, as indeed you know it does, even in a little wind. How then could it withstand the blow of a gun? Soldiers stood there, at least twenty of them, and one shouted, 'Where is Liu En-lan?'

"When I heard my name I stood up at once. No one said anything.

" 'Are you Liu En-lan?' the sergeant shouted.

" 'Yes, I am,' I answered quietly, though I was very much astonished.

" 'You are under arrest!' the sergeant roared. 'Come with us!'

" 'But why—why—' I stammered, and could not talk. I could not imagine why I was arrested, nor indeed that even my name was known except to my teachers and a very few of my fellow students. 'I think there is a mistake,' I said to the sergeant.

" 'No mistake!' cried the sergeant. 'Liu En-lan of the Liu village in the province of Shensi!'

" 'That is certainly I and that is my village,' I replied, 'but why should I be arrested?'

"At this the sergeant grew very red in the face. 'You dare to talk to me!' he bellowed, and rushing to me he seized me by the collar and jerked me off my feet. I felt to my horror that my collar was torn and I would have to buy a new coat. But I had no time for anything more than the bare thought, because the sergeant was a large man and very angry. He shook me and shouted, 'You dare—you dare!' I wanted to fight back, but I knew it would be foolish, with all the guns of the soldiers pointed at me.

"At this Miss Maitland grew very angry. You know her small mild face, under her parted white hair—it is always gentle and proper. None of us had ever seen it otherwise. But suddenly she flew at the sergeant and grasped his arm and shook it.

" 'You stop behaving like that in my classroom!' she said severely. 'I say stop it—do you hear me?'

"Since she spoke in English the sergeant understood nothing that she said. He looked at her as a tomcat looks at a furious mouse.

" 'What is this foreign female saying?' he asked me.

" 'She begs you to desist,' I translated.

" 'Tell her you are arrested,' he ordered.

" 'I am arrested,' I said to Miss Maitland in English.

" 'What for?' she demanded.

" 'I do not know,' I replied truthfully.

" 'That's silly!' Miss Maitland cried. 'Ask him, the big beast! And tell him I say he is a beast!'

"But I dared only say to the sergeant, 'This honorable foreign lady, who is our teacher, asks why I am arrested.'

" 'Tell her it's not her affair,' the sergeant replied loftily.

" 'He says he is not allowed to say,' I translated to Miss Maitland.

" 'Now that's just too silly!' Miss Maitland said. 'Tell him to get out and stop interfering—tell him he can't come arresting my students like this—I'll speak to the British consul!'

"I hesitated.

" 'Tell him all I said!' Miss Maitland commanded.

" 'She says,' I began, 'she will ask her consul to inquire—'

"The sergeant glared at Miss Maitland, but she glared back, and he turned away with dignity.

" 'I was told to arrest you,' he said more loftily.

" 'But why?' I now demanded for myself.

" 'Oh, what's all this about?' Miss Maitland cried.

"But before she could say another word the sergeant shouted to the soldiers, 'Forward, march!' Instantly the soldiers seized my arms and I was hustled out before anyone could help me—

41

if, indeed, I could have been helped. The students all sat silent and still as stone, and Miss Maitland only screamed.

"I was marched down the street, and then into a great gate and thrust into the jail. I had written of this jail in my composition.

" 'We have also a model prison in our country,' I had written. 'It is said that prison is one of the best in the world, and American and English visitors go to see how well China treats her captives in her model prison.'

"Now I was thrust into a cell in this prison and the door was locked. It was, as a matter of fact, not uncomfortable at all. I think I must have been the first one there. It was clean—not as you saw it when hundreds had been through it. The cell was much better than most of the little earth huts in which the villagers lived in my home village, and indeed quite as good even as the tiny room I had been able to afford when I had first come to school in Shanghai, before I was given a room in the dormitory. In the cell there was a board bed, a dark blue cotton quilt, quite clean, and some bricks piled into a seat, and the small window. The house in which I had spent my childhood had no window at all. But then the door was open to the threshing floor, which was also the dooryard, so that the wide sky was always to be seen. As a small boy I sat on the high doorstep and watched my father and mother threshing wheat or beans and sifting out the chaff and husks in the strong dry winds. But the food in the prison was certainly better than what I had as a child.

"The food, in fact, was so good that I enjoyed it and when I had finished my breakfast of rice and salt fish, with a bit of bread, on the second morning, I could not believe that in such a beautiful prison I would not receive the utmost justice. Besides, I told myself, this new government was just. They would allow me to explain at the trial. Every morning I thought, 'Today I shall be summoned.' I had long prepared in my mind what I would say.

Lying upon the board bed at night, and staring at the square of sky by day, I planned every word until it was put together something like this.

" 'Sirs, I beg you, of what am I accused? I belong to no revolutionary party.' For at that time, I-wan, I did not. It was only afterwards that I truly was a communist.—'I work hard every day and I do not leave the school grounds. I have only one ambition. It is to graduate with honors, to get a good job, and to pay back debts. When that is done, I wish to establish a school in my home village. The people are very poor. The winds are dry and the crops are scanty. The earth gives barely enough food against starvation, and not always enough, so that sometimes we have famine. And the taxes are very high—military taxes, taxes on opium—all taxes. For though we can sell all our opium quite easily to the government, the government taxes us first and so heavily that it pays us only a little better to grow opium instead of grain. All these difficulties keep my people poor, so there is no money for schools. But I have always been for learning. From my childhood I have wanted to learn all that there is to know. So my people saved and pinched and gathered enough to send me to this beautiful city to school. Here I have been happy. Sirs, where is my fault?'

"I practiced saying all this and much more, as I imagined myself standing before the judges—grave, kind, intelligent men who would soon see they had made a mistake. Then I would be set free. When I went home next summer it would be a thing to tell, how I was arrested by mistake—I would tell them what a fine prison this was, how comfortable the quilt was, and how twice a day I had quite good food. Nobody ate more than twice a day in my village, and in winter when work was slack, perhaps only once a day. Then, the winter days being short, we all slept a good deal. I tried to sleep in the cell, but though it was quiet and

43

comfortable, I could not sleep, expecting at any moment to be summoned for trial. I kept hot on the end of my tongue what I would say.

"But I was not summoned. Day followed day, and the only face I saw was that of the guard who brought me my food. To this man I cried out at last, 'Are they not going to give me a trial?'

" 'I don't know about such things,' the guard replied. 'Here is your rice.' And he went away.

"I grew mad at last with impatience. I began to beg the guard. 'Please find out about my trial! I beg you—I beg you!'

"But the guard only shook his head. 'I am forbidden to speak to the prisoners,' he said, and went away.

"I always carried in my belt my little store of money for the term. This I still had, because when I came, although it was the rule in this prison to make the new prisoners bathe and change their clothes before going to their cells, they had let me pass, saying that the bathroom keeper had gone out that day to drink wine at his brother's wedding feast, and so I was put straight into the cell, locked up and forgotten, and I still had my money. One day I took out my money, divided it in half, and putting one half in my hand, I said to the guard, holding it out, 'Please inquire when I am to be tried. Here is a little small silver.'

"The guard opened his eyes very wide at this, but he took the silver, without reply. The next day he said abruptly, 'There is to be no trial. You are a political prisoner and your crime is proved.'

" 'But I do not even know what it is!' I cried.

" 'That I did not ask,' the guard said.

"I tore off my belt and poured all I had into the guard's hand.

" 'Find out what my crime is,' I begged. 'This is all I have.'

"When the guard went away I sat on the bed, my body tense and sweating. I should not have told the guard I had no more.

Perhaps he would keep the money and do nothing, knowing there was no more to expect.

"But the guard had a good enough heart. He said to me next day, 'I asked a guard whose brother is a scribe in the court and has to do with records, and he says you wrote something in a foreign paper where foreigners could read it that our country was poor and full of famine, and that the government taxes the people too heavily, and that they buy the opium which the farmers raise. And so the foreigners read it and laughed at us and despised us. This is your crime.'

" 'But—it is not what I said!' I cried in horror.

" 'The record is so,' replied the guard, and went away.

"I could not sleep at all that night. I sat up remembering every word of that composition. I had been very proud of it, and Miss Maitland had praised it greatly and had read it aloud to the class. She said, 'This is so beautiful a piece that I wish English people could read it to see how young Chinese love their country. Liu En-lan, suppose you send it to the English newspaper for the prize competition.'

"I had felt the blood run all over my body under my skin, until I was warm with pleasure, and I had spent my spare hours for weeks copying the composition with all the corrections. Then I had sent it with a letter to the editor of the English paper. It was given the prize and the editor printed it with a note, saying, 'It is not often that we receive so honest and thoughtful an analysis of a country as this young Chinese patriot has sent us.' When I saw these words I was joyful with pride."

I-wan paused in his reading. Yes, he remembered that essay. From his school also that year they had all written essays for the competition, and Liu En-lan—that had indeed been the name of the one who wrote the best. But nobody had ever heard of him and it was soon forgotten. He himself had not thought of it until this moment.

He began to read again.

"For this I was now in prison. Day followed day in an endless chain of morning and night which were different only in dark and light. I lost count of the days and the nights, so that I did not know how long I had been in prison. I had no friends and no one came to visit me. Miss Maitland tried, but she was told they had sent me home, and she believed then I was safe. She told me afterwards. And there was not even any reason to speak to the guard any more, since all my money was gone.

"I sat, therefore, hour after hour, or I stood, my face against the bars, staring at the bit of sky, and thinking over and over of what I had said in my composition. . . . I had written it one day in spring, a beautiful day when the winds were warm and flowers were for sale in the markets. The streets were gay and motor cars were flying back and forth, the rickshas swerving out of their way. Time and again I had stopped to watch the quick beauty of a motor car, speeding along the wide street. In the afternoon after school I had walked outside the city and I had stood looking over the miles of green country, my heart full of a strange great feeling I did not understand. It was like the ache of love—not love for a girl, for I knew no girls, but love for my country spread before me, spread so far to the north where my home was, spread here in this new modern city, spread further still to the southern seas I had never seen. And as I stood this great love began to distil itself into words. I wanted to put down all that I felt about my country. The words began to shape like drops of shining water from a glorious mist. I hurried back to my small room and began to write, word by word, what had been my vision.

"It was not easy to do this. I remember I was sweating with the effort to write exactly what I felt and saw. Night came but I did not eat. I lit a candle and wrote on by its small light. All over the city there were bright electric lights and neon signs springing out of the darkness, though I was too poor to rent a room in a house with electric lights. But this made no difference to me. I was proud that there were such lights. If I had not been working I would have been out on the streets, staring at them as I never tired of doing.

"I put the electric lights into my composition, I put the whole city, the strong new city growing out of the sea. I put in motor cars and motor trucks carrying the heavy loads that human beings had once carried. I put in the schools, the fine markets, the luscious imported fruits, the flowers from greenhouses. I smiled and put in the beauty shops where women curled their hair. I put in the fine new buildings, finer than any palaces of emperors. I put in the miles of country, the fields, the skies I had seen that afternoon, and I laid down my pen.

"When I read it over I found that it was still not all of my country. There was also my home village, my father and mother, the dry stubborn fields of the north, the desert winds, the famine we had suffered two years ago, the little earthen huts, the opium we grew instead of grain, hopeful of a little more money. But there were the taxes—the taxes which went to build the government. I put them in, too. Pondering on all these things, I did not at all feel that the taxes had not been well spent—not at all. Only I wished, as I remembered them, that the faces of my parents and of the others in the village were not quite so weathered with harsh winds, their bodies not so lean with scanty food, their hands less scarred with grubbing in cloddy earth for roots for food and fuel. . . . So I put all these things in also.

"And I could not forbear to put down, too, my longing that somehow this wonderful new learned government which Sun Yat-sen had begun, might think of some way to make it possible

for my village to have a little more share in all the fine new times
—if, say, the taxes were lightened somewhat, or a few country
roads built—not great motor roads such as were being built about
the city, but simple earthen roads they could drive an ass upon
or push a wheelbarrow—or if, say, they need not grow opium—
or be so taxed—

"It came to me therefore in prison that this was what had made
them angry at me. This was why they called me traitor. I had
never thought of it. I had written it all down, all I felt about my
country. I wrote it first in our own language, and then because
I was proud of it I translated it carefully into English.

"And so the authorities had seen it thus in English and grown
angry with me. It came to me slowly, after much thought, that
here was my crime. I had written my composition in English.
They were ashamed of the things I had told of my village and
my people, and they did not want the foreigners to know of
taxes and opium, of famines and earthen huts. If I had only left
it in Chinese, if I had not put it into English—but then I could
never have dreamed of such an outcome to that one spring
afternoon.

"It was not to be believed, even in the prison, morning after
morning. Each morning I got up in a different mood. Every night
was the same—I was desperately lonely, desperately afraid. But
in the morning when the bit of sky was light, I thought, 'This
cannot happen in these new times—this is impossible—' or I
thought, 'At worst they have simply forgotten my case. My time
will come. It is not as though we had no justice these days. We
have a whole new code of modern law.' I had studied in a history
class this code.

"But nothing happened for a long time—nothing, indeed, until
one day they began to fill the cell full of others. The search for
revolutionists must have been very severe. Every day the cell was

filled full and at every dawn it was emptied. The nights were horrible. They were afraid, at first cursing, and then as the night came near dawn they began crying and wailing. At first I used to talk to them. And it was out of this talk that I became a real revolutionist, I-wan. For they all had stories to tell me of how they had done nothing that was a greater crime than to help the poor to get more money for their work in mills or shops, or how they had helped girls to escape out of brothels into which they had been sold, or how merely they wanted to make a better country and had joined a band of patriots such as ours. I came to see that the government ought not to have imprisoned them at all. They were all young—many of them younger than you and I. And as I watched them go out to be killed I grew so full of hatred towards those who ordered their death that I swore I would revenge them if I escaped. When you came, I was already a determined revolutionist. Then I talked no more with anyone. When new ones came in I was silent. The cell grew used and filthy. But I cared for nothing. I could not sleep. Each night I, too, only waited for the dawn. Then when the cell was still dark, there would be a rattle of a key in the lock, and a round cylinder of light would be shot into our darkness. And a rough voice would call out the names one after the other of everyone—of everyone, that is, except me. Day after day I waited, sweating, my heart tight, for my name. But it was never called. I was only forgotten.

"The cylinder of light was fastened upon one miserable creature after another. They were nearly always crying as the soldiers handcuffed them one to the other. Then they were marched down a corridor. Only I was left, and there I always stood watching them go, knowing where they went. I imagined them always, every day, crowding down the corridor, feeling the air suddenly fresh on their faces as I had not felt it in many days. But it was still dark. In the darkness hands they could not see would push

49

them, jostling them against a hard wall. There would be a shout, a noise, a flash before their eyes. They would fall, huddled.

"An English sentence kept springing out of my brain. 'I wandered lonely as a cloud—' I longed to cry out to them, to tell them something. But no one even knew what became of them. Day after day I died with them, forgotten, until you came one day with the new ones, and with you I was found."

I-wan, reading these pages far into the night, over and over again, could not burn them. These things En-lan had put down were a precious record. He folded the pages and put them away in his drawer, underneath some old books which his grandfather had given him and which he never read. But he could never put away what he had read. En-lan had given him a part of himself. What could he give in return? He lay awake thinking what he could give to En-lan, and he could think of nothing worthy in return, except his own blood, sworn to brotherhood.

When he saw En-lan the next day he did not speak of what he had read. He saw En-lan was now shy, having told him much. So without speaking of it he asked him, "Will you be my blood brother?"

At this the shyness went out of En-lan's look, and he answered, "Yes, I will."

Then they went to En-lan's room and after the old rite of blood brotherhood, they drew blood from their arms and mingled it together, and clasped their hands and took the vow. And though neither ever talked of it, the vow remained between them.

This was how En-lan had become a secret revolutionist and I-wan with him, so that they met with these others in a deserted classroom when school was over each day. . . . He came out of his thoughts in this meeting to hear En-lan say, as he now stood up before them all, "We have been given the task of organizing the district of the silk mills in the northern part of the city. These are the mills for which we are responsible."

He read a list of names, one after the other. I-wan had only heard of them. He had never in his whole life been into those parts of Shanghai where thousands of men and women and children worked in the silk mills.

"You, I-wan," En-lan said, "must take the furthest section, the Ta Tuan mill, since you can hire a ricksha and need not go on foot. Those who must go on foot may take the nearer places."

And En-lan went on to tell them how the revolution must now be taken into the factories, so that the people who worked there might understand and prepare for the day when the government would be overthrown, and a new rule set up, the rule of the people for themselves. It was, as En-lan showed it, a true and right plan. I-wan thought of the villages in En-lan's story—they ought to be freed from taxes and from having to grow opium. And if the people in the mills were so sorrowful as En-lan said they were, they should be helped to a better life. He was glad to do this, and he took his orders, as they all did, willingly and without reply. All over the country, in many cities, young men and women were taking such orders against the day to come, the day of hope for all. . . .

Peng Liu at this moment came running in. "Someone comes!" he cried.

There was the sound of footsteps on the stair.

"Run!" En-lan cried.

They scattered as though the wind blew. But I-wan, even as he ran, noticed something. Peng Liu did not run. Instead he stood alone in the room as though he waited for someone. And after a moment he had come for them and, grinning, he told them it was no one—a carpenter come to change a broken windowpane. So they had gone on with their meeting, and I-wan forgot to think about Peng Liu, the more easily because Peng Liu was of a sort that everybody forgot rather than remembered—he was so small and indistinct in his looks and ways, and so seemingly harmless. None ever thought to give him any work to do except his spying, and I-wan was glad not to think of it because he did not like him.

And indeed after this day I-wan began another life.

"What are you so busy about?" I-ko demanded. "You are in some mischief."

I-wan now came home so late that several times in the last few weeks I-ko had come before him. Tonight he had met his brother on the steps. I-ko stepped out of his handsome private ricksha and gazed at I-wan with scorn.

"On foot!" he said. "Like a coolie! You never used to walk everywhere." For I-wan, in spite of what En-lan had said, took pride in setting forth each day after school as the others did in his old uniform and unpolished leather shoes for the silk mill.

He did not answer I-ko and they went up the steps side by side. He could smell the heavy musky fragrance of the oil I-ko used to smooth his long straight black hair. It was the fashion among all of I-ko's friends to let their hair grow long to the neck and to smooth it straight from the forehead and the ears. This was because a popular young poet of the day wore his so, "The Chinese Byron," he was called. I-ko was proud to know him and he said constantly such things as, "Tse-li and I—" "Today I said to Tse-li—" Everybody rushed to read Tse-li's latest verse. I-wan read it also, but he could not see anything in it. There was nothing but talk about flowers and death and escape into the misted bamboo hills and always to a woman, waiting.

"Besides, you ought not to go about alone," I-ko scolded him. "You might be kidnaped. Anything happens now. Then it would

52

cost a great deal to ransom you—far more than you are worth," he added, teasingly.

It was quite true that in the disturbed times when the breath of new revolution was everywhere this sort of thing happened. His father had hired two tall Russian guards to go with him every day in his automobile. They kept their hands upon pistols in their pockets, and I-ko's private ricksha puller was once a soldier and he also carried a pistol in his bosom.

"The poorer I look the better, then," I-wan said.

"Oh, a clever kidnaper would make sure of who you were," I-ko said.

They entered the house. Across the hall Peony's face looked out from behind a curtain and disappeared. He heard his grandmother's cracked voice cry out their names.

"I-ko! I-wan!"

I-ko shrugged his shoulders and lifted his eyebrows and did not answer.

"I am dining with Tse-li," he muttered. "I have no time for the old woman."

"Why do you call her that behind her back?" I-wan whispered fiercely.

And then not because he wanted to, but because he hated I-ko's flippant look, he turned aside into his grandmother's room once more.

But he stayed only for a moment and then went on to his own room and threw himself on his bed. Tse-li—Tse-li! What right had young men to be like Tse-li in times like these? He would ask En-lan, "Ought we not to put Hua Tse-li's name on the death list?" He hated the young aesthete whom his brother loved.

This death list was like a weapon to the band. They had none of them any real comprehension that it meant massacre. As yet it was only a hope of revenge against people whom now they

53

could only hate. When anyone made them angry, a teacher or a fellow student or an official whom they could never meet but who made some foreign treaty of which they disapproved, or if they heard of one who took public money for himself, they put his name upon the death list. Peng Liu even wished to put the name of the young science teacher, who was an Englishman, upon the list because he disliked Peng Liu and made no bones of it.

"Stand up!" he had roared at Peng Liu one day. "Don't cringe like a filthy Hindu!" Peng Liu had not understood "cringe" or "filthy Hindu," but he had looked up the words in the dictionary, and after that he had wanted to put the name of James Ranald on the death list. But En-lan had said with scorn, "There is no use in putting foreign names down, because naturally when the time comes all foreigners will be killed."

When this time would be no one knew, but by late autumn everyone in the band felt it was coming soon. The revolutionary government at Hankow was growing stronger every day, and at a certain moment Chiang Kai-shek would sweep down the Yangtse River. What would happen would happen. No one spoke of it loudly. But I-wan heard it talked about secretly and with hope in the band, and at home, scornfully, by his father. In the band En-lan explained to them that it was not enough to talk. They must take their share of the preparation. All through the city bands like theirs were getting ready.

"Getting ready," he had said, "means preparing the people, their minds and their bodies. We who speak the language of the people must prepare their minds. You, I-wan, because your grandfather is a general and because you have learned military drill, must now organize also a workers' brigade in the Ta Tuan mill."

For a moment I-wan could not speak because he was so astonished. En-lan knew who he was and had always known. But how did he know that at home his grandfather had had him tutored by a young German officer for three summers?

Then he shouted loudly, "I will!"

He said no more than that, but afterwards once, when he passed En-lan alone in a corridor, he asked, "How did you know I knew military drill?"

And En-lan grinned and answered, "I see you goose-step like no one else every day at the school drill!" and went on.

Thus it came about that I-wan began to organize that strange secret army among the pallid men of the mills. For two months now he had been going daily to the mills. It was not easy. He was not allowed to go into the great ramshackle buildings from which poured the hot filthy stink of silkworms rotting in the steamy heat. But about the mills were many straw huts where the mill workers lived, and he loitered near them and waited for the people to come home—the men, the women, the children.

At first he felt awkward and strange with them. He could scarcely believe these were people, these crawling, sickly creatures, coughing, blear-eyed, their hands swollen and red. It was the hands of the women and the girls which were worst. They held them out, stiff with pain. When I-wan first saw them he could not keep from blurting out, "What is the matter with your hands?"

It was a young girl who answered, a slight child who looked less than twelve. She spoke in a mild, pleasant voice.

"It is the hot water."

"Hot water?" he asked.

An old woman broke in. "The cocoons must be put in very hot water, young sir, to kill the worms and to soften the silk, and we must take them out with our hands and find the end of the silk the worm has spun, so the cocoon can be unwound.

The water is kept hot by foreign electricity and so our hands are like this."

He could say nothing more, feeling sick at the sight of the raw swollen flesh. That first day he went home having done nothing. When he entered his home he thought, "There is one smell worse than the opium in this house—it is the smell of the silk mill."

And that night he had said to Peony, "Let me smell that scent of yours."

She brushed her scented palm across his cheeks and his eyes. "It is sweet, after all," he murmured.

She put her palm upon his lips, and for a moment he did not move. Her small clean fragrant hand was grateful to him.

"It's like a flower—your hand—" he murmured.

He did not love Peony at all. He knew now he did not love her, and would never love her, but hers was a girl's hand, delicate and sweet, and its fragrance and softness stood to him for a moment for some delicacy and sweetness to come sometime to him, as to all young men, though from another hand than Peony's. He longed for it a moment vaguely, then put the thought away from him. There was no place for any girl even in his mind. He must use his mind only for the people.

But how could Peony know this, and how could he tell her?

She leaned against him delicately and he allowed it, and he felt her heart beat against his shoulder as he sat at his desk with his books. And in a moment he was not thinking of her, nor of anything except again the people he had seen for the first time that afternoon. They were more real to him than any girl's hand, even than Peony's.

"You are not going to bed yet?" Peony asked him. Since the night when he had locked her out of his room she had come in early with his tea, and gone away again. He shook his head.

56

"Don't sit up," she coaxed him. "You work so hard—and you don't need to work. You aren't a poor man's son."

"I can't sleep," he said. He thought, "That is why I can't sleep—because I am a rich man's son." He wished it were to-morrow, so that he could go again and somehow help those people.

"Go away," he told Peony, "I must work."

She went away then, sighing, not teasing him as she usually did. At the door she waited. But he did not look at her, and so she left him. When she was gone, he pushed his books aside and went to the window and stood a long time staring out into the night-filled garden. He knew every foot of the garden. It was a place famous for its beauty. His grandfather and his father had put much money into its making. Huge rocks from the far north beyond Peking had been brought to it, strange and fantastic, and colored pebbles from the hill of the Blue Porcelain Pagoda near Nanking were scattered over winding paths between them. There were streams and bridges and a lake, summerhouses and small boats. And around it all was a wall so high that even from his window he could not see over it. There was no gate from the garden except a small postern gate for the gardener, who lived just outside. He kept it locked and he only carried the key.

"That's the way I've lived," I-wan thought, "in the garden with the wall around."

And gazing into that silent darkness he determined that he would put away all thought of anything for himself and learn only of the people in the mill.

Soon there was nothing he did not know about the life of these mill workers. From all over China they had drained down to Shanghai. Out of famine and poverty and civil war, they had come here. Their lot was no better except that now they barely escaped starvation and there were at least no soldiers to maraud them. They lived, somehow, in their huts.

How to help these people now became I-wan's chief life. At school he studied barely enough to escape reproof, and at home he took care to do quickly what he must in order to escape without notice. Everything was becoming a dream except these people.

He could do very little for them, and when he discovered this they possessed him more than ever. For they were at once so grateful to him and yet so hopeless. He crouched under their miserable matsheds with them in the cold late autumn rain. They looked at each other and at him and shook their heads, and a man said, "You speak out of your heart's goodness, and yet it is no use. No one can help us. The truth is, there is no other way for us to get even our poor food. Who wants us? No one, anywhere. Who cares whether we live or die, or has ever cared?"

"Then you yourselves must care," he told them.

"What can we do?" they said. "We can do nothing—and we know it."

Little by little he began to try to teach them they were of some worth.

"You must be strong enough to hope," he told them. "To have no hope is to give up tomorrow as well as today."

But it was a long time before he could persuade them there was any reason even for hope that there would ever be anything better. Bit by bit, over weeks, he persuaded a few men to come to an open place beyond the huts, where not many people passed, and there he began to teach them the military drill which he had himself been taught. They shuffled their heavy feet and hung their heads shamefaced, but he compelled them and scolded them.

58

"Hold up your heads!" he commanded them. "Some day you will have to fight for yourselves."

By now he had explained to them often the whole plan of the days to come, how the revolutionary army would sweep down the river, how there would be a general strike declared in all the mills—everywhere they were working for that strike— and in each place there must be a workers' brigade, men who could march and shoot and be ready to attack from within while the revolutionary army attacked from without. They listened, doubting everything.

"We are like men who flee from a dragon to find a tiger in the path," one said.

In the end I-wan had cried, "Let only the men who believe what I say, stay to learn!"

Instantly the older men had gone back to their huts, choosing the miseries they knew. But seventeen young men remained and with these I-wan began his brigade. But even they were doubtful until one day I-wan gave them each a gun. For plans were growing quickly real, as autumn grew into winter. To a certain shop whose master had been bribed, a certain number of guns was sent for their band, not all at once, but ten by ten. And I-wan had claimed eighteen, one for himself and one for each of his seventeen young men. He gave them by night one by one, here into a hut and there into a hut, and they were hidden in the piles of straw upon which the people slept and under the rags of their garments. One by one he taught his men how to shoot, meeting them far outside the city in the fields. If anyone asked them what they did, they said they were hunters.

On the piece of open ground they had marched without their guns. But it was different now when they marched. They had new strength because each thought of the weapon he now had been given.

And I-wan came and went secretly at night through the gate in the garden. He had bribed the gardener, and the gardener laughed and gave him another key.

"You are like I-ko, too!" he said. "Ah-ha, young sir!"

I-wan smiled. Let the old man think he was going out to pretty girls and flower-houses as I-ko did!

Each worked blindly in his own place through that autumn and the winter. En-lan knew what every one in the band did, but beyond that he, too, knew nothing, except that all through the city there were bands like theirs, each doing its allotted work. Somewhere there were those who knew the whole, but where they were or who they were, no one knew. I-wan felt himself part of a great secret body, through which the life blood flowed, whose heart they could all feel beating, whose brain directed, and yet they knew no more.

All that had seemed real in his life before now became of no importance. His family he scarcely thought about, knowing the day now inevitable when he must renounce them all and say nothing when their names were called for death. Much of the time he felt strong enough for this. When he was working, when he was caught up into that secret life force and felt himself a part of the great specific energy which was to heal all the troubles of the people, he thought, "Why should I save alive even my father when I know that he would condemn men like En-lan to death if he knew them? Even me—he would condemn me." For this was now a time when a deeper unity than blood united. Blood could divide now, when men were dividing themselves into these two parts between which there is no bridge, those who stay in the ways they know and those who must go on to other ways. And coming and going, with every day he felt this deeper cleavage. Sometimes in the winter night, in the silence of his bed, with the curtains drawn, he lay imagining. And then he felt as though the great ocean were beginning to divide slowly and inevitably, from the bottom. Though the surface was still unmoved, in the deeps, among hidden caves and watery foundations, a bottomless fissure was growing which would one day be a bridgeless chasm between these two kinds of people. It would not be race against race. No, it would be something else. For Mr. Ranald and Miss Maitland would not be with white people on one side. Mr. Ranald and his father and his grandfather would be on one side, and he and En-lan and Miss Maitland on the other. I-ko would be with his father, because he would feel safer there, and his mother and his grandmother. And little creatures like Peony—it was only chance where they would be when the moment struck, whether with him on his side or with another. East and west, they would all be mingled together on the two sides of the chasm.

He would be with En-lan, and with them would be all these others, the ones in his band and the ones he did not know in other bands. And with them would be all the poor, the peasants and the workers in mills and apprentices in trades and shops— from all over the world other young men, too, and young women, whose language they could not understand, but whose hearts and purposes were one with his and En-lan's. When there was to be such brotherhood as this, why should he cling to a few whose blood he shared by chance? The old ways were gone. And from such meditation I-wan rose to every day like a sword drawn from its scabbard and he compelled the young men in his brigade to his own spirit.

Through the winter, in spite of cold winds and frequent

rain, this brigade had now grown to thirty-seven men. He knew them each by name and he knew where their huts were in the mass of huts which lay like scales of huge fish around the mills. At first they had all looked alike to him. All were so pale and fleshless, and their faces so same with their black hollow eyes and haggard mouths. Even the stories they told him seemed the same. For though they were born in many parts of the country, still the same causes had driven them here—the wars and famines, the many taxes of greedy and unjust rulers—there was nothing new. When one man said, "I was the youngest son of a farmer with less than two acres of land, so how could I be fed? The others could not stop eating because I was born—" it was in essence the story they all told. They drifted seaward, following the river, and at its mouth Shanghai was spread like a net. When they reached Shanghai there was the sea, and one could go no further. So they came into the mills.

When I-wan heard what their wage was and how they worked from before dawn until long after the winter dark had fallen, so that until summer they could not see the sun, he cursed in anger. "We will change that!" he shouted.

Then one of them said, "Why should they pay us more when there are so many clamoring even for what we have? It is not reasonable."

This also was what he had to fight, this gentleness they all had in them. They were rough in speech and not one of them could read or write and their ways were as simple as the beasts', so that when nature needed, a man turned where he stood and took relief. But they would have been abashed and humble before any rich man, not from fear so much as from their own timidness because they thought the gods had not made them equal to him. I-wan struggled to break down this gentleness.

"You are as good as any man!" he shouted at them. "You have the right to all that any man has!"

To this they laughed amiably and replied so peaceably that I-wan gnashed his teeth at them.

"It is your kindness to say so," they said courteously, "because we know we are nothing."

Yet he could not keep from loving them because they were so faithful in their trying to learn from him. They had to steal the time to come to learn from him, two or three coming at a time, and the others filling in their places for an hour or two in the mill. They tried hard, and by the end of the winter they could march together and each one could shoot well enough. With his own money I-wan had bought cartridges for them to practice with, and they were fair marksmen. Then, though they were proud of this, like children they longed for uniforms to wear. They fingered the rough stuff of his uniform and asked, "Shall we some day wear warm cloth like this?"

"Yes," he said, "that I promise you. You shall all wear warm clothes and eat all you want."

They clustered about him that night in the cold winter's moonlight. He was ashamed that he had put on his greatcoat. He wished he had not, so that he might have been cold, too. He stood there, warm and well clad, his belly full of food such as they had never seen and which he ate every day, and he felt tears hot in his eyes. Their eyes were a little hopeful now, sometimes, when he spoke. But their wistful faces broke his heart, and the wind fluttered their cotton rags and pierced to his own bones. He cried in himself, "If my father's house were mine, I would open the doors and take them in!" Then he thought, "It would be no use. They would come in and come in until there was no room to stand, and still they would be coming, millions of them." No, if all the houses of the rich were opened it would not be enough, he thought, for all these poor. The poor filled the earth.

"When shall it be?" a man asked. I-wan knew him well, a poor coughing young fellow who had not long to live. It would not be soon enough for him, however soon it was.

"Soon," he said, "very soon. Perhaps in the spring."

No, the only thing that could save them was the world made new for them, a world made for the poor and not the rich—a world whose laws were for the little man, whose houses were for him, whose whole thought and shape was for him, so that there could be no rich and strong to prey upon him.

"Don't stay here longer," he said to them. "Go to your beds."

"When you speak," a voice said out of a shadow, "we feel warmer and as though we had eaten something."

"Good night—good night," he cried. He could bear no more —his heart was too full, and he turned away.

That night, late as it was, he felt it impossible to go straight from their want to the plenty and waste of his own home. He strode through the cold, half-empty streets of this part of the city toward the school. He would go and talk awhile with En-lan.

He found En-lan alone in his cubicle, not studying, but reading a sheet of closely written writing. When I-wan came in he put this under a book.

"Come in," he said. "Why are you so gloomy?"

En-lan was never gloomy. His black eyes were bright and he looked as though he could scarcely keep from laughter. Indeed, in these days he made excuse to laugh at anything, as though he were so brimming with inner pleasure that it must overflow.

"I have come back from—" I-wan paused. They never spoke aloud anything that had to do with their work. He sat down on the little iron cot and reaching for a bit of paper on the table, he wrote, "When do you think the day will really come?"

"Not later than the end of the third month of the new year," En-lan wrote in answer. Then he took the paper and lit a match and burned it to ash and blew the ash away.

"It is moonlight—will you walk?" I-wan asked. He craved from En-lan some of his brimming sureness, and some, too, of his hardness. En-lan was hard and sure and never moved by anything. Now he nodded, rose, and put on his coat and cap of rabbit's fur, such as the northern peasants wore. Then he took up the paper he had put under the book and folding it away from I-wan's eyes, he burned it, also, and blew away the ash. Then they went out into the street.

"Let us turn this way, out of the wind," En-lan suggested. "On a night like this the wind snatches one's words and carries them to other ears."

They turned down a quiet alley where they had talked before and squatted in the lee of a wall. I-wan began at once. There was that about En-lan which sifted out extra talk before it was spoken.

"How shall I persuade my men they are worth anything?" he asked. "All my life I have lived among people who thought they were valuable and should have everything." He paused and thought of I-ko. I-ko had never in all his life been worth anything. He had done nothing except consume food and goods, and yet I-ko thought he must have the best. "These poor," I-wan went on, "believe somehow that they deserve to be poor. I can't get them to see that they have any right to live. I can't get them even to hate the rich. They simply say, 'One is rich and one is poor—it is fate.'"

He waited to hear En-lan's laughter. But En-lan did not

laugh. His face looked stern in the moonlight and his voice was grave when he spoke.

"You have hit on the kernel of the matter. Our real difficulty is not with the rich. They can be killed and their riches taken from them. The trouble is with those who have been born in such poverty that they cannot hope. They will have to have something in their hands—food—money—something to feel and know they have, before they will believe." He paused and then went on. "You are an idealist, I-wan, and that is your weakness. The poor are no better than the rich."

I-wan looked at him. What was this En-lan had said?

"Then why do we work for them?" he asked.

Now En-lan laughed.

"Do you believe that if any of those poor were in your father's house he would share what he had with the others? No!" En-lan shook back his rough hair. "They would be worse than your father, because your father has never had to be an animal. I-wan, prepare yourself!"

"For what?" I-wan asked.

"For the time when the poor get what they have never had," En-lan said in a whisper.

"Why?" I-wan whispered.

"It will be worse than wild beasts," En-lan said. "On the day when we tell them the city is theirs, they will kill not only the rich but each other. Much of what they take will be destroyed simply in the struggle to possess it. We must let them alone. It will pass."

"And then?" I-wan asked.

"When it is over and they are bewildered because nothing is left, then we must come in and force them to obedience and order."

"Force them?" I-wan asked. "I thought everybody was to be free."

"Free!" En-lan echoed harshly. "Such freedom is foolishness. No one is free. We are not free, you and I. We work in a planned system. So will they. There is one man—"

"Who?" I-wan asked. As far as this they had never gone.

"One," En-lan replied, "one man, a great man."

"Who?" I-wan asked.

En-lan leaned to I-wan. Against his cheek I-wan felt En-lan's fresh hot breath.

"Chiang Kai-shek," he said.

It was the name of the head of the revolutionary army.

"When he comes into this city," En-lan's breath was swift against I-wan's ear—"it will be the day. The plans are made. In twenty days the general strike is to be declared. It will give the workers time to meet and to complete the final organization. They will fight from within while he attacks from without. It was written on that paper I burned—secret orders. All that we have been working for is coming together now—the end for which all has been planned—a new country—our country!"

They sat shivering a little from the cold night and their own heat within. The moon was setting and the walls threw black shadows over the alley so that they sat in darkness. But it was nothing—this present darkness. They did not see it. They were gazing into the brightness of what was to come, into that day when all that was now wrong should be made right. I-wan could see it all—the victorious army of the good. It was now gathered, already waiting.

He had seen a picture of Chiang Kai-shek in his plain revolutionary uniform. At the time he had thought, "He looks a little like En-lan." There was the same bold clear look in his eyes that En-lan had, the same strong peasant face. Now as he

67

thought, his wandering idealism gathered about this figure. A man like that, so young and strong and full of noble power, leading the army of the young and strong. . . . He drew in his breath and was choked by something—tears or laughter. He stood up abruptly.

"I am glad you told me that," he said. "I shall work harder now. We will be ready."

En-lan did not answer. He rose and they walked hand in hand down the alley.

"How soft your hand is!" En-lan said curiously. "You've never done any work, have you?"

"No," I-wan answered. He was ashamed, feeling En-lan's hard hand in his, and after a moment he pulled his away. "But I'm strong enough," he added.

At the school gate he left En-lan and turned homeward. It was strange how heavy-hearted he had gone to En-lan and how light his heart now was. En-lan could always do that for him. The trouble with him, he thought, was that he let himself be lost in the present moment, and En-lan never did. To En-lan a moment was but a moment, and only the future was real. En-lan opened the doors of the present and showed him what was ahead and what they were working for together. He could think now of those creatures blown in the cold wind and feel pity for them and not agony.

"Poor things," he thought. "I am glad they will have their freedom for a while, at least, to take what they like."

He let himself in at the garden gate and entered the house and went upstairs. It would be strange when these sumptuous rooms were full of the poor, tearing at the curtains, dragging the rugs away, snatching and pulling. Would he mind?

"No," he told himself stoutly. "Why should I? I have never cared for such things."

And then he heard someone weeping. He listened. It was I-ko, crying like a boy. There was a light shining through the transom of his grandfather's door. Before he could wonder, he saw the door of his own room open, and Peony came out silently.

"I have been waiting for you," she said in a low voice. "You are to go at once to your grandfather. I-ko has done something wicked."

It was like coming into a cage again to enter this room of his grandfather. It was hot and close. They were all there except his grandmother. His mother was weeping softly, her round face swollen and her cheeks trembling. His grandfather sat erect in his large chair, holding one of the cigars he loved between his thumb and finger. But he was not smoking. I-ko was standing by the table, leaning on his hands, his neck bent, his head hanging. Before I-wan opened the door he had heard his father shouting. But when he came in the voice stopped. They all looked at him except I-ko, who did not move. But his father began again at once, as soon as he saw I-wan.

"It's you—you, too—where have you been? It's long past midnight. But I don't know why I expect better of my younger son than of my elder! Where have you been?"

"To see a schoolmate," I-wan answered. He could see I-ko. Now that his father's attention was not on him, I-ko took his handkerchief and wiped his eyes and blew his nose. I-wan felt in the midst of his disgust a sort of pity for his elder brother. It was horrible that a young man should be so weak and whimpering. Somehow I-ko had been made into a useless being, but it was not altogether I-ko's fault. He would keep his father's attention a little longer to help I-ko.

"The moon is so bright," he said. "My friend left his room in the dormitory with me and we went out into the street."

69

"Don't tell me you ended at that!" his father shouted.

"We talked awhile and then he went back and I came home," I-wan said quietly.

"I think you ought to believe I-wan," his mother said in her sudden hurried way. "You should believe I-wan, because he is a good boy."

"You always say your sons are good," his father now shouted at her. "Two months ago I thought something was wrong in the bank. But no, you said, I-ko is so good—I-ko could do no wrong! And so everybody knew but I—I have been made into a fool by my own son!"

He had mimicked his wife's high soft voice, and she began to cry, and I-ko hung his head again.

"I-ko," his grandfather commanded him, "sit down!"

I-ko sat down by the table, without looking up.

"Do you know what you have done?" his grandfather inquired. "It seems to me you do not."

"I don't think it's so bad," I-ko said in a sullen half-whisper.

His father started. "You don't—" he began.

"Be quiet," the old man commanded. "I am speaking. I-ko, you have taken a great deal of money that was not yours."

I-ko did not answer at once. Then he said in the same sullen voice, "It's not as if my father were not the president of the bank."

I-wan saw his father set his lips without speaking.

The old man put his hand to his head.

"Do you know whose money is in the bank?" the old man inquired. "It is the money of other people—of many people. There is even government money there. People trust your father. They trusted his son."

The room was quiet except for the old man's stern voice.

I-wan thought, "I-ko has done this!"

70

"Why did you do it, I-ko?" he blurted out. "You always have money."

He saw I-ko's eyes steal toward him hostilely, but I-ko did not answer.

"Why did you do it?" his father suddenly bellowed at him. "We have all asked you, and I-wan asks you, too. Have I ever denied you anything? You had only to come and ask me!"

"I didn't want to ask you," I-ko answered, goaded.

There was silence to this. They all looked at him. He looked from one to the other of them.

"I—I—" he began. He stopped, then rushed on: "Why do you all look at me so? I—I—I didn't take it all at once—for any one thing. Tse-li said, 'Let's do this—or this'—some little thing—I don't know—and he hadn't the money, so he said, 'I-ko, you always have plenty of cash.' And they all got to saying that— and I was ashamed to say I hadn't plenty—" He was half crying again. His smooth hair was falling over his face. He turned on his father. "You—you say, why don't I ask you—it's because you scold me—you're always scolding me—ever since I can remember. I—I'd rather take the money than have to ask you and have you —you yell at me, 'Again—again!' "

"It's true," his mother cried at her husband. "You have always been so harsh to him!"

"And who was to save him otherwise in this house?" his father shouted at her. "A lot of women spoiling him, teaching him to cheat, to lie, by pretending to obey me when I am here! You are to blame—women like you are to blame for all the corruption in the country! Do you think I don't know? I was a rich man's son, too—in a house full of women and slaves!"

I-wan said not one word. He had his life elsewhere now, and though this house fell to pieces, he would not fall with it. But when his father said what he did to his mother, he thought with

71

a sort of curiosity of him as a man, to wonder why he was not spoiled, then, as I-ko was. Something had come to save his father just as he himself had been saved by happening upon certain books and then upon En-lan and the band and the men in the mill, and through all of these upon the whole age of revolution which was to come. In a sense the revolution had already saved him.

"What can I do with you, I-ko?" his father asked. His voice changed to sadness. "What can any man do with a worthless son?"

His grandfather spoke.

"Nevertheless he is your son and my grandson, whatever he does. We must return the money. And let us send him abroad to some school where he must work and where he can leave these idle companions."

I-ko did not speak. But I-wan could see he was waiting to hear what his father said.

"That is the best thing to do," his mother said in her soft eager way. "No one will know—and so many young men go abroad to study now. It is exactly the thing."

"Cover it all up—cover it all up," his father said bitterly. "That is the way—no one need know, and so he will never learn the difference between evil and good!"

"I will never do it again," I-ko said in a whisper. "I have learned. I will do whatever you say."

His father rose suddenly.

"Get out of my sight," he said to I-ko, not loudly, but his voice low and cold. "Put your things together. You will go to Germany —go to a military school and let them see what they can do with you. I will have your ticket bought, or you will spend the money."

"Yes, that's right," the old man agreed, "that's best. The Germans will teach him."

72

"Get away from me," his father said to I-ko.

Without speaking, I-ko turned away and went out. They heard him cross the hall and the door of his room opened and shut.

In this room nothing was said. Then his grandfather struck a match, lit his cigar at last, and smoked a moment. Until he spoke no one would speak.

"I will go to bed," he said, and he rose to his feet.

"Let me go with you," his son said.

"No," the old man replied. "I can go alone—"

When the door shut behind him, I-wan's father turned to his mother.

"Will you retire?" he asked.

And she knew he meant she must, so she rose, wiping her eyes, and went into the next room.

Then I-wan was left alone with his father. He had risen while his grandfather and mother left the room.

"Sit down," his father said. So he sat down, and his father looked at him.

"Will you take your elder brother's place?" he asked abruptly. He had a small toy in his hand, a paperweight made like a pagoda, and he played with it restlessly. I-wan's eyes moved to his father's strong smooth hands. They were powerful hands, though the flesh on them was as soft as Peony's cheek.

He felt his father near as he had never done before. He felt the depths of his father's disappointment in I-ko, and that now he needed comfort. He thought, "I wish I could tell my father everything." But the fear that hangs between the generations would not allow him. He could not forget that his father was the same man he had always been, and that if he did not like a thing he could not comprehend it, however good and right it was. So I-wan held back his desire to confide in him, but still

73

he could not wholly refuse his father. So he said, "Will you let me tell you, Father, at the end of the school year?"

Before then, he thought, it will be another world.

His father stared at him and nodded.

"Let it be, then," he said. "Now you go away, too. I don't know why men want sons now-a-days. In the past men had sons for their old age, so that they could be sure of care. But no one can hope for such care now from the young."

He rose and without looking at I-wan, he also went into the other room. And I-wan, left alone, went back to his own room. His father, whom he had thought of always as a proud man, satisfied and able to have anything he liked, he now saw was neither proud nor satisfied, nor had he what he wanted. He thought, puzzling, "It still is not enough to feed men and give them enough money for all their needs." The men in the mill wanted only food and shelter secure, and they would be happy. No, but plenty of people had these things and they were not happy. How would the revolution help these? Pondering this, he opened the door to his own room and Peony sat there by his table, waiting. Her pretty oval face was solemn.

"What is it?" she whispered. "Has I-ko killed someone?"

"No," he answered, "not that."

"Then what?" she urged him. "I know it is something wicked. Your grandmother kept weeping. She said your father was going to beat I-ko to death."

"Of course not," I-wan said scornfully. "But he is to be sent abroad."

"Sent abroad!" Peony cried joyfully. "At once!"

I-wan nodded.

"Then he did kill someone!" Peony cried. "I am sure he did!"

"No, he didn't," I-wan said. "He took some money."

"From the bank?" she exclaimed.

74

"Yes," I-wan said. "Why do you hate him so much?"

"I can't tell you," she said. "I don't want to tell you. You can't imagine how hard it has been to be a slave in this house—with I-ko growing up—and always at home—not away at school."

She turned her head away.

"You haven't been treated as a slave," I-wan said.

"You don't know!" she cried with passion. "You don't know anything about me!"

And to his astonishment she put her face in her hands and began to weep in great loud sobs.

He stood helpless, watching her.

"Don't cry, Peony," he said, "I beg you not to cry."

But she cried through her sobs, "I have been only a slave—an old woman telling me to do this and to do that—getting me up in the night to rub her old sticks of legs, and to make her opium ready. I'm so sick of that smell—"

"Do you hate that smell, too?" he asked.

"Yes," she sobbed. "I run into my room so sick—but I have to come back again to it—and your mother at me—"

"Why?" I-wan asked. He began to see a whole life going on in this house of which he had not been aware.

Peony stopped crying. "Because of I-ko," she said in a low angry voice. "She says I must do what I-ko wants—who am I, she says, but a slave?"

"My mother said that?" I-wan stared at her and felt his heart begin to thump in a slow thick beat.

She nodded.

"But you haven't?" I-wan demanded.

She shook her head.

"I've thought of eating some of the opium and killing myself," she said. "I've often thought of it. Because what have I to live for, I-wan? I'm not a servant, to be happy among servants. I've been taught to be something more—but still not enough to be free. I suppose you think I ought to be grateful your mother let me learn to read and write when you did. I used to be grateful, but I'm not now. I wish I had been left ignorant if I am not to—be any better than this. Then I could have married—someone lowly—and been content. It's so wrong!" she cried. "It's so wicked to let people know there are good things in life and then deny them!"

He could not say a word. Peony had been living like this for years and he did not know it! He thought she was happy and well-treated. That she had to serve them was only, he had thought, what she should do in return. But now he saw what she meant. She was not free. This house where she had plenty to eat and silk robes to wear was still only a prison. He thought, "She needs the revolution, too, to set her free."

In that moment he made up his mind that he would tell Peony everything.

"Peony—" he began. His heart was beating like a clock now, very fast.

She looked at him.

"I want to tell you something," he went on.

"Yes?" she asked. "What is it?"

"Peony, have you ever heard of the revolution?"

"Of course I have," she said. "It's not a good thing. I've heard your father talk about it. He said revolutionists are like bandits."

"No, they're not!" he exclaimed.

"How do you know?" she asked.

Now he would tell her, straight out.

"Because I am one of them."

They looked at each other, and neither moved.

"I-wan!" she whispered.

He nodded.

"If your father knew! He would think you were more wicked than I-ko!"

This struck him. "I believe he would," he agreed.

"You must never tell him," she exclaimed. "Oh, I wish you hadn't told me! I feel as if you had put your life into my hands. I-wan, you will be killed! Why did you?"

And then he began to tell her everything, how in books he first discovered that men's minds had thought and dreamed of a new world. He told her of En-lan and of the band and of the mills. She listened to everything without a movement or a word. And he talked to her as he had never talked to anyone, not even to En-lan, because he had no shyness before Peony. But the strange thing was that he spoke not only to her but to himself. He was giving shape as he talked to all his faith in what was to come, and to all his hope of it.

"When is all this to happen?" Peony interrupted him.

"Soon," he whispered, "as soon as Chiang Kai-shek comes."

She stared at him a moment. Then she shrugged her shoulders. "I don't believe it," she declared.

"You don't believe—Peony!" he cried. "I tell you it's true."

"I know you think it's true," she retorted, "but you're only a boy. I don't believe people will do things for other people for nothing. And all your revolutionists—what are they but people like everybody else?"

"You don't know them," he insisted. "You've only known people like—like my family. Naturally you think everybody is selfish. But that's because they're capitalists."

"I don't know what you mean by capitalists," she said, pouting. "I know this, though, that when people have money they don't mind giving some of it away, but whoever heard of poor people being unselfish? They want everything then for themselves."

77

"But you don't understand," he cried at her. "There won't be any rich and poor!"

"Oh, don't be silly!" she answered.

He was so angry with her he wanted to slap her cheek.

"I wish I hadn't told you," he said shortly. "I told you to make you happy—and let you know soon you will be free. There won't be any slaves after Chiang Kai-shek comes."

"Oh, him!" she said, and laughed. "He's only a man, isn't he?" Then she was sad again. "No," she went on, "where would I go if I were free? I don't know anything except this house. Where could I find shelter? No, if I have been born to be a slave, I am a slave."

It was the old hopelessness of the mill workers, coming from Peony's red lips as she sat, a little satin-clothed figure, there in his chair. Her pretty hands with jade and gold rings were playing with the things on his desk. Was all the world hopeless except himself and those like him? He was clouded with a sort of sadness, watching her hands. It came to him again that there was more to all this revolution than merely feeding and clothing the poor. There was much more. What answer, for instance, could he give to Peony, when she asked him where she would find shelter if she were free? He could not say because he did not know.

"I suppose," he said aloud, hesitating, "that food will be given to everyone somehow. Certainly in the revolution no one will be allowed to starve. Things have to be organized, of course."

She did not answer. When she spoke again he was not in the least prepared for what she said. She looked up brightly, as though she had forgotten herself, and she said, her voice cosy and warm and full of interest, "Tell me about that En-lan—is he handsome?"

He was too disgusted to answer. To think of En-lan thus was to insult him. Girls—why did anyone think a girl could hold any-

78

thing in her mind? Peony was not fit for revolution. She was as she said, born to be a slave—thinking about nothing but—

"I don't know," he answered curtly. He got up suddenly. "I want to sleep, Peony. It must be nearly dawn."

She rose, hiding a small graceful yawn behind the back of her hand, her painted rosy palm turned outward. She had not understood the importance of anything he had told her. And it was true that he had put his life in her hands.

But she leaned forward and touched his cheek with her finger.

"Don't think I shall forget what you have said," she told him. "I never forget anything you ever say. I lock it all up in me and take it out only when I am alone, to see and to think about. It's all I have— Oh, but, I-wan, you won't let them catch you!" She locked her hands together tightly.

"No, of course not," he answered and relented a little toward her. "Besides, it's only a little while."

"I have no faith in all that revolution," she broke in. "It only frightens me. I wish you hadn't told me—except that—it helps me understand something."

"What?" he asked. There was another look now in her face, a look of stillness.

"It helps me to understand you," she said, "and why your heart is not to be touched." She waited a moment. Then she said, "You are like a young priest, I-wan. I saw that when you were telling me. It explains—everything."

She was at the door now and she smiled at him, a flicker of a smile.

"Good night," she said, and closed the door between them.

He had not the least idea what she meant, and he forgot it instantly, because it could not be important.

What Peony had said, that he was like a young priest, he really did not hear, even when she said it, because he was so centered on what he was telling her. If he had comprehended it he would have been angered, for it was part of the plan that all priests should be driven out of the temples, since they deceived the people. I-wan had tried to drive them out of the minds of the men whom he taught. Whenever they said, as the poor will say anywhere, "Heaven will protect us," he cried out, "Heaven will never protect you, because there is no heaven!"

The first time he said this not one of them answered him. It was a holiday, the three days' holiday of the New Year, which is given even to the poor, and they had met together in an open field beyond the town. I-wan had taken his own money and bought tea and New Year's cakes for them at a country tea house, and then they had come away where there were no walls.

"What is that above us, then, if there is no heaven?" a man asked, and he pointed to the sky.

"Air—and cloud," I-wan answered.

"And beyond that?" the man persisted.

"Nothing," I-wan answered.

They thought about this in silence.

"Then all the priests in the temples have told us lies?" the man asked again.

"Yes," I-wan said. And when no one said anything to that, he asked them, "Can any of you point to a single time when you spent money before the gods and they gave you what you asked for?"

They thought awhile again in the way they had whenever he said something they had not heard before.

"It is true," one of them said, a young man with crossed eyes. "At every New Year I have begged the gods to let me grow rich —and look at me, how poor I am!"

80

"Not even the gods can make a man rich if he is born to be poor," a sad voice said.

"Then what is the use of them?" the cross-eyed fellow said hotly. "I'll ask no more of them! If this revolution will make us rich we don't need gods!"

Everyone laughed at this and they all felt merry and brave with good food in their bellies. I-wan had indeed learned already that if he wanted them to believe what he said, they believed better if he fed them first. Every time he fed them they believed more in the revolution.

"Why should he spend his money like this," they argued, "if he is not telling us the truth? He is a good young man."

They helped I-wan to believe, too. Every time he talked to them he came away more sure of that in which he believed, that after the revolution there would be no more trouble or sadness. Whenever he passed a beggar in the street, he gave him a penny and he thought, "A few more months and there will be no more beggars—for no one will be in need." So that winter passed.

One night he was awakened by a noise in the house and the garden lights shone out beneath his windows and he heard his father's voice calling loudly, "Tie him—tie him! I have already sent for the police!"

He got up quickly and drew on his robe and went out and in the hall his mother stood, too frightened to go down.

"They have caught a robber," she gasped, "in the garden!"

He went downstairs and outside in the chilly darkness he found his father and the servants staring at a miserable ragged man who had somehow got over the high wall, a thin dark agile fellow, starved in his looks, and now afraid for his life. He was on his knees whining and crying while the gardener held him by his long hair.

"I heard him," the gardener kept roaring bravely, "I heard the tiles on the wall clatter and one fell to the rocks below, and I said to my wife, 'That's more than wind can do,' and I—"

"Have a kind heart, sir—" the man moaned. "I have not eaten for two days. I thought I would see only if I could find a little food thrown out of the kitchens. I swear I would not have entered the house."

I-wan was about to cry, "Father, I am sure he is hungry," but he caught the man's eye and it had such a cast of evil and malice in it that he was aghast and he said nothing. And at that moment the police came and took the fellow to prison. He went sullenly away and as though he were used to it.

"We might have been murdered," his father said when they were in the house again. Everybody was up now, his grandparents and the servants and Peony, and they all fell to talking together.

But I-wan went to his bed, not to sleep, but to lie wondering why the man's eyes should have been so full of malice. He had seen a look like that before, and when he tried to think, he remembered. It had been the way I-ko looked before he went away a few days ago upon a great ship. They had gone to see him sail, and I-wan and his father had stayed on the dock until the ship had left the shore.

"I cannot trust I-ko," his father had said. "He might leave the ship secretly and hang about the city—"

I-ko, alone on the ship and going alone to a foreign country, had looked like that caught thief, his eyes dark with malice and despair. I-wan felt confused again. What if food and plenty for all were still not enough? But he turned away from this question now as often as it came to him. He must believe that everyone would be better, somehow, after the revolution came. He must believe that Chiang Kai-shek would set everything right. It was all as simple as the difference between night and day. When the sun rose, it was day.

He and Peony did not talk again. She had withdrawn herself from him since that night and she came no more to his room when he was there. Nothing was changed except she did not come. The quilts were spread, the tea was hot, there were his favorite sweetmeats in the box, and new flowers were in the windows or on the table, but it was all done before he came. Once she passed him on the stair and leaned to him and he smelled the jasmine scent.

"Still dreaming?" she asked, her smile small and shadowy. "When will you wake?" she murmured, and went on her way.

He was not sorry he had told her, no, because she had the right to know of coming happiness, even if she would not believe in it, and he knew now his life was safe with her. She would never betray him.

Besides, the time grew short. It was already the middle of the second month, and although the mill owners did not know, the strikes were to be called in fourteen days. No one knew how far these strikes would go, because none knew how many revolutionists were in the city. But in the band each rose and told in numbers what he had done, so that if by chance there were ears in the walls, they could hear but not understand. A girl rose and said, "Of the women to whom I was assigned, sixty-three, prepared eighteen."

This told them that in her band there were sixty-three women, of whom eighteen knew how to use a gun and had guns. For in this work there was no difference between men and women, and women were to be soldiers, too.

Two days before the strike they held their last meeting. En-lan so declared it.

"We must not meet again," he said. "The police have grown so wary that it is not safe. Nor is it necessary. We know our way, hour by hour. If it must be that any of you need to speak to me, mark a round sun on a bit of paper and put it in my hand, and I will set a time and place. Otherwise let there be no meeting between us or any sign of recognition, until after the day. Each in his place, and on that day the whole will come to life. Until then, each goes alone."

But the next day in their English class, where he and En-lan sat side by side, En-lan had drawn a round sun on his notebook, and under it had written an hour. So he had gone to En-lan's room, and En-lan had opened the door. When he came in En-lan said, "I am more afraid of you than the others. I want to warn you especially, in that house of yours, to say nothing to anyone. These last days are the most dangerous. And your father is powerful. All our lives depend on secrecy."

"I?" I-wan asked impetuously. "But I—"

En-lan said, "You are so innocent—you tell without knowing it. You do not know how to conceal."

He was about to deny this when he remembered that it was true. He had told Peony. He stared at En-lan, his mouth open.

"You have already done it," En-lan remarked. "I see it in your face. Come with me into the open, where we can talk."

So they had gone out on the streets and seeming to buy peanuts and sweets, to stop and watch a wandering actor's show, to laugh at some children, En-lan questioned him at such moments as no one was close, and he drew out of him everything about Peony and what he had told her.

He had never seen En-lan so angry.

"A woman and a slave!" En-lan muttered, his voice low, but his eyes like a tiger's. "Was there ever such a silly as you!"

"But I tell you, you don't know Peony," I-wan said eagerly. "She is like my sister." He hesitated, then stammered, "Why— why, she—she loves me!"

"She isn't your sister," En-lan said, "and it is the worse that she

84

loves you. She will want to hurt you—because you don't love her —even though she kills you."

"Peony is not like that," I-wan protested.

En-lan said nothing for a while. Then he sighed. "Well, it is done!" And after a while he said again, "I cannot rest. I am responsible for you all. Can you send this girl to meet me somewhere, so that I can see what she is and threaten her into silence?"

"I don't know," I-wan stammered. "I don't think she would— I think she would be ashamed to come to meet you."

"A slave?" En-lan asked scornfully.

"She isn't just a slave," I-wan said. "We've not treated her like a slave."

"Ask her," En-lan said. And again he said, "It is more than your life, remember. We might all be seized and killed."

It was true that not a day passed now that there were not those whom the police seized and killed as revolutionists. Their names were not published and people did not hear of them. But from schools and from homes young men and women were marched away by police and by soldiers appearing suddenly and demanding them, and they were never seen again, nor could anyone save them after they were taken.

"I will ask her," I-wan had said.

But Peony did not come near him that night and when he sent for her, she returned word by the servant that his grandmother needed her.

The next day the general strike was declared. In his home I-wan at the breakfast table heard his father roar out over his newspaper.

"What next? The silk mills are closed!"

I-wan put down his chopsticks. His father went on reading aloud, furiously, his eyebrows frowning over his eyes.

"In the Ta Tuan mills, three hundred workers on strike. In the Ling I mills, four hundred and twenty-five. In the Sung Ren mills—" he banged the paper with his fist. "We have money in every one of them! What is the government thinking of to allow this? It's the students—they have been fomenting this!"

"The government doesn't kill enough of them," his grandfather remarked.

"What is this communism?" his mother asked. "I never used to hear of it. Is it some kind of foreign religion?"

Peony, bringing in a bowl of hot eggs in broth, faltered and spilled a little of the broth.

"Careless child!" his grandmother scolded her, "You grow more careless every day!"

I-wan met Peony's eyes, full of terror and meaning, and smiled at her. He must give her En-lan's message. Now he watched for a chance to speak to her secretly. His father had risen from the breakfast table without finishing his food.

"I must get to my office," he exclaimed. "How do I know? It may be I shall find the whole place upset. At any rate, we must stir up the government. I for one shall refuse the new loan to the Ministry of Education if they cannot control the students better."

"Will you not have a little more hot tea?" Peony asked, coming to his side with the teapot in her hand. He went on talking without answering her.

"Wait until that Chiang Kai-shek gets here!" he cried.

I-wan looked up. Peony went around the table and filled each bowl with hot tea.

"What do you mean?" I-wan asked.

His father laughed harshly, drank his tea, and pushed his chair back and went out.

"As if they could do anything to Chiang!" I-wan thought, ardently. Chiang was afraid of no one. He had driven his victorious way up from the south, a man full of the power of his own integrity. "As if he cared for bankers!" I-wan thought

86

proudly. Then he remembered Peony again. He had for the moment forgotten her. But she had gone and when he went about the house he could not find her. He heard her voice in the kitchen at last. He looked in. She was there, stooping over a basket full of fish a vendor had brought in.

"Peony!" he said.

She looked up.

"Where is my school cap?" He had not been able to find it and had not looked very far, needing excuse to see her.

But she looked back to the fish. "On the third hook in your closet," she said.

He could think of nothing else and so he had to go on to school. In the English class he shook his head slightly at En-lan.

Twenty-one days the strike was to be held, that he knew. And the twenty-first day was the day. The city went on its seeming usual way, but nothing was the same. Everyone made his face calm and all came and went as usual, but the strikes spread into newspaper offices, into great shops and business places. The working people were gay, for from somewhere they were being given money, and for the first time since they were children they could go out by day to the amusement places and see all the wonders of animals trained to do tricks and foreign moving pictures and all such things they had only heard of before. By night they loitered about tea houses and gambling dens. I-wan could scarcely gather together his brigade. In these days when he himself was in such a pitch of waiting that he could not sleep except in bits and snatches through the nights, these men he had taught were children freed from their tasks. They were idle all day, but at night he could not get them together. They came, a few of them at a time, and when he asked where the others were they laughed and pointed to the city.

"We have all been seeing what we have never seen," one said.

"As for me," another said, "I don't care if nothing better than this comes to me. Do you know what I saw today? Three monkeys, dressed like little men! I laughed until my stomach turned on me."

He could not get them to listen to him, and there was nothing for him except to go home, still to wait. He was so helpless with them that he grew afraid lest at the time when all must come together they would refuse to come. So one day he made the sign to En-lan and En-lan met him on the green spot on the campus, but at an hour when most students were in classes, and I-wan told him, "I don't know what is the matter with my brigade. Ever since they have not had to work they have been like silly children."

Then he went on and told him how they seemed to have forgotten the revolution. En-lan only laughed at him.

"What did I say? You are an idealist," he answered. "You know nothing at all, I-wan. Do you think that people who have had to work all their lives will not play when they can? Let them alone. There will be no order anyway on that day. It will come like a great storm—no one can tell its size or shape or what the destruction will be. It is only afterwards that we can begin to think of order." Then he said, his voice lower, "What about that girl? One word now in these last few days and we are all lost."

"I have had no chance—" I-wan began.

"Make it—make it—" En-lan said imperiously. "What right have you to risk our lives?"

He went on, leaving I-wan there to go home again.

And again there was nothing for I-wan to do except to wait. The air was restless with new spring, too, and waiting was the harder. He entered the house and his grandmother called and he went into her room listlessly and stood there.

88

"What is it, Grandmother?" he said as he always did.

"Where have you been?" Her thin old voice was exactly as it had always been, everything was as it had always been, and yet he felt it all as insubstantial as a dream from which he was about to wake.

"At school," he answered.

His grandmother coughed, and then she began to complain as though he had not spoken.

"This pain in my joints grows worse every day. I can't walk. But nobody cares. They just leave me here—nobody cares about me. What is the use of having sons and grandsons? You don't care whether I live or die."

He thought, "En-lan would laugh at her and say, 'You're right, we don't care.'"

But he lacked some hardness that En-lan had. He said gently, "Yes, we do, Grandmother."

She stared at him a moment longer. Then she put out her hand.

"Let me feel your hand, little I-wan."

So though he hated it he put out his hand once more and she took it in both her old claws.

"Such a warm young hand," she murmured.

He could not bear her touch and yet he knew, in his too quick imagination, for a moment, what it might be to be old and lonely and feel one's body growing cold and feeble and eager to cling to someone warm and young. And he could not pull himself away from her, though he longed to leave her.

"You don't want me to die, do you?" she murmured.

"No," he said. And yet he knew it did not matter if she died. All old people had to die, to make room for the young, and it seemed right to him that this should be.

At this thought of death he did pull his hand away.

"I have to go and study, Grandmother," he said as he always

did. He could not bear this smell, this room closed against the spring outside.

But when he turned and rushed to the door and opened it, there outside he met Peony, bringing in a bowl of soup for his grandmother. And he remembered.

"Peony," he said, "come to my room tonight. I have something to tell you."

She looked at him and nodded and went on.

He said to her, "Of course I know that you would not go out to meet him."

Peony was stooping about his bed, unfolding the quilts adroitly and smoothing the sleeping mat while she listened. Now she took a silk cloth out of a drawer and began dusting the table.

"Did you tell him I wouldn't come?" she asked without stopping.

"Yes, I did," I-wan said. He sat in his foreign easy chair. In the whole house only the beds were Chinese, and that was because his grandfather said he could not sleep wallowing in springs and feathers as the foreigners did. He wanted firm boards beneath his body and a wooden pillow under his head.

"No, I wouldn't tell anybody what you told me," Peony said, and then added after a moment, "but I think I will see him."

I-wan stared at her. The edges of her mouth were curled and her eyes were full of mischief.

"Why?" he asked.

"Oh, because," she said, flicking her cloth about his books. "Maybe," she added, "I want to see for myself all this revolution you've been talking about—or maybe it is only that I want something new to happen. Nothing happens to me here in this house."

He felt a strange confusion in himself. Peony was a girl in his family and she should not go out to meet a strange man. It was against tradition. And yet was not tradition what they were all against? He had a moment's flying doubt of himself. When the revolution really fell upon this house would he be strong enough not to lift his hand? He thrust this away from him.

"I will tell En-lan tomorrow I was wrong," he said stiffly. "He will appoint an hour and a place."

"Why not here?" she asked. "Why should your schoolmate not come here? And why should I not serve you tea? Isn't that my business?"

He did not answer. En-lan here! He had never thought of bringing any of his schoolmates here. Peng Liu once had come to the gate and he had not wanted him to enter. Since that day, too, Peng Liu had not liked him as well as before and they had seen little of each other. That Peng Liu, there was something mean in him. Everybody felt it, and En-lan gave him no authority, and yet no one could dismiss him from the band. So he came and went with them and they avoided him. Why should one poor man's son be such a small mean creature and another poor man's son be fearless and good like En-lan? But there was also the meanness of I-ko, who was a rich man's son. They had had one letter from I-ko, complaining because he hated the sea and had got only so far as Bombay. He asked permission to stay in Bombay, but his father had cabled him, "Proceed to Germany. Funds forwarded there." So I-ko had gone on to where those funds were. Whenever he thought of meanness such as Peng Liu's he thought also of I-ko. There was something alike in those two.

Into these thoughts Peony broke.

"You never did tell me whether this En-lan was handsome or not."

"I don't know," I-wan said shortly. He thought, "How foolish I was to tell her everything!"

"Ah, well, I shall see for myself," Peony said.

She went out singing a little under her breath, and he said to himself again, "She is not thinking of the revolution at all." He wished more than ever that he had never said anything to her. But it was this endless waiting that made everything seem wrong to him.

Nevertheless the next day, so that he might not bear the weight of the chance, he took advantage of a moment after a class when they copied an assignment together from a bulletin board, to tell En-lan what Peony had said.

En-lan listened and went on copying as though he did not hear.

"At least she is not stupid," he said. Then he smiled, "I have never seen the inside of a rich man's house. And after the revolution there will be no more of them to see." He went on copying. "So, I will meet you at the gate at four o'clock. As she says, there is nothing remarkable in going to visit a schoolmate. That was clever of a slave to say." He closed his book. "There, I am finished!" and went down the hall.

All day I-wan was uncomfortable. And now, when they came to his home, he was very uncomfortable. En-lan's bright dark eyes were looking at everything quietly and fully. He had put on a clean school uniform and he had smoothed his hair and thrust a blue cotton handkerchief in his pocket. The uniform had shrunk a little and left his strong wrists bare and two buttons across his chest would not fasten so that his blue shirt showed. But it also was clean. Inside the door he paused and looked down at the thick red carpet.

"Am I to step on this?" he asked.

I-wan laughed. "It is foolish, but so you can," he replied. He felt nervous and afraid of what En-lan would think of everything.

"If I had it I would sleep under it," En-lan said. Nevertheless he stepped upon the carpet.

I-wan had told Peony that morning, "If I bring him home today, you are to manage so my grandmother does not make me come into her room."

Peony had managed, for no sound came from his grandmother's room. She was sleeping, doubtless, under her opium. He could smell it. En-lan sniffed.

"That here!" he remarked amiably. "I used to smell it in my village."

"Did they use it there, too?" I-wan asked, surprised. He thought, somehow, that farmers only sold this opium for food.

"Didn't I tell you rich and poor were alike?" En-lan said calmly.

They were going upstairs now. I-wan had told Peony, "If I bring him home today, manage it so I need not go to my grandfather's room or my parents'—"

No one called and he led the way straight to his own room and En-lan followed.

"Now!" I-wan said, shutting the door. "Here we are free. You can say anything you like. The servants never come here unless I ring for them. And Peony will bring us tea herself in a little while." He spoke quickly because he felt so ill at ease with En-lan here. He was ashamed of all that he had.

En-lan did not answer. He stood on the edge of bare floor, looking around the room.

"This is the place you come from every day!" he exclaimed.

I-wan could not bear the amazement in his face.

"I am used to it—I never think of it," he stammered.

"My father's whole house could go in this room," En-lan said. Then he stepped to the carpet. "I should always feel it was wrong to walk on this," he said. He stared down at the heavy fabric, blue and velvet beneath his feet. "How much does this cost?" he asked.

"I don't know," I-wan muttered. "I didn't buy it—it's been here always.

He turned away and took off his coat and cap. But En-lan kept staring about him.

"Is that your bed?" he asked.

"Yes," I-wan said.

"I never saw such a bed," En-lan whispered. "I never saw anything like this—all that silk stuff—what is it for?"

"Curtains," I-wan said shortly. Then he cried, "I can't help it! I was born into this house. I don't know anything else."

En-lan sat down on a small chair and put his hands on his knees.

"I'm not blaming you," he said slowly. "I am asking myself—if I had been born into this—would I ever have run away and joined the revolution? I don't know. I can't imagine any life except my own—having to work bitterly hard and not having enough to eat. If I'd been you—I don't know." He looked at I-wan. "I-wan, I think more of you than before."

"Oh, no," I-wan said, abashed. "It's—I'm used to this—your life seems more interesting to me than this—"

"You have by birth what we are fighting for," En-lan said. "Why, then, do you fight?"

I-wan had never thought of this before. Did he have everything? Why was he fighting, indeed?

"You have everything—" En-lan repeated, "everything!"

"I feel uncomfortable," I-wan said. "I can't tell you how I feel. When I am with my brigade I wish I could bring them here. But I don't think they would like it here, either. Do you like it, En-lan?"

They looked around the room. For the first time I-wan saw it as a kind of life, and not a place in which to sleep and work.

"I don't know," En-lan said slowly. "It's beautiful, but I don't know. This thing soft under my feet all the time—it feels wrong. But then, I'm not born to it."

"Do you wish you were?" I-wan pressed him.

En-lan did not answer for a moment. Then he shook his head. "No," he said firmly. "No. I am glad I was born as I was. What would I do here? I like to take off my coat and to spit on the floor."

It was like a door shut in I-wan's face. He felt suddenly cut off somehow from En-lan and from all for whom En-lan stood. He felt as a child feels shut into a garden alone when outside in the dusty open street other children are shouting and screaming in living play. But before he could speak the door opened and Peony came in with a tray of steaming bowls. She did not look up. She went to the table, and cleaning one end of it of books and papers, she set out bowls and chopsticks and between them a dish of small pork dumplings and another of balls of rice flour in a syrup of brown sugar.

"I thought you and your friend might like these," she said in a quiet voice.

I-wan had not expected this of her, and he said gratefully, "Thank you, Peony." Then turning to En-lan he said, "This is Peony, of whom I told you." And to Peony he said, "This is En-lan."

They looked at each other. Then En-lan rose to his feet and stood, twisting his cap round and round, and suddenly Peony said to him, her voice very silvery and cool, "You need not rise to me. I am not one of the family. I am only a bondmaid."

"As for that," En-lan said, "I am only a peasant's son. I have never even been in a house like this before."

They looked at each other and I-wan felt himself more than ever the lonely child shut into the garden.

95

"You thought I might tell on you," Peony said, slowly, "but I will never tell."

And En-lan answered, his voice as low and slow as hers, "I don't know why I thought you might tell—except I didn't know you."

Then Peony recalled herself. She looked away from him and she said to I-wan in her usual voice, "I-wan, you must eat while the dishes are hot. Sit down, both of you."

"But," En-lan said merrily, "why not the three of us?"

Now in all the years Peony had been in the house she had never eaten with I-wan. He had never thought of such a thing, and it was a surprise to him now, and Peony saw it was. She said quickly, "Oh, I am used to serving and not sitting."

"I won't sit down," En-lan argued warmly, "unless we sit down together. In the revolution there is no such thing as one to be served and the other to serve, eh, I-wan? We are all equal!"

A light came into I-wan's mind. How had he not thought of this before? He had been dreaming of revolution outside and he had not known how to make it come here in his own room. He forced away a foolish shyness he suddenly felt toward Peony.

"Yes, Peony," he said, "sit down with us. Why not?"

So wavering between them, looking at one and the other of them, she grew as pink as her name flower. She said to I-wan, "And what if your father and mother should come to the door and see me sitting down with you? We couldn't cry revolution to them!"

En-lan strode to the door and turned the key.

"Sit down," he commanded her.

So she sat down across from them, her face still pink, and she began, a little stiff and grave, to serve their bowls full of the pork dumplings.

"So," En-lan said, looking at them cheerfully, "how pleasant this is! I am hungry as a starved dog!"

I-wan was shy for a few minutes more and he struggled with this curious strangeness toward Peony, whom he had never seen sit down at a table with him. Then he forgot it. And he forgot his being the lonely child, for they were all eating together, and he was hungry, too. And Peony, daintily touching her chopsticks to this bit and that, let them eat for a little while. Then she leaned toward En-lan.

"Tell me," she said to him gravely, "more about this revolution. I want to believe in it."

So En-lan began, and listening to him, and seeing Peony's face as she listened, I-wan thought, "I believe in it, too—more than ever."

It seemed come already, here in this room.

When En-lan was gone, Peony sat down again for a moment.

"You never made it plain to me what it was all about," she said.

"You wouldn't believe me," he retorted.

She laughed. "Perhaps I didn't. It's hard to believe such big things coming out of a boy one knew when he was small. But that En-lan—he makes you believe it." She mused a moment, her face changing with her thoughts. He could not read it and he felt vaguely jealous.

"I'm glad you believe, anyhow, Peony," he said. "Now we can talk together. It won't be so hard to wait."

She rose. "Meanwhile I must go on as I always have," she said. "Your grandmother will be waking."

She collected the bowls.

"How he ate!" she said. "I like to see a young man so hearty."

"Come back," he begged her. "I want to talk some more."

For when they talked it was all real and inevitable and nothing could hold back what was to come. But she shook her head.

"No—not tonight," she said firmly.

Nothing could stop the marching of that triumphant figure of Chiang Kai-shek. He had left Hankow and was proceeding down the river with his great army. Kiukiang, Anking, Wuhu—the cities on its bank fell like fruits into his hands. Shanghai grew hot with expectation and fear. The people on the streets were arrogant and noisy. Ricksha pullers idled and would not hire their vehicles and vendors did not care whether they sold anything or not. They threw dice on the sidewalks and played all day.

"Why should we work when Chiang Kai-shek is coming?" they said.

It was as gay as a festival. Even in I-wan's home the servants grew impudent and careless. They were away for hours and when Madame Wu scolded them they said, "We have joined the union and we can do as we please."

She complained to I-wan's father and he said, "It is the same thing everywhere. But it can't go on—we won't have it."

"How can you help it, Father?" I-wan asked. He was a little ashamed, as a matter of fact, because he too was inwardly astonished and even indignant when the dinner was not ready, although he knew that servants also must have their rights in the revolution, and indeed months ago he had listened to the plans for this very union of which they now spoke.

"This sort of thing cannot be tolerated," his father replied shortly. "How can a nation prosper if its ignorant people are allowed to do as they like?"

He wanted to argue with his father. But he felt Peony touch his shoulder, warning him.

It was like the coming of a storm. There was the disturbance among the people like the first rufflings of the wind over the country and sea, and then there was the intense waiting stillness. Again I-wan felt shut off from everyone. The schools of the city suddenly declared a holiday at the mayor's demand in order that students could be dispersed and could not hold meetings. The strike continued at the mills. En-lan had told I-wan to go there no more until he had the command, because they were all being watched. There was nothing for him to do except to wait in this quiet house and garden. But he could feel the end of waiting near. Now he was glad that Peony knew. They could talk sometimes, here and there, when no one was by. When a city fell and the news was cried in the streets and printed across newspapers, he looked at her triumphantly.

But he could never be quite sure how Peony felt. One day he asked her outright. She had come into the garden, where everything was breaking into bud. He had gone to look at a hawthorn flowering.

"Are you a real revolutionist, Peony?" he asked her quietly, fingering a budding branch.

"I don't know," she answered. "I shall wait and see how it is." She put out her hand and touched a red blossom.

"No, but what do you believe?" he urged her. "You must believe in right or wrong."

"I am not a priest like you," she said. "You believe in Chiang Kai-shek as though he were a god. I know he is a man."

"No, I don't," he denied. "I don't believe in any gods. But I believe in the revolution."

"The revolution is still only what people do," she replied. "If they do well, then I am one of them."

He knew she was wrong. It was wrong to measure one's belief by what people did. A thing was right or wrong in itself. But he could not forget what she had said. That night before he slept he locked his door and from a secret place in his desk he drew out a picture he had once cut from a magazine. It was a picture of the young Chiang Kai-shek. He sat looking at it. It did look a little like En-lan. It was a face at once bold and kind, harsh and dreaming.

"I don't worship him," he thought, "but I believe in him."

They all believed, thousands of young men and women intellectuals, thousands of men and women who were ignorant and poor. It had been a long time since they had anything in which they could believe and hope. Since the last corrupt dynasty had died in Peking, the people had had nothing. And the young, especially, had had nothing since Sun Yat-sen had died. Before he could become known to them he was only a memory. Therefore all their hopes fastened upon this young leader of the revolutionary army.

And now there was only one last great city to capture before he entered Shanghai. It was the ancient city of Nanking where once the Ming Emperors had ruled in such power and such glory and where they were buried. Everybody waited for Nanking to fall. The gates were locked in the great walls and the government soldiers were holding the city. But it would fall. For within the walls it too was honeycombed with people who wanted the revolution.

I-wan lived these last days in a sort of ecstasy, full of an excitement which was both pain and joy. There was the knowledge that everything he did was for the last time. He knew exactly what was to happen. As soon as the news came of Chiang's victory he was to leave this house, never to return to it. He was to join En-lan and all the others at the revolutionary headquarters, to report for duty. He told Peony one night, whispering to her in his room. She listened steadily. She was different these days.

He liked her better than he ever had. She did not touch him or tease him or arouse in him that warm sweet discomfort of which he was afraid. She was quiet and busy and he was not disturbed by her presence.

"You must come with me, Peony," he told her at last.

"Tell me the name of the place," she said. "Perhaps—"

So he wrote down the place and she looked at it. Then he burned the bit of paper.

"I do not promise," she said. "I promise nothing."

But she had seen the writing. And he knew she never forgot anything.

Of the moment of his own leaving he thought continually. He wanted to be sure to get away at the instant, so that he need not be here when the people were loosed. He knew now he did not want to see them here. Sometimes in the night he woke and then he lay awake and trembling, tempted to warn his father. But whenever he prepared to warn him he was held back because he knew his father would demand to know everything and then En-lan and the others would be lost. So he had to keep silence, though it was the hardest thing to keep.

And then one night, after three days of this intense waiting, the news flew into the city. Nanking had fallen. He went early to bed so that he need not hear his father's talk, but it was impossible to sleep. This was his last night in this house. Tomorrow he would be he did not know where. And tossing on his bed, he made up his mind at last—or half made it up—before he went— no, he would leave it to Peony—he would tell her if she went she was to warn his parents and let them escape. Nothing could happen before noon. Twelve o'clock was the hour set for proclaiming the revolution. Between dawn, when he would leave this house, and noon, they could escape. He struggled a moment in himself. Was it betraying the revolution to warn them? But if Peony warned them and not he? Long after midnight he fell into a shallow half-dreaming sleep. In a few hours. . . .

He was awakened before dawn by his father, shaking him by the shoulder. He opened his eyes and there was his father's face, black and white in the shadows, above him.

"Get up!" his father said. His voice was so cold that I-wan woke instantly.

"Get into your clothes," his father commanded him.

I-wan got up. "What is it?" he asked. "What is the matter?"

"Stupid, foolish boy," his father cried. "Wicked, deceitful boy!" I-wan did not answer. From his childhood he had feared his father and loved him, too. I-ko had only feared him. But I-wan knew that his father was good and he had tried always to obey him, even when his grandmother or a servant said, "Never mind —your father isn't at home."

"What is it, Father?" he repeated. But he knew.

His father drew a paper from his breast. It was a long sheet, folded over and over. He handed it to I-wan. Upon it were hundreds of names. I-wan read them, one after the other. They were clustered under titles of schools. He saw the name of his school, and under it En-lan's name, and his own and the names of all the band. No, one was lacking—Peng Liu's name. He remembered suddenly that he had not seen Peng Liu for a long time. He had been sick, he sent word, and unable to come to their meetings. Then somebody said he had left school and gone home because he had no more money. And no one cared, because no one had liked him. But his name—it was not here!

"Do you know what this is?" his father asked him.

"Yes," I-wan said. He was telling himself that he had done nothing of which he need be ashamed. He would not be afraid. He handed the paper back to his father.

"Where did you get it?" he asked.

His father stared at him sternly.

"That does not matter," he replied. "Dress yourself quickly. At any moment soldiers may be here to seize you. Chiang Kai-shek has come."

I-wan felt his body grow weak.

"Chiang Kai-shek—" he faltered.

"He is here in the city," his father repeated. "He was here yesterday."

"But Nanking—" I-wan stammered.

"He left Nanking to his subordinates," his father said. "He himself came straight to Shanghai. I tell you, dress yourself!"

"I can't—how do you know, Father?" I-wan asked. His heart was thumping in his side. How did his father know all about Chiang Kai-shek? He could not know—

"I saw him yesterday," his father said.

A terror darted into I-wan's mind like a thread of lightning. His father and Chiang Kai-shek—

"He met with us—with all the bankers," his father went on in quick short jerks. "We told him Shanghai must not be disturbed —our businesses—if he wants money, that is, to go on with his government. Will you dress yourself, or do you want to be killed?"

"He never agreed!" I-wan stammered. How could he get word to En-lan—to his friends—to everybody who—?

"Of course he agreed," his father replied. "The man is no fool. I was impressed by him—clever and strong and reasonable. Everything is arranged. He is to purge the city of the communists."

The blood which had drained away from I-wan's heart now rushed back. He felt suddenly strong and furiously angry.

"He has betrayed us," he said loudly, and then he turned away from his father and began to sob wildly. "All of us he has be-trayed—we who believed in him!" He snatched at his clothes.

"I must get out and find them all—find En-lan—they'll all be killed!"

His father leaped up and seized him by the arm.

"You are going nowhere except straight to the docks—to a ship for Japan," he declared. "The car is waiting—ready—"

"I won't go," I-wan sobbed. He wished he could stop sobbing—it was childish.

"You will!" his father whispered fiercely. "You are going at once. It is not only you—it is the family. I gave my personal word that if they would erase your name from the list you would leave the country today."

He stared at his father and felt as though he were choked.

"You are making me into a traitor!" he cried. He was struggling, but his father held him. He could feel his father's fingers like steel clamps on his shoulders.

"You are already a traitor," his father retorted. "The government has condemned all communists to death. The revolution is to be purged. They have thousands of names—"

The room turned slowly before I-wan's eyes. He saw his father's black eyes in the midst of it, staring at him. It was all meaningless—everything was meaningless.

"Peony!" he heard his father shout, "come here quickly, Peony!"

His body was so loose he could not hold it together. He fell into his father's arms.

"Where is Peony?" His father's voice bellowed around him in waves of noise. And like an echo he heard a servant's voice screaming, "She's gone! We can't find her—Peony's gone!"

PART TWO

II

THE ship was moving slowly among small green islands, threading its way through a shimmer of bright blue water and sunshine. The air was warm and still, except for the fall of water at the prow, and in the vistas between the islands he could see flights of small Japanese fishing vessels, their sails white against the blue sky. He lay in his chair, gazing at it, empty of thought. That was the only way to endure his complete helplessness—simply not to think, not to remember.

Sometimes he felt, pushing through the emptiness, the old wish that at least he might have told En-lan—and then he summoned the emptiness to wash that away, too. There was no way whereby he could tell En-lan. En-lan perhaps was dead already. He could not even write to Peony. Peony was gone. He wondered dully when she had gone and where. He remembered so clearly his father's unbelieving shout, "Peony gone!" Then he summoned the emptiness again to wash it all away.

All of it was gone—all the hopes they had had together. He felt a sharp remorse when he thought of the brigade. They were doubtless back again at the mill, working as they had before in their old hopelessness. They would think he was a liar after all—perhaps even that he had betrayed them. But perhaps they would only think he was dead. He hoped that was what they thought—that he was dead. He never, never wanted to see them again.

But lying in the emptiness of the sky and water, watching the dreaming islands slip by, he had come at last to cease hating his father. He had come to see it would have been impossible for him to have stayed in Shanghai, even if he had not been killed, especially if he had not been killed. To have had to go back to the old life, shorn of its plans, back to the round of school and home without the hope of anything to come, back to his grandmother and the reek of that opium—no, it could not have been. And Peony gone. They would not look for Peony in that house. No, his father would simply say, "Let her go—she is nothing but a bondmaid. Get another to take her place."

It was all impossible to think about. He shut his eyes and his lids smarted. His heart felt crushed in his breast. There were many ways of breaking a heart. Stories were full of hearts broken by love, but what really broke a heart was taking away its dream —whatever the dream might be.

He lay in the emptiness, giving himself up. The soft sea air swept over him. He heard a sailor call a sounding somewhere, his voice musical in the silence. There was no meaning now to anything. He closed his eyes. Let nights drift over him and days pass him by.

He would have liked to stay on the ship forever, but that of course he could not. In a few minutes the ship would dock at Nagasaki, and beyond that his ticket did not go. He had his father's written instructions and now he read them over again. Since he cared about nothing he might as well follow them. At the dock, he read in his father's heavy writing, he would be met and taken to the home of Muraki, the merchant. "Mr. Muraki is an old friend," his father wrote, "and he will keep you in his home. I have asked him to give you a place in his business. Of course you need not be dependent on your earnings. Let me know what you need, after you have spent what I have given you. But

I want you to go to work, and when I think it is safe you may return."

"I will never return," I-wan said to himself in his cabin. If he could not return to such a country as he had dreamed of, then he would be an exile forever. He had no country. He closed his bag and took it and went up on deck. It was already noon, and the ship was slowing to anchor in the bay.

The land looked strange to him. A steep mountain range pressed almost to the sea, but between its foot and the shore there was a small city, stretched long and narrow. The houses were angular and squat. The tiles on their flat roofs were gleaming in the sun, but over the mountain tops a cloud hung, black and full of rain. Around the ship coal barges were beginning to flock, and short thick-bodied Japanese coolies, men and women, were stooping themselves ready to heave from shoulder to shoulder the baskets of coal. He could hear them chattering, and it did not seem strange that he could understand nothing of what they said. Nothing was strange any more—everything had already happened to him, and everything was over.

He took up his bag and followed the others along the swaying ladder down the ship's side into a small launch. He had spoken to no one on the ship and he knew no one. Most of them were Americans, going ashore for sight-seeing. Their English he could barely understand, since he was accustomed to Miss Maitland's sort of English, and Mr. Ranald's. When he thought of Mr. Ranald he thought for a second of Peng Liu and how he had wanted to put Mr. Ranald's name on the death list. That death list! A very different one had served at last. He thought dully, "It was Peng Liu who betrayed us." Then he drew emptiness resolutely about him again. Peng Liu did not matter. Miss Maitland and Mr. Ranald were doubtless teaching their classes as usual, except that certain seats were empty. . . . Was En-lan dead? He would never know.

The launch was puffing through the smooth bright water. Suddenly across the sunshine a slanting rain fell, silver and cool.

"Regular Nagasaki weather," an American voice said.

"Gives 'em the most glorious gardens in the world," another answered.

Above them the cloud had stretched a dark arm toward the sun. In a moment it was gone and the rain stopped. The launch was at the dock now, and among them all I-wan stepped off. The land rocked a moment under his feet. He stood looking around him. Then he saw a young Japanese in western dress come to him, and he heard his voice, speaking Chinese, strongly accented, "Is it Wu I-wan?"

"Yes, if you please," I-wan answered, "I am that humble one."

"I am Mr. Muraki's son," the young man answered, "Bunji, by name. My father invites you to our house."

He smiled, his teeth white and his eyes pleasant. He took off his hat and his stiff black hair stood up about his square face like a circular brush.

"I say," he said suddenly, "shall we speak English? It's easier for me, though I speak it badly, too."

"Yes," I-wan replied, "if you like."

To himself he thought, climbing into a small motor car with this Bunji Muraki, that he never wanted to speak his own tongue again. He wanted to cut off his whole life and begin from this moment. He would dream no more world dreams and hope for nothing and trust no one. He would live from moment to moment, never thinking beyond. In such a mood he seated himself beside Bunji Muraki and allowed himself to be driven away.

They stopped before a thatch-roofed gate in a low brick wall. Bunji opened the door of the car and leaped out. He moved with an angular sharp precision, as if his muscles had been drilled to a count of one, two, three, four.

"We live here," he said, his white teeth shining again in a smile. Then he reached for I-wan's bag.

"No, don't—I'll take it," I-wan said.

"No—no, I—" Bunji protested.

They ended by carrying it between them for a few steps until at the gate a stooped old man in a short-skirted cotton coat took it from them.

"He is our gardener," Bunji said. "Let him have it."

He led the way through a garden laid out in a landscape of miniature hills and lakes. A tiny red-varnished footbridge carried them over a stream and the path led them around a curve where at the far end they could see the house. It was a low-roofed building whose white-papered lattices gleamed through the dark-leafed flowering trees. Everything in the garden was so perfect, that it was impossible not to be diverted by it. There was not a leaf upon the moss planted under the trees, not a rock out of place in the stream tinkling in little artificial waterfalls.

"My father's garden is quite famous," Bunji said. He pointed ahead. "There is my father now."

I-wan saw in the distance a slender old man in a silk kimono of silver gray, standing under an early flowering cherry tree. He had pulled a small branch downward and was looking at the buds. As they drew near he turned.

"Hah!" he said to his son, "you are here!" He spoke in Japanese. But when Bunji said, "This is our guest," he said in a stiff old-fashioned Chinese, such as he might have learned from books, "In this little house, the son of my old friend is welcome beyond any others."

III

I-wan liked this old man at once. In that other life before this emptiness fell upon him En-lan had said, "When we get our own world set right, we must fight the Japanese and get back what they have taken from us." Ever since the Twenty-one Demands it was one's duty to hate the Japanese and to talk of war one day to come. But he could not hate this old gentle man. His skin was a pale gold beneath his silver-white hair, but his eyes were black and young. He was so small that I-wan looked down upon him as he might a child. Who could dislike him?

"It is very kind of you to accept me. I do not deserve it," he replied.

"Hah—your father is my friend, and all we have is yours," Mr. Muraki said. He was still clinging to the branch. "You see," he said, "the cherry trees are about to bloom. You have come at just the moment. In six days all Japan will be in blossom."

"My father lives for this each spring," Bunji said to I-wan, "and then he lives for the chrysanthemums in the autumn."

They stood a moment, half awkwardly. Mr. Muraki was smiling a little at his son.

"Hah," he said with his soft, indrawing breath, "you had better allow him to go in and refresh himself, Bunji."

He nodded and turned to the tree, dismissing them.

"My father is retired," Bunji said. He was leading the way again. "My two brothers are heads now of his business."

"And you?" I-wan asked.

"Oh, I am a clerk there, only," Bunji laughed. "I see to packing and billing. It is import and export business."

They were at a wide door, and two pretty servant girls fluttered out in brightly flowered cotton kimonos. Bunji stopped and thrust out one foot. One of the girls dropped to her knees and began unlacing his leather shoe. I-wan had heard of this, and when the other knelt at his foot, he, too, tried not to feel it strange to have women there serving him. He felt his shoes drawn off and his feet slipped into soft straw slippers. Then he followed Bunji up the steps into the house. He had never seen one like it. There were many rooms, only partly shut off from each other by the white-papered lattices, which were screens. It was like stepping into a huge clean honeycomb. There was the smell of the clean matting on which they walked, the fragrance of un-painted woods. And through all the open rooms floated the airy fragrance of the garden coming into spring.

"My father likes to live entirely in the old-fashioned Japanese way," Bunji said. "So—you see—but in your room we have put a chair. In my room, too. My married brother, Shio, however, has chairs in each room in his house in Yokohama. He is quite modern!"

Bunji laughed loudly and I-wan smiled. Within himself he still felt complete quiet. Moment by moment, that was how he wanted to live now. He found this moment amusing, but nothing could excite him, however strange.

"Here is your room," Bunji said. "It is next to mine—see, it opens on the garden!"

He drew a latticed screen aside, and I-wan saw a small square room. There was no bed, nothing but a bamboo armchair and table and in a recess a scroll upon which was written a poem, and beneath it a branch of budding hawthorn in a green vase. There was no other decoration, until Bunji slid another screen away, and there was a corner of the garden. The wall was only a few feet away, but a dwarfed maple tree grew against it, its buds scarlet, and beneath was a small pool scarcely two feet square, and beside it a rock.

"No one will come here except the gardeners," Bunji said. "It is quite your own. And when you are ready to sleep, clap your hands and a maidservant will spread your quilts on the mats.

113

Our midday meal will be ready in half an hour and a maid-servant will bring you water to wash yourself. I will come back." He put out his hand in a quick foreign fashion and I-wan put out his and they shook hands.

He sat down when Bunji was gone and looked about him. The house was still. Everything was so still. He could hear the soft sibilance of distant sliding screens, and a low murmuring voice somewhere not near. The house was ordered, like the garden. There was no dust anywhere. The bit of garden seemed a part of the house. The few feet of grass were green and clipped, lying like a carpet where the polished floor of the room stopped. He felt wrapped about in peace. Life here was planned. There were light-ness and clarity and absolute cleanliness, and in spite of fragility a feeling of long-settled stability. Precisely this life had been lived here for generations.

He was glad he had come. He had no plans now of his own. Perhaps he never would have again. Why plan, when hopes and plans could disappear in a night, as if they were mists? He felt very tired and he sat down on the edge of the floor, his feet upon the grass, and sat gazing at the water, his mind empty and his heart still.

At last he heard someone cough beyond the screen, and he called "Come!" and then Bunji came in wearing a soft dark silk kimono. He looked entirely another person, gentler and some-how more the son of Mr. Muraki. On his arm he carried a dark purple length of silk.

"I thought you might like to put this on," he said.

He held up the garment and I-wan saw it was another kimono. But he did not want to put it on.

"If you will not count it rudeness," he said, "I will put on one of my own robes."

"Do," Bunji replied. "I thought only to rid you of the stiff

114

western clothes. Good for business but not for pleasure!" He laughed. Then he turned to look into the garden while I-wan put on the robe of blue silk he had brought with him. The last time he had worn a robe had been in his own home.

"Now," he said, "I am ready."

Bunji turned. They stood, two young men, looking alike in their darkness of hair and eyes, and yet so different. I-wan was taller by half a head than Bunji, and his body was more slender, his face more oval, his hands and feet more delicate. But Bunji's body was the more powerful and strong.

"In reality," Bunji said, "our clothing is not so different. What I wear is the ancient dress of your people. You wear their modern dress. Ah, I have not seen it! Is it comfortable? Yes, I see it is. It fits you closely, and the sleeves are not so wide. That is what I dislike—our wide sleeves. But of course our dress is very pretty on the girls. Wait until you see my sister. She is a moga—that is, a modern girl—at heart, but at home my father will not allow it. I, too, think she is not so pretty in western dress. Come on—you're hungry. I'm always hungry!"

He ended everything with a laugh, this Bunji. Now he led the way to a large square room, facing the main garden. At the door he paused and bowed to his parents who were already there.

"Mother, this is I-wan," he said.

I-wan bowed to Madame Muraki. He thought, "I have never seen anyone so beautiful." She did not look at all like his own plump mother. She was very slight and her face was sad and her eyes were full of a strange dead patience. Yet although she was more than fifty and her pompadoured hair was gray, her face was smooth and she wore a faintly purple robe of plain heavy silk. When she bowed her little body seemed to crumple at the waist over the wide sash of deeper purple satin. Then she straightened herself like a flower after wind.

"Hah," she breathed, "I am so glad you are come! Will you sit down? And forgive my poor English, since I shamefully never learned Chinese."

"I hope I can learn Japanese quickly," I-wan said. "Then I may speak in your language, Madame."

"Hah!" she answered softly, smiling. It was assent and echo.

They sat down upon the silvery mats about a low table, facing the garden. There was no decoration in this room either, except for latticed screens and a scroll in a recess and a long low dish of narcissus in flower beneath it. The air was cool and fresh and the whole atmosphere light and quietly gay. A rosy young girl came in with a tray of bowls. No one spoke to her. She set a bowl before each of them and went away. As soon as she had gone Bunji burst into such laughter that his parents smiled.

"That is my sister," he cried. "She is shy and she won't eat with us today. But she will get over it."

"Shall I speak to your sister?" I-wan asked, smiling. "Is it your custom?" To be courteous, he had not looked at the young girl.

Madame Muraki in her soft voice spoke a few words I-wan could not understand. Bunji translated, "My mother says, 'Wait until afterwards. She will come in again.' Her name is Tama."

But she did not come again. Bunji laughed again when a maid brought in the next course of fish.

"Tama knew we would tell you who she was, so she doesn't come in again."

They laughed together then, and I-wan suddenly felt at peace. He would stop thinking. There was nothing to remember. The air in this house was clean and pure, and the light poured in everywhere, and the unpainted polished woods gave off that delicacy of fragrance in every room. It was all open and clean and everybody laughed easily as though they were untroubled.

"Can you eat our poor food?" Madame Muraki asked him.

"I like everything," I-wan said. Then he blushed because he had spoken, perhaps, too warmly.

"Hah," Mr. Muraki said, "that is the way the young should feel."

Mr. and Mrs. Muraki smiled again gently and he felt himself liked. It was pleasant.

And though there was little talk, no one felt ill at ease. It was as if each person knew exactly what he should do and did it. The meal proceeded to its end of bowls of rice, dipped from a lacquered container, and then tea, and after that Madame Muraki folded herself into a bow like a butterfly closing its wings, and went away. As though he were prepared for it, Bunji looked toward his father, and Mr. Muraki said to I-wan, "Your father has written me that he wishes you to learn our business. If you like, I have planned this for you—that you spend half your time at the business. In the morning you will have a place beside Bunji. Bunji will help you. In the afternoon you may study or play."

"I am grateful," I-wan replied. Yes, he was very glad to have his life taken out of his own hands and planned for him, hour by hour. That was the way he wished to live now.

Mr. Muraki rose. "Then it is arranged," he said. "If you are not happy you will tell me." It was half question, half command, but wholly kind.

I-wan said, "But I am sure I shall be happy, sir."

"I like all my house to be happy," Mr. Muraki murmured. He went toward the garden, hesitated, and then he murmured again, "Those irises—they should be trimmed. They are excessive." He stepped down upon the moss and turned the corner and was gone.

"Now," Bunji said, his eyes shining with mischief, "Tama will come in. How shall you behave to her, I-wan? As a mobo—that is, a modern boy—or as an old-fashioned young man?"

I-wan felt half alarmed and half shy.

"What will she like?" he asked. But he could not somehow feel excited about this young girl. She had not even lifted her head when she came in.

"No, I won't tell you," Bunji replied. "You shall judge for yourself. Only let us be talking."

They were silent a moment, and then Bunji exploded again into laughter.

"What shall we talk about?" he asked.

"I can't think," I-wan replied, unable, too, to keep from laughing at Bunji.

"Oh, how silly we are!" Bunji said, wiping his eyes. "Now, let us be dignified."

"Will she like that?" I-wan asked. His heart was dancing, too, with the nonsense. He had not felt so pleasantly foolish since he and Peony used to tease each other long before he had ever heard the name of revolution.

"Hush," Bunji replied. "I hear her." He raised his voice a little and sobered his face. "The question of foreign exchange," he began, "is in itself extremely serious. You see how it is. When we accept a large wholesale order, say from the United States, we must insure ourselves against a drop in the exchange which might nullify all profit."

The screen slid and Tama was there, hesitating. I-wan looked up. He saw a girl in a rose-colored kimono, her feet in Japanese shoes and spotless white stockings. Around her waist was a gold brocade sash. But her hair was not done in the shining oiled Japanese pompadour. It was drawn back smoothly from her round and pink-cheeked face, and it was not oiled at all. It lay soft and straight about her head and was fastened into a knot at the neck. She bowed a crumpled butterfly bow exactly as her mother had done. Madame Muraki's head always drooped, but after she had bowed Tama stood upright.

Then she said in English, "Bunji, please?"

"This is my sister, Tama," Bunji said, his eyes dancing. "And this, Tama, is I-wan."

I-wan stood up to bow. But Tama came forward, her hand outstretched.

"We shake hands, yes?" she said in a soft rushing impulsive voice. "Bunji told me you were a mobo—yes? I also like to be new, though my father does not wish it. I attend the University of Kyushu."

He took her small firm hand in his and shook it and let it fall quickly. She did not seem shy now. But he was shy. He did not look at her face as she seated herself beside the table gracefully and felt the teapot.

"Now we will have some hot tea together," she said cosily. "What were you saying, Bunji? I never heard you talk about exchange before!"

They all laughed again.

"You see how she is," Bunji said to I-wan. "Only you must understand she is two girls, Tama is. Before our parents she is very proper and so shy—"

"Bunji!" she murmured. "You mustn't—"

"And the other Tama," Bunji said remorselessly, "is a moga, bold and brazen, liking to talk to young men at the university—"

"I'm not—I do not!" she cried. "Don't believe him!"

"I shall believe only what you tell me yourself," I-wan said, "no one else!"

He was charmed by this gaiety and by this pretty girl, at once blushing and natural, and for the moment he forgot everything else. He had never sat in a room like this with a young girl—except Peony, who was only a bondmaid.

"I am so lucky," he blurted out. "I feel myself very lucky to have come to your home. I can't tell you how unhappy I was—

I thought nothing could be any good. Just this morning I thought that. And now just being in this house has made me feel happier."

They listened with an air of delicate understanding. Tama sighed.

"I know—sometimes I also—I am quite overcome with melancholy. But not for long."

"I should think no one could be melancholy here," I-wan said.

He saw the other two look at each other in a common thought. Bunji answered him, his face more thoughtful than I-wan had yet seen it.

"In this house," he said, "it is true—we are very fortunate. Don't you think we are, Tama?"

Tama nodded. "Yes," she agreed. Then she added, "But I think women are never so fortunate in any house as men are."

"You are far more fortunate than most," Bunji replied. "You are lucky to be the only daughter. You are a petted child, Tama."

"That is why I am melancholy," Tama said, sighing.

No one spoke for a second. Some sort of shadow, indeed, seemed to gather like a faint mist out of the air about them, something which they knew but did not tell I-wan. Then Bunji said abruptly, "I suppose, Tama, we ought to go. Akio is expecting me at the office. And I have been away all morning. Akio is my second brother," he said, turning to I-wan.

"Ah—yes," Tama agreed. She rose in quick acquiescence.

"There will be plenty of time for talk, because I-wan is going to live here," Bunji went on.

"And I—I have so many questions to ask you about your great country," Tama said to I-wan. A sort of pretty formality had fallen upon her. "We owe everything to your country, we Japanese."

I-wan did not answer. He thought, "I don't want to talk about my country," but he did not say it. The shadow was palpable now. Laughter was gone. They were very formal.

"If you are ready?" Bunji said.

"Yes—but my clothes?" I-wan replied.

"I must change too," Bunji said.

"So," Tama assented, "until you all come home." She made her little drooping bow and seemed to disappear rather than to depart. I-wan, watching her, thought he had never seen anything so pretty as her bow, except the spring of her head upward when she had made it.

But Bunji did not notice her. He said briskly, "Now for work!"

He seemed another person—perhaps because he did not laugh when he spoke of work.

There was no laughter in the office of Muraki and Sons. The long low cement building which carried on the work of six great curio shops in the main cities of Japan was as close to the sea as it could be, so that the docks could be near. I-wan followed Bunji into the gate and across a cemented yard.

"We have tried to persuade my father to move to Yokohama," Bunji said, "but the most he would do was to send my eldest brother Shio. My father was born in our house, and his grandfather before him, and he will not leave this island of Kyushu. It is very inconvenient because since the largest steamers now burn oil, they don't stop here for coal as they once did. We have almost no tourist business here, though once we had much business with the Americans. But—what can we do, my brothers and I? He will not go. So we do all the business here except the actual selling in the shops."

They entered a door. Inside it the building was very clean and very ugly. It was all cement. On the cement floors were no mats or any covering, and the cement walls were bare except for a few maps. In a huge room twenty men worked at desks in complete silence. All were in western dress.

"Our accountants and bookkeepers," Bunji said. "Here is my office. Your desk will be here for a while. But first I must take you to my elder brother, Akio."

He tapped at a closed door and listened.

"Enter," a deep voice called.

Bunji opened the door wide.

"Akio, this is Wu I-wan," he said.

A man in Japanese dress sat at a low desk. He was the only man in the building whom I-wan had seen who was not in western business dress, except the runners in coolie garb. He looked up without smiling and nodded, and I-wan saw a strange, melancholy, intense face. The temples were sunken and the cheekbones high, and the mouth was exquisite and sad. He did not look in the least like Bunji.

"Come in, please," he said in English. "I am sorry I cannot speak Chinese. But you will soon learn Japanese."

His voice had resonance, as though it were full of echoes.

"I hope so, sir," I-wan replied.

"Undoubtedly," Akio murmured.

They stood there for a moment, uncertainly.

"Shall I—show him his desk?" Bunji asked.

"Yes, that will be best," Akio replied. And then, as though he feared he had been discourteous, he rose and bowed. "I hope everything will be as you like it," he said vaguely.

"I think it is already," I-wan replied.

But Akio seemed not to hear. He sat down again, his eyes curiously without light.

"Come," Bunji said, and they went on and he closed the door. When they were walking down the corridor again, he sighed and said in a low voice, "My brother has a trouble—he and my father do not agree. Someday when you know us better, I'll tell you."

I-wan did not know what to say and so he said nothing. Certainly Akio did not seem to belong in that cheerful house.

"Here is our office," Bunji said.

They went into a square barren room, furnished with two desks and a few straight chairs. But upon one desk was a spray of hawthorn.

"That is your desk," Bunji said. "I had it placed so you could look toward the sea." I-wan looked and there beyond the window was the sea line, rocky and curving sharply inward. Upon the rocks were a few pines, shaped into flat and stunted shapes by the wind. "If your eye could see straight from your window," Bunji said, "you would see your own country."

I-wan turned away. His country never was and never would be. He had cut himself off from it.

"What are my duties?" he asked sharply. There was a pile of books upon his desk.

"They are all records," Bunji replied. "At my father's wish, I had them brought here for you to examine. Here is ten years' business. If you will study them a few days you will see the principles upon which we work and how the business has expanded. My brother Akio," he went on, "is the best business man among us. Although my eldest brother, Shio, is the titular head after my father, Akio is the most active. Shio is too much of an artist. He judges the quality of our goods and is the one who buys our antiques. Sometimes he won't sell them—then Akio goes to see what is wrong. Well! Are you ready?"

"Yes," I-wan said—as well this as anything.

He took off his hat and coat and sat down and opened the books. A servant brought him paper cuffs and showed him

123

how to put them on. Bunji had them also. He was already at his desk, a shade over his eyes, an abacus in his right hand while his left traced a column of figures. His face was not smiling now. It was shrewd and intense and his lips moved as he muttered figures. I-wan had seen the abacus all his life in Shanghai shops and he knew how to use it somewhat himself. But he had never seen such skill as Bunji's. That short thick hand moved with an amazing speed over the beads. Then with a fountain pen Bunji put down totals in thousands of yen.

I-wan took up the books before him and began to read slowly the records. At first he thought, "This will be stupid." And then he forgot himself in the descriptions, minutely made, of all that passed through the house of Muraki—paintings and silks, fine furniture and porcelains, embroideries and ivories and filigreed silver and cloisonné, bronzes and lacquers and rugs. It was like a great fish net, this business, scattered far and drawn together with all its gathered richness into this building, the riches to be sorted and sold and sent away. He grew curious and looked rapidly through one book after the other to see the direction. The net was cast over India and China and the South Seas, and the goods flowed out again to the West, and especially to America. He read, his eyes sorting out the Chinese names he knew—Canton ivory, Canton blackwood and teak, Canton silver and jade, blue kingfisher's feathers from Foochow, ancient Fukien paintings and images, potteries from Kiangsi and Szechuan curiosities, and scrolls from Peking, from the imperial palaces.

He was astounded. "How can they get these things?" he wondered. Who sold the imperial scrolls? They were national treasures and could not be sold. He thought, "When I know Bunji better, I will ask him."

He felt indignant somehow. And yet he could not justly

blame the house of Muraki. They paid for what they bought, even if they sold for great profit. He was about to look up the matter of profits, when Bunji said, "I-wan, it is time to go home. You have sat for three hours without getting up. Has it been interesting?"

"I forgot the time," I-wan said.

He looked up. It was true. The lengthening rays of sunlight were shining over the sea. They walked back together and entered the garden. In the distance he saw a girl dressed in blue, standing upon a footbridge across a small pool. She was gazing into the water.

"Tama is back before us," Bunji remarked. He called, but she did not hear. "Ah, well," he said comfortably, "she's dreaming about something."

He led the way into the house and I-wan followed. His heart grew lighter again, inexplicably, and he went to his room and stretched himself out upon the mats and lay gazing into his tiny garden. Every pebble in it was perfectly placed. The little rill of water was guided over a flat rock to fall with its small exact music into the miniature pool. It was so small and yet it continued to give, in its proportion of one thing to another, the effect of a larger nature. He lay, idly thinking of it.

It was strange how in a few hours he felt he could call this place home. There was a close security here into which he longed to fit himself. It was a fairy world—not his dream, but exquisite enough if one gave up one's own huge dreaming. And he had given up.

This room of his became a refuge to him. He thought of it pleasurably as he worked at his desk. At the end of the day he went to it and stayed there, happy and alone. He had begun to buy a few books, such books as he had never read before, poems and novels in English. In the small second-hand book-shop where he found them he never looked for such books as he and En-lan used to read. But indeed they were not there. The shopkeeper would have been afraid to sell them, since they were forbidden.

And so instead of these I-wan now read for the first time in his life stories of love and passion openly given and taken. He lay on the mats in his room, and read and paused to look out into his garden and think of what he read. There were other worlds than those he had dreamed of with En-lan. He thought of I-ko. But I-ko could not think of such love as was to be found in these books, love so pure and powerful. He was enchanted with the books.

And then, one summer's day, not knowing why, he felt restless. He had been four months in Japan and he was used to the shape of the days. Now on this day it was almost time for the evening meal, and he rose and changed his clothing and went into the dining room.

Someone was there arranging flowers in a vase—a woman. She turned, and he saw it was Tama.

"Ah, I am too early!" he stammered in a sweat of horror. She would think he had come early on purpose to intrude himself upon her while she was alone. In all these weeks he had never come upon her alone. He backed away, awkwardly.

"No, never mind," she said quickly. "Why should we be afraid?"

She was quite at her ease, he thought, amazed, so much more than he was. What could they talk about alone? He could think of nothing. What was in a girl's mind? He could not imagine. He had never in his life really talked with a girl, except Peony, and he could not count Peony.

She thrust a budded fruit branch into a tall green vase and arranged it.

"How beautiful it is!" he murmured.

She took a pair of scissors and clipped off a twig or two.

"We are taught all such things, we Japanese girls," she answered. Then she added, half pouting, "But no one teaches me the things I really want to know."

He was about to ask her, "What things?" when a screen slid back and Mr. Muraki came in and looked at them.

"Hah!" he breathed softly, astonished.

She bowed to him, a quick half-willful little bow, and nodded at the flowers.

"Is this right, Father?" she asked.

Mr. Muraki's face changed. He forgot his astonishment. He seized the scissors and began clipping twigs sharply while they stood and watched. When he had finished he had reduced the spreading blossoms to a design of bare branch, spare and grotesque, upon which a few flowers hung like exquisite ornaments.

"Hah!" he sighed, his eyes full of peace. "That is as it should be—no exuberance, Tama. It is the rule of art, and of life."

It was all nothing, I-wan told himself that night when he came back to his own room again—it was less than a moment. But it had been long enough for him to feel his heart beat hard with something he had not felt before—something shy and sweet. He laughed at himself, too, when he remembered it.

"It's those love stories," he thought. "I read too much."

And yet, there the content was. It stayed and it made him more nearly content to go on as he was.

Yes, this content pervaded his days and made everything pleasurable. He did not connect it with Tama, but still to know

127

that she was part of the life in this house somehow deepened his content with it.

He seldom saw her, and never again alone, and he would not have so violated hospitality as to try to see her. She spent the whole of every day at her school, and often he and Bunji and Mr. Muraki dined alone at night. But still sometimes Madame Muraki came in, and then Tama was there, too.

And so the months moved smoothly into each other toward a year. I-wan was beginning to feel he knew this small clean city very well now, having seen it in summer and autumn, and at its most beautiful under soft, quickly melting snow. Instead of the crowded streets of Shanghai here were clean narrow roadways, following the contours of the rocky hills, winding into bridges over deep ravines, and coming out again into vistas of the islands. These roads climbed up the mountains to temples and people's parks, or they swept downward to the sea. There were no crowds anywhere. People went their way and there was space and everything was clean.

He had to confess a good many things to himself. Certainly this country was very clean, much cleaner than his own. He saw no beggars and no very poor. Or was it that here the very poor were still clean? A cotton kimono flowered like the spring cost still only a few cents. No one looked poor and no one looked rich. Even the rich went barefoot in their wooden shoes if the day were mild. One snowy day he saw a thing he had never seen before. Two restaurant boys on bicycles speeding past knocked each other so that the dishes of food which they carried in baskets on their heads fell to the ground. He looked for them to curse and quarrel, as it would have happened anywhere. But these two bowed and drew their breath softly through their teeth.

"It is my fault," said one.

"No, no—I can't allow that; the fault was mine," said the other.

They stooped, each to pick up the other's basket, and went on their way. I-wan stood astonished, never having seen such courtesy.

The truth was that already he was being won by this small country which seemed simple and ordered in all its life. He came to love everything—the nights when he slept upon a thick clean mat upon the floor, wrapped in a clean silken quilt, the mornings when he woke to the fresh smell of the sea and heard the soft *shir-shir* of the sliding screens. Breakfast he ate alone in his room, after he had washed himself. Then he went to the office.

In the afternoon, two or three times a week, as spring came on again, he went with Bunji to a bathhouse and they bathed in a great square pool, having first been cleansed and scrubbed in soap and water by a man who threw buckets of water upon them. In the pool there were women too, and I-wan at first could not bear this. He said to Bunji, "It couldn't be like this in any other country."

Bunji opened his eyes.

"Why?" he asked. "A gentleman does not look at a lady in her bath. If I should look at a woman here she would take it as an insult."

I-wan said nothing. They were strange, these people. They must be very strong and good and far above common flesh, he thought, able to control these warm rushing feelings which somehow troubled him now more than ever, now that his old inner absorption was gone.

And yet, there was Akio. Akio came and went as quietly each day as though he did not belong in his father's house. At the evening meal he was always there, punctilious, silent,

129

answering only questions put to him but never speaking first. But months passed before Bunji told him about Akio.

Then he said in a calm voice, "Akio fell in love with a courtesan, and my father is angry because he wants to marry her. Akio is so stubborn—it is nearly five years since it happened. My father engaged him long ago to the daughter of a friend. So it is embarrassing to him now. But Akio will not hear of any wife but Sumie. Well, Sumie is a good woman for her place, but not to come into our home. I think my father is right. It is time for Akio to marry. But he will not. It is ridiculous. . . .

"I tell you this," Bunji went on, "because you must not mind if Akio is melancholy and pays no attention to you. He pays no attention to any of us. It is so strange when he is painstaking and good in the business and obedient to my father in everything else, that he will not marry."

"Have you seen her?" I-wan asked. Love—Akio in love! Yes, Akio would be able to love as it was done in books.

"Yes," Bunji replied. "She is good enough for her position. But I don't know much about that. Although I am old enough I have not yet begun that sort of thing. It takes time and money. Also I am a mobo, and many mobos don't. Perhaps I'll marry a moga and she wouldn't like it. Old-fashioned women don't mind, of course." He laughed. "That's why my father is so angry at Akio. His betrothed is not a moga. It is a disgrace for her that Akio will not marry."

Every time after that day when I-wan saw Akio's quiet face and sad eyes, he thought of what Bunji had told him. He felt somehow fascinated by Akio, nearer to him, and yet further, too, for Akio was not in this world. In this house there was a strange union of rigor and relenting. Akio maintained his own way in a fashion, and was often away from home, but no one asked where he was. And there was never one moment, at least that any other eye could see, when courtesy failed between him and his father. Each yielded and did not yield and would never yield. Whatever had been said was said and needed not to be said again. Life went on as it was.

As for I-wan, even with content he could not of course fill at once the great emptiness of his inner life. Not even all the newness of his present life could do it, and there were times when he felt all his reading and dreaming only increased his inner want. I-wan was one who by nature needed to worship somewhere, and now he had nowhere to worship. His life had been filled with large things, his friendship with En-lan, his part in the revolution, his hope in Chiang Kai-shek, the leader —and all these had been taken away together. He could not even think of En-lan as alive. He searched himself superstitiously, asking himself if he had any premonitions now about En-lan. But there was nothing, and this nothing he took to mean that En-lan must be dead.

Even Peony had perhaps been swept into that death. The papers here in Nagasaki were full of stories of the purge. There were no names, only numbers. Thousands of young men and women were being killed. He belonged among them, he told himself; he too should be dead. He had been saved only by his father's power, that power which he had so despised because it was the power of money. He had betrayed, against his will, the revolution, as he had been betrayed. What of those promises he had made to the mill workers? He could still see them back at their hopeless tasks, accepting their fate again, muttering to each other that after all they had known there was nothing for them.

There was nothing left to worship. He could be diverted upon the surface of his days by a strange country and new ways, by

Bunji's nonsense and laughter and by work and by his real happiness in this house. But there was the great inner emptiness. He did not know what to do with that. When he was alone he was faced with it. What was there to dream about any more outside of books? And what could hope mean again?

He would never, he felt, hope for anything very much for himself. He read his father's letters with a strange sadness, as though they were written long ago by one dead. They came regularly, once a month, but nothing in them seemed real, though his father said everything was coming back to what it had been. Business was improving quickly, now that it could be sure the new government was to make no great changes. Credit was established abroad. Foreigners were anxious to make loans for reconstruction. The radicals were in full flight. Indemnities had now been arranged and paid for the few foreigners killed accidentally in the fighting at Nanking a year ago. All was being stabilized; the old peace and order would soon be restored. The family was as usual. I-ko was still in Germany. He had arranged wisely that I-ko could procure funds only through the military school he attended. His mother was lonely without her sons, but they were grateful to have them alive when so many young men were dead. His grandfather was in excellent health. Only his grandmother was disturbed because they could find no one to take Peony's place. The servant girls were idle and impudent now. As for I-wan, he was to learn business and some day his father would intercede personally with the government to allow him to return. Only he must be sure that I-wan was first cured of his radical ideas.

He folded the letters and tore them up small and threw them away.

"I do not wish to return," he wrote his father. "I like this country well enough."

Well, he would be a good business man at least. At the beginning of his second year he began working all day, as Bunji did, taking only the holidays that all clerks were allowed. Mr. Muraki said one night at the dinner table, "I have written your father how well you do." He bowed in thanks, and felt someone looking at him. Tama was there that night. Across the table she was looking at him, and now he noticed her clear black eyes. She looked away, and he went on thinking with difficulty. He did not hate his father now.

No, his father and Mr. Muraki, he was coming to see, were perhaps right. For nothing made Mr. Muraki more angry than anything at all communistic. When he saw in the papers that the government had arrested some student as a communist, he drew his breath in through his teeth. "Dreamers!" Mr. Muraki would mutter. "As if anything can be accomplished by dreams!" Perhaps he and En-lan had been wrong. And yet the thought gave I-wan no comfort. It increased rather the isolation of his spirit to distrust the reality of that upon which he had once put his life. But he could make nothing of it and at last he tried to think no more. He settled himself steadily into the pattern of his days. They made, he told himself, a sort of life.

All life, I-wan told himself now in the steady round of his days, went on as it was. If one struggled against it, it was not life that broke, but he. Sometimes in the solitude of his work or in his hours of reading and walking, for there were many solitary hours in his life in this quiet house, it seemed to him that all that had been until he came here was something he had dreamed and never done.

And his father's letters kept coming. Everything was as it had been, his father always wrote. Chiang Kai-shek was a man of great sense and he had cut off all the revolutionists, and they would be driven into the interior and not allowed to come into the prosperous river cities, certainly not into Shanghai. The bankers, therefore, were solidly for the new government. Everything was turning out well and far better than it had been hoped, because this man Chiang, with his strange power over the people, had chosen the way of wisdom rather than of folly.

Three or four times I-wan had said to Bunji, "I ought not to live on here forever. It has been two years. I ought to find some rooms outside." Each time Bunji cried out against this and told Mr. Muraki, so that Mr. Muraki made an opportunity to see I-wan and say in his delicate quiet fashion, "Do not leave my house. I like to have my friend's son in my house."

So through two winters I-wan had stayed on. He had waked many mornings to see from his warm quilts snow in his bit of garden, soft thick snow that looked scarcely cold. The sea mists kept back ice and sharp frosts, and when snow fell it clung where it lay, melting slowly underneath upon the warm earth. The paper-latticed house which was so cool in summer could be warm, too, in winter. In his room there was a sort of shallow pit sunk into the floor and into the pit was put a pot or cauldron of red coals, covered with ash, and over it a frame, and over this a thickly-stuffed quilt, and here he sat in the evenings when he and Bunji did not go out to some place for pleasure, his legs and his whole body warm and comforted. Sometimes Bunji came in and thrust his legs under the quilt, too, and they read or talked together. Sometimes in the main room where a large pot of coals was burned, they all sat under the big quilt as though around a table. Only Tama was still not often there. She had always, she said, to study, since this was her last year at the girls' school.

But sometimes she came, and on such evenings I-wan sat quietly, much more quietly than when she was not there. He did not look her in the face, but he saw her, somehow, between his looking here and there as Mr. Muraki or Bunji talked. She never sat by him. That he knew she could not do. She sat by her mother, her eyes bright and rebellious under her quietness and her cheeks red with the warmth. He knew now she was pretty, though he dared not look at her. In all this seeming freedom there was no real freedom. He had now learned that, too. Mr. Muraki might take off his garments before them and put on others in the presence of them all. But he turned his face to the wall first and when he did this he put a curtain between himself and everyone. Maidservant or family, they all turned their own faces away from him.

So also with Tama. She came and went as she liked, or so it seemed, but now I-wan knew, with none having told him, that if by one word or movement he let it be seen that he thought her free for him to speak to or to touch, he must leave this house, where he, too, came and went freely, only as long as he took no freedom for himself.

Then in the early summer of that year Tama left school. No one spoke of it to I-wan, but there she was, always at home. In the mornings she had been used to put on a straight plain foreign dress before she went to school. Now all day long she wore her own soft Japanese dress. It had been that when I-wan came back from work she was never there, since she seldom left school before nightfall. Now she was always there when he came home, not waiting or even where he could meet her.

But he knew she was there. He saw her sometimes in the garden, cutting a branch from a flowering tree, or he saw her arranging a vase or a picture in the alcove of a room. If they met in passing, she smiled at him, he imagined, a little sadly. Certainly she looked gentler now that she went to school no more, and she was quieter than she had been. He was glad she was in the house, but he did not know why she seemed so quiet. No one said anything to him. It was as though it were taken to be none of his business whether Tama went to school or stayed at home. And it was none of his business. But he could not keep from blurting out to Bunji when they left the house together one rainy day, "Why does Tama seem changed now that she has finished school?"

Bunji, splashing through the mud, did not stop. "She is at home now," he said carelessly, "preparing for marriage."

"For marriage!" I-wan repeated. "Is she going to be married?"

He had not thought of Tama's marrying. But she would be married, of course—she was almost his own age, though she looked so young.

"Oh, nothing is decided," Bunji replied. The wind had caught his black cotton foreign umbrella and he was struggling with it. "It is our way when a girl has had enough school, to keep her at home to get ready for marriage—you know, cooking, sewing, arranging flowers, making tea, music—everything, in fact, about a house and a husband." He jerked his umbrella down and folded it and let the rain splash in his face. "What an umbrella!" he remarked. "The old-fashioned oiled paper ones are better after all."

"Tama is to be married?" I-wan asked, his mouth suddenly dry.

"Of course," Bunji replied. "But not for some time. She has a great deal to learn, you know—especially about men. That's the trouble with a moga. She doesn't really know men. Take Sumie—now she makes Akio perfectly happy. She's content to do it—it's what she wants. But Tama has a lot of moga ideas—she'll have to forget them before she's ready to marry, my father says. She'll take lessons, probably, from some good old retired geisha girl. It's part of the training."

136

To this I-wan listened with a horror which amazed him. What was this to him? And yet it seemed to him intolerable that Tama must give herself up to nothing but the amusing and solacing of one man, some man—what man? He now perceived that though he saw her almost never, yet she was a part of the life of this house, and so of his life. He thought of her round pretty face and pleasant ways which until now he had not known he noticed. Now he knew he noticed everything about her.

"Are you sure she isn't—engaged?" he asked, knowing he ought not to ask it, that even Bunji would feel it ought not to be asked.

"It is not my affair," Bunji replied. Then he turned in the street to look at I-wan. The rain was streaming down his big flat face, over his upturned collar and down his oilcloth cape. "I'll tell you this, though, I-wan. You are like our brother. My father wants her to marry General Seki."

Now I-wan had lived here long enough to know this General Seki. He was known to everyone on the island, for Kyushu was his native place and they were all proud of him, though no one thought of loving him. He was a man past middle age, whose wife had died two years before, and he had given her a mighty funeral. I-wan had seen the funeral procession soon after his coming. Everyone had seen it since there had never been such a procession before in the city. General Seki had been driven slowly at the head of it in a motor car, covered with rosettes and streamers of coarse cotton cloth. He sat as squat and thick as a bullfrog, his shaven head sunk into his collar, his breast covered with ribbons and decorations. Everyone stared at him, while behind him in a smaller car came a little pot carried in an old maidservant's arms. In the pot was a handful of human ash. This had once been his faithful wife.

"I don't think young girls should marry old fat men," I-wan muttered, remembering all this. He felt sick. Tama learning how to amuse and care for that old fat man!

"General Seki is my father's old friend," Bunji replied. Then he laughed. "Don't think about such things, I-wan!" he cried. "It does no good. Don't let love be important—look at Akio!"

"I'm not thinking of love," I-wan said slowly. "I'm thinking of Tama."

And then for the first time he thought, what if they were the same thing? But it had not occurred to him really to love Tama until this moment.

He did not, of course, love her, he told himself. Had he not lived in the same house now with her for more than two years without thinking of it? Whenever he saw her he looked at her secretly to convince himself of this. All through the summer he told himself that she was too short, that her shoulders were square and her lips too full. She was not even so pretty as Peony.

No, but there was this difference. He had not wanted to touch Peony. But Tama he longed to touch. Day after day when he looked at her he forgot to see the faults of her face, her hands, her body, and he longed only to touch her. Her eyes were so pure in their clear black and white, her too full lips so red.

It seemed once he had thought of her that there was nothing else in the world about which to think. His work, a book he read, all that he did seemed useless beside this question to which he now leaped: did he love Tama? At first he let it be a matter to be balanced and weighed. He could love Tama or not love her. If he loved her, then he must ask to marry her. Marriage —that was serious. To marry Tama—but why not marry her?

He never wanted to go home. He could make his home here in this pleasant country where he had been so kindly cared for. He and Tama would make a new home.

He began dreaming. Suppose it were for him that Tama was preparing? When he thought of this, everything changed. If it were for him, then of course it was quite right that Tama should leave school and learn how to cook and to place flowers with meaning and how to play the lute and how to make love to her husband. He saw, off in the clouds somewhere, a little new house and himself and Tama there.

His father would not like it at first. But then perhaps he would, since he and Mr. Muraki were old friends. Mr. Muraki was always speaking of his father. "A strong man—a fine man," he murmured when he spoke of Mr. Wu. "The sort of man China needs—that any country needs—a friend to Japan."

Mr. Muraki might be glad to have the son of such a man for his own son-in-law. As for Tama, he was indignant that she should even think it possible to marry General Seki. But no, of course she did not think it possible. Perhaps she did not even know of it. But the danger was that she might think it her duty. She was so strange a mixture of willfulness and duty.

All through the summer and into the autumn I-wan argued with himself. Sometimes he was sure he loved Tama and then he made up his mind firmly that he would speak to Mr. Muraki himself about Tama, in the new modern fashion, but then whenever he saw Mr. Muraki he knew he could never do this. There was such fearful dignity in that small old figure. To be too bold would be to spoil all. And how could he speak at all when he did not know Tama's own heart? To her he might be only repulsive. He felt sometimes, staring at himself in the small mirror in his room, that he must be repulsive. His face was too long and always pale. He did not get enough exercise.

He did not love to walk as Bunji did, but he must walk more. And then, shrinking from himself, he was not sure, after all, that he loved her—if she did not love him, certainly then he would not love her. But whether he would let himself love Tama or not, he thought finally, he must at least let Tama know that she ought not to marry General Seki. He would find some chance time in which at least to tell her that, and once he had told her, he would feel eased.

But such chance was not easy to find. He saw her, it had seemed, so easily, in such glimpses here and there, and yet when he tried to speak to her about a private thing, there was no privacy. Somehow a maidservant was suddenly there, or Madame Muraki seemed by chance to be passing and she stopped to speak pleasantly, and when she went she always took Tama with her, for a special need. Or he saw her when the whole family was there, and she was always the first to excuse herself.

It seemed all accident, but after weeks of trying to speak to her even a moment alone he perceived that there was no accident in all this. They did not want Tama to speak with him alone. He felt hot for a moment. Was he not to be trusted? And yet nothing was changed. Everyone was to him as ever, and he could not be sure he had not imagined they did not want him to speak to Tama.

Then one afternoon when he came in, he saw her bending over a rock at the edge of a pool in the garden. It was already cold again, and there was thin ice on the water. He went to her quickly. Now he could catch her alone. He would waste no second of time.

"I want to tell you—" he stammered. He could speak Japanese very well now— "I have been trying to tell you—"

She looked up at him, her dark eyes full of surprise, her

hands still upon the stone she was arranging in the thin ice. She should not, he thought, get her hands so cold—then he was driven on by her soft direct look.

"You mustn't marry an old man," he whispered. "Tama, don't, I beg you—"

Before he could say another word he saw Madame Muraki, a shawl over her shoulders, coming toward them from the house, more nearly hurrying than he had ever seen her. He was about to go away, and then he stood still. Why should he go? He was doing nothing wrong. And Tama, seeing her mother, rose and moved toward her. But she found time for one sentence before she went.

"Do you not think I shall marry whom I please?" she said. Her soft face and her soft voice were pervaded with stubbornness. And immediately happiness fell upon him like light.

He watched her join her mother and they stood talking a moment. He could hear nothing, but he saw Tama shake her head quickly once, twice, three times, about something. He went on to his room, laughing a little, and greatly comforted over nothing in particular when he came to think of it, except that he was glad Tama was stubborn.

It was a good thing to educate women. He believed in it. It made them willful. He reached his room and sat down without even taking off his hat. He smiled and remembered her face as she leaned above the pool. She was not really pretty. He could see that. She was not pretty with Peony's invariably exquisite prettiness. There had been days, he remembered, when he had been perfectly able to see that Tama's school clothes were not becoming in their plain colors and tight foreign fit. But now she did not wear them any more. She wore her brightly flowered robes with wide sashes, and above the silken folds her fresh colored face was as beautiful as his heart could wish.

Besides, there was more than prettiness, wasn't there, to marriage? He had heard his mother when she talked about daughters-in-law.

"Women ought to be pretty, but not too pretty," she used to say like an oracle. "Extremes are always evil, and a woman too pretty is a curse to everyone, even to herself."

She used to say this before I-ko again and again, for some reason which I-wan did not know. Now he could see what she meant. A man should be able to count on his wife. There was that about Tama underneath all prettiness, something he could trust—if he loved her.

Was he truly in love, or not? How did he know? He wanted to be with her—was that not love? He would like to come home and find her there—that was love, wasn't it?

"If I could be alone with her even for one hour," he thought, "I would know."

But there was not the least chance of such a thing. She was like a bird fastened to a length of invisible thread, flying, it seemed, hither and thither. But there was always the length of the thread to which she was tied.

He rose abruptly and took off his hat and coat and lit his Japanese pipe. He had only recently begun to smoke a pipe. It was, he had heard Mr. Muraki say, a calming thing. He stepped down into the bit of garden outside his room and stood looking down into the basin of the small clear pool. Everything about it was fresh and neat as always. He took this for granted. But now he saw someone had scrubbed the stones since the rain last night. They had been picked up, washed, and put back again. He took one up out of its frame of thin frosty ice and looked at it. Even the underside was clean. Only a few grains of the wet sand in which it was set clung to it. He put it back carefully. In this house it would be known if so much as the position of a small stone were changed. He would wait, he decided. He would wait until he knew his own heart and Tama's.

"I want to climb a mountain," Bunji said suddenly on one day of spring, looking up from his desk. "Why not? We have not had a holiday since the New Year. My legs are growing soft."

I-wan was used to these sudden moods of Bunji's. For weeks and months Bunji worked as though there were nothing in his life but work. And then one day, without any warning, he would put down his pen and pound his desk with his fists.

"A mountain climb," he declared in exactly the same way each time.

I-wan looked at him and smiled. It had taken a long time for him to learn to climb with Bunji even after he had made up his mind to do it. Those bowed crablike legs of Bunji's, so ludicrous in puttees and leather boots, were able to clamber up rough mountainsides with a speed which I-wan could not reach however he tried. He grew used to seeing Bunji leaping along in his crooked fashion to pause on a rock high above him and wait.

"Tomorrow," Bunji said decidedly, "the azaleas will be in bloom. We will go to Unzen." He paused and grinned at I-wan and then he added as though it were nothing, "And we will take Tama with us, shall we? She used to go with me always before you came."

I-wan felt for his pipe. He must not show excitement. If it were between his teeth he could occupy his hands with it. He could light it and seem busy with it.

"Will she come?" he asked coolly. He had lived so many months now waiting that he could control his voice, his eyes.

143

"I don't know," Bunji said. He glanced at I-wan, his eyes full of teasing. "It depends on whether she thinks it worth while." I-wan did not answer, and Bunji went on, "That is, worth while to stand the storm afterward."

"You mean—" I-wan could not keep from asking.

Bunji shrugged. "My father," he said simply.

"Oh," I-wan murmured.

"We'll see," Bunji said calmly. "I'll ask her, anyway. She can do as she likes."

He suddenly began to laugh loudly.

"Why do you laugh?" I-wan asked him, though he knew.

"Oh, for nothing," Bunji said mischievously. "I don't like General Seki—that's why."

I-wan turned his back and did not answer and began to whistle without a tune. They went back to work without speaking again. But this, I-wan thought, bending above the invoices, this must be love, this heat in his bosom. Suddenly he felt tomorrow would be intolerable if Tama did not come with them. If she did not come, he would make some excuse to Bunji that he did not feel well. He would stay in his room, and perhaps, somehow, if he were in the house with her a whole day— But she might come.

He worked steadily on. There was nothing he could do or say to make tomorrow. She would come or she would not. No, what he had in his breast was hope. He hoped with all his heart—it was foolish to hope. She would or she would not. It might rain. Rain would not stop Bunji, but it might stop a girl. He really knew very little about Tama. Was she the sort of girl who would go up a mountain whether it rained or not, if she decided to go?

He became obsessed with the possibility of rain. It seemed to him that all these three years in the Muraki house he had

144

been only waiting for this one day, which was tomorrow. After his work he went and walked along the sea. It was from the sea that the rains came—that is, if they did not come from the mountains. He stared up at the mountains. Sea or mountains, at least now there were no clouds. He went home, for the moment calmer.

But in the night he woke convinced that he heard rain on the roof. He dashed to the edge of the garden. There was no rain. The spring moonlight filled the tiny space and what he had heard was only the ceaseless trill of the tiny waterfall, translated by his dread into rain in his dreams. He sighed enormously and went back to bed.

Yet when he saw her in the morning he felt that all the time he had known she would come. She looked sweet and familiar, as he had often seen her. She was still wearing her own dress, but it was a cotton one, flowered in blue and white like a peasant girl's. From its crossed folds on her bosom her neck rose creamy soft, and her face was a warm rose when she saw him and her eyes were full of pleasure.

"She wants to come," he thought, and this excited him so he could not speak. But she was calm enough after their greetings were given, and then he grew calm, too. After all, they were old friends, having lived so long in this house together.

"Where are the sticks, Bunji?" she asked. "And here is our lunch, and some cloth soles to put over our leather shoes so we won't slip on the rocks."

They set off, like any two brothers and a sister, and all of I-wan's thoughts of her during the last few days seemed now foolish and unreal. She was too healthy and natural and free to be in love with him. Girls in love—he remembered against

145

his will things I-ko had told him about girls in love. She was not thinking of him at all.

For a moment he was cast down by this. She ought not, if she loved him, to look so gay and healthy.

But it was impossible to be long cast down on such a day. The farmers were in their fields at work and called as they walked past, and children ran out to laugh at them, and the green hills were bright with sunshine.

"There has not been such a day in all these years since I came to Japan," I-wan declared.

"There are not many such days, even in Japan," Tama said, "nor, I think, in the world."

It was such a day when everything they saw seemed right and beautiful and fitted to the clear windless sunshine. And they passed scene after scene like pictures, each lovelier than the last. It was still early morning, and they had passed the fields and were at the foothills. Then they reached a certain point where the road took a sudden turn inward, and there was a small stream splashing down into a pool, and in the pool a country girl stood bathing herself. She was naked, and the water was about her ankles, and she was laving herself, her long black hair knotted upon her head. I-wan saw her unexpectedly and he looked her straight in the eyes before he could stop himself. But though he was instantly ashamed for her, he saw not the slightest shame in her wide dark gaze. She looked at them in most innocent wonder and called out a spring greeting. Bunji did not speak, but Tama called back to her.

Then the girl cried, "Where are you going?"

And Tama called back, "To the hot springs!"

"It's a fine day for that," the girl replied.

They went on, then, and now I-wan was ashamed before Tama. But Tama said with much pleasure, "How pretty she

146

was, standing to her ankles in the clear water and her skin all wet!"

"Yes, she was," Bunji agreed.

Then to I-wan, this, too, became beautiful and fitted to the day, although not to be wholly comprehended.

So by noon they reached the top of the mountain, and there was an inn and in the inn the hot-spring baths. I-wan thought to himself, "If Tama bathes with us—" He thought of the pretty naked peasant girl. At that instant he found himself possessed by his imagination. It came like a rush of music heard when no music was expected, and he felt his face grow hot. He wanted Tama to bathe with them and he did not. He could not ask Bunji a word. He did not answer his chattering. Tama had waved to them and gone one way and he and Bunji another. If he should see Tama in that great pool of steaming water, so clear that it was blue, and sparkling with silvery bubbles as it flowed from the earth, it would be the most beautiful sight on earth. He wanted to see it, and he was afraid, too. Could he keep from gazing at her?

But when he and Bunji came out, scrubbed and wet, she was not there. They stepped into the pool and Bunji cried out with joy, "Did you ever feel anything like this? Aren't you light—so light and clean?"

"It is beyond anything I have ever known," I-wan said. They played in the water like two little boys, splashing and teasing each other. Yet inside of I-wan was nothing but intense waiting.

Tama did not come. When at last they came out and dressed themselves and went into the garden, she was there. Her face was pink and fresh and her hair wet.

"Did you have a good bath?" Bunji asked her.

"Yes," she replied. "I had a little pool all to myself."

Yes, that was the way it should be. I-wan was glad it had

147

been so. He was relieved now that she had kept herself away from him. He was, after all, not a Japanese. He felt clean and strong and suddenly very happy. And yet he did not know why. There had been other days before, days when the sunshine was as bright and when he felt as well and ready to laugh. But today everything seemed more perfect than he had ever known it. The mountain air was so clear, the little inn so clean, and the old bare-legged man who was its keeper so courteous.

"Amuse yourselves, sirs," he called, "while I make your dinner ready! Those curious rocks I carried up from the sea with my own hands."

So while they waited for their food to be ready they ran about among the rocks in the garden, and exclaimed like children over the strange water-washed shapes. Everything was to be laughed at, the rock which the water had carved into the lines of a shrewish face, the crab in a little pool scuttling to hide when they looked at him, and especially all that Bunji said was to be laughed at. And every time Tama and I-wan laughed they looked at each other. At first their eyes met only to say, "Isn't he absurd!" But each meeting was so pleasant that I-wan made every chance to look into her dark eyes, and he discovered that when he looked at her the day sprang again to its perfection.

Then a voice called and they went in to eat their meal. The old man had placed a low table near the edge of the room and they seated themselves about it. The old man paused.

"I have waited until you came," he said, "to finish the decoration of the room. Look, if you please!"

He waited until their eyes were turned toward him. Then he drew back the screen. There, like a picture, was a hillside of burning maples, their rosy red soft against the clear blue sky.

I-wan's eyes leaped to meet Tama's, and hers were waiting for him. Her eyes were not full of laughter now. They were very soft and shy. She was beautiful! He felt his heart suddenly move out of its place and the blood poured out into his cheeks. He spoke to hide it. "You must sit here, Tama," he said, "where you can see." He pulled the cushion to a place facing the hillside.

"I will sit wherever you say," she replied.

He felt her docile and this made him giddy. Tama was not usually like this. She had a clear firm way of doing what she wished to do and of arranging even a small thing as she liked. But now she knelt upon the cushion. The sight of her smooth black head, bent before him as she knelt, sent I-wan into silence.

Bunji was playing the clown. He seized his chopsticks and pretended he was famished, holding his bowl and begging for food in the way that beggars do. But now I-wan could not laugh. He was trembling because of Tama. She knelt there, busying herself with the bowls and the cups, smiling, glancing up now and again at the hillside. He wanted to think of something to say, a verse to quote, or some ancient saying out of all he had learned. But he could think of nothing. His mind was empty of everything except the way Tama looked at this present moment. He said, stupidly, "Isn't it beautiful, Tama?"

He thought, "I am so stupid she will hate me. What is the matter with me?" For all morning they had all been full of talk.

But she nodded her head quickly and joyously, and again their eyes met for a deep moment. Then she took his bowl and filled it with the hot white rice and handed it to him. He took it with both his hands and instantly the moment was full of meaning between them. He did not know what the meaning was.

"Tama—" he began. And when he said her name it seemed to him that the moment rose like a beautiful rocket into the sky and burst into a thousand stars of light. Of course it was she who made the day wonderful, it was she who could make anything wonderful! He grew grave with this discovery. He was almost afraid of it. And yet, was it not for this very certainty that he had so long waited?

All the way home Bunji bantered him.

"What's wrong with you, I-wan? You've gone as quiet as an old man. Tama, the old man of the mountains has bewitched him."

"Don't say such things, Bunji," Tama said. "There are really spirits in the mountains."

They were walking quickly down the rocky steps of the path hewn into the hillside. Tama was ahead. She had kept ahead ever since they left the inn. He was watching her quickly moving feet. She put her feet down so surely with every step that she never slipped once. Bunji was always slipping on the loose stones. He wore the thick clumping soldier's shoes that he had worn when he was in military training.

"The only good I ever got from all that drill was these shoes," he had declared when they set forth in the morning.

"Bunji, don't," Tama had said. "It is the duty of every man to be ready to fight for his country."

"I'll never fight anybody," Bunji said stoutly.

"You will if you must," Tama rejoined practically. And now she said there were spirits in the mountains.

"You don't believe that, Tama?" I-wan asked.

She turned and pushed back her tossed hair. The sun and wind had burned her face a dusky red.

"Yes, I do," she answered.

"And you call yourself a moga!" Bunji laughed.

"Yes, I am," she said. "But I believe in spirits, too."

"Then you aren't a moga," Bunji insisted.

"I am—I am!" she cried, running away from them. She ran down the steps, her skirts flying, and suddenly I-wan ran after her in the rich afternoon sunlight. Behind him he could hear Bunji's clumping footsteps. But I-wan's feet were for this moment as swift and sure as Tama's. He ran, gaining on her with every leap. When she saw this she stopped and turned to face him. And he ran flying past her, not able to stop, so she put out her hand and he caught it hard.

"How you two run!" Bunji panted, coming up.

They all laughed again and because they were laughing it seemed he could hold Tama's hand for a moment. He had never touched her before. Now, though they were all laughing, he was only thinking of her hand, how it felt in his, so firm and soft. He remembered suddenly Peony, who used to slip her hand into his sometimes. Peony's hand was not in the least like this. It was slight and narrow and thin, the palm hot and the fingers quivering. Once he had said to Peony, "Your hand makes me think of that bird I caught. It's trembling."

But Tama's hand was strong and cool. When he held it, it did not fold and crumple. It held his, too. Before he could get the whole feeling of it, she drew it away and they all began to run once more. Then suddenly they were down the mountain, and there was the bus line, and they stood waiting for the bus.

"I'm hungry again," Bunji yawned. "Oh, how my legs ache!"

"Do yours, Tama?" I-wan asked.

She shook her head. "I'm used to walking," she said. Her voice was quiet, but she stood alert and buoyant. He could feel her brimming with a sort of private happiness.

"Have you liked this day?" he asked.

"Yes!" she answered quickly.

"It's been the best day of my life," he said. He waited for her to answer. Then when she said nothing, he asked, "And you?"

"I don't know what this day has been in my life," she said, "but it has not been like any other day."

Before he could speak the bus came clanging around the corner and they climbed in. And then they were at home again. This was home, this house of polished unpainted wood, spreading among the pines of its garden. The lights shone pearly through the rice paper screens as they came in.

The day was ended. And yet it could never be ended. He found a letter waiting in his room. It was from his father. He did not want to read it and he put it aside. It was not for today. For today had brought him to the knowledge of himself. He loved Tama and he wanted to marry her. Now that he knew, he wondered at his stupidity and cursed his own slowness. How was it he had not known the very first moment he saw her?

"My father," Bunji said the next day, "is angry with Tama."

I-wan, at his desk, was still in the dream of yesterday. In the night he had waked once to hear rain pattering on the roof. Let it rain, he thought, lying in the darkness. It did not matter tonight. "She hears it, too," he thought, and listening in deep content, he had gone to sleep. When he woke the tiny garden of his room was green and dripping with freshness. "She sees it, too," he thought. He could scarcely wait until he saw her.

He could not ask about her. That would have been to be rude. "She is tired and sleeping," he thought. He saw Tama, sun-flushed, asleep in the soft flowery quilts. There was still a little slanting rain when he and Bunji left the house, and a maid, bowing deeply, handed them wide umbrellas of oiled paper. The dream of yesterday still held. He must make his plans now. He must go about asking Mr. Muraki—not himself, but by someone as a go-between.

He had been pondering as he sat at his desk whether or not he should tell Bunji, when Bunji spoke. I-wan looked up, startled, at Tama's name.

"Angry with Tama?" he repeated.

"Yes," Bunji said. "But I expected it, you know." The abacus was clacking under his fingers and he was jotting down figures.

"He is not pleased that she went with us yesterday," Bunji went on. "He scolded her, too—hah, how he scolded last night!" Bunji's eyes danced. "I can laugh this morning, but I didn't laugh last night. He said I should know better, too." He pursed his lips. "I know what he meant," he added.

"What?" I-wan asked. He felt himself grow hot.

"He is determined now that Tama shall marry General Seki," Bunji said, and added, "Seki says he will wait no longer."

I-wan's head began to grow dizzy.

"But she won't marry him in a thousand years," Bunji said gently. He rattled thousands off and put them down. "Those little ivory toys we sent to America—" he said, "fifteen thousand of them."

"She won't marry him?" I-wan repeated. His mouth was dry.

"Oh, it's an old story," Bunji said. "None of us like it. My mother doesn't like it, even, but being an old-fashioned woman she can't say so. She has merely postponed it time after time. When my father begins to say, 'Now positively, we must decide this thing,' she always thinks of something. She says, 'Oh, I'm very busy now—all the heirlooms must be cleaned, so let us wait until next month.' But it's getting harder."

"Next month!" I-wan whispered.

"Oh, Tama will never do it—she will kill herself first, of course," Bunji said cheerfully. "We all know that, but my

153

father won't believe it. Under all that gentle look of his, he is so stubborn. But she is as stubborn as he, and that he can't believe."

Bunji opened a drawer and drew out another ledger.

"You mean—all this is going on—and you—" I-wan stammered.

"Love difficulties are very common now," Bunji said, laughing. "In these times almost any young person has love difficulties. The old want their way—and the young want love. Only I!" He burst into fresh laughter. "I have no troubles. I am not in love."

But I-wan could not laugh with him, for once.

"Why does this—Seki—want Tama, of all women?" he asked.

"Oh, he's a man of power and money," Bunji answered, clacking his abacus. "Samurai stock—like my father—Japan's honor and all that. He wants a young wife who will give him sons. Tama is so healthy—that's why he wants her. And my father says it will help the country—old Seki's blood and Tama's health. The old ones worship the country, I can tell you—and the Emperor."

"Do you think—" I-wan began in a whisper.

"I don't think," Bunji said quickly. "I tell you, I-wan, I don't think about anything. It doesn't pay. When I was in school some of the fellows took to thinking and I never saw them again. One day soldiers marched in—they were Seki's soldiers, too—and marched them off. Seki won't have any thinking going on in this prefect where he lives. So I made up my mind to enjoy my life."

I-wan thought it did not seem there could be anything under the spectacled, rather stupid-looking faces of the students he passed every day upon the streets.

154

"Do you mean there are revolutionists here?" he asked.

"Hush!" Bunji cried under his breath. "Don't speak that word! Someone might hear you!"

The door was shut, but he went to it and opened it and looked out. No one was even passing.

"I don't talk about such things," he said hurriedly. "I don't listen to them. I have my work to do."

He went back and began to work determinedly and I-wan turned back to his books dazed. His thoughts whirled about in his head. He got up suddenly, trying to think of an excuse to go back to the house to see Tama—to tell her—why had he not said something more to her yesterday? But he had been so happy that he had forgotten everything else. He felt compelled to turn to Bunji. "Bunji, can I—will you help me to see her—today? I must see her—"

Bunji looked up. "Tama?" he asked. "My father ordered her to stay in her own room for three days."

"Three days!" I-wan repeated. He could not see Tama for three days!

"Once before he made her stay in for three days," Bunji said. "There was a time last winter she told him that she would marry Seki in order not to be disobedient to her father, but that she would stab herself afterwards. He had to believe her and he punished her because he was so angry."

"That was the time you said she was ill," I-wan cried. There had been such a time, he now remembered.

"Yes, that was it," Bunji said. "Tama does not disobey in small things—only in great ones, like refusing to be Seki's wife."

The door opened and Akio came in. He looked tired and sad, as he almost always did.

"Here is a letter from that Paris dealer," he said to Bunji. "He complains that the blackwood stands to the Han pottery horses were crushed in shipment. Did you pack them as I told you to do?"

"In rice straw, chopped," Bunji said, leaping to his feet.

"I told you to wrap them first in shredded satin paper," Akio said.

"I forgot that," Bunji said, struck with horror.

"Ah," Akio said, "I thought so—we must replace them. It will cost hundreds of yen."

"I could shoot myself," Bunji said in a low voice. "I am a perfect good-for-nothing!"

"You laugh too much," Akio said.

He went out and shut the door. Bunji sat down and leaned his head on his hand. "I'll never be worth anything," he said contritely. "I'm always forgetting the important thing. Akio told me—and probably I was thinking about something else."

"Do you think I could see Tama somehow?" I-wan asked abruptly.

Bunji stared at him.

"What's that?" he asked.

"I must see her," I-wan repeated.

"What for?" Bunji asked, astonished.

I-wan did not answer. He looked at Bunji steadily, feeling the blood rise up his neck, into his cheeks. Bunji stared at him.

"You don't—you aren't—not really—" he stammered.

"I know I am," I-wan said.

Bunji's mouth fell ajar. Then he began to laugh suddenly and loudly. I-wan waited.

"Why do you laugh?" he asked coldly.

"Oh—it's funny," Bunji gasped. "It's very funny! Our house —a nest of love tangles—Akio—Tama—you—poor old father mixed up in it all—trying to—to—be the dictator—"

"It's not funny," I-wan said coldly. He waited for Bunji to be quiet.

"Well," Bunji said, "if you want to hurry on the Seki business, try to see Tama, that's all."

I-wan hesitated, but Bunji's look discouraged everything he wanted to say.

Beyond his window he could see the long roll of the sea, gray this morning under a gray sky. He would have to think. . . . But though he thought all day, he came to no conclusion except this —that now certainly he was in love with Tama.

They were in the dining room doing exactly what they did every night; yet it was all different because they were different toward each other. I-wan felt them different to him. Even Bunji seemed withdrawn. The night meal had been strange and quiet. Madame Muraki excused herself early. And then Akio rose to go.

"Akio, have you finished the monthly inventories?" Mr. Muraki asked sharply. He had said nothing all evening. Because the night was cool and wet he had commanded a small open brazier to be filled with coals and he sat smoking a short bamboo pipe.

"Yes, Father," Akio said quietly. They looked at each other, father and son, a long steady look. Mr. Muraki looked away.

"Very well," he said, and Akio went out.

Then I-wan and Bunji were left alone with him. Usually I-wan liked to hear Mr. Muraki talk, or if he were quiet and did not talk, merely to see him sitting quietly as he smoked was pleasant. He had looked until now a figure of goodness. But tonight I-wan was confused by him. This gentle-looking old man had made his love a prisoner. Somewhere in this house, in her own home, Tama was locked up. No, there were no locks on these doors. The screens would be open to the garden. But for Tama they were locked by her father's command as surely as though a bolt had been drawn. Then suddenly Mr. Muraki spoke.

"Bunji, go to your room," he said. "I want to talk with I-wan. I have a message from his father."

Bunji, startled, glanced at I-wan. But there was nothing he could do except to bow and go away, so I-wan was left alone with this old man. His heart began to beat swiftly.

He thought, watching the composed aging face, "I need not be afraid of him." But he was somehow afraid. This face was so sure, so carven in determination to maintain its own life, the life it knew. It would never be aware of any other life. He had thought for a moment that he might speak directly to Mr. Muraki. Now he put this thought away. He must approach him in the ways the old man knew, or he would have no chance at all. Again he must wait. He sat motionless in silence.

"Your father is pleased with your progress," Mr. Muraki said slowly. "I told him you were doing well." He paused, seemingly to light his pipe again with a fragment of hot coal which he picked up with small brass tongs.

"Thank you, sir," I-wan said.

"Your father writes me," Mr. Muraki went on, "that there is great improvement in China. The revolutionary elements are purged. The communists are driven into the inner provinces. Order is quite restored."

I-wan did not answer. He was not sure whether Mr. Muraki knew why his father had sent him abroad.

"Order will always prevail," Mr. Muraki went on in his even, old voice. "It is what the young must learn—not desire, not will-fullness, not impetuous wishes for—for anything. These must be checked. There is the course of right order which must be rigidly followed—" Then in a moment he added, "—for the good of all." He cleared his throat and said a little more loudly, "Therefore, since you have done very well, I-wan, and have learned so much here, I have decided to send you to Yokohama, to help my son Shio in our offices there. It is time you learned the rest of the business. Besides, there is a good university in Yokohama, and you may want to study a little more. You will live not in Shio's house, but in the hostel where the other young clerks live."

"Yes, sir," I-wan whispered. He wanted to cry aloud, "I know what you mean—you want to send me away from Tama!" He wanted even to cry out, "Why should we not marry?"

But he could not say one word. There was such dignity in this erect old figure sitting beside the brazier that he could only murmur his assent—for the moment, his assent.

"Since I always do at once what I have decided upon at length," Mr. Muraki said, "you will leave tomorrow. It happens that Akio is going to Yokohama on his usual monthly trip to consult with his brother. Have you ever been in an airplane?" Mr. Muraki lifted his eyebrows at I-wan.

"No, sir," I-wan muttered. Tomorrow!

"Ah," said Mr. Muraki, "then it will amuse you to fly. The Japanese planes are excellent. So—hah!"

His soft final ejaculation was a dismissal. He nodded, and I-wan hesitated. He should express thanks of some sort, but he could not. Thanks would choke him.

"Good night, sir," he said.

"Good night," Mr. Muraki said.

Outside the door Bunji was waiting for him.

"What did he say?" he inquired.

"I am to go to Yokohama," I-wan answered. They looked at each other.

"I thought something would happen," Bunji said. "The minute I came in tonight I knew by the feel in the house—everything was so promptly and exactly done—even the servants feel it when he is angry. Everybody is afraid of him."

I-wan did not answer. Against his own father he could rebel. His own country was full of rebellions—children against parents, people against governors. China was used to the lawlessness and unruliness of people who loved freedom. But here not a leaf could grow in a garden where it was not wanted. Ruthless scissors snipped and trimmed the least detail to the appointed shape. He began to see that the great peace of this house, the exquisite order of everything, was the result of ruthlessness.

"What shall we do now?" Bunji asked.

"I don't know. I can't go to bed—"

"It's raining, or we could walk," Bunji said.

"I don't care for rain," I-wan answered despairingly. Tama would not be free until day after tomorrow. He would have to go away without seeing her.

"Put on this raincape," Bunji said.

They put on the oilcloth capes that hung behind a screen and went out into the quiet cool rain. The cobbled streets were empty except for a servant maid gone out on an errand, a ricksha hooded against the wet. They walked down to the sea, lapping upon the cobbles. In the darkness they could hear the roar of surf against the breakwater. But it was held back and here in the harbor the sea lay as quiet as a pool.

They had said nothing, but now Bunji spoke suddenly.

"You wouldn't think that once a tidal wave rushed over that breakwater twenty feet high and came roaring through the harbor, crushing great ships together and sweeping the little ones out to sea."

"Can't the breakwater hold it?" I-wan asked listlessly.

"Not when the sea really rises up," Bunji replied. "Nothing can hold back the sea then."

"It is hard to believe," I-wan said dully.

They went on, seemingly without direction. I-wan felt the rain on his face. His hair was wet and he felt a trickle run down his neck. But he was thinking, "I shall probably never see her again." He was thinking, "What will become of her?"

Bunji stopped before a small square house, set exactly in a small square garden.

"I-wan—" he began.

"Yes?" I-wan answered.

"This is Akio's house," Bunji said.

"Akio's?"

"Where Sumie lives," Bunji explained.

I-wan paused a moment in his endlessly circling thought. Akio, that mysterious man, so strange and reserved, as even as a machine, lived here.

"Would you like to go in?" Bunji asked.

"Should we?" I-wan inquired. This was nothing he had ever known. Such things were, of course, but not to be recognized.

"Oh yes," Bunji said, shaking the rain from his cape. "I often come here. Sumie and I are quite good friends. She is a good woman. Even my mother has visited her."

"As you like," I-wan said, doubtfully. How would he behave before Akio? As for Sumie—old as he was, he had not seen such women as she. His father had said to him, "Stay away from such women!" That was in some trouble of I-ko's. But he had been interested in the revolution then and had no time for anything else. And since he had come to Japan—he had not wanted Japanese women. He wanted only Tama.

Bunji was knocking at a screen. It slid back.

"Bunji, is it you?" a very soft voice asked in the darkness.

"I and my Chinese friend," Bunji replied. A light flashed on above their heads, and I-wan saw a short plump woman, no longer young, though still very pretty, standing looking out into the rain.

"Come in, come in," she said warmly. She drew Bunji in by the sleeve.

"Oh, how wet you are!" she exclaimed. "Oh, is this I-wan? Akio has told me. I am so glad. Now take off your capes. Oh, and your wet shoes! Are your feet wet?" She stooped when Bunji kicked off his shoes and felt his feet. "Oh, your feet are wet! I have plenty of Akio's socks here. You must change—oh, you naughty boys!"

She was so warm, so soft, so natural that she was wholly charming. I-wan felt vaguely comforted and for the first time in the day his heart lifted. They followed her into a lighted room, dry and warm with a glowing brazier. There by the brazier, reading a newspaper, sat Akio. It was an Akio that I-wan had never seen, a cheerful Akio who looked up to say, "Bunji, come in. And you are welcome, I-wan."

He stirred himself as though they were guests.

"Sumie, two more cups, please!"

She had gone into the other room and now her soft voice called, "Yes, yes! I am bringing everything, so impatient man!" Akio laughed. I-wan had never seen him laugh before.

In a moment she came running in, her footsteps noiseless on the deep woven mats, in her hands the wine cups, and over her arm two pairs of clean dry socks. Here in the light she was prettier than ever in her kimono of deep apricot silk, patterned with white pear blossoms. Her hair was still black and dressed in the old Japanese butterfly style. Her cheeks were round and her lips soft and red.

"Now, then, here is everything. You pour them hot sake now, Akio—don't be slow, Akio—and change your socks at once so you won't catch cold, the two of you."

In a few minutes they were all sitting about the brazier sipping hot sake and feeling warm and secure and free. Yes, there was a sort of freedom within these walls, whatever it was. Akio was talking, he who never talked at home. And Bunji was listening, attentively, without laughter. Sumie rose silently and fetched a small lacquered box and took out a piece of silk embroidery and fitting a thimble ring to her finger, she sat down again a little away from them all, and sewed. Every now and again she looked at Akio and filled his cup or mended the fire.

At first I-wan could not talk for feeling this secret life into which Bunji had opened the door. The room was Japanese. There was not a single touch in it of anything new or western. It might have been the home of any middle-class Japanese man— a few books in a low case of polished wood set on the floor, a simple flowered scroll hung in the alcove and beneath it a red lily and two long leaves springing from a bottle-shaped vase. The mats on which they sat were shining clean. Akio's paper was the only touch of disorder. He had thrown it down when he began to talk—to talk, of all things now remote to I-wan, about war.

Afterwards I-wan could not remember what Akio had said. It did not matter. The miracle was Akio himself, talking quietly and freely in this warmed and lighted room. Inside the mold which I-wan had thought of as the man Akio, was this other living man who was Akio. He said something about war and how foolish it was, and yet how men must sometimes do things which were foolish, because it was not possible for any man to judge except for himself.

"War?" Sumie's soft voice cried. "We don't have to fight anybody. There is always another way of doing it."

Whenever she spoke, Akio paused to listen to what she said, and he smiled peacefully as though it did not matter what she said so long as he heard her voice.

"That's it, Sumie," Bunji cried. "When it comes to that, you can always do something else. But nobody will want to fight us."

Sumie sprang to her feet and took up the sake jug.

"Now don't please talk about such things," she coaxed them. "It is evil to speak of them. No, not war! My grandfather was killed before I was born, in our war in China, and then we grew so poor. Even though we won such a quick victory, he was no part of it. When everybody was out on the streets to welcome the soldiers home, my grandmother stayed at home and drew the screens shut and cried and cried. . . . See, I will sing while you drink! It is so nice to be happy!"

So she fetched a little lute and sat down and sang in a fresh pretty voice, a song of snow on plum blossoms. "I learned it in the village where I grew up," she said. I-wan felt quiet and good here in this house which Mr. Muraki had forbidden to be. But here it was, all the same.

They said good-by at last and he and Bunji turned homeward. All the way I-wan kept thinking of the last moment when he saw Sumie bowing at the door. He thought of her smiling simplicity, her childlike eagerness, and of Akio standing beside her, looking so different from the Akio he had known.

"It's a shame!" he burst out to Bunji.

"Yes," Bunji agreed, "but it can't be helped."

"She is good," I-wan insisted.

"Yes," Bunji agreed again. "We all know that. But she was not fated to be born as Akio's wife."

"Do you believe people are born for each other?" I-wan asked.

"Oh, yes," Bunji said simply, "my mother says so. Not for love, of course—that is another matter. But certainly two persons are born under certain stars to be man and wife. Then their marriage is successful and good. You see, that is really Akio's fault. He won't marry the woman who is his fate."

"Do you know who she is?" I-wan asked.

"Oh, yes," Bunji replied. "It is the daughter of a friend of my father's. Everybody says she is good and dutiful. But Akio defies his fate. My father says that will bring ill luck on us all. Oh, it was very bad at first, especially because Akio himself is good—my father was surprised at his disobedience more than at anything."

Home again in the quiet house, they nodded good night, and I-wan went to his own room. The screens had been drawn against the night. Suddenly he felt shut in by them. He opened them. The garden was full of mist, as white and enclosing as a screen itself. It shut him in alone.

He did not know when it was during the night that he first thought of seeing Tama. He had been asleep—no, he had not really been asleep. But suddenly after long lonely hours everything seemed reasonless and foolish. Only Akio was wise in his disobedience to an old man.

"Why should I not simply go to her?" he asked himself. He sat up. Why not? If he saw Tama once, he could go more easily to Yokohama.

The moment he thought of this it became a necessity. He knew where her room was, though he had never seen it. It was on the other side of the house, beyond the rooms of her parents. He knew that Mr. Muraki dreaded the night air. They had talked about it once, and Mr. Muraki had said that the night air was poisonous, especially to the old. And Tama had cried, "As for me, I always open my screens at night!" Madame Muraki had said in her even low voice, "Hush, Tama! It is not suitable for you to talk about the night." Tama had said to him once by chance, "Last year on my birthday my father asked me what I wanted, and I said, to have for my own the room facing the little waterfall. So I sleep and wake to the sound of the water, splashing upon rocks."

I-wan had thought of her listening to the falling water. Now, it occurred to him, in the misty darkness he could, if he stepped into the night, be guided toward Tama by that same sound. Why not? He thought of Akio taking his own quiet determined way. And at the same instant he knew he must do it.

He rose and put on his robe and stepped into the garden. The grass was soft and wet and he trod lightly. There must be no footsteps. Mr. Muraki's screens would be closed. So much would be safe. He crept past them, nevertheless, until he felt the corner of the house and turned to the right and stood, hidden in mists, and listened. There was the sound of the waterfall. He could hear its steady tinkling splash, and he went toward it, feeling with his hands outspread for trees and shrubs. Then he felt stones under his feet. That was the path toward the waterfall from the summer house—now he was close. The sound was clear. He reached the fall and put out his hand and felt the slight spray of it.

Now he must stand with his back to it and he would be facing Tama's room. There was no light whatever. If she were asleep he would have to scratch a little on the lattice to waken her. But he must take great care to walk in a straight line, lest he miss the spot. What if he happened upon Mr. Muraki's room?

He counted to himself, "One—two—three—" Now that silly goose-step would be of some use to him—goose-stepping helped one to walk in a straight line. He lifted each foot high and put it down carefully. In his excitement he laughed a little, under his breath. This was fun—dangerous fun, perhaps. He looked very silly doubtless, if Tama could see him. Lucky there was the mist! He felt his foot strike something and he put out his hand. It was the wooden edge of the narrow veranda. He felt upward with both hands, and, as he thought, the screens were open.

He was about to scratch on them a little, like a mouse, when he thought, "I'd better listen again."

Yes, the waterfall was directly behind him. Then this was Tama's room. He scratched on the screen softly. The night was so still he dared not call or cough.

What would Tama say? Now that he was actually standing before her door, he was doubtful of her. Suppose she would not be disobedient at all to her father? She was such a strange mixture of new and old. No one knew when Tama was old-fashioned Japanese and when she was moga.

At first he heard nothing at all. The room was so silent that it was as if no one were there. Then he heard a long sigh and the sound as of a hand flung out in the darkness upon a sleeping mat. Perhaps she was asleep. No, for he heard a wakeful little moan, a sigh again, but now made articulate.

He tapped quickly, little rhythmic taps on the wood. Then he waited a moment and tapped again. A light flickered palely behind an inner screen placed about her bed. Behind its thin silk he saw the shadow of Tama, her long hair flowing behind her. She rose from her mat on the floor and listened. He tapped again. Now she knew someone was there. He could see her shadow, undetermined, move a little away. She would be frightened perhaps.

"Tama!" he said softly, and instantly she was there, holding her long robe about her.

"I-wan!" she whispered, aghast.

"Tama," he begged, "I had to—I am to be sent to Yokohama—tomorrow, Tama! I don't know when I'll come back. Bunji told me your father was angry with you. How can I go away like that?"

167

"But you—my father would send you back to China if he found you!"

"He won't find me," I-wan urged her. "Tama, please—help me!"

"Help you?"

"Don't be Japanese, Tama—let's just be us, you and me—such good friends! Didn't we have a good time on the hills? That was only yesterday."

"Yes—yes—we did—"

"Tama, I went to see Akio tonight—with Bunji—Akio and Sumie. I never admired Akio so much before. It is brave of him to love Sumie like that. People ought to be brave when they know they are right."

Tama was holding back her hair in one hand. She stood, staring at him, listening, in her rose-colored sleeping robe.

"Is it—I don't know if—" she began.

"I won't come in," I-wan said quickly. "I'll stay here. But come to the edge of the garden close to me, so we can talk a little. Please —I am going away tomorrow!"

She did not answer. Instead she made one swift movement and blew out the candle.

"I am afraid someone will see you," she whispered. Then he heard her beside him. She was sitting on the edge of the veranda floor. When he put out his hand he could feel her shoulder.

"Tama!" he whispered. His heart began to beat hard. He longed to put out his arms and hold her close to him. But she shrank away and he did not dare.

"Sit down beside me," her voice said, so softly he could barely hear it. "No, I-wan, please—a little away from me. I—I-wan, if anyone hears us something terrible would happen to me. You must hurry."

"Yes, I will," I-wan promised.

168

It was true. If they were discovered, the penalty would be fearful. Once, even in China, he had heard his grandfather say that a sister of his was killed by her father's orders because she was found with her lover—innocently enough, in a garden, talking. And Mr. Muraki was sterner than anyone in China. "Tama," he said quickly. "About General Seki. You wouldn't ever give up, would you?"

"Never!" she said stoutly. He was sitting beside her now, and his shoulder touched hers again.

"I couldn't bear it, Tama. I'll come back, somehow. You'll see."

"I shall be here," she whispered.

"Don't—you know—marry anybody—" he begged. He wanted to say "Only marry me," but he could not.

It was so enormous a thing to say. They were so young, and there was so much against them. And this was against all lawfulness.

After a moment he heard her little whisper at his ear.

"I don't want to marry anybody."

He felt such happiness rush over him at this that he could scarcely sit still beside her. He leaned to her ear.

"Isn't it wonderful there is this mist?" he said, choking a little. "It's like a curtain to hide us."

"A good spirit sent it," Tama whispered back.

"Will you let me write to you?" he asked. "I have so much to say. No, but how—where shall I send letters to you?"

"To Sumie," she answered. "Sumie will keep them for me. I go there sometimes." She said it as quickly as though she had thought of this before.

"How it all fits together!" he cried joyously. "I never thought tonight why I went there to Sumie's. I had planned nothing!"

"It is fate," she said solemnly. "There is a fate for us."

"I wonder what it is," he answered.

169

"We cannot know," said Tama, "but it is waiting for us."

He wanted to cry out, "I know what it is! It is that we shall love each other!" But he could not.

He had never in his life spoken that word aloud, or indeed heard it spoken with the meaning of the love which he now felt born in his heart. This was so new a thing, so deep and huge in him, that he could not speak of it in the haste of this dangerous moment. There must be time to tell of it. It was not a word to crowd between second and second.

"We can't hurry fate," she went on, "and we can't avoid it."

"Do you believe, too, in—in two people being born to—to marry?" he asked, stammering.

"Yes," she whispered.

They were silent. In the darkness they sat, only shoulder touching shoulder. He felt a little shiver down his arm and into his hand and he moved his hand and it touched hers; their hands sprang together.

"Now you must go," she said, hurrying. "I will write to you, too, as soon as you tell me where—and we will meet again—if it is our fate."

"It is our fate!" he said firmly.

Their hands clung a little longer. Then she sprang up and a second later there was the sound of the screens sliding softly into place. Alone he fumbled his way into the mist.

Well, he could go now, even to Yokohama. . . . He was so excited he could never sleep. He would lie awake and think of her. . . . Instantly he was asleep.

He was in the airplane with Akio. They left Nagasaki in a big tri-motored plane. As soon as the inland sea was crossed, Akio said, they would change to a small plane. The big one was only for safety over the water. From it he now looked down on the island of Kyushu.

"Tama is there," he thought, gazing down into its greenness.

The mists were all gone this morning. He had waked from deep and pleasant sleep to find sunlight streaming into his room. Last night he had stolen through the mists to Tama, the heaven-sent mists. This morning they needed no mists. Everything was clear between them.

Akio was peering down through glasses.

"See that line of gray buildings and forts," he remarked, handing I-wan the glasses. Looking down, I-wan saw a dotted line of forts facing east and south and west. He laughed.

"You seem to expect enemies from everywhere," he exclaimed.

"When a nation is the smaller among larger ones," Akio said, "it must be ready on all sides."

"Surely you don't expect war!" I-wan exclaimed.

"I suppose," Akio said, hesitating, "we Japanese always expect war." His face grew serious. "At least we have been so taught."

I-wan was scarcely listening. He was searching the island with the glasses to see if he could find the house. People could still be seen—suppose he saw her in the garden! But no, the plane was mounting swiftly across the sea. Tama was there, hidden on the green island, like a jewel, the jewel of his heart. He gave the glasses back to Akio.

Akio was pleasant this morning. Neither of them spoke of the evening before, and yet because of it they knew each other as they had not. Akio was really talkative. I-wan, not wanting to talk, sat back in his seat by the small window, listening and gazing down at the brilliant blue sea. They were so high now that a great ship seemed to crawl like a snail on the surface of the sea, its wake like a tail behind it. Akio looked through the glasses eagerly.

"That is a warship," he announced, "a Japanese ship going westward—probably to China," he added.

"To my country?" I-wan asked idly. It seemed now a thing of no importance that once En-lan had exclaimed bitterly, "Why should foreign gunboats come into our waters? We send no such ships abroad."

"We have no such ships," I-wan had felt compelled to say honestly to En-lan.

"That's not the point," En-lan had argued. "We wouldn't if we had them."

I-wan, remembering, half-dreaming, thought, "I wonder if we would. I wonder if having them would make us want to use them."

"Why do you send ships of war to China?" he asked Akio aloud.

"To protect our nationals," Akio said, and added, "At least, so we are told."

"I am not protected here," I-wan said, smiling.

"Ah, but you are quite safe here," Akio said. "We treat you well—we treat everyone well—" he hesitated and went on, "that is, I sometimes think we treat everyone better than we treat ourselves. We are very harsh with ourselves, we Japanese. We are devoured by our sense of duty."

But the words scarcely fastened themselves in I-wan's ears. He was thinking, "How pretty she looked last night in the candlelight, holding back her hair!" It seemed to him he could think forever of the way Tama had looked.

He fell into a dreaming reverie. He did not mind going away —very much—if he could have letters from her and could pour himself out in letters to her. They would tell each other more in letters, not having the bodily nearness to distract them. In letters they could draw mind closer to mind and spirit to spirit. . . . The time went quickly while he dreamed like this. Almost before he knew it the plane was dropping swiftly upon a crust of shore that appeared suddenly beneath them. Then in a few minutes they were on the ground, and being hurried by sturdy blue-coated men into a much smaller plane. Almost instantly they were mounting again, but this time flying so low they could see the farmers harvesting the yellow rice in the small fields which fitted as neatly together as the pieces of a puzzle.

"This," Akio said suddenly, "is a convertible scouting plane."

"Why so much preparation for war?" I-wan asked.

"It is our philosophy," Akio said.

"Do you want war?" I-wan asked curiously.

"No," Akio answered. He hesitated, in his frequent fashion, and took off his spectacles and wiped them very clean and put them on again. "I myself am a Buddhist," he said. "I do not believe in taking life."

"But if you were ordered to war?" I-wan asked.

"I have not yet decided," Akio answered. He looked so troubled that I-wan made haste to say, "There is no need to decide—it was a silly question."

But Akio said nothing to this. And I-wan did not notice his silence. He was only making talk. Inside himself he was already planning his first letter to Tama.

If he wrote in Chinese Tama could read it, because classical Japanese and Chinese were the same, and Tama wrote beautifully—he had once seen a poem that she wrote on a fan with delicate clear strokes of a camel's hair brush. Well, but he would not use the old stilted Chinese forms of letter writing. He would simply begin straight off, "When I was there so high, soaring up in the blue, that was only my body—my heart like a wounded bird had never left the threshold of your room." They must write like that, straight out of themselves. . . .

Then again the plane was drifting like a leaf to the ground,

173

and they were over Yokohama. He was shaken out of his dreams. . . .

Yokohama was a busy, noisy city. There was no quiet garden here, no screen-shadowed house. He had found himself hustled into a crowded bus and hurried into the city along barren ugly streets, to a mushroom-like house of gray cement blocks.

Their bags were thrown on the sidewalk and he and Akio stepped down beside them. A uniformed doorman came and picked them up.

"These are our offices," Akio said. "Shio will be waiting for us."

He followed Akio through the door.

"I have never seen a building like this," he said.

"Earthquake-proof," Akio explained. "All Yokohama is earthquake-proof now, since the great earthquake."

They went into a bare new office. A young woman met them.

"Mr. Shio Muraki begs you to be seated," she said, hissing a little through her prominent front teeth. She was very ugly, I-wan thought, in a plain black skirt and a white blouse like a uniform. The skirt was too short and showed her thick, curving legs in black cotton stockings and heavy wide black leather shoes. But her ugly spectacled face was earnest with her effort to please them. She said, still hissing through her teeth, "Please—he is just now talking to an American gentleman from New York."

They sat down as though they were guests. But Akio seemed quite accustomed to this. He went on: "That year I went to America on some business, I forget—ah yes, it was on the matter of a gold lacquered screen from the palace in Peking, and the American collector in New York wanted it, among other things. So I took it over myself. My father was afraid to send so valuable a thing. And also there were reasons why he wanted me to leave Japan for a while. When I left I stood by the steamer's rail, looking back at Yokohama." He stopped a moment and went on.

"Sumie had come to see me off. And I watched the skyline as long as I could—long after I could not see Sumie, I could see the buildings lifting themselves against the sky. There were many fine tall buildings." He lit a cigarette and smoked a moment. "Then we had the earthquake. I hurried back. And there was no skyline at all."

"No skyline?" I-wan repeated.

"It was all flat," Akio said. "Every building was gone. I stared and stared, and I could not believe it. But there was nothing. Also I had not heard from Sumie—she was to wait in Yokohama."

Akio laughed suddenly.

"But when the ship came near, I saw a small plump woman standing among the ruins of the dock. Sumie! Well, I could spare the rest!"

They laughed together.

"And immediately," Akio went on, "everybody began to rebuild. So we have our skyline again. We know our fate, we Japanese—we are not cowards."

The door opened. "Now, if you please," the young woman said.

A large American man came out and behind him a small slight figure in a gray business suit. That was Shio. He looked like Mr. Muraki made young again.

"All right, Muraki," the big American was saying in a great rumbling voice, "it's up to you. Seventy-five thousand dollars, good U. S. money—but you take the risks of breakage."

"There will be no breakage," Shio's high clear voice declared.

"Well, that's your pidgin," the American said. "G'by, pleasure to do business with you, 'm sure—" He put out a large red hand and Shio laid his small unwilling brown one in it for a second. When the door had shut behind the American, Shio wiped his hand, half secretly, on his handkerchief.

"Hah!" he said to Akio, smiling and showing very white teeth under his small black mustache.

Akio smiled. "This is Wu I-wan," he said.

"Hah!" said Shio pleasantly. "My father wrote me about you. He spoke very highly. I am sorry I was busy."

"It is nothing," I-wan said politely.

He felt suddenly shy. Shio was really too much like Mr. Muraki.

"Will you come into the office?" Shio said.

They followed him into a square ugly room with gray cement walls and uncomfortable wooden furniture painted yellow, and the young woman poured tea for them. But there was no time to look about. Shio was unwrapping something on his desk.

"Look!" he said eagerly.

It was an ivory figure of the Chinese Goddess of Mercy. She stood two feet high, benign and exquisite, her tranquil presence diffused from quiet eyes and flowing ivory robes. She must be very old, for the ivory was creamed.

"Ah," Akio exclaimed, "at last!"

"At last," Shio said. He gazed at the beautiful statue. No one spoke. Then Shio said sorrowfully, "If only we could keep her! But she is to go to America with the rest. A museum has bought the collection entire."

"The great Li collection from Peking?" Akio asked, surprised.

Shio nodded. Then he said in a lower voice, "But tell me— how is all in my father's house?"

"Well enough," Akio answered. He hesitated and I-wan caught his eyes looking at him as though he wished I-wan were not there. So in decency I-wan took up a newspaper that lay upon a small table near him and began to read it, so that he need not hear what Akio was now saying to Shio of family matters.

Then suddenly he heard through all he read, these words:

"So now he is very angry and he says he will tell General Seki that the wedding may take place at once."

These words I-wan heard and instantly understood. In the crash and confusion of his own being he sat staring at the ivory goddess, speechless. She stood facing them, enigmatic, benevolent, ageless, eternal. He clung to her. She was quite helpless, of course. People could do with her as they liked. But in Japan, in America, wherever she was, whatever happened to her, she would be herself, unchanged. "I am insane," he thought, "thinking about ivory idols. . . . He wants the wedding at once. . . ."

"You will go to your room first, and rest," Shio was saying kindly.

"Yes, if I may," I-wan said. His voice sounded thin and far off.

"Don't hurry," Shio replied. "Have your meal. I want to talk with my brother. Tomorrow I will show you your desk. Just now of course we are very busy. Treasures are pouring out of North China."

What, I-wan thought, did that mean?

"This way, please," the young woman said. He took up his bag and followed her across the street toward a long one-story gray building. This was the hostel.

"Earthquake-proof," she said proudly.

She led him to the desk where a clerk whisked a card catalogue to his name.

"Room fifty-one," he said.

He went to room fifty-one, and opened the door to a small cell of a room. There were a bed, a chair, a table, a washbowl stand. Floor and walls were gray cement.

He sat down heavily and put his head in his hands. He must write to Tama at once. He opened his bag and snatched out the paper and pen he had put in this morning. That quiet room seemed a thousand miles, a thousand years, away.

177

"Tama," he began, "I have heard a terrible thing. Akio says—" He scribbled on and on incoherently, trying to tell her what to do —only what could he tell her? "Postpone—pretend to be ill, Tama —anything. Tama, could you run away? Think of something and write me. I can't sleep or eat until I hear."

He sealed it hastily, marked it for air mail, and rushed out to the desk to post it. When it was gone, he suddenly felt very faint. He must, after all, have something to eat.

He went into a restaurant and ordered a bean-curd soup and a little fish. As he waited he remembered the letter he had planned to write to Tama, when he was flying through sunshine over a blue sea. How different was the one now flying back to her, perhaps on that very plane on which he had come this morning! He felt a strange premonition that was like the memory of terror. He remembered his father bending over his bed and shaking him out of his dreams. He felt as though now, again, something had shaken him from a dream.

When he opened his eyes the next morning there was the sound of laughter in the hall outside his room. Young men were shouting with laughter. He heard them approach his door and pass, their laughter growing fainter as they went. A streetcar turned and screeched outside the window. He heard a crab vendor's call, "Fresh crabs from the morning sea!"

He lay a moment, remembering the mood in which he had fallen asleep. His fears had woven themselves into broken dreams in which he and Tama seemed always about to meet, and yet he never found her. It was all not true, fears or dreams. Everything was going to be all right. He could trust her—that soft stubbornness of hers.

The sun falling through the bamboo curtains was making little dancing waves of light on the wall. He leaped out of bed. He was going to work so hard that Shio would tell Mr. Muraki how good he was, and then perhaps Mr. Muraki would let him marry Tama. Well, his own grandfather might say he would rather his son married a Chinese, but then he had often heard his father say that China and Japan should be allies and friends. He laughed silently as he brushed his hair carefully before the mirror. He agreed with his father!

Tama would have his letter today. Perhaps she would not expect so immediate a letter and would not go at once to Sumie? He paused, his hand on the door, framing mentally a possible telegram. No, it was impossible. He would trust to her going at once to Sumie to tell her there would be letters. He could trust Tama.

He went on to his restaurant breakfast almost blithely. If she answered also by airplane, he might have a letter tomorrow. He ate rice gruel and an egg and salted vegetables and drank a glass of American malted milk without knowing what he ate or drank, then rose and paid his bill and crossed the street to the Muraki building.

The door of Shio's office was open and I-wan stood before it and coughed slightly.

"Come in!" Shio answered. His voice was so exactly like Mr. Muraki's that I-wan felt a little daunted. But he went in. Shio was at his desk already, a small, intensely neat figure with spectacles and a close stiff black mustache. He looked a straight militant little man until one saw his eyes. Behind the heavy lenses his eyes were, for a Japanese, unusually large, and their gaze was as naïve and mild as a child's. The militancy was all on the surface and because he had gone to military school, as every Japanese man had to do.

"Good morning," he said kindly. "If you will follow my secretary, she will show you your office. And please check the lists you will find there against the bills of lading of the shipments we expect today from China. Later, if you please, help to unpack the articles and check again. If there is any uncertainty, call upon me for help. I am glad to give it. When all is unpacked, I myself will come and examine everything."

"Thank you, sir," I-wan murmured. This little man was so calmly full of authority, in spite of his childlike eyes, that one's instinct was to obey him. Shio touched a bell, and the bowlegged girl in her black skirt and white blouse appeared, and I-wan followed her into a square hall where ten clerks bent over their desks.

"Here, if you please," the girl said in a smiling hissing whisper. She paused by a desk near the window and, bowing slightly, went away.

I-wan found himself looking down into a wide clean treeless street, edged with squat houses and open shops. Beyond was the brilliant blue harbor, where ships lay resting. Around him in this room no one moved. There was absolute silence. As he looked he met hasty secret glances from the corners of eyes turned for an instant in his direction. He felt suddenly for the first time a stranger in Japan, and that he missed Bunji very much.

Here he knew no one. The heads were all studiously bent now. No one moved except to open a drawer or reach for a pen. There was the atmosphere of a rigid discipline. He hesitated a moment, then felt his gaze caught toward a door. It was open, and a man stood there watching him. "Have you your assignment, Mr. Wu?" he called.

"Yes, sir," I-wan replied.

"Hah!" the man said.

It was a command to work, and I-wan opened the folder before him. Not a head in the room had moved.

When he came to his room three days later he found Tama's letter.

"Wait," she said, "we must wait. It will be made clear to us what our fate is."

Yes, but what of her father's haste to marry her, he thought impatiently. His eyes raced ahead. "My mother knows how to delay what she does not like," Tama wrote. "She has delayed this many times and she will again—and again, until—" Madame Muraki, so silent and scarcely seen—it was strange to think it was she upon whom he and Tama depended. And yet when he thought of it, he felt reassured. Tama was not alone in her father's house.

He wrote to her throughout the long year, often impatiently, sometimes angrily, and sometimes, in the long gray winter's days, in the apathy of delay and discouragement. He knew that she could not always get his letters when they reached Sumie. Sometimes, she told him, there were five or six waiting before she found a chance to go to Akio's house and then she had to wait until night to read them. But her letters were always the same. They were short, even when his were long, but they carried always the same steady words. "It will be made clear to us what our fate is. And my mother still delays."

Well, he must learn to be content with delay, he told himself. . . . That year in Yokohama was the longest of his life.

For hours he had stood checking with a pencil the things which the clerks drew carefully out of the sawdust and rice straw—potteries and ivories, carved agate and rose quartz, crystal and cloisonné, carved blackwood and redwood, and silver, inlaid with the sky-blue feathers of the kingfisher bird. But he paid no heed to anything.

All through the spring and the summer he had forced himself

to be content with delay, but now in this first month of early autumn he was miserably anxious again about Tama.

He had not simply imagined that her letters had grown careful. It was more than that. Last week she had told him to write less often and less freely. What did that mean except that she was afraid and uncertain—that she was changed? He had remembered then that she had never said that she would surely marry him, whatever happened, and he had decided desperately that he would wait no longer for Tama's "fate." He must know why she had changed to him. And instantly he had sat down and written her all his fears and had begged her to tell her father everything and let him come. He had told her that he would wait four days for her answer. This was the fourth day. If tonight there were no letter he would leave for Kyushu tomorrow. And now he could scarcely wait until the hands of his watch crept to six, and yet he dreaded to know the hour was there.

The door opened and Shio came in.

On great tables put there the treasures stood. Shio went over them in an ecstasy.

"Hah—" he whispered tenderly, "hah—all this—"

His small stubby fingers touched as delicately as a breath one thing after another. He knew everything, murmuring as he went. "This now, is Sung white—and this is a green they never made so well as in the Ming—and yes, I see it—the white jade landscape—ah, I have tried for ten years to get that!" He seized upon a lump of jade carved into the likeness of a snowy mountain. He was laughing and half tearful with joy. "It's here!" he cried. "I cannot tell you what it means! I will not sell it to any American, even if he offers a million for it! It shall stay here in Japan! Such things belong in Japan. It is only we who appreciate them—"

I-wan watched, astounded. Why, Shio was like a man half mad! He was caressing the mass of jade, muttering and grunting. It was

182

revolting, I-wan thought to himself, horrible! Suddenly a question cracked across his mind again like a whip. Where had these things come from?

He stood a moment, then he turned and silently and quickly he went out of the warehouse. He brushed his way through the crowds of clerks leaving for their buses. Everybody was laughing and merry as they put away office coats and slipped off paper cuffs. But he went on swiftly, entered the hostel and went down the hall and opened the door of his room. . . . If there were a letter it would be on the table.

It was not there, he saw instantly. But, peacefully asleep on his bed, he saw Bunji.

His first thought was to shout, "Bunji! What are you doing here?" But he checked the cry. He had never taken any thought before of how Bunji looked. He knew Bunji was not handsome. Bunji himself made fun of his looks.

"I look like the clown in a street show, of course," he always said cheerfully. "Well, what of that? I don't have to worry about that—all the mogas will not love me—so I can have a peaceful life." He always declared he would marry the ugliest girl he could find, since being still uglier himself, he would make her happy in feeling she was beautiful by comparison. Nobody needed to think how Bunji looked when he was laughing and joking, because he was always a pleasant sight in spite of his thick flat nose that was bridgeless and his small bright eyes and big smiling mouth.

But now for many months I-wan had not seen him. And he had never seen him asleep. Bunji gravely asleep was someone else. His face looked low-browed and the jaw was too heavy and the mouth was thick. Now I-wan could see—Bunji was very Japanese. His body was squat and his arms long and his hands short and powerful. Even his feet, without shoes now, looked short and thick except for the prehensile Japanese toes. I-wan had heard children on the streets of Shanghai call after a Japanese, "Monkey—monkey!" The word came to his mind now. But Bunji opened his eyes, stared, and leaped up, laughing.

"I-wan!" he shouted.

"Why are you here?" I-wan asked quietly. He was forcing himself to think, "This is the same Bunji."

Bunji was yawning loudly and rubbing his eyes with his fists.

"I don't know," he said cheerfully. "All I know is Akio and I were told to report at Tokyo at army headquarters. We got here too late to go on tonight. So I said, 'I'll go and find that old I-wan and we'll have fun once more together.' "

"Where is Akio?" I-wan asked.

"Oh, of course Sumie came, too, and they are somewhere together, I suppose, looking at Fuji-san under the moon or something like that!" Bunji laughed. "You know them! Besides, they love Fuji. Every summer they make a trip together up Fuji—"

"Why should Tokyo headquarters send for you?" I-wan asked.

Bunji was putting on his shoes.

"That's what I shall ask them," he said cheerfully. "Every year or so we reserve officers have to go and get registered in case of war—generals are like old grannies, always thinking about war."

He was on his feet now, brushing his hands through his stiff hair.

"Yokohama has good geisha dancing," he roared. "Come on, I-wan! After all, it's months since we met!"

I-wan thought a moment. Bunji could tell him of Tama. . . .

"I'm coming," he answered.

The theater was bright with lanterns and the seats were full of gaily dressed people, placidly eating sweets and staring at the brilliant stage, their faces serene with pleasure. It was an ancient dance, full of stateliness and pomp and historic meaning which I-wan could not understand. But everybody else seemed to understand it. When it was over there were cries and shouts of praise. Bunji leaned back, beaming and perspiring with his pleasure.

"I never saw it done so well," he cried. "Ah, that little Haru San—the one in the middle—she is famous! Everybody knows her. I have heard of her and never seen her."

"I did not listen too well," I-wan confessed.

Everybody was talking and laughing and moving about until the curtain rose again.

"It is the story of how the daughter of a great samurai disguised herself as a man and led her father's armies out in his place," Bunji explained. "She takes the enemy general captive, you see, and falls in love. Her heart bids her spare his life. The struggle is terrible. But her country prevails and she kills him with her father's sword. Then, seeing him dead, she kills herself." Bunji wiped his face which instantly burst out into fresh perspiration in his excitement. "It's beautiful—" He sighed and looked about him. "It is a famous play. Everybody knows it, but still they want to see it over and over—" His round absurd face grew suddenly shy. "If I had any courage," he said, "I would ask to see that little Haru San—and tell her—how I—how I—"

"Why don't you?" I-wan said, smiling.

Bunji turned red.

"I know my own face," he said humbly. "I wouldn't ask her to look at it."

I-wan burst into a laugh. Monkey or not, it was impossible not to like this Bunji. And in this return of affection he walked back with Bunji and asked him what he had wanted to ask all evening and had not, because the strangeness of the day separated him somehow from everyone.

185

"Bunji," he said as soon as they were in his room again, "what of Tama?"

He stood by the table waiting. And Bunji sat down on the bed and looked at him honestly.

"I'll tell you," he began. He fumbled in his coat pocket. "Well, there's a letter she gave me, but she said, 'Don't give it to I-wan until you tell him everything first.'" Bunji pulled out a long narrow envelope scattered over with the tracing of delicate pink blossoms which I-wan now knew so well. He put out his hand, but Bunji drew back.

"She said—" he began doggedly.

"I'll only hold it," I-wan said hastily. "I promise!" he added to the doubt on Bunji's face.

"We-ell," Bunji agreed. He gave it to I-wan and watched him a second. Then he cleared his throat. "It's this way with Tama," he began. I-wan, waiting, bit back his need to hasten him. This Bunji was so slow it would be dawn before he got to any point.

"Let's see," Bunji was saying very slowly and thoughtfully, "two days ago she seemed just as usual. She arranged fresh flowers and dusted the rooms. Well, then, when she was alone with me she told me to tell Akio to tell Sumie that she would come to see Sumie just before twilight. So she went to see Sumie. I don't know why, except that something was between them. . . . But that was afterwards."

"After what?" I-wan groaned.

"After General Seki came to see my father," Bunji said.

"He came to see your father?" I-wan cried.

Bunji nodded. "And my father called her into the room and they talked to her and talked to her. I was late myself that night because I had gone to see an American film called—let me see, what was it called?—"

"Ah, in Heaven's name!" I-wan groaned.

186

"No," Bunji said brightly, "you are right—it doesn't matter, though I can think of it if I give myself to it—a pretty girl, and a robber in her bedroom, who she finds afterwards is a man she once knew and they marry—it was— Well, about Tama— when I came home the light was still on where they were talking to her. So—"

"Had she my letter then?" I-wan broke in.

Bunji stared at him, his eyes blinking questions. But I-wan had no time to explain now. He tore Tama's letter open.

"I didn't say—" Bunji began.

"I can't wait," I-wan replied grimly.

"Well, I was about finished," Bunji said amiably. He threw himself back on the bed. "All these tangles of love—" he began to laugh.

But I-wan did not hear him. His eyes were eating up the words on the patterned paper.

"I-wan, I said to you I wanted to marry no one," Tama wrote. "But my father has told me there is going to be war with China. And so everything is changed. Even my mother says that now it is my duty to marry General Seki, since he has to go to fight for our country. She delays it no more. And I see my duty. It is fate. Tama."

She had brushed out a word before her name. But he knew what it was. "Your Tama," she had written. Then she had brushed away the word "your." Duty! It was like a drug, a poison in them all. But if Madame Muraki—he must not waste a moment.

"Will the train or the plane get me there first?" he demanded of Bunji.

Bunji sat up.

"Where?" he asked.

"To Kyushu," I-wan cried.

Bunji shook his head. "My father won't let you see her," he said pityingly.

"I'll see her somehow," I-wan swore.

"Well," Bunji said, hesitating, "the night train has gone, and of course the plane is quicker than the morning train, if it goes. But there's the chance of storm or something."

I-wan threw open the window. There were no clouds and the moonlight was clear and still over the city.

"You can see Fuji-san!" Bunji exclaimed.

"I'll go on the plane tomorrow," I-wan decided. Only there was the rest of this night to be passed somehow!

"I shall sleep," Bunji said with firmness.

"Then you may have my bed," I-wan replied. "I can't sleep."

He sat down by the table and put his head on his arms. What could he do—what could he do?

"I would help you if I could," Bunji said comfortably, "but then I have to report tomorrow."

"The through plane doesn't go until noon," I-wan muttered.

"No," Bunji agreed. "Well, if Shio doesn't want me for anything, I might go back with you after I have registered. If you wanted to write a letter or something, then, if you haven't been able to see her, I could give it to her."

"Yes!" I-wan cried, looking up, "that is a good thought. Bunji, how good a friend you are to me!"

"Hah!" Bunji answered. "Well—yes—I like you, you know." He laughed and began to undress.

But I-wan had already found paper and pen. He would see Tama, of course—but in case he could not find an immediate way, Bunji could give her this letter. He wrote on and on into the night, begging, pleading, pouring out his love.

"Even if our countries should go to war, my Tama," he wrote over and over, "it has nothing to do with us. You and I, we are ourselves. We belong to each other. It is an accident that governments—" He felt no loyalty to that government now in China—it was not his!

To the sound of Bunji's steady deep breathing he wrote everything to Tama. Then for a long time he sat reading all he had written. When he folded the pages at last the moon had gone, and it was the dark before dawn. He turned off the light and lay down, dressed as he was, beside Bunji, and fell asleep as a man stumbles exhausted and falls into a well.

He waked the instant Bunji moved.

"What time is it?" Bunji asked thickly. Sunlight was streaming into the room.

I-wan looked dazed at the watch still on his wrist. "Half-past-eight," he answered.

Bunji leaped across him.

"Akio and I must catch the train at nine!" he shouted. He began flinging on his clothes and dashing to the water basin; he laved the running water over his face and head.

"It's a long way," he sputtered. "I'll have to buy a bit of something and eat it on the train as I go."

He brushed up his spiky hair as he talked. "I'll be back as soon as I can," he promised. "If Shio doesn't want me, I'll go—" He was knotting his tie crookedly and buttoning his coat and searching for his hat, all at the same time. Now he was at the door. "So—hah!" he grinned and was gone.

And I-wan got up slowly, still exhausted in spite of sleep, and undressed and washed himself and put on fresh garments. Then he sat down and read carefully again Tama's letter and his to her. Then exactly as though the day were like the one before, he went to the restaurant and ate and then went to the warehouse.

The great jade piece which Shio had so caressed was gone. Shio had taken it, doubtless, to his own home. He felt suddenly angry, as though he himself had lost a treasure. But he worked doggedly, checking and rechecking. Nothing now mattered except the one thing—could he reach Tama in time, and having reached her, could he persuade her . . . ? Then, it occurred to him, persuade her to what? What would he tell Tama she must do? Where could he take her? He paused, in his hands a twist of the root of an old cherry tree, carved and polished and stained into the appearance of an ancient impish face. When he looked down at it, it seemed to peer up at him with the mocking eyes of a merry and cynical old man. Where in the world was there a place for Tama and him . . . ?

Then before he could answer, he heard someone crying and shouting for him. It was Bunji. He burst into the door, his eyes wild and his face twisted with weeping.

"I-wan," he gasped, "Shio—where is Shio?"

"I haven't seen him," I-wan said, frightened. The old man dropped from his hand, "Bunji—don't—what—"

"Akio—" Bunji sobbed. "Akio—Akio—"

He held out a sheet of paper to I-wan. Upon it was written in Akio's fine neat brush strokes:

"To my father and to my brothers, this: I have considered well this step which I now take. I know why I am called to register myself again as a soldier. We are to be sent to China to fight. But there is nothing in life for which I care to fight. Especially I wish to have no part in killing innocent people of any race. Yet it is not possible to refuse the Emperor when he commands except by the one means which I now take. When this comes to your hands, I shall have given my body to Fuji-san. And with me now, as ever, is Sumie."

"When—when—" I-wan stammered.

"When I reached the station to get my free ticket," Bunji sobbed, "when I had declared my name, they said this had been left for me. So I took it and read it, and when I burst out weeping—an officer took it and read it—he was so angry—he said—he said Akio was a traitor—and he had no right to—to kill himself at a time when—when the Emperor needs men—" Bunji's tears were streaming down his face.

"Does Shio know?" I-wan asked in a low voice.

Bunji shook his head.

"Come," said I-wan. He put out his hand and took Bunji's, and felt Bunji's short wide fist clutch his own slender hand. Then without a word they went to Shio's office. He was there at his desk. Before he could do more than lift his head to look up, I-wan put Akio's letter before him. He read it, his eyes blinking, his face changing from surprise to consternation, to a quivering understanding. Then he put the paper down.

"I always knew Akio would do this some day," he said quietly. "He was so continually poised between life and death. Death seemed as sweet as life—" he paused and swallowed. "When we were children—if anything went wrong—he used to—want to die." They were all silent. Then Shio said heavily, "Bunji, you must go home at once. I must see if—there is anything to find of their bodies. Sometimes they—people—don't leap clear of the rocks into the crater—"

"I cannot," Bunji said. "I am to report for duty this afternoon. I was given these few hours only—"

They looked at him, startled.

"I must sail in three days," Bunji said simply, "to Manchuria—"

They stood there, not knowing what to say to each other.

"As a Japanese," Bunji said thickly, "I have to go."

"I know," I-wan said slowly. "I understand that."

He turned to Shio. Even now he had thought of something.

"If you will trust me," he said, "I will go in Bunji's place to your father." He had a strange sense now of an arranging fate. What if indeed there were such a thing?

"Then go," Shio said. "And tell my father not to be too angry with Akio."

So death opened the door for him to Tama.

She sat there on her knees, quietly, a little behind her parents, while he told them what had happened. Mr. Muraki had received him first alone. When he had heard, when he had read the letter, he said nothing for a while. He folded the letter carefully into a small square and put it in the pocket of his sleeve. Then he said, "Let my daughter and her mother be called."

So I-wan went out and found a maidservant and told her. Then he went back into the room where Mr. Muraki sat. He had not moved. He did not speak as I-wan sat down.

In a few moments the door opened and Madame Muraki came in. I-wan rose, without looking up. It would not be courteous to look, and he stood turning a little away. But he knew, he could feel, that Tama was in the room. Then he could see from under his lowered lids the edge of her blue kimono upon the floor. At least she was here!

"Sit down," Mr. Muraki said.

So they all sat down. And Mr. Muraki drew out of his sleeve Akio's letter. He paused a moment, his teeth clenching and the muscles working in his jaws. Then he began to read, quietly and clearly, what Akio had written. When he had finished he folded the letter again and put it in his sleeve. They sat in silence. Once I-wan heard a sob, instantly choked. But he knew it was Tama. He looked up quickly. She was biting her lips and her hands were folded tightly together. Madame Muraki sat rigidly, her tears flowing down her face. She took up her sleeve and wiped her eyes, but she said nothing.

"For a son disobedient to his Emperor and to his father," Mr. Muraki said in the same still voice in which he had been reading, "there can be no mourning. Let there be none, therefore, in my house."

His hands, lying palms upward on his knees, were trembling a little, and he coughed. "That is all," he added. Then he turned to I-wan. "You will want to sleep a night before you return," he said. "Your room is as usual."

"Thank you, sir," I-wan murmured.

Beneath all this repressed sorrow his heart suddenly began to beat wildly. He knew the path now to the waterfall that splashed outside Tama's door. There was no need for his letter now.

"If you will excuse us, sir," Madame Muraki said faintly.

Mr. Muraki nodded, and I-wan rose again. He lifted his eyelids quickly, once. He met Tama's eyes, wet with tears, and yet imploring and full of warmth, and he knew she expected him.

He stood at a little after midnight at her door, and shrinking out of the moonlight into the shadow of the heavy overhanging eaves, he scratched his little tune upon the lattice. Instantly it slid back. She was there. He saw her face, pale in the shadow of the edge of moonlight. She put her fingers on his lips for silence and he smelled the fragrance of a rose perfume. He stood, not moving, scarcely breathing, feeling only her.

"Come into the shadows of the veranda."

Her whisper was lighter than the flutter of a hummingbird's wing. Silently he stepped from the moss to the mat she pulled forward to catch the sound of his footstep. They stood, face to face, gazing at each other, speechless. Then he put out his arms to her. He had never in his life put out his arms to hold a woman. He did not know a woman's shape or form. But he held her to him, wondering in the midst of love that a woman's body could lean like this against his own, and being so different could yet fit against him and be a part of him. They stood together, motionless.

Then she drew away.

"Oh!" she cried softly. "And I said, 'I won't—if he comes—I won't see him.'"

"I would have found you," he said solemnly. "You are not safe from me—anywhere."

"No, don't, I-wan."

"Yes, I will, Tama!"

"Do you know—there is to be war?"

"Never between us!"

"I can't—I can't—but there is no help for us. I must do my duty."

"You never thought it was your duty before—to—to—marry an old man whom you hate!" he whispered hotly.

"No, but now everything is different. In war Japanese men fight and Japanese women bear sons," she pleaded.

"Tama—you a modern girl!" he scolded her.

"No, but it's true—what else can we do?"

He held her more tightly. His heart was beating fearfully, so that his breast ached.

"No," he said thickly, "not you. You and I are going to run away—somewhere where there are no wars—where no one can find us—where it won't matter that I am Chinese and you are Japanese!"

"There is no such place in the world," she moaned.

"There is—there is—" he promised her. "Only promise me—you won't marry him. I'll plan everything—and tell you—"

There was the sound of a footstep. A twig broke. They clung together in instant terror. They saw Mr. Muraki turn the corner of the house. Tama clutched I-wan's arms and pulled him silently into her room. They stood behind the drawn screens, scarcely twenty feet from him. For he had paused before the waterfall and stood there, his head bent. They could see his hair shining in the moonlight. In his hand he held a spray of white crape myrtle flowers which he had broken as he passed the tree. He stood so long their bodies were tense with waiting. Then he stooped and laid the myrtle in the pool beneath the waterfall. They heard him sigh and saw him turn away and walk on feebly into the further garden.

But they dared not linger. I-wan stooped to Tama's cheek. It smelled as fresh as an apricot, and felt as downy smooth beneath his.

"Promise!" he whispered.

"Oh," she breathed, "you must go!"

"Promise only to wait!" he begged. "At least until we find out whether there really is to be war or not. It may be nothing."

He felt her lips move upon his cheek, soft and warm.

"Go—go," she whispered, "I hear something."

He slipped out into the moonlight and darted to his room. Surely, he thought, surely there were islands in the sea, far from any wars and troubles that other people made! He lay tense on his bed. Surely there were such islands! And then he remembered that she had not promised.

"This," Mr. Muraki was saying, "is General Seki."

I-wan had eaten his breakfast alone the next morning, and afterwards, not knowing what part of his still unformed plans should come first, he had gone into the room which the family called the modern parlor. He still preferred chairs to sit upon rather than mats, and in this room there were large stiff foreign chairs, upholstered in bright green plush. Years ago, before the main offices had been moved to Yokohama, Mr. Muraki had seen the room in a department store and had bought it entire, in order to have a place in which he could entertain American and European customers. It was seldom used now, and there I-wan had sometimes gone when he wished to read or to be alone in this house of sliding screens, since the room had walls and doors in the western fashion.

He had scarcely sat down this morning, however, and lit a cigarette, when the door opened suddenly and he saw Mr. Muraki and behind him a thick short figure in uniform. I-wan leaped to his feet. And Mr. Muraki looked astonished for one instant. I-wan bowed. All his blood seemed in one second to rush to his brain to whirl there in a frenzy, leaving his body cold and weak.

"This," Mr. Muraki said to General Seki, "is the son of the Chinese banker, Wu Yung Hsin."

General Seki nodded his head sharply at I-wan.

"I was just going, sir," I-wan said to Mr. Muraki.

"No," General Seki answered. "You will stay." He sat down with difficulty in his stiff new uniform and his sword clanked against the chair.

"As you please," Mr. Muraki murmured to General Seki.

So I-wan could only sit down uncomfortably upon the edge of a straight wooden chair. From the tumult in his brain certain thoughts began to sort themselves. This disgusting, thick-necked man! He looked strangely like a turtle, his neckless, bullet head sunk into his big collar. He had a square, flat-surfaced face and a short brush of gray mustache. Yet he did not look old, I-wan thought, cursing him. He looked, though not young, vigorous and harsh and domineering.

"It may be you can give me some information," General Seki said, turning to him. "Can you tell me in what cities in Manchuria your father's bank has branches?"

Instantly I-wan thought, "I will tell him nothing." He remembered now that he had heard En-lan say once that Japanese were always asking questions and trying to find out even small things that were apparently of no use. But this was stupid, to think he—

"I don't know," he said.

"It seems strange you don't know," General Seki said, after a second's pause. He stared at I-wan hard. "But it does not matter. I have the information at my headquarters. I merely asked as a detail in discussing plans with Mr. Muraki. Perhaps then you can tell me how far, in hours, Peking is from Harbin?"

"I have spent most of my life in Shanghai," I-wan answered.

A small purple vein began to beat in General Seki's forehead. He turned to Mr. Muraki and spoke in a loud voice.

"Let the plan stay as I have said. It will not be a real war— three weeks will be enough to crush a few rebellious Chinese. There is too little time now—I leave at once. But when I come I will take a holiday"—he paused to grin hideously—"it will be the happiest of my life."

I-wan sat staring at this man. He began to feel that General Seki wanted to punish him because he was a Chinese, or at least to frighten him. In his heart a furious anger began to burn. Suddenly his head felt clear and cool. Three weeks would be enough, would it? A few minutes ago he would have said it would be impossible for him to hate Japan. But now he had found something in Japan to hate—it was this man, this militarist, this arrogant, overbearing, ambitious overlord sitting before him, who wanted to marry Tama.

"You expect no resistance?" he asked quietly.

"If there is resistance from the Chinese," General Seki said haughtily, "we will begin bombing—"

All the hatred of which he was capable rushed to I-wan's heart. He stood up. The important thing was not his hatred—it was that there would be no war.

He turned suddenly and walked, a little unsteadily, out of the room and shut the door. Outside he stood a moment. He felt sick and short-breathed. Yet his head was perfectly clear. He must find Tama and tell her that Seki himself had said it would not be a real war.

A maid passed bearing an oblong bowl of freshly arranged flowers.

"Where is Tama-san?" he demanded.

She looked at him, surprised. "In the east veranda, sir," she answered, "arranging the flowers."

He had never been in the inner parts of this house, for it was not customary for the men to go there. But now he went east through the kitchen. And there beyond, upon a small square veranda, he found Tama alone, flowers and grasses heaped on the table before her. She was choosing a handful of silvery grass to put in a vase with the red spider lilies, but when she saw him she stopped.

"I-wan, you—" she began.

But he broke out ahead of her. "Tama," he cried, "he is horrible!"

She stood there clutching the silver grasses. He saw her eyes sicken.

"Yes, he is horrible," she whispered. "I saw him yesterday, after I had said—"

198

"There is to be no war!" he broke in. "Seki says there will be no war!" He told her what he had heard and then he thought of his father and used him shamelessly. "Men like my father —they will never allow a war with Japan. And my father has power, Tama—enormous power—money—"

He felt a faint reminiscent rising of old gorge in him. How En-lan would have despised him for such an argument! En-lan would never be able, either, to understand how he felt about this Japanese girl, how he loved her. En-lan would not understand how anyone could love a Japanese.

"Of course, if there is no war—" Tama said, slowly, "then everything is changed. If it is only my father, trying to force me—"

"I swear there will be no war!" he exclaimed.

The maidservants were beginning to flutter about them, seeming to be busy about sweeping and dusting. "Shall I help you, lady?" one piped, and then another.

He looked at them grimly.

"They make me think of wasps," he told Tama. "They are determined not to leave us alone. But I shall not leave you until I know you are safe—in yourself, I mean. For I know if you make up your mind—"

She looked at him steadily, her dark eyes large. She was very pale. In his agitation he had not noticed this until now.

"If there is to be no war," she said, "of course I will not marry him."

So at last he had her promise!

"Then I shall ask your father for you," he said gravely. "Count upon that. I shall be as old-fashioned as he likes. I'll find a go-between and make the proper presents. You will hear nothing until it is all arranged."

She put the silver grasses to her cheek and said nothing. He bowed, looked deeply into her eyes, and went away. When he turned back once to see her, she was surrounded zealously by the maidservants, and in the garden he saw Madame Muraki, hurrying so fast her robes seemed to weave about her as she glided. But he did not care. All that needed to be said was said.

With no further farewells and seeing no one, he left the house and returned to Yokohama.

At last the newspapers declared and it was cried upon the streets that there would be no war in Manchuria. As he had guessed, "arrangements," the papers said, would be made. The League of Nations had been invoked. That meant the government—that was Chiang Kai-shek—did not want to fight. He could see his father behind this, manipulating peace.

He turned his thoughts away—no use thinking of those things which he could not control or change! Peace! Peace for him meant only Tama—Tama and long happy quiet years together. He was glad now that he had not come to love Tama quickly or impulsively, but slowly through four years of acquaintance and friendship and love. He had had time to face everything in that marriage before it took place. Now when it came, as it must, with this peace, it would be eternal. He would live his own sort of life apart, working, studying, enjoying, he and Tama together, years of individual peace and fulfillment. Let the nations take care of themselves. In such a world an intelligent being had no hope of life unless he enclosed himself in a small world of his own making.

He said nothing to anyone, but he went about his private plans, sure of Tama. He had already found an old professional matchmaker and now he went to him, and for a fee the man agreed eagerly to go to Mr. Muraki and put forth I-wan's request.

"But your photograph!" the old man cried.

I-wan was about to say, "They know how I look." Then he was silent. Let it all proceed according to custom. In seeming conformity a man was safe. He had had enough of rebellions. They had brought him nothing. He went out and had a picture taken and when it was finished—and he paid to have it quickly done—he gave it to the old man. There was nothing unusual about his pictured face, he thought. He looked pale and solemn and commonplace in his western clothes, and the Japanese photographer, trying to improve him, had retouched his features and given them a curious Japanese look. His eyes seemed to stare and his mouth was drawn out of its real likeness, but these things did not matter.

"And I will bring you back her picture, too," the old man said slyly.

"No need," I-wan replied quickly, "I have seen her."

"No, but a picture is your due," the old man insisted. "Besides, you can look at it as long as you like. That's better than peeping at her."

He was making a great show of justice to be done his client, and I-wan smiled and let it pass and went away.

No war! Life fell out wryly enough, he thought, walking along the gay, narrow streets. He stopped and bought a newspaper and read it as he strolled along. But he could make nothing of it. He knew by now that the papers said only what men like General Seki wanted them to say. There were headlines here about renegade battalions, bandits that were creating disturbances because they would not surrender to the Japanese. If En-lan were alive, he would have been among them. But doubtless he was dead. Because of these bandits, the paper said, the Japanese had only with difficulty restored order and safety for their nationals. It was impossible to know what those words meant—order and safety!

At least, they meant peace, and above everything now he wanted peace and the things of peace. He wanted Tama to be his wife, to make his home. He was done with all causes. When it was all settled he would write to his father. He tossed the newspaper away and the wind caught it merrily as though it were a kite and rushed it flying and crackling down the street.

He did not expect an old man to move quickly, and he waited for a while, therefore, in some patience. In the night when he awoke and lay thinking, the darkness oppressed him and he feared that he had been too hopeful and that Tama was not so sure as he had counted. But when day came he remembered again how sure she had looked when he left her. He felt an enormous stability in her. There was none of Peony's light waywardness and teasing. If Tama said she would do a thing he could be sure of it. Duty she would do, as she would have married General Seki, for she had been trained to do her duty. Yet she was not like an old-fashioned Japanese woman who gave blind obedience to the man over her. The same stubbornness which could carry Tama one way, could carry her away from it, too, if she thought it right. He trusted her and was comforted and went quietly about his work.

New shipments came in every day and others went out. He grew hardened to seeing boxes unpacked and pouring out all sorts of Chinese treasures. He grew used to Shio hovering over everything and choosing what he wanted to keep. Shio's instinct never failed him. Whatever was priceless he kept.

"Those white men," he explained to I-wan, half apologetically, "do not know the difference between what is merely rare and what is unique and perfect. I will keep in Japan that which is perfect. Here it belongs, and here is its home. In times to come, all that is perfect in the world will find its home with us. No one values beauty as we do."

I-wan did not answer. He never answered Shio. It was true that he had never seen any one eat and drink beauty as Shio did. He did seem actually to feed upon the porcelains and the ivories, the paintings and the tapestries which he loved. When he was tired, and he was easily tired, for he worked long hours and ate little and was a small thin man by nature, if he sat for a while caressing a jade or a smooth pottery bowl or a bottle vase, a sort of peace came over him and he looked stronger, as though he had been fed. In the palm of his hand he held continually a piece of old white jade, oily smooth with long handling and as warm as flesh. When he sat counting and muttering over his figures, he leaned his cheek upon the hand holding this jade. He said it kept his head from aching.

I-wan, looking at him with a new curiosity now, saw nothing in his pallid face of Tama's round cheeks and healthy looks. Yet they were of one blood, and he must call Shio brother, and something of Shio would go into his children, perhaps. Well, he was a harmless man, at least, and if he went dazed with beauty, there were others who went dazed for less. This whole country was a little mad for beauty, I-wan thought. Men so poor they ate a handful of cold rice for a meal found a few cents somehow to buy a flower pot and seeds to plant. Tama would keep his house beautiful with flowers, too, because she had been taught that a room was empty if it held no flowers.

It was not until the eighteenth day of the next month that

the old matchmaker came back, and I-wan was beginning to lie half his nights awake, wondering what had gone wrong. He had all but decided to go himself and see, when suddenly one night when he went to his room he found the old man there in the one big chair, smoking his pipe peacefully enough.

"Hah!" he said when I-wan came in, and rose and bowed.

"Where have you been?" I-wan cried impetuously.

"At my business," the old man answered serenely, "at my business. There has been a good deal of it. There was the old suitor—" he nodded. "He had to be arranged. But the young woman managed that very well. The father objected, you see, on the grounds of offense to the old suitor. But she managed it."

"How?" I-wan demanded.

"By saying she would kill herself," the old man answered, without excitement. "Yes, and she went at once to it. I saw her. She said it, and then she took a knife she had ready in her girdle and drew it across her wrists before our eyes—"

"No!" I-wan cried.

The old man nodded profoundly. "Across one wrist and then she prepared to do it to the other, and the mother wept and fainted, and her father bade her wait. She stood, the blood rushing out of her arm and soaking into the mat."

He relished telling the tale, but I-wan could not speak for horror.

"And her mother came to herself and moaned something about her having no children left. I thought you said there were sons?"

"One is newly dead," I-wan said, "and one, the youngest next to her, is gone to China in the army."

"So!" the old man answered, his mouth open with interest. "Then the father said, 'Wait, we will talk it over.' So I waited, and by arranging another young girl for the old suitor, which I did, the daughter of a baron in a prefecture near Kyoto, who was glad to have a general for a son-in-law, and their daughter's fiancé had run away last month and married a moga, causing such shame as cannot be wiped away, and after all the wedding garments were prepared, and they were casting about for some way to save them. So in their extremity it was sent from heaven to get a general, however old and fat. So I thought of them and arranged it. So what with one thing and another, it all went together, and you are to go not to the house, but to the hotel that is on the sea at the south side of the city, and there meet with the family, and talk and take tea together, as the custom is. Then the wedding day will be set, soon, as the custom is, also, and the thing is as good as done."

"But her wrist?" I-wan asked. He could not forget Tama's wrist, bleeding.

"It was bad," the old man admitted. "And yet, I think she knew that only shedding her own blood would make them yield. The old man had been stubborn until then. But when she did that, he saw she was more stubborn than he. . . . Well, now that it is as good as done, I will advise you. Hasten to make her way yours, before she knows it, for when a woman is stubborn, the ocean itself is not so sure as her own will."

He coughed and took a bit of paper out of his sleeve and spat into it neatly and laid it under the table where it would be swept away by a servant. Then he sat waiting for what remained of his fee.

I-wan laughed and rose to give it to him. "I will give you as much again on the day of the wedding," he said.

The old man took the money and folded it small and put it into his belt.

"You Chinese," he said, "you never look beyond tomorrow.

But tomorrow is only the beginning of time. And a wedding is only the beginning of marriage. Ah, yes, so it is."

He rose, coughing and nodding, and went away. It was all nothing to him. He made his living by such things, and in this case it was merely his luck that the young girl was willing to kill herself to marry the young man.

But after he had gone I-wan began packing his best clothes quickly. Tomorrow morning he would go to Shio and ask leave of absence and tell him why he went. He could not imagine Shio caring half as much as he would if he found a piece of old jade. Nevertheless he must consider Shio as his elder brother and give him his due courtesy. He wanted to do all that he should do for Tama's sake—Tama, who was willing to die for him!

For Tama's sake he went through the formal party at the hotel, where as though he were a stranger he met Mr. Muraki and Madame Muraki, also, dressed as he had never seen them in stiff dark formal robes of thick silk. With them were friends and relatives he had never seen, and among them for one moment was Tama, a Tama whom also he had never seen. Her hair was brushed and oiled in the old Japanese fashion, and her face was painted red and white. When she bowed she smiled the vacant empty smile of the well-taught Japanese virgin, and he did not know what to say to her. Only when he caught the look of her eyes once, when she swept up her lashes, was he comforted. They were bright and shining and full of laughter.

"We will go through with the play," they seemed to tell him, laughing.

So he went through with it for her. Even when Mr. Muraki decreed that they must wait for a letter from his father giving

206

consent, I-wan said nothing. For he was sure of the consent. His father would be eager enough now to show his friendship for Japan. He would reason that after all I-wan remained Chinese, and that a woman, Japanese or not, was of little matter, and Tama's chief importance was as a daughter-in-law and not as a Japanese.

The letter, when it came, was as I-wan thought it would be. Mr. Wu wrote to Mr. Muraki that he was honored to deepen the new peace between the two countries. "We ought," he wrote, "to bind these two brother countries together, and what better way than this?"

To I-wan he wrote, "There are no better trained women in the world than the Japanese. They are docile, humble, obedient, home-keeping. You will have a good family life. When a little more time has passed, bring her to us to see. But not yet—the people here have an unreasoning hatred against Japan because of the recent troubles. But the common people are always ignorant and mistaken. The Manchurian situation will be adjusted reasonably. Nevertheless, wait a little while before bringing back a Japanese wife to China."

I-wan smiled as he folded his father's letter. He did not want to go back with or without Tama. Certainly he would not go back without her.

For Tama's sake he had waited without seeing her again until the wedding day, which was appointed as soon as his father's letter came. And then he went to his wedding, held in the same hotel where the betrothal had been acknowledged. Here in strange cold formal rooms, half Japanese, half foreign, he found the same people waiting. And soon Mr. Muraki came and Madame Muraki and Shio and with him a small quiet gray-toned woman who was his wife, and at last Tama.

They drank the mingled wines and obeyed the rules which the old matchmaker set for them.

He felt inexplicably lonely for a little while, though Tama was at his side. But this was the silent painted Tama he did not know, and not for weeks had he heard her voice or seen her as she was. He had to tell himself even as he felt her stiff silk-covered shoulder touch his as they stood together, that indeed it was she and that only by obeying the old rules had he won her. For Mr. Muraki would never have wanted him for a son-in-law if he had taken his own way and married Tama as he would like to have married her, simply and quietly and as though it were their own marriage. No, marriage belonged to a family.

When it was over he looked about at them all, these small grave courteous people behind Mr. Muraki and Madame Muraki, aunts and uncles and cousins, all staring at him and smiling anxiously and shyly. They looked alike, he thought. Even Tama looked like them just now, he thought. He had, he felt suddenly, married not Tama, but Japan. He felt in some strange sickening fashion that he had betrayed something or someone, somehow. Then he heard the old matchmaker at his elbow.

"If you will now change your garments," the old man said in his matter-of-fact way, "the bride will be ready. The automobile is at the door."

This recalled him. He had decided, he remembered, that they would go into the mountains to the small hotel by the hot spring, and there he and Tama would spend the first week of their marriage. He had forgotten in his daze of the moment what lay ahead. Now he turned, instantly restored to himself. The wedding was over. When he and Tama were alone at last, their marriage would really begin. He forgot everything in this thought and rushed to the room in the hotel, where upon the bed he had carefully spread out only this morning before he dressed for the ceremony the new dark blue foreign suit he had bought. It was the fashion for a bridegroom to wear western clothes. Everything was new, even the red silk tie which lay beside it. He hurried into it and taking his new hat, rushed downstairs. Tama was waiting for him. He found her in the closed and curtained automobile. Someone had opened the door in time for him to leap inside, and then the door slammed and the car started with a great jerk and they were thrown at each other. She laughed, and when he heard her laughter everything turned in that instant warm and real.

"Tama!" he cried.

She had washed the red and white paint from her face, and her hair was drawn smoothly back again, and she had on a plain dark green dress and leather shoes.

"Do you know me?" she asked, still laughing. Here was her own face, rosy and brown and pretty in the old way.

He put out his arms, speechless, and she came into them and for the second time he felt the shape of her, strong, a little square but still slender, in his arms. She was more real than anything in life. That was her quality, a strong reality. She had no perfume even upon her. He put his cheek against her and smelled the faint smell of clean soap-washed flesh, and from her hair a piny smell of the wood oil with which it had been brushed.

"Tama," he whispered, half suffocated with happiness, "are we married?"

She nodded. He felt the strong quick nod of her head.

"Yes, of course," she said in her pleasant practical voice.

He did not answer. In his arms he felt the affirmation suddenly run over her body, a quiver through her blood.

"Now I-wan," Tama was saying sternly, "it is necessary in our marriage that you always remember this—I am a moga."

He laughed and she turned on him with mischief bright in her eyes. "You don't believe me?" she demanded.

"Yes—yes, I do," he said quickly. "I believe anything about you."

"Ah," she said, "that is a good beginning."

He laughed again as he lay on the bed watching her. She was combing out her long black hair. It was still slightly wet from the bath they had taken in the pool of the hot springs, though she had coiled it up on her head to keep it dry. But they had laughed and played and splashed each other so much.

Now they were back in their rooms and he had sent the bathmaid away impatiently so that he could be alone with Tama. He knew the maids were all laughing at him, but he did not care. He had tipped them well to keep other bathers waiting until he and Tama had finished. He had not told her, but he had made up his mind before they went in that Tama was never to bathe in any other presence than his own. He was Chinese and he would not have it.

She was standing now, quite naked, as she brushed out her long hair. It was an innocent nakedness, he could see, as innocent as had been that peasant girl's the day they had climbed the mountain with Bunji. It was as if she were unconscious of any difference in being covered or not. He felt vaguely jealous of this innocence. It was too childish. He could not endure the thought that she might have stood like this even before servant maids. But it was impossible to explain this to her. He knew by instinct that she would not understand.

"Let me see your wrist," he said suddenly.

She came over to him and held out her wrist. Upon it was the long scar, still red. He laid his cheek upon it.

"Do mogas often cut their wrists to get their own way?" he asked. If ever he grew impatient with Tama—though it was impossible—but if he ever did, he would only need to see this wrist of hers.

"It was what my father understood best," she said quietly. "When I did that he knew I meant what I said—that I would marry you."

This was sweet enough, he thought, to fill a man's heart. But he wanted more.

"And even if there had been a war," he said, coaxing her, "you would have married me—I know you would."

He looked up at her, still holding the wrist, to see her eyes when she acknowledged it.

But she shook her head, her eyes too candid not to be believed.

"No, I wouldn't, I-wan," she said. "If there had been a war I would have married General Seki. Don't you know I said I would?"

He could not believe even her eyes.

"I can't believe you," he said.

"Then you still don't understand," she replied quickly. "If there had been a war, I-wan, I would not have belonged to myself, but to my country. In times of war everyone belongs to the country."

"Old Seki isn't the country," he said with scorn.

He still held her wrist, but he felt strangely that it was different. Why had she cut it? A moment ago it had seemed pathetic and wonderful to see this red line across its amber smoothness.

"He is a very great general," she said simply. "The Emperor trusts him."

When she said "The Emperor," it was as though she spoke of all the gods. He felt suddenly again jealous of something he did not understand.

"You must love only me," he cried. He dropped her wrist and sitting up, he put his arms about her waist as she stood by him. Under his cheek he felt her firm soft belly and he could hear her heart.

"I do love only you," she answered quietly. She took his head in her hands. "I shall always love you."

"Then why do you say 'if there had been war—' " He wanted her to say that this closeness would have been theirs, inevitably, though the world divided beneath them.

"That would have had nothing to do with my loving you," she said. She was touching his hair softly. "I-wan, see—as a Japanese, if it is my duty—"

"Hush!" he cried. He did not want to hear her talk about duty.

"I am your duty," he muttered, "I—I! You have no other!"

He seized her wrist again and moved his tongue along the scar, feeling its slight roughness with all his being.

"Don't talk," he whispered, "don't let us talk."

He wanted nothing except to feel. In feeling there was no division between them. Their blood flowed together in the same rhythm, to the same desire. That was the essential between man and woman—that only. She obeyed, saying nothing, but by delicate touches and movements accommodating herself to him. Suddenly after a few moments he drew back at a movement of her hand, half shocked. It occurred to him that it was strange, surely, for a young girl only newly married to know how to do such a thing. He drew back, stammering.

"What did you say?" she asked.

"I said, how do—you know—to do that?"

She looked up at him from where she lay, her eyes full of pure and innocent surprise.

"But I was taught, of course," she exclaimed, "by a very good old geisha. My mother hired her to teach me."

She was so guileless, so innocent in her sophistication, that he was fascinated and horrified together. He sat up for a moment, struggling with himself, not knowing which was the stronger in him.

"But what is it, I-wan?" Tama asked.

"Your—realism," he managed to say. "It's—it frightens me."

He thought, "She will not know what I am talking about."

But she did. She watched him for a moment. Then she said in her calm practical way, "See reason, my husband. Would it be reasonable to allow a young woman to marry in ignorance of what will please the man she loves? I have been taught to make your clothes, to cook the food you like, to tend your house and your children. Should I know nothing of how to love you when we are alone? But that is the heart of our life. When the heart is sound, all the body is full of health."

But he muttered, "It is like—a courtesan."

"Oh, no!" she said quickly, and dropped his hand. She leaped up and reached for her robe, and he saw that now it was she who was shocked. These strange differences between them! What did they mean? He remembered the first time he had seen women in a public bath and how he had been horrified and how Bunji had said so calmly that the only harm was in looking at a woman naked. He had not understood that, but he had accepted it. Now she went quite away from him. She was standing by the window, fastening her robe tightly about her, tying the wide sash fast. He could see her hands trembling over the bow. Her back was turned to him.

"It isn't in the least—like a courtesan," she said, her voice full of sudden weeping. "I am your wife. It is I who will bear your children."

She took up the end of her sleeve and wiped her eyes quietly and then smoothed back her hair.

Standing there with her shoulders drooping, she was suddenly intolerably pathetic and childish to him, a child doing as she had been taught. He went over to her impulsively.

"You are to forgive me," he said. "I command it," he added. Her shoulders straightened.

"You needn't command me," she said, without turning her head. "After all, am I not a moga? A moga resents being commanded, even by her husband. Besides—I only want to do what you like."

He could see her lips quiver. Suddenly he wanted to laugh. This woman was dear to him, the dearest being in the world. He did not care what she was or how inexplicable her ideas and behavior. He did not care whether or not he understood her or what she thought. He only knew that his whole being accepted her.

"Come back to me," he said with determination.

She turned her head then and her eyes stole around to his and they looked at each other. Then he saw in their deeps a smile rise like the ripple of light over water. She gazed at him a moment, and without a word, while he waited, she began loosening the sash which she had just tied so firmly about her waist.

When he let himself think apart from her it was only to build higher in his soul the wall between the world and

214

themselves. He had cut himself off from his own country and by marrying her he had in that measure cut her off also from hers. They were two creatures separate from all others as any two must be who mate out of their own kind. Chinese and Japanese, they were foreign to each other. The blood of their ancestors had not been the same blood. Their very bones were not the same. He knew when he looked at her body and at his own that their clay had never come from the same soil. They met and mingled now for the first time. Dearly as he loved her body, close as it was to his own, it was not the same flesh. His skeleton was slender and tall, and hers was short and strong. She was not fat, but she could never be slender as he was. He loved her for the very earth quality which her body had and his had not, even as he loved her for the very simplicities at which he often laughed.

He loved her for simplicity the more because he knew complexity was his own curse. There was nothing he did which he might not have done in many different ways, but for Tama there was only one way to do everything, and she had been taught that way. Even her pride in being independent and what she called modern, it seemed to him, only in reality made her more determined to do the thing as she had been taught to do. When he teased her for this, she could not understand what he meant, as he had teased her the evening it came to him when she was setting out the dishes of their meal in their hotel room. It was the last day of the seven he had allowed himself for their wedding pleasure. The next day they were to return to Nagasaki. He was to take Bunji's place now, Mr. Muraki had decided. Tomorrow he and Tama would be in the small house they had taken for their new home on a hillside in a suburb of the city. Tonight, therefore, was an occasion, a feast, and Tama had ordered an especial dinner, and when it came, she dragged the low table to the open screens at the end of the room which overlooked the valleys and hills and far below under the night sky the twinkling lights along the seacoast. She would let him touch nothing.

"No—no," she explained, "please—it is I who will arrange everything, I-wan."

He sat down then and watched her, smiling inwardly. She was so serious, so busy, and every trifle was important. All afternoon when they were wandering about the hills together she had been searching for certain flowering grasses with which she planned to make a bouquet for the feast. When they came back she spent an hour arranging them, discarding almost all she had brought, and cutting and trimming in absorbed silence the few she had chosen. But he could not deny the perfection of what she had done. A few silvery-plumed stalks, standing, it seemed, in natural growth among their own long and graceful leaves—if he had not seen the intense care with which she had placed each leaf and each stalk, he would have said she had thrust them into the square pottery vase exactly as they grew. All her effort and the art which she had been carefully taught were merely this—to make it seem not art but nature. It explained, he thought, much of Tama.

So she arranged the table and the dishes and the pot of tea, so she planned how they would sit and in what order eat the courses served them. Only when all this was done and there was nothing left to place did she suddenly laugh and clap her hands.

"Now!" she cried merrily, "Now let us be happy!"

"But you have been very happy, my Tama," he said, laughing at her. "I have been watching you. You have been very happy arranging everything."

She stared at him across the tiny table at which they were sitting on the soft floor mats.

"What do you mean?" she inquired. "I was only doing what should be done."

"No, what you liked," he said gaily. "Do you think it is necessary to do all you did? The food could have been brought in and eaten."

"Oh, I-wan!" Her voice was full of pain. "But there is a way in which to do each thing in life—even the plainest. Why, I have been taught there is a way in which to sweep a room, that makes it more than mere sweeping, a way in which to serve tea, a way in which—"

"Moga—moga!" he cried joyously.

She stopped. "You mean—as a moga—" she faltered, "it is not necessary—I suppose," she said very slowly. "I am really somewhat old-fashioned. It is true—I am, perhaps—more than I think."

He had hurt her, he perceived. He had taken the joy out of all her small arrangements, and he hated himself.

"No—no," he insisted, "I love it. I love all you do. Don't mind my teasing you, my heart. No, I won't tease you any more."

"Yes, you must tease me, I-wan, if you like," she said quickly. "I will learn to be teased."

She was so grave that he could scarcely keep from reaching across the table for her. He would have, indeed, except that a maid was bringing in a fish. Instantly Tama forgot.

"I-wan, here is the fish!" she cried. "I chose it myself today in the pool. Now you must like it, I-wan, because it is a beautiful fish, and I myself gave the recipe at the kitchen."

"I shall like it," he promised, "and it is beautiful."

She separated the fish with a pair of silver chopsticks and

217

he held out his bowl for her to fill and she filled it and he took it and looked at her.

"I take whatever you give me," he said.

She blushed and he saw, or thought he saw, alarm in her eyes.

"But you know I want to give you only what you want," she said.

"Yes, I know," he said. He must, he perceived, make his way delicately with this young wife of his. She was old and new, child and woman together. He must treat her as each and all together.

In a moment she was laughing at him. Then they spoke of Bunji and of how he would have enjoyed such a feast as they were having, and how out of all the world they would have minded him less than any other. Where he was they did not know, except now somewhere in China. And then Tama said, "Tell me about China. Is it like our country?"

I-wan shook his head first, and then said, "Yes, it is—no, I don't know. No, it is not like." He thought of the strong racial difference between Tama's body and his own. That difference went into mind and thinking and feeling. They would hurt each other again and again because of that difference.

He waited for Tama to ask him more. But she did not. Instead she rose and put out all the lights except one. The maid had taken the last dishes and left them fresh tea, and Tama brought her bowl and sat beside him at ease, now that the feast was over. She had forgotten China and whether it was like what she knew or not.

Instead she was gazing out across the mountains, her whole look one of peace and pleasure. His eyes went with her and for a moment they were silent. And in the silence all differences faded and they were simply together, man and wife.

This union of man and woman—it was the deepest in life—deeper than race and ancestry. He was not afraid of his marriage. He would give himself to it, for it was his only world. He had no world into which he could take her, but he would enter as far as he could into her world. But the real world would be the new world which they would make. A new world—he put the phrase away with the shock of old pain. No, nothing so important and large as a new world. What he and Tama would make would be a small secure place, large enough only for themselves and their children. Their children would be like them, without a country of their own. They would need the more the small close security of home. It occurred to him now, for the first time, that his children might not thank him for being their father. They might even have preferred an old Japanese general. In Shanghai, he remembered, there were certain people, born of mixed blood, who were nothing. But that was white blood and yellow—intolerable mixture. His children and Tama's would at least not look as those did.

"Tama!" he cried, "what are you thinking about?"

It seemed to him suddenly necessary to hear her voice.

"I am thinking of our house," she answered peacefully. "I am thinking of how I shall arrange everything."

"Ah, I wish we need never go down from this mountain!" he cried with passion. "It has been so safe and so quiet—we have been alone together as though there were no one else in the world."

It seemed to him at this moment that the whole world lay in turmoil about this one peaceful spot where they sat alone in the stillness of evening.

"Oh, I wouldn't like to live all the time on top of a mountain," Tama said. "It is too difficult."

"Difficult?" he repeated.

"Yes," she said, "to get meat and vegetables and charcoal and all the things we need every day."

"Ah," he said, thoughtfully, "of course it would be difficult." The things of every day—they had not occurred to him.

The days ran after each other so quickly that before he could lay hold of one to treasure it another had come. They went nowhere, except he to his work, now again in his old office, but alone since Bunji was gone. From it he hurried back to Tama in their small clean house. And day followed day, and month slipped into month, and they wanted no change, he because it was such sweet change to have this house and this woman for his own, and she because surely Tama was the goddess of everyday things. He thought, "I have never known her really until now."

For now he perceived that it was in doing her everyday tasks that she seemed most free. When they had been together on the mountain she had been, he thought, perfect—a little more than perfect, he had sometimes felt, as though she had set for herself a pattern of what she would be at such a time and had faithfully followed the pattern. But now in her eagerness and in her being so busy in making the house as she wanted it, she forgot to keep her hair always smooth and her sash straight and uncrumpled. Instead she ran about in a cotton kimono girdled with a strip of the same cloth instead of a sash, and she tied back her long sleeves in the way the small maidservant did, and her hair was loosened, and more than half the time when he came home those first days to his noon meal she had a smudge on her nose or her cheek from the charcoals upon which she cooked his dinner.

There was always a good dinner for him. She was a zealous

cook because, he found, she loved cooking. A soup, different each day, and two dishes at least, awaited him. And each dish was a surprise. She made great excitement over lifting the cover and disclosing a boned fish or tiny balls of meat or chicken steamed to tenderness and hid under a sauce of fresh bean curd smoothed into a gravy.

"How can you know so much?" he cried.

"Ah, you don't imagine how much more I know!" she answered proudly. "I still have scores of things I haven't made for you."

He had always thought eating was of no importance. And since he had lived alone he had taken a sort of pride in eating anyhow, as if in an unconscious expiation for the wastefulness of his father's house. Often he sat down in a cheap restaurant to a bowl of noodles in meat broth, such as a ricksha puller might eat also, and he thought, doggedly, "It is good enough for anyone."

But this was better. Tama was frugal enough to satisfy him. She cooked enough to make him well fed, and yet there was no waste. It amused him to see her calculate, with a pretty frown, how much the small maidservant would need. In his father's house the servants robbed the stores and no one heeded it. He liked to think that in his house Tama's careful hands measured and took account. He thought sometimes of En-lan, and he wished that En-lan could see him now. There was nothing to be ashamed of now in his home, before rich or poor.

This small house set upon a terraced corner of the hill beyond the city came to be to I-wan the place of perfection in the world. It was so plain, so clean, so quiet. The floors were covered with silvery white mats, and the walls were latticed paper screens that were drawn back and thrown into one great space for the day's living. But at night they were drawn together again and made small, cosy, separate rooms, one for his books, where he might read and study and smoke a pipe while Tama finished the evening meal, and one where he and Tama slept together the deep secure sleep of those eternally in love with each other. And around the house was a small uneven garden where he and Tama worked and planted on Sundays and where Mr. Muraki came and sat and gave them endless advice.

And beyond was the sea.

"The sea," Mr. Muraki murmured after long pondering, "the garden must be shaped to the sea. The sea is the scene set for it. It must, therefore, lead the eyes beyond its own confines toward that horizon."

He came Sunday after Sunday up the rocky winding street which led up the hill to their house, and with him they laid the garden, plant by plant, rock by rock. In these peaceful hours it was hard to remember that this happily excited old man was that stern one who had ordered no mourning for his dead son, the one who had been ready to give up his only daughter. But in this old man there was this gentleness and all that other sternness, too. There was no reconciling them. They were only to be accepted, as everything was to be accepted. To his accustomed hands they left the final trimming away of the branches and old shrubberies. And his hands with their old delicate ruthlessness cut and cut again, until I-wan in a panic thought, "There will be nothing left. After all, it is a very small garden."

But when it was finished it appeared that Mr. Muraki was right. He had left what was essential. And only now indeed could they see what was essential. For he had so cut and shaped that the trees looked gnarled and bent with a strange beauty as though the sea itself had disciplined them to these shapes.

"Come here," Mr. Muraki said, his face all shining with sweat and excitement. "Come here to the house."

They stood with him, then, where the screens were drawn back in the house. Before them the garden lay like a path, and at the end of it the trees divided as if the winds had driven them apart to make a gate forever open to the sea.

It was autumn so quickly that I-wan could not believe it. But one morning when they rose Tama said, "There was frost last night." When he went to work she came into the garden with him and it was true that the grass blades were edged with frost, and the moisture around the stones had frozen into silver sprays. When he came home in the late afternoon he found her again in the garden sweeping the first fallen leaves.

"Is it autumn?" he asked unbelievingly.

She nodded joyously. Her cheeks were red with her work in the sharp pure air, and she looked younger than ever—especially when suddenly she thought of something and looked indignant.

"The chrysanthemum heads are showing their colors," she said. "Two of them are not the right color."

These chrysanthemums they had planted together from pots they had bought from a vendor a month ago. There were six of them, which was as much as they could put into a corner of their garden. She took his hand and pulled him over to see.

"Those two—they are common yellow ones," she said, "and we wanted all red and gold."

"I suppose he had too many," he said, smiling at her indignation.

"If I ever see him," she said vigorously, "I shall make him pay us back."

She began sweeping again as she spoke.

"I am sure you will," he answered laughing. "Wait until I get a broom."

He went into their small kitchen and found a broom and they

223

were sweeping together, when suddenly she stopped and sat down to rest on the bamboo bench.

"Are you already tired?" he asked, and was surprised when she nodded her head. It was not like Tama ever to tire.

"Are you well?" he asked again.

"Very well," she replied.

He kept on at his sweeping, looking up now and then to see her. Each time she was gazing out across the quiet evening ocean.

"What do you see?" he asked at last and went to her to see what she saw.

"I wish I knew your parents," she said suddenly. "I wish I knew what your family is and how your home looks over there." She pointed across the ocean.

He had not thought of his parents in months. After his marriage he had written to them and had sent them a picture of himself and Tama in their wedding garments, and his father had written back courteously. His mother never wrote letters but she had sent presents of silk and embroidered satins. Tama had admired them and kept them now put away with their precious scrolls and paintings which had been given them at their wedding.

Now he seemed suddenly to see, far across that water shining in the twilight, the great square house in which he had grown from a child. He could almost smell the odor of it, that odor which used to be waiting for him as he opened the door when he came home from school, compounded of his grandmother's opium and the old smell of long hung curtains and deep dusty carpets and polished old woods. He breathed in this clean ocean air to cleanse that other from his memory.

"Why do you want to see them?" he asked her.

"Because," she answered solemnly, "I am about to become truly one of your family."

At first he could not understand what she meant.

224

"I mean," she said, seeing this in his eyes, "that until now I have belonged only to you. I have been a part of you. But I am going to have a child. To us that means that I shall belong altogether to your family and no more to my own."

He had thought sometimes in the night of this moment. They had never spoken of it. He had been shy of speaking of it, and she had seemed to think only of their life together.

He had wondered, "How will she tell me?" For he had thought a good deal about his own sons, and even whether or not he wanted any sons. Daughters mattered less. He could marry them to good young Japanese men. But if he had sons, would they not be Chinese? And how could he explain to them why they were not living in their own country? There were times when he was afraid of his own unborn sons. And now Tama, when she told him there would be a child, spoke first of his family. He had told her very little about them and nothing of why his father had sent him away. None of his past, it seemed to him, had anything to do with her.

Besides, he was never sure she would understand if he told her. She had been taught so great a terror of the word revolution that whenever he had thought of telling her about himself, and he longed to tell her everything, he was afraid to do it, even though he now perceived he had never been a true revolutionist, as En-lan had been.

For En-lan was one of those who are born to be in rebellion somewhere and anywhere. If it had not been in his own country, it would have been abroad. In revolution he found his only satisfaction and peace. He did not love the people for whom he fought. He only loved the fight. But I-wan had loved the people more than the fight, and he perceived this in himself, that in his heart he hated fighting. It was more true, he reasoned, to tell Tama nothing and let her see him only as he now was, because this was he more than that I-wan had been who had gone with En-lan. He had never even told her why he had not taken her to his home.

"Shall we go to your home now?" she asked. "I-wan, why are you silent? Don't you want the child?"

She had taken alarm at his uncertain looks, and he made haste to assure her.

"Of course I want the child!" he exclaimed. "I have thought a hundred times of this moment. No, I shall not take you home."

"Why not?" she persisted. "It would be suitable for me to meet my father-in-law and my mother-in-law."

"I thought you were a moga!" he retorted, trying to make his voice gay. "I thought modern girls didn't want to meet their mothers-in-law."

"I am moga, I-wan," she declared. It always made him want to smile to hear this favorite declaration of hers. But now he would not even smile lest she be hurt. He was learning that this little Japanese wife of his did not like him to laugh at her.

"But there are some things which are only right," he finished for her.

"How did you guess my words?" she asked.

He might have answered, "Because I have heard you say them before." But this also he had learned not to say. Instead he said, "It is what you think, isn't it?"

"Yes, and especially now," she replied very gravely. And after an instant's pause she went on, "When a woman is to have a child, it is strange, but her moga feelings are quieted. She thinks instead of old ways and of how she can protect the child. She thinks of family."

"My family cannot protect him, I think," he said in a low voice.

"But I thought your father was rich?" she inquired. "And you said he was powerful."

He ought, he felt, to tell her that even his father's wealth and power were perhaps not enough to protect a child born of a Japanese woman. But he could not. The words would destroy something in this quiet secure home. They would stay in her mind and hide in her heart like a disease. She would not be able to forget them, and at last she would hold them even against him. No, he could not say, loving her as he did with his whole heart, "My people hate yours, Tama"—not when together they were to unite into this child.

"I want you for my own," he muttered, and put his arm about her shoulder. "Stay moga, Tama. I, too, am mobo. We live apart, you and I. We don't need any family. We are enough for each other—we will be enough for our children."

She looked at him doubtfully. "They cannot always live just with us," she said. "We will grow old and die."

"But there will be a lot of them then," he replied, "and we will teach them to be enough for each other."

"The house will be too small for them," she said.

"We will cut back the hill and add more rooms," he retorted.

"It would be cheaper to move into a bigger house," she said thoughtfully.

But he would not have this.

"No, Tama, no," he declared. "We will never leave this house. I should feel it an evil omen to leave it."

"Oh, and you a mobo!" she cried. "A mobo believing in omens!"

They laughed together so heartily over this nothing that at last she wiped her eyes on her sleeves and demanded of him, "What were we talking about before we grew so silly, I-wan?"

"I believe," he said, "that you had said we are to have a child —a daughter, Tama."

"No, never—a son, of course!" she corrected him quickly.

"I should like a small girl," he told her.

"I shall certainly have a son," she declared.

They were laughing and again forgetting everything.

Bunji had not yet come home. A year before there had been a disturbance in Shanghai. It was not important, the papers had said then. A renegade Chinese battalion had clashed with some Japanese soldiers.

It had not seemed important when a few days later Mr. Muraki said Bunji had been ordered to Shanghai. It did not seem important when now, a year later, Bunji was still away and Mr. Muraki said it would be summer before he came. For in the midst of this spring I-wan's first son was born.

He had never seen before the cycle of birth. If he had been a village child as En-lan had been it would have held no mysteries. Among common people, he knew, the union of man and woman and the coming of a child were as usual as food and drink and sleep. Nothing was hidden. But in the great foreign house in which he had lived, none of these things were seen. If a slave girl conceived by accident and could not cast the child by any herbs and medicines, she was sent away, his mother declaring she would not have dogs and cats and crying children in the house. And I-wan himself was the youngest.

So he came freshly to the birth of his own child, and so it was a miracle to him. It was a miracle to see Tama at this work of hers, eating and drinking one thing and another to make the child wise, to make him strong, to make his teeth grow out straight and white, to ensure the blackness of his hair and eyes and that his skin be smooth. And yet he must not be too large to be safely born. On a certain day, when she announced his coming to her own family, she bound a girdle about herself and changed her food to keep him strong and yet small. And though

I-wan wondered how she knew all these things, she hired an old midwife to help her as the time went on.

But nothing would persuade Tama to cease her work at cooking and cleaning, at sweeping, and tending the garden. She did these things until the moment of the child's birth. "It will keep me strong," she declared and would not spare herself. Nor would she have a doctor to help her.

"If you hear I am to die, then call a doctor," she told I-wan, "and put it to him that he is to save me. Otherwise this midwife is good enough. I have taught her to wash her hands and to boil whatever she uses."

He would have protested that she ought, as a moga, to use more science in the birth of their child. "After all, a midwife—the women of past ages did no better." But she silenced him with her hands folded against his lips.

"I want our son to be born here in our home," she pleaded with him. "If we have a doctor he will make me go into a hospital and our child will lie in a room with scores of others. I want to give birth to him here. I will take care, I-wan. I have been taught about germs, too."

He had to yield to her then. Yes, he too would like his child born in this house.

"And when I know the time is come," she said, "you are to go away, I-wan, where you can't hear me. And you are not to come until I send the maidservant for you."

"I leave you?" he cried. "But—"

She would not let him go on.

"Yes, you are to leave me," she declared. "It is my task."

And she would have it so. On that mild day of early summer when he rose in the morning, he saw her changed.

"It is begun!" she said. "Hurry, hurry—go away."

"But where?" he cried, dismayed. "Where shall I go?"

"Why, to work, of course," she answered.

"As I do any other day?" he cried, astounded. "I can't work today!"

"Yes—yes—yes," she answered in little gasps. "You can—you must. Don't think—just work—as usual. Say to yourself—'What Tama is about today is very usual. It will happen again and again. I must go on with my work.'"

"I shan't be able to," he declared.

"But you must, as soon as you have eaten your breakfast."

And she served him, though he tried to make her rest, because she said it would be good for the child and make him strong if she were strong. When at last he saw that indeed he could do nothing with her, that every few minutes she turned white and held back a groan and the sweat burst out on her clear skin, he rushed off as she had commanded him to do. She would have her own way, he perceived, forever. And he loved her and would let her have it, he thought, remembering that sweat at the edges of her dark hair and upon her nose and soft upper lip. She was always right, in herself.

And before noon the little maidservant came and told him he had a son. He left everything at once as it was and hastened as he had never in his life for any cause. Rickshas begged him to ride, but he pushed them aside.

"I can go faster on my own legs," he shouted and they roared after him their laughter. "He goes to meet a beloved mistress," they said.

This he could not stand. He stopped one moment to shout back at them, "I have a new-born son!" and rushed on up the narrow hill road to his house.

Madame Muraki was there and came out to meet him, her soft face flushed.

"It is a strong child," she said. "I had none better, except perhaps Akio."

He checked his speed and remembered to bow to her and then wished she had not spoken of the dead Akio at such a moment. It was an ill omen to speak of the dead, his mother had always said, on the day a child was born.

But when he saw the child he forgot it. He was compelled to laugh. For this son of his, with the trick the new-born have of looking for a few days like the old, looked exactly like his own grandfather, the old general. There was not a trace of Tama in his small frowning majestic face. I-wan's own blood had prevailed.

When his son was a little more than three months old, in the midst of Tama's enormous preparation for the Feast of the First Meal, when, as Tama explained to I-wan, the baby was to be given rice boiled in milk and also a little broth, and when everyone in the family must be invited to dine, Bunji came home.

Years later I-wan was to look on Bunji's return as the beginning of what was to come. But on that day it seemed of no importance, except the pleasure of his presence. Tama said, "How luckily it comes about that Bunji is here for the feast!" And I-wan himself thought of it only with joy in seeing Bunji, and in showing him the child. He went himself, the morning of the feast day, to meet the ship which was to bring back the soldiers being returned from Shanghai, and waited, with Mr. Muraki, for Bunji to separate himself from the stream of brown-clad men who poured across the gangplank as soon as it was put down.

Bunji was among the last. They saw him before he saw them. They saw him pause, as though he were bewildered, as he stepped upon the shore, and he did not hear I-wan's shout. He started away and was about to go on with the others when I-wan ran after him and caught him by the shoulder, shouting to him, "Bunji, where are you going? We are here."

Bunji turned, and I-wan saw instantly that the many months of being a soldier had changed him. It was not merely that I-wan had never seen him in uniform with his bowed legs in puttees. Bunji's face was changed. It was no longer an open tranquil youthful face. It had hardened and his big mouth, which had only been laughing and somewhat shapeless before, now seemed coarsened and even cruel.

But he laughed when he saw I-wan, with something of his old laughter.

"I was about to keep on with those fellows I have been with so long," he exclaimed.

"Your father is here, waiting," I-wan said, "and you are to come to my home today for our son's feast."

"So!" Bunji exclaimed. He went with I-wan and met his father, bowed and laughed and shouted, "But I must bathe, I-wan, and dress myself. I haven't had a good bath since I left home."

"Everything is waiting for you," Mr. Muraki said. He was very quiet, but his eyes never moved from his son. They all climbed into a waiting taxicab.

"And so you and Tama have a son," Bunji said.

"As like my grandfather as a small photograph," I-wan said. "You will laugh when you see him—though he is less like than at first. I confess, when I first saw my son, my impulse was to put a Chinese general's uniform on him and hang a medal on his breast. I felt I owed it to him."

Mr. Muraki smiled dimly and Bunji laughed as though he knew I-wan expected it. Then he said with sharpness, "A Japanese general's uniform will one day be more suitable, I suppose."

I-wan did not answer. He looked at Bunji, not knowing

232

whether he meant to tease him or whether he was in earnest—to tease, he decided, after a moment.

Everything was the same about Bunji, I-wan thought, still not having answered him, except something completely changed within him. He talked, he laughed, he moved as he always did. But the old Bunji had seemed to be showing himself as he was. Now when he talked, he seemed to be thinking of something else. And even his laughter seemed only a surface stir as though beneath it there was gloom.

But nothing could be said of this now. I-wan went with them to the gate of Mr. Muraki's house, and there they parted.

"We meet in less than an hour," he said.

"At two o'clock," Mr. Muraki agreed.

But Bunji said nothing. He seemed still thinking of something else.

In the midst of the crowded hotel room while the feast wore on, Bunji said very little, though he sat beside I-wan. The rite of feeding the child had taken place, and all had gone as it should. Everyone had admired the small boy, and especially when he sturdily refused to swallow the strange food thrust into his mouth and spat it out again upon his new silken robe and burst into a roar of weeping. He wore a boy's coat for the first time, and his head had been freshly shaved, bald in a circle at the top, and then a fringe of straight soft black hair. Bunji, watching him, turned to I-wan.

"I would know he was not Japanese," he said.

"Yes, that's evident," I-wan answered.

It was at this moment that he caught Bunji's look, fixed on him with a strange and secret hostility. He was astonished, as though Bunji had drawn a dagger against him. But he could say nothing in this room full of murmuring and admiring people.

He withdrew his eyes and moved a little away from Bunji and tried to imagine why Bunji should have changed to him.

Had something happened between Bunji and his own father in Shanghai? Yet so far as he knew they had never met. He had written to his father and given him the name of Bunji's regiment and station. But his father had written to him that it was not safe to receive Japanese callers. There was a band of young men who had organized themselves for assassinations, and they had only recently killed another banker for seeming to be friendly with a Japanese captain. To Mr. Muraki he wrote regretting that an illness prevented him from returning the kindness shown to I-wan. But he hoped, in time to come, when mutual understanding increased—and Mr. Muraki had replied saying that between them, at least, now that they were united in their grandson, all was understood.

Tama had said, opening her eyes, "Why doesn't your father like Bunji?"

And I-wan had hastened to say, "How can he dislike him when he has never seen him?"

"I don't know," she answered, staring at him thoughtfully, as she nursed the baby at her full young bosom.

"Neither do I," I-wan said, and before she could speak again he had knelt beside her and put his arms about them both. "You make me completely happy," he whispered. And she had taken up his hand and laid her cheek in its palm and forgotten what she had asked.

He could not talk to Bunji here or today—it was not suitable—but he would talk with him and know what Bunji meant. He gave himself determinedly to being the host, deferring to the elder guests, and especially to Mr. Muraki at the head of the table and to Madame Muraki. Everyone was gay and full of courtesy, and Tama had seen to the dishes and busied herself

234

with directions to the hotel cook for each one, and to look at them all on this late summer afternoon it seemed that none of them had any thought beyond the pleasure of eating and drinking and looking at the baby, who slept peacefully in his nest upon the maidservant's back.

"He sleeps like a Japanese, at least," Bunji said once to I-wan.

"How—what do you mean?" I-wan paused to ask.

Bunji nodded at the child's bobbing head.

"We can sleep anywhere, we Japanese, because we begin like that. We can sleep in noise and movement and any confusion. We can sleep even in the midst of cannon firing, if we are off duty for a few moments. It is the secret of our endurance in war."

I-wan looked at the peaceful innocent face of his small son. His eyes were closed and his little mouth was pouted and rosy.

"He doesn't look as though he were being trained for war," he said, laughing.

But Bunji was sipping his wine gravely and he did not answer. And I-wan felt suddenly alone, as though he had been separated from everyone. He was conscious for the first time in the day that after all he was different from all of them, even indeed from his son.

He could not, he found, immediately ask Bunji what was changed in him. In the first place he was not sure, after a few days had passed, that Bunji was aware of change. Then also it was impossible to assume the old relationship until Mr. Muraki had made it clear who was to be the head in the office. I-wan had resigned from his own place, in order to make this decision easier, and yet he was, he felt foolishly, somewhat hurt when Mr. Muraki accepted it and placed Bunji over him, and gave him only the second place. Their salaries were so nearly the same, it is true, that I-wan could not complain of that. His was not decreased, but Bunji was given a little more.

And I-wan, again he felt foolishly, was the more hurt because at home Tama accepted this as a matter to be expected.

"Father is very kind not to give us any less now that Bunji has returned," she said.

It was impossible for I-wan to tell her that it was difficult for him to take the lower place now and to have to ask Bunji if such and such were the right order to give and to see the clerks begin to go to Bunji instead of to him. But most difficult of all was still to perceive the change in Bunji himself. Where once he had been careless and easy to please, he was now become meticulous and careful of every detail of I-wan's work. Once he rebuked I-wan sharply for not overseeing himself the packing of a consignment of cheap dishes to be shipped to a great New York department store. I-wan made himself smile. But he could not forbear saying, "You yourself have done worse, Bunji. I seem to remember Akio complaining of that."

"The army has educated me," Bunji retorted, and turned to his own office. He had wanted an office alone, and I-wan had been moved into another room with two clerks. It was not so easy to see Bunji as it had been.

But indeed this change in Bunji, manifest in many ways, became a great hurt to I-wan. His only resource was to go home more steadfastly as the months passed to find refuge in Tama and in their small son. In her bustling and busy care of them both he found his comfort. She had the genius of reality. By her warm matter-of-fact ways and her ready speech and quick response to his least need, she made him feel rooted and secure and able each morning to go out to his work. Through her he had union with life and people. Her people were his because she was his and made all that was hers his. She could so tell the story of the small

236

happenings of the day while he had been gone that through her very telling he felt close to life and near to people, though in reality he knew almost no one.

And then there were all the things which the growing child did. He had been given the name of Jojiro, and they called him Jiro. He knew his name already, and Tama complained proudly that he was troublesome because he was wanting to creep too early and that meant he would want to walk before he was a year old and he must not, and it would take someone's whole time to keep him from it, and he would cry when he was prevented because he was so willful he went into a rage if he were denied anything.

"That's because you are a Chinese, Jiro," I-wan told his son, who at that moment was sitting erect upon the mat, chewing at the large dog of papier-mâché which had been given him as the guardian of all his dreams while he slept.

"Is that what is wrong with him?" Tama cried, and then seeing what he was doing, she shrieked and snatched the dog away. "No Japanese child would eat up his guardian dog, at least!" she cried, while Jiro wept with all his might.

No, I-wan was never lonely in his home. For that matter, it was difficult to put a name to any moment when he was treated less well by anyone than he had been before. The people on the street were as courteous to him as ever. When he went into a shop to buy cigarettes for himself or a toy for Jiro, the shopkeeper was as eager as ever to please him. Why, then, did he feel that the courtesy was not quite what it had been? It was not the courtesy, he imagined, at least, which people gave to each other, but that which they gave to a guest. He was not sure whether even this was true, any more than he could be sure that it was quite true that Mr. Muraki was more withdrawn than he had been. Once he mentioned this to Tama, and she said robustly, "I-wan, you are always too ready to imagine. Father is growing old, that is all, and age cools him as it does everyone. He forgets me, too."

He accepted this, and yet as time went on he still felt a change. He examined himself, then, to discover what it was he really felt, and decided that it was altogether Bunji who made the difference, and the only thing to cure it was to tell him so. For it was necessary to I-wan to feel about him the support of those who liked him and were faithful to him. He wished sometimes now that he had made other friends outside the Muraki family. But he had not, beyond a few men to whom he spoke a few words when he met them at a café or a theater. To them all, he knew, he was known as Mr. Muraki's son-in-law. It now occurred to him that after Mr. Muraki died, if life went on as it was, he would be known merely as Bunji Muraki's brother-in-law. It would not be pleasant unless Bunji went back to being his old self.

Then he put these thoughts aside and went doggedly on with his work. He had made his place here, and as the world was now, it would not be easy to do it again. He must bear with Bunji. And he learned to do this.

And when he came home and saw Jiro walking and heard him begin to talk and when Tama began to fret because now Jiro was past a year old and it was time she had another child, so that he laughed at her impatience to be about her business, then it seemed nothing was really too hard to bear in the daytime, if it brought him this at night.

Bunji, before he went to the army, was a youth who could drink scarcely a cup of wine without growing dizzy from it and wanting to sleep. But now he was able to drink a great deal and liked to do so. More than once he had come back

238

to the office after his midday meal, his temples red, to shout out his commands and to laugh too loudly. On one of these days he thrust his head into I-wan's room.

"There you are!" he roared. "Working like an old man! What has Tama done to you? You used to be a companion, but now you are nothing but Tama's husband!"

Bunji bellowed out a laugh and the two clerks made themselves busy over their desks as if they saw and heard nothing.

"I am also Jiro's father," I-wan said, smiling a little, and looking up from his desk.

"A man is always someone's father, sooner or later," Bunji retorted. "Come, stop work, I-wan."

"To do what?" I-wan inquired.

"Come out with me to a café," Bunji said. "No more work —you may also stop work," he declared to the two clerks. They rose instantly and bowed and remained standing. I-wan said nothing. He knew that as soon as Bunji went away they would return to work until five o'clock, which was the proper end to their day. But, it occurred to him, here might be his good chance to talk deeply with Bunji and to discover what had come to change him. He rose therefore and put on his hat.

"I will come," he said. He nodded at the two clerks, who perfectly understood that he was humoring the son of the proprietor of the business, and then walked with Bunji out into the street.

It was autumn, and vendors were carrying on poles across their shoulders baskets of potted chrysanthemums of every size and color. Two years ago when he and Tama were first married they had bought them to plant in a corner of their garden, and now they had spread until this year they were a knot of color. Mr. Muraki looked at them and disapproved.

239

He said, "There should be no temporary distraction of flowers in a garden." But Tama wanted them and so they had been kept. At this moment I-wan saw a vendor carrying an especial flower which she loved, whose petals were red and gold together, and he stopped and said to the man, "Do you know the road which winds up the west side of the mountain from the city?"

The man nodded vehemently.

"Go up until on the right you see a small house roofed in green tiles which looks out between two great pines to the sea, and go in and tell the mistress her husband sent you."

"How will she know I saw you?" the man asked shrewdly.

"Look at me," I-wan replied. "Tell her how I look—and say also, if she doubts, that I am a Chinese."

"So," the man said wondering, "you are a Chinese! But you look much like us. I have never seen a Chinese before. But of course everyone has heard of them."

He looked as though he were long of wind, and I-wan nodded to dismiss him and went on with Bunji.

"I suppose Tama is an obedient wife now and no longer a moga," Bunji said, half sneering as he spoke. "I suppose she will buy the flowers like a good Japanese wife."

"She won't buy them if she doesn't want them at his price," I-wan said reasonably. Bunji was just drunk enough so he must not mind what he said.

"You Chinese!" Bunji said scornfully. "Hah, you Chinese!" He shook his head largely.

They were passing a small café now with a few outdoor tables and chairs, and he sat down heavily at a table and slapped the metal top so that it sounded like a tin drum. A thin-faced girl ran out.

"Beer!" Bunji shouted. "I suppose you can drink beer?" he inquired of I-wan.

"Certainly," I-wan replied.

"Beer for one," Bunji cried to the girl. "For me, whisky."

"So—" the girl whispered.

"At once!"

She disappeared.

"I hate the English, so I drink their whisky," Bunji explained when she was gone.

"You used not to drink much," I-wan replied.

"Oh, so," Bunji retorted, "yes, I used to be a very good boy, didn't I? Well, now I am better. I know how to drink and I know other things also."

The street was quiet in the afternoon sun, but it was a small street. Across it a woman bathing her child looked up curiously.

"Let us go inside," I-wan suggested. "That woman is listening to you."

"Women," Bunji declared in a loud voice, "are all fools." He laughed senselessly, rose, stumbled, and would have fallen if I-wan had not caught him. They went into the little café and sat down in a corner and the girl came with bottles and cups. I-wan paid her and gave her an extra coin.

"Turn on the phonograph as long as it will last for that, and when it is used, come to me again and I will add another to it," he said. In a moment the room was full of scraping noisy music, and no one could hear Bunji except I-wan. I-wan began to sip his beer and Bunji poured himself whisky and drank it by mouthfuls.

"Nevertheless, I am going to be married," he announced to I-wan.

"Have you so decided?" I-wan inquired politely.

"Yes," Bunji declared, "it is the only thing. Poor Akio!" he sighed and shook his head. "He never learned that all women are alike."

I-wan did not answer and he hiccoughed once and repeated, "Women are alike, I say!"

"I don't know women," I-wan replied.

"It is not necessary to know women," Bunji repeated. "I tell you, they are alike!"

I-wan did not reply to this. It was, after all, he thought, a waste of time to talk to Bunji drunk and growing more drunk.

"So," Bunji went on, "I invite you to my wedding. Who is the bride? I don't know, I don't care. I told my father yesterday, 'It is time I married. Please get me a wife.' That is what I said, 'Get me a wife.' He said, 'Who?' I said, 'Any woman, any at all. They are all alike.'"

Bunji glared at I-wan, poured his glass full of whisky, spilling it and drinking it together, as I-wan looked away. He had seen men in Japan drunk often enough, farmers along the roadside roaring their way home from the markets, half their day's profits burning in their bellies and their brains, young men in restaurants and old men even. He had grown used to a sight he had never seen in his own country, where men drank while they ate, without drunkenness. Even though they drank more than men did here, they were not so easily disturbed by it. Perhaps their natures were in greater equilibrium.

Suddenly, to his surprise, he saw Bunji begin to sob. Bunji sat upright, his face working hideously and the tears rolling down his cheeks.

"I swear I didn't want to do it," he sobbed. "Why did I do it then?"

This he inquired of I-wan in a broken and piteous voice. I-wan was wholly bewildered, having an instant before seen him shouting and boisterous.

"What did you do?" he asked.

"They were all doing it, you understand," Bunji said. He leaned forward and put his head in his hands. "That is— all except the captain of my regiment. You understand, I was lieutenant. I kept my eyes on the captain. I said—"

He was fumbling for his glass, found it and swallowed a mouthful and coughed and shook his head and shuddered.

"Tell me, I-wan," he whispered. "Have I drunk enough, do you think?"

"More than enough," I-wan replied gravely.

"Ah, there you are wrong!" Bunji cried in triumph. "I drink until I see the tables begin to circle in the air. Then I know it is enough. But they are still in place. So—I must keep on." He sighed, and drank again. "What was I telling you?" he asked abruptly.

"You said you kept your eyes on the captain," I-wan reminded him.

"I did," Bunji said eagerly. His thick lips were trembling constantly, and a twitch began to jerk his left eye. "The men, you see, I considered beneath me. After all, my father is a man of wealth. And influence. General Seki—is my friend. Through him—I was lieutenant. So I said, 'I am not a common soldier.' I was right, wasn't I?" he demanded angrily of I-wan.

"Perfectly," I-wan replied, not knowing what all this was about.

"So when the men did it, I said it had nothing to do with me. I said, 'Their common nature compels them—' wasn't I right? So long as the captain didn't, I didn't."

"Didn't what?" I-wan asked.

"I tell you, don't I?" Bunji retorted. "You are stupid, I-wan. That is because you are Chinese. All Chinese are stupid."

I-wan felt his anger rise, and put it down again. Bunji was drunk.

"Stupid and cowards," Bunji said loudly against the blare of the music. "We routed them as though we ran about in play. We gave them money to go away, and most of them went. The rest we routed. They all ran—you should have seen them run!" Bunji laughed, tears still wet on his cheeks. He shook his head and tried to pour whisky into his cup. But now he was not able to find it, and I-wan did not help him. He watched Bunji while he searched for the small white cup.

"Hah, at least I know where my mouth is!" he said, and stood up, and put the bottle to his lips. When he set it down, he was sobbing again.

"Still it was the captain's fault. You see, I had seen the men at it night and day. I tell you, I-wan,"—he leaned toward I-wan, twitching and sobbing—"war twists a man too high. He needs everything strong—wine, much food, many women. He has to have everything heaped up. That is because of the noise of the cannon in his head all the time—and then, he may be dead in an hour—in a minute—no time for anything but the things he can snatch." Bunji was in such earnest he seemed almost to have sobered himself with his earnestness. "At first I thought it was horrible—you know—the men snatching at women everywhere—young and old—I said to the captain, 'Shall we allow this?' He said, 'We must—if we want them to fight tomorrow.' You see, he was my superior officer. So what could I say? I looked away from the men and watched him only. I said, 'So long as he does not—'"

He was beginning to shake again.

"So, I-wan, I ask you, why did he do it, too? I saw it, myself—he had them bring a woman into his tent. She was crying and fighting, but he went at her, not caring—I was crazy. I ran out into the street—I—the first woman I saw—a child—say twelve—though perhaps she was only ten—or perhaps fifteen—she might have been only small for her age—I dragged her into an alley." He was shuddering and shaking and staring at I-wan as he talked. "All the time I knew I didn't want to do it—but I had to go on—you see that? It was the captain's fault, you see that, I-wan? Her fault, also. She screamed so. She screamed out that I was so ugly—monkey, she called me! I said, 'Be quiet,' and she kept on screaming and struggling. So I said, 'Be quiet, or I will have to kill you.' I warned her, you see. But she was not quiet. So—afterwards— I killed her." He was weeping and weeping. "You see, I-wan? And only when she lay dead it occurred to me—she did not understand what I said—I spoke in Japanese—without thinking—I didn't think in time—how could I not have thought of it? That is my fault in the matter, I-wan."

He sprawled over the table, sobbing. A few people looked at him, and looked away again, and the curtain of noisy music kept them from hearing him.

I-wan sat perfectly still, dazed, sick, seeing everything that Bunji had told him.

This, then, was how they had behaved in China. His father had told him none of it. But then his father's letters had been very few then, and such letters as had come had had more lines than ever blocked out by the Japanese censors. And the news-papers had said that the Emperor's army had behaved with perfect order! He had believed it, he a Chinese! He despised himself. He rose.

"Come home, Bunji," he said. And stooping, he put his arms about Bunji's slack body and lifted him to his feet and helped him to the street. Then he called a ricksha, and putting Bunji, now sound asleep, into it, he walked at his side to the gate of Mr. Muraki's house. The old gateman was there, and he told him, "See if you can get your young master to his room unseen."

The old man nodded, and I-wan went on to his house.

A turmoil filled him. What had really happened in his own country? How much did he not know? What was the truth? He had been so absorbed in his own marriage that he had simply let it be that there was no war and so he could marry Tama. But he was a Chinese.

He mounted the steep rocky steps from the street to his home and Tama ran out to meet him, Jiro in her arms. She looked wonderfully fresh and pretty, her hair newly brushed, and her skin like the cheek of an apricot.

"We are just bathed, Jiro and I," she announced, "and we have on new kimonos—that is, Jiro's is all new and mine has new sleeves—and I bought such beautiful chrysanthemums —the man said you had sent him, and I said, 'What is the token?' He said, 'A Chinese gentleman,' and I said, 'I am not married to all the Chinese gentlemen in Nagasaki,' and he said, 'Ah, he told me to look at him, and I saw a small mole by the hair of his left temple,' and I said, 'Right!' "

She laughed and Jiro laughed and I-wan smiled.

"You are tired!" she exclaimed.

"Very tired," he admitted. No, he would not tell Tama what Bunji had said. It was not for her to hear. It was a Bunji she did not know and could not know. Besides, it was all not clear to him yet.

"Sit down," Tama begged him.

He sat down and she drew off his leather shoes and then

246

his socks and rubbed his feet with her smooth strong hands. There was ease and rest in her very touch.

"Now your coat, and here is a kimono, and your bath is ready," she murmured. "And I will see to everything and you are only to rest. Jiro will be so good and so quiet and not trouble you."

Jiro, sitting on the floor, was staring at all this with large eyes.

He let her do everything, seizing the excuse of his weariness to say nothing, to do nothing, except to think and think of what Bunji had told him. Routed armies, bombs, raped women—he had heard nothing of these. Had there been no punishment, no reprisals? He longed with sudden impatience to go home and see for himself what the truth had been. He remembered fragments of old hatreds—people on the streets spitting at Japanese and calling them dwarfs and monkeys, the demands of Japanese officials in the northern provinces, En-lan saying over and over, "And when the revolution is over we must fight the Japanese." But the revolution had never come and he had put away with it everything else that had never come to pass.

He could, he thought at last, soothed in the hot water of the deep wooden bath, go home alone even for a few days and find out. He had more than half a mind to do it. He rose and wiped himself, his flesh soft and warm, and even the tension of his mind relaxed. It would be easy enough to go home. He ought to go and see.

At the supper table while Tama leaned over him to fill his bowl, he looked up at her.

"I think I must go home for a little while," he said.

She put down the bowl.

247

"We will go, too," she cried joyfully. "Jiro and I, we will see your home."

He shook his head. "No, only I," he said. "It might not be safe for you."

"But why?" she asked, wondering at him. She had Jiro on her knee now and was feeding him with her chopsticks.

"There was fighting at Shanghai, you know, not many months ago," he said carefully. "I am not sure of the temper of the people toward Japan."

"Oh, but the Chinese people like us," she declared eagerly. "I do assure you, I-wan, I see it in all the papers that the common people run out to welcome our soldiers. They have been so oppressed by their own officials and armies, the papers say. I read the papers every day, you know, I-wan—more than you do."

He could not deny this. She read a great deal so that, she said, she would have something to talk about with him when he came home, "so I won't be only a stupid old-fashioned Japanese wife," she said.

"Nevertheless, you cannot go," he said firmly. He did not often so command her. She looked at him across the table. Then, Jiro still in her arms, she rose and came over to him and put Jiro on his lap.

"Jiro," she said, "tell your father what I told you today."

Jiro, struck with shyness, looked from one face to the other.

"Say, 'My mother says in the spring, if the gods permit'— only I know there are no gods, of course, I-wan, but I like to say it at such times—'in the spring I am to have a little brother.'"

"Tama!" he cried.

She nodded. "Yes, and yes, and you mustn't leave us now, I-wan. If something should happen—and I have such a super-stition, I-wan. I know it is silly—but I look at the ocean so

248

much and I feel it must never come between us. It wants to come between us, I-wan. I feel it—and if you leave me now, I shall be afraid that it will spoil the child. He will sicken in me and die."

He looked at her uncertainly.

"Wait until we can all go together," she begged him. "Not you alone—never without us!"

She seized his arm and clung to it and Jiro began to cry with fright.

"Hush, Jiro," he said, and he put his other arm around Tama. After all, why should he go? What could he do, anyway, if he found out the truth. What had happened had happened. Tama was crying now, too, against his shoulder.

"Hush, you two," he scolded them. "Was ever a man so beset by his family?" He put his arms around them both and locked his hands together behind them and rocked them back and forth gently.

"There," he soothed them, "stop your tears. I am not going. Tama, be quiet. You are terrifying the child."

She sobbed more softly and more softly until she was quiet, and then Jiro was quiet, too. And I-wan sat rocking them gently to and fro. This was his world, here in his arms.

And the next day Bunji remembered nothing, or, at most, nothing except a fear that he had said more than he should. He came in late, looking pale and tired, but trying to be jaunty in his old way. I-wan saw him pass his door, but he had no wish to speak first and he let him pass. Then at noon when the clerks were away eating their meal, Bunji came and stood in the door and said to I-wan with a sort of coaxing, half frank, half ashamed, "I was drunk yesterday, wasn't I?"

"You were," I-wan replied, looking up.

"I talked a great deal—what did I talk about?"

He saw that Bunji did not remember, and he was at once relieved of the burden of such confidence between them.

"You said you were going to be married," he replied.

"Is that all?" Bunji said. "So I am. I am going to be married in the old way, I-wan. I shall look at many pictures of young women of suitable age and family, put my finger on one, and tell my father, 'That one!' "

He laughed and I-wan smiled and said nothing.

"I will announce the wedding day," Bunji declared. "It will be soon. I can't have your son too far ahead of mine."

"Sons," I-wan corrected him.

"What—another!" Bunji cried.

I-wan nodded.

"Good Tama!" Bunji exclaimed. "Hah, the mogas still do very well, don't they?"

"Excellently," I-wan replied.

"A boy, eh?" Bunji asked.

"Tama says so," I-wan answered. "She thinks she knows."

"Then she knows," Bunji rejoined. "At least, the child itself will have to prove her wrong before she will believe it. Well, I shall choose a milder woman."

"I am well suited," I-wan answered.

Bunji nodded, and went away.

I-wan sat thinking a moment longer. He was greatly relieved that Bunji did not know what he had told. He had seen behind a curtain drawn for a moment from Bunji's memory. He knew that if Bunji had been conscious he would never have drawn that curtain. But he would never tell Bunji what he had done. Yet nothing could ever be quite the same again, now that he knew. He was different today from what he had been. He had, for instance, wanted daughters, but now since yesterday he wanted only sons. Tama had said to him this morning, "I feel the child in me is a boy. We will hang two paper carp over the house at the Festival of Sons when this one comes!"

"Good!" he had said.

Sons would follow their father some day, but daughters must be left behind.

The birth of Ganjiro, his second son, the Festival of Sons, and the earthquake, were all one confusion forever after in his mind. They happened together in the middle of the next spring after Bunji's wedding, that strange wedding, which took place so quickly and informally in the Japanese fashion to which I-wan could never become accustomed. It was simply one of the differences between his own country and this, that in one a marriage ceremony lasted for days, and here it was soon finished. Bunji himself behaved as though it were nothing, and the little Setsu Hajima whom he married looked like millions of other little Japanese women behind her bravely painted face. And once married Bunji never mentioned her. In a few days it seemed as though she had always been in the Muraki house. One forgot that she had not always been there, and now that she was come one forgot that she was there.

And then, less than a month later, Ganjiro was born. He had been born in the middle of the day, in the most easy and tranquil fashion, without I-wan's knowing anything about it. He had bade Tama and Jiro good-by on a morning late in April, when the last of the cherry blossom petals were floating down in the garden. The streets were wet with a sudden rain, and the sky was as he loved it best, clear blue behind huge soft white clouds billowing up from the ocean. The trees and leaves were green in every garden, and people on the street looked happy and content in the mild damp air.

There was a deep sweetness in this life of the people and he felt it and valued it. Human beings liked each other and showed it in their courtesies. It occurred to I-wan as he walked along in April sunshine that in these streets he had never seen an old face unhappy or a child angry because he was beaten. He loved these people willingly and unwillingly, too. He grew nearer them, and yet more alone.

Bunji, since he had married Setsu, was nearer and yet further away than he had been. He had immediately given up his drinking, although on his wedding day he had been very drunk. But none ever saw him drunk now. And certainly he played the lordly husband over stocky plain Setsu, who did not so much as sit in his presence. In these days Bunji was given to loud opinions on foreign policy, especially the policy of Japan in China, where he insisted the communists were again seizing the control. I-wan had listened to a great deal of this the night before, when he and Tama had dined at Bunji's new house.

"Sooner or later we shall have to put them down," Bunji had declared.

Well, he had learned not to answer Bunji. It was no use. Besides, he did not believe what he said. Men like his own banker father owned China and they hated the communists. And had not the Japanese papers reported again and again the rout of Chinese communists by their own government? Bunji was growing middle-aged with prejudices. He dismissed such things from his mind and entered his office as usual. He had hoped, at the new year, for an advancement, at least in his salary, but there had been none. Mr. Muraki explained at the annual new year's feast for his employees that there could be no increase in salary this year because of an unexpected and heavy rise in taxes, in order to strengthen the Emperor's army defenses by sea and land. He had only to say "The Emperor," and all was accepted—that is, by everyone except I-wan. He felt no loyalty to this sacred emperor, and it was not in him any more to worship anything.

He sighed a little as he sat down. When the second child came, Tama would have to twist her wits to make the money stretch over him, too. His own father had not sent him any money for a long time, and he did not like to ask unless he were in need. Why, he wondered, did the Emperor want more defenses now that Japan definitely possessed Manchuria? The military party, probably, growing in power—but he cared nothing for Japanese politics, or indeed any politics since the League of Nations had let Japan do as she liked. Politics he had put behind him as a waste even to think about.

He had worked nearly the morning through on classifying the inventory of goods held still unsold, when the maid-servant who had come running in to call him to Jiro's birth now appeared, serene and demure, having stopped to brush her hair and put on a fresh kimono and clean white cotton socks.

"Well, what is it?" he said, looking up at her, surprised.

"Honorable, I am to tell you Ganjiro's come."

"What do you say?" He leaped up and seized his hat.

"He is here, very fat and so healthy," she beamed on him. It was lucky to be the bearer of such good news. The two clerks were bowing and hissing softly through their teeth with pleasure.

"Just before the Festival of Sons!" the maid said, laughing.

He went off at once, stopping only to put his head in at Bunji's door and say, "My second son is come and I am going home." He took pride in saying it coolly as though every day

253

he had a son. "What?" Bunji roared. But he went on, only nodding to affirm it.

He did not let himself hurry along the street, and he listened to the maid's chatter as she clacked along behind him. "It was as sudden as today's sun and rain. One moment Oku-san was as well as you are, sir. The next, she said, 'I feel changed —it's beginning.' I ran for the midwife, and soon as she came the child arrived, sound and so handsome. And Oku-san said, 'If this is all the trouble of having a son, I can do it any time.'" She laughed heartily at her mistress and was very proud of her.

And indeed there was nothing unusual in the house. The smell of the food which Tama had been cooking before she lay down was fragrant, and he was hungry when he smelled it.

"I'll have your dinner when you want it, sir," the servant said, and knelt to take off his shoes.

"In half an hour," he replied.

Behind screens he found Tama on her bed holding Ganjiro in her arms and Jiro, now able to run, much astonished beside her. I-wan could not believe she had done with the birth. She was not even pale. She lay on the soft mattress spread on the mats and looked up at him mischievously as though it had all been a trick. In a corner of the darkened enclosure the midwife was hastily putting away something.

"Tama!" he whispered.

"Here we all are," she answered. "It is a boy, as I said."

"So!" he answered. He scarcely knew what to say. Jiro's birth had been a tremendous event. But this boy had come tranquilly into the world. At this rate, he thought, in a few years the house would be full.

"I wanted it all over before the Festival of Sons," Tama said proudly.

"So you arranged it," he replied.

And she laughed.

"Go on and have your dinner—it is carp, too, today. That's another lucky omen."

"Shall I not stay home this afternoon?" he inquired.

"What would I do with you?" she asked. "I shall sleep and Jiro will play in the garden with the maid. That is all."

So he had eaten his excellent dinner and gone back to work. Tama was one of those fortunate women, he thought, who breathe out health with every act. Nothing was too hard for her to do. And with all else she found time, too, to be free of everything when he came home. Long ago he had ceased to wonder at anything she knew. He expected her to know everything. He had come to take for granted that his house was always neat and the flowers fresh every day, and the food delicately prepared and Jiro's face always clean and happy. Whatever came, he could never be sorry he had married Tama. If sometimes he felt himself yearning beyond her for some sort of spiritual stir which had nothing to do with her, he put his discontent away. He wanted nothing to do with dreams if Tama were the reality.

On the Festival of Sons they went nowhere, since Tama's days of uncleanness after birth were not yet over. Ganjiro was less than a month old. But she made great preparation for the day. Over the house that morning he had helped her to raise the two paper carps, which were the symbol of the day, a big black and white one with gold eyes for Jiro and a small red one for Ganjiro.

It was a fair day on the fifth day of the fifth month of the sun year, and Jiro was shouting as the wind blew the carp. There was an extraordinary wind blowing in from the sea that day. Tama had taken Jiro up in her arms, and then I-wan took him, saying, "He is too heavy for you yet, Tama."

"Hold him up, then, so he can see," she had replied. They had stood looking at the carp, the wind tearing at their garments.

"A home with sons," Tama said proudly.

He did not answer her. It occurred to him at this moment that his sons were growing up with festivals he had never known as a child. Tama loved festivals and made the most of every one. He remembered his own joy over the new year and over the Dragon Festival and the Festival of Spring—all days Jiro and the little one would never know. After all it was the woman who shaped the life of the house.

"So, Jiro," Tama was saying to the child, "remember, the carp means boy—because it swims upstream against the current, in the cold mountain streams."

It was at that moment he saw, or imagined he saw the pole from which the carp flew, sway. At the same instant the wind, which had all morning been growing higher, fell utterly quiet. He and Tama with one movement looked out to sea. It looked strange and dark and swollen. There was a low deep roar, whether from the sea or from inside the earth they could not tell.

"Tama!" he cried, frightened.

"Earthquake," she said. Her voice was small and quiet and her face went white.

He had learned to take tremors of the earth as nothing, an earthquake as a matter of constant possibility, and yet he had never seen a great one. Sometimes in the night he and Tama had awakened to feel a shudder beneath their mattress and dust falling on their faces from the ceiling, and to hear the crack of beams and wood. Tama always got up and dressed

256

and waited in watchful silence. He knew that all over the city in every house people waited like that, helpless and yet prepared. But each time the earth had subsided. Today, though, there had been this fierce wind.

Now she ran toward the house, but the maid was already running out with Ganjiro in her arms. From the house behind her came sudden creaks and then loud cracks. There was no doubt that the pole bearing the carp was now swaying with something that was not wind.

The maid, without a word, thrust the baby into his arms also and ran back into the house. Tama came out with the drawers and boxes into which their clothing was folded, and in a moment the maidservant followed, her arms full.

"Where shall I put these children?" I-wan gasped. "I must help."

"Please—stay with them," Tama replied, quietly.

He wondered at these two women, they were both so quiet. It was as though they had rehearsed many times the thing which they now did. Back and forth they went until in a very few minutes in the open space about them were all their chief possessions. There were not many. Their most precious things, the best of their scrolls, some fine pottery Mr. Muraki had given them, jewelry that I-wan had given Tama when they were married, the silks his mother had sent, she had put into a warehouse in the city, built for safety in earthquakes.

"Where shall we go?" he asked her when at last she stood beside him and reached for the baby.

"Where can we go?" she asked simply. "There is no escape when the earth heaves."

They stood, waiting, their faces to the sea. He held Jiro hard. But Jiro was not crying. He, too, was looking at the swollen ocean. And then Tama gave one moan of horror and put her hand to her mouth. The sea was gathering near the horizon into one great wave, no, not so much a wave, as a tide, a great bank of water, stretching across the surface of the ocean. There was no crest upon the wave. It was simply there, immense and dark, lifting against the sky.

"It can't reach us," Tama whispered.

"It will cover the lower city," he answered, and felt his gorge rise in him to make him sick. But he could not turn his head away. On it came, seeming motionless and as though it were simply swelling more huge. But in reality it was rolling toward the shore at greatest speed, gathering the waters with it as it came. Far below them they could see people running out of their houses and climbing the hills everywhere—away from the sea.

"It always comes quickly," Tama said.

He had never seen her like this—so still. He did not know whether or not she was afraid. He wanted to run, to escape somehow, but she held him there.

Then the wave struck. There was still no crest until the instant when it crashed with such a roar as shook the whole island. Then it broke and surged in a mass of foam. Houses and streets disappeared. The whole sea seemed to have rushed in.

"This may sweep as far as my father's house," Tama said in a low voice.

They watched. And more horrible than the onward rush was this next thing, this outward backward moving of the same tide, which seemed to suck out to sea in its enormous flood houses, people, trees, everything it could reach. The whole island indeed seemed to be moving out to sea.

I-wan groaned and buried his face in Jiro's shoulder. And at that instant the earth shook under his feet. He heard rocks crashing down the hillside and he put out his arm for Tama. Even at this moment her body was firm and strong.

"Our rock will not move," she said. "That is only loose rock. And there are the fields above us—not rocks."

It was true. Above them lay a valley running almost to the top of the mountain and because a small stream ran through it, it had been terraced for rice fields on both sides.

He felt once more the sickening unsteadiness of the earth swaying beneath him.

"The wave is coming again," Tama said, "but it will not be so great."

He heard it strike, this time a lesser roar, but he did not look up. Jiro clung to him, his arms about his father's head. Still he did not cry, and the small child was sleeping. I-wan remembered how Bunji had spoken of Japanese sleep, how nothing waked them, used as they were to noise and movement in babyhood, upon their mothers' backs.

There was a soft slithering sound, a loud cracking of falling wood, and the sound of tearing paper. He looked up. With surprisingly little noise and less dust the house had fallen into a heap.

But before he had time to cry his dismay, Tama said, "There, it is over. And we are alive."

She turned her back on the ruined house. Only then did she sit down. The sea, full of wreckage, was subsiding, and now the wind was beginning once more. He felt his legs begin to tremble.

"I have seen much worse earthquakes," Tama said. She wiped her face with her sleeve and then uncovered her bosom and began to feed her child. He sat down on the box beside her and let the maid take Jiro from him. Now that it was

259

over sweat was pouring down his whole body. He could feel himself wet under his clothes.

"It is worse than anything I have ever seen," he said.

"Oh, there are far worse," she repeated.

He looked at her. She was sitting there as calmly as though the house which she loved were not in a heap behind her.

"Now what shall we do?" he asked, after a moment.

"Rest a while—and then see if my father's house is harmed," she said.

A man in a short blue coat came climbing up the hill and appeared among a clump of bamboos. It was a ricksha puller from her father's house. He bowed before them.

"I have been sent," he said, "to see how you are."

"My father and mother?" Tama asked.

"All is safe," he replied. "The gate house is fallen and part of the kitchen, and the garden we do not know, but the main part of the house is safe and no one was even hurt except the young mistress who was in the kitchen and was held by a beam over her thigh. But she is now resting and in less pain. The ceremonial teahouse is not touched."

"Ah, how fortunate we are!" Tama cried.

They rose and stood for a moment and I-wan could not but turn and look at what a little while ago had been his home. Tama's eyes followed his.

"We can easily build it again," she said.

"Not here," he said, not knowing why, except it seemed not safe ever to build his home here again. But Tama insisted.

"Yes, here. The sea reached for us and could not get us. It is a good place to build again."

He was too shaken to argue it with her and he followed her, carrying Jiro, down the hill by the way the man led because the road was gone. And behind them came the maid, her arms full of whatever she thought precious enough to be taken. She had said nothing from first to last.

He never forgot that day. The safety of the Muraki house, the comfort of a roof standing over their heads and of food hot and ready to be eaten, the quiet and the kindness—these were miracle enough. But unforgettable above all was the miracle of silence—Mr. Muraki's silence as he walked about his ruined garden where the streams had raced over broken walls and had swept over tended mossy slopes and torn them away and uprooted the dwarf trees as priceless as any curio, Bunji's silence over his young wife's broken thigh, Setsu's silence in her own pain—I-wan was never to know Setsu well, but her eyes, fine eyes in a plain face, he never forgot—the silence of the people on the streets whose houses and relatives had been swept out to sea, the silence of the little clerk in his office, solitary now that his brother was dead—this silence he never forgot.

And the next day everything had begun again, the building of houses and the cleaning away of wreckage and the putting up of the torn sea walls. Everyone worked as though at an old task, often done. And Tama said, "Now that we have to build again anyway, we may as well make the house bigger."

He was ashamed of his own question. "But if it happens again—and again?"

"That is as it will be. We can always build again," she answered.

He had not the face to complain of anything for himself when all over the city people were going back to wreckage and ruin. And those missing who had been swept out to sea. . . . He was drawn again and again during those days to the part of the city which lay on the shore.

261

"Are you building your house again exactly where it was?" he asked an old fisherman.

The man turned small somber black eyes upon him.

"Where else?" he answered. "My father's house was here and my grandfather's."

"But if the same thing happens again?" I-wan asked.

"It will happen again—we know that," the man said.

This took on a meaning for I-wan that was far beyond what he could then express. It seemed to him he saw Tama far more clearly than he ever had before. Beneath her woman's ways and her gaiety there was something desperate and resolute, something that had nothing to do with what she might wish to have or to do. So, beneath the playfulness of these people who knew how to enjoy as children enjoy, was also this dogged resolve which made them able to endure anything if they must.

Years later when he heard it sworn that soon the war would be over he shook his head. No, not soon, and perhaps never. These island people had been trained to vaster foes than man. They had fought earthquake, fire, and typhoon. These had been the enemies who had trained them in war. He was always proud that through it all his own two sons had not once wept or been afraid.

It was not a war. The papers made that clear. It was not to be called a war. It was, in the Emperor's name, nothing but an incident.

Certainly it seemed not so important to I-wan as the fact that to the house built new after the earthquake two years before he had this summer added a study for himself with firm wooden walls which could not be moved away. For the last year Tama had been urging him to it, since the two little boys were growing so noisy. He should have a place, she said, of his own. And when one day he found they had taken his paste and smeared it everywhere over his desk, in the main room, while Tama was bathing herself and the maid preparing the supper, he agreed. And it was pleasant to have his own room. . . . Besides, the papers made little enough of the incident—a few soldiers in a quarrel at a small town in North China.

"It will not last three months," Bunji had declared the first day.

It was this which first made I-wan pause to wonder if this incident were graver than was said. Else why so long as three months? He waited for letters from his father, but his father did not write so often as he once had. I-wan wrote asking for what his father's opinion was, but no answer came. This seemed strange, and yet he knew that it might mean nothing.

One day the clerk in his office resigned. He was, he said, called to army service, though he was his mother's only support now that his elder brother had died.

"What will she do?" I-wan asked.

"Mr. Muraki is so kind," little Mr. Tanaka replied. "He gives a weekly sum to all who must leave their families without support to fight for the Emperor."

Two young women came to fill his place, and a partition was put up between them and I-wan, so that he had after a fashion a room of his own. He had a good deal of time now. Business began to decrease. There were few shipments. This, too, made I-wan wonder. If it were only a matter of a few soldiers, then why did Chinese exporters at once cease sending their goods to Japan? Shipments came in as usual during that month. Then suddenly nothing came in. Ships came to port and went on, and there was no business for the house of Muraki. But they had great stores unsold and these continued westward to America and to Europe. I-wan busied himself in checking off inventories and arranging for packing and shipping boxes and crates of rugs and tapestries, potteries and china, furniture and scrolls, and all the confusion of the cheap and valuable which made the business.

Then one day he received a cable from his father. Afterwards it seemed strange to him that it had come to him through Bunji. But at the moment he had not had time to think of that. Bunji sent for him one morning, and when I-wan went to see why he was wanted, Bunji handed him an envelope and sat watching as he tore it open. It was from his father. "I-ko arriving seventeenth at Yokohama on S.S. *Balmoral*. Meet him at dock." The seventeenth was two days away.

"Your brother is coming?" Bunji asked.

"How did you know?" I-wan asked surprised.

"My father wishes to send a present to your father, if your brother will be so kind," Bunji replied obliquely.

"How did Mr. Muraki know?" I-wan asked.

"He received the cablegram, of course," Bunji said calmly. "It was sent to the house and he read it."

"Why?" I-wan asked.

"To know whether it was important, of course," Bunji answered as if surprised.

I-wan was about to retort, "But it was my cablegram!" but this would be rude toward Mr. Muraki, who perhaps had no sense of wrong done. So instead he said, "Please thank Mr. Muraki."

Did he imagine Bunji was watching him strangely?

"I suppose it is necessary for you to go," he continued.

"Certainly I feel it is," I-wan replied firmly.

He had been half thinking as he stood there that he might

take Tama and the boys to show them off to one of his own family. Now, going out of Bunji's office, he decided against it. He had better meet I-ko alone.

He stood craning his head to watch as the ship came into the harbor with the smooth slow grace of a great swan. He did not run instantly to the gangway. He suddenly felt very shy of I-ko. They had never been close. I-ko was too much older. And I-wan remembered still that Peony had hated him for things of which she would never speak. That hatred had long made I-wan feel that I-ko was mysteriously evil, so he could not love him, even yet. And now there were these years in Germany. Who knew what they had done to him? Still, he was excited, too, at the thought of seeing his brother. For the first time he felt he had been a long time away from home. While the ship docked he stared at the row of people along the ship's rail, recognizing no one.

Then he saw I-ko coming down the gangplank. He could not believe this upright cleanly-cut figure was that I-ko who had gone away, the slender slouching young man with thin peevish lips, who could pout like a child when he was denied and even weep to get his own way. What had Germany done to I-ko? He saw I-wan and shouted, and now I-wan saw a straight upright man, a head higher than the swarming Japanese about him, a hard-looking man with a firm mouth and haughty eyes and a foreign bearing. Behind him was a white woman dressed in some sort of shining green silk, her arms bare to the shoulder, but I-wan did not look at her. There were other men and women coming down the gangway.

He went up to I-ko shyly and put out his hand.

"I-ko," he said.

"I-wan!" I-ko cried, and then he seized the arm of the white

265

woman behind him. "Frieda," he said to her, in German, "here is my brother."

This I-wan heard. He remembered a little of the German he had learned long ago from the tutor his grandfather had hired for him. But who this woman was he did not understand. He looked at her and at once hated her. She was young but already too fat and her cheeks were too red. Her eyes were a hard bright blue above these red cheeks, and her hair under a green hat was yellow. She put out a hand covered in a yellow leather glove.

"Ach, it is so wonderful to see you!" she cried in a loud voice. I-wan felt her seize his hand in a sharp upward German clasp, and then to his horror he saw her lean forward and upon his cheek he felt her painted lips. "Brother I-wan!" she said and giggled.

"This is my wife, I-wan," I-ko said haughtily. "Her name is Frieda von Reichausen, and her father is a German military officer of high standing."

His voice, his eyes fixed upon I-wan, were daring I-wan to say anything. There was nothing to be said, I-wan thought. If they were married, what could be said? He merely bowed, therefore. But within himself questions were whirling. Did their father know? What would their mother say? How could this stout, hard young woman fit into their family? Why had I-ko done this? And then he remembered Tama, whom all these years he had not wanted to take home. If he should ever say a word of disapproval to I-ko, would not I-ko say at once that at least he had not married a Japanese? And yet Tama—he knew by instinct that this woman was not fit to stand beside Tama!

"We are only bride and groom," she was saying. "Everything is so wonderful!" And again she giggled, her eyes arch upon him.

He thought, "I must not look at I-ko. She is so silly he will be ashamed of her before me."

Something, he felt, must be said quickly to help I-ko. They were standing on the dock waiting awkwardly for nothing, and people swept against them as they hurried to and fro. And yet what could he say? He was still dazed. He took out his handkerchief and wiped his face and secretly rubbed his cheek, lest her red lips had left a stain on him.

"I-ko," he said at last, "I scarcely knew you." He spoke in Chinese and his tongue felt stiff and strange. Not for years had he spoken his own language. And now he was glad to speak it because it shut out this foreign woman.

I-ko looked pleased.

"No, I am changed," he replied. "In fact am I not improved?"

"You look—much older," I-wan said diffidently.

"Oh, I am a man now," I-ko replied, smiling slightly. "I am very grateful to my father. I hated Germany for the first year and then liked it. I-wan, where can we talk? I have much to say—and the ship's stay is very short. They are staying one hour instead of four."

"But can't you wait over a few days and take another ship?" I-wan asked politely. What would he do if I-ko accepted—with *her!*

I-ko shook his head. "There is no time," he answered. "It is imperative that I get home. Where can we go?"

"I suppose we could go to that little restaurant," I-wan said, doubtfully. A small restaurant was near the dock and it had a few outdoor tables. I-ko nodded his head vigorously.

"Yes, that will do," he decided. "Come, Frieda!" he called in German. He strode across the street ahead of I-wan, his shoulders set square, and when they sat down he beckoned imperiously for a waiter. Behind them she came. They sat down and I-wan at once felt the stare of people—a white woman with two Chinese men! But I-ko seemed not to notice.

267

"Beer," I-ko said to the waiter, and scarcely waiting a moment, he leaned toward I-wan.

"I-wan," he said, "you cannot stay here. You must come home at once." He spoke in Chinese and he paid no heed to his wife. But she seemed used to this and while they talked she sat looking about her with hard and curious eyes. If she cared that other people wondered at her she made no sign of it.

"But—but—," I-wan stammered, meeting I-ko's look. He drew back a little. I-ko's face was almost menacing. "I—it is impossible —my family—"

"Can it be you, too, don't know?" I-ko exclaimed.

"Know what?" I-wan asked. The old premonition had him by the throat and his mouth went suddenly dry.

"Haven't you heard?" I-ko cried.

"I haven't heard anything," I-wan faltered.

"The Japanese are going to take Peking!" I-ko whispered.

"Peking!" I-wan repeated stupidly.

"Has there been nothing told even about that?" I-ko exclaimed. Around them Japanese were sitting at the small tables, talking and laughing, and drinking tea and wine. Above them the sky was blue, without a cloud. There were women in bright kimonos, and at one side sat a little group of Americans, having tea with an officer from the ship. And beside them the German woman sat, her plump elbows on the table. She had already drunk her beer, and now she sat eating small cakes.

"It was just troop movements, they said," I-wan replied, looking away from her. No, but perhaps he had missed something. He did not always read the papers these days. He dreaded them. And Tama never spoke of such things. No, rather it was as if together they did not speak of them. But he could not tell I-ko this.

But I-ko was hurrying on. "Father foresaw everything weeks

ago and cabled me. The Generalissimo wants me to come home. The army is being reorganized on a huge scale. There will be war! We will resist to the end. At last it has been decided!"

I-wan could scarcely comprehend what I-ko was saying in his low hurried whispering Chinese.

"But—no one knows—anything here," he stammered. He felt as though his breath had been driven out of him. "There hasn't been much in the papers—people are just going on—some mention of a little difficulty, but not—"

"These people!" I-ko said contemptuously. "The ones at the top don't tell them anything. I tell you, I-wan, mobilization has begun. It's going to be the greatest war of our history. I-wan, come home with me!"

"Now?" I-wan cried.

"Now!" I-ko said strongly. "I have money for your passage. We can get your ticket on the ship, if need be. Father told me—"

"But my family—" I-wan began.

"There are no claims on you now but this one," I-ko insisted. "You have no obligations to any Japanese except to hate them forever!" I-ko's teeth shone as white as a fox's teeth in a dramatic snarl. Even at this moment, while they stared at each other, I-wan could stop to remember that I-ko loved to be dramatic, and this made him the more cautious.

. . . Tama, I-wan was saying to himself, Tama was a Japanese and he loved her. She seemed more than ever gentle and faithful and good, now that I-ko had—had married such a one as this. He could not leave Tama. He would have to think what to do.

"I don't understand," he said. "I can't see why—why should there be war? We aren't enemies—"

"We are enemies!" I-ko answered firmly. "Where have you been, I-wan, not to know that this war has been hurrying upon

269

us for months—years? Have you heard of the outrage at Lukow-chiao?"

"The papers said it would be amicably settled," I-wan said.

"Settled! By the loss of Peking?" I-ko asked passionately.

"I tell you, they—they didn't say it was like that," I-wan stammered.

"Has your marriage made you Japanese, too?" I-ko demanded.

"No—no—" I-wan said quickly. "No—only it is so quick—I haven't known—I have had no letters from home." Why did he not retort, "Are you German?" But he did not want to hear I-ko say, "At least my wife is not a Japanese!"

"How do you know?" I-ko interrupted him. "Letters don't get through here unread. I am sure Father did tell you and you never had the letters. He cabled me that he couldn't understand why you wrote as you did, and that I was to stop and see what was wrong."

"Mr. Muraki told me he had heard my father was taking a journey into Szechuan to see about organizing a branch bank!" I-wan exclaimed. "So I thought the letters were delayed."

"There is not one Japanese you can trust!" I-ko declared. "Come, I-wan!"

They talked far longer than they knew, with long silences between.

Whenever they fell silent the German woman asked a question about something she saw. Once she exclaimed, "Ach, so—see the funny little people—they are so little, the Japs, are they not?"

Whatever she said it was I-ko who answered her and not I-wan. He scarcely heard her. He sat thinking and trying to realize what I-ko had told him had happened. The afternoon deepened and the sun was half-way to the sea. The hour was gone. The

German woman was yawning. They rose, and she sauntered ahead of them to the ship.

The Americans were getting up now, too. Their clear, sharp voices carried across the tables as they talked to each other, oblivious to everyone else. Two of them were going with the officer, and the others were staying. A pretty girl cried, "Be careful, you two, in Shanghai! Red, take your hat off, when the air raids begin, so they can see your flaming top and know you're not a Chinaman!"

A red-haired young man laughed.

"So long, Mollie! Sorry you aren't coming, but I guess it's no place for girls just now."

The ship's whistle roared in warning.

"Do you hear them?" I-ko demanded. "Everybody knows, I tell you, except these stupid common people in Japan. I-wan, hundreds of people have been killed—and it will only grow worse. Our whole country has to wake up—we have to fight as we've never fought!"

They were walking now to the ship. I-ko stopped.

"Will you come?" he demanded.

"I can't," I-wan said. "Not now—not like this—"

"Why not?"

"I can't just—leave them—Mr. and Mrs. Muraki—they have been good to me—"

"They're Japanese," I-ko reminded him in a whisper.

"They've been good to me," I-wan repeated.

"Then I tell you this," I-ko retorted. "As your elder brother speaking for our father, you are to come as soon as you can. That means days, I-wan—not weeks. And hours are better than days, I tell you."

The crew was busy on the decks. The passengers were mounting the gangplank.

"Hours," I-ko repeated. "Of all countries, you cannot stay in Japan. It's—indecent!" He put a hand hard on I-wan's shoulder and shook it a little. "Good-by, then—for a few days only. Meanwhile, I will write you at once the truth about all I see."

I-wan did not answer. He stood watching while the ship began to edge away from the shore. From the deck he saw I-ko's wife wave her yellow-gloved hand. He took off his hat and bowed. The ship moved, turned south, and then west . . . He had asked I-ko nothing, and I-ko had told him nothing. They were further apart than ever.

He returned to his home by train that same night. When he entered the house in the morning Tama came to meet him with soft welcoming cries and they walked together along the garden path. He thought with fresh disgust today of I-ko's wife. And yet it came to him how Japanese Tama looked. In the old days of her girlhood he had not thought of her as looking very Japanese in her school clothes and her leather shoes. She seemed then only a young girl.

"You wear kimono and geta now all the time," he said abruptly.

She gave him a laugh soft with apology.

"Do you mind? They are so comfortable!"

He could not say he minded, since until now he had not noticed. Certainly the bright orange-flowered kimono was very becoming to her apricot skin and dark eyes. At the door she dropped to her knees as though she were his serving maid and untied his shoes and took them off and then slipped over his feet the loose cloth house slippers always ready. He had protested often at this service until she had persuaded him that it was a way of expressing her love for him.

"I do it for no one else," she insisted.

So he had grown used to it, and indeed there had come to be

272

a sweet intimacy in the sight of her dark head bent before him. Today he thought, "But no other woman would ever do it."

At that moment Jiro came running to meet him. "Where is Ganjiro?" he asked him, for the two were always together.

"Asleep," Jiro replied.

Tama had continued to make Jiro wholly Japanese in his dress and looks, and even in the way she brushed his hair. I-wan said abruptly, "Jiro's feet are beginning to turn in from wearing geta. Get him some leather shoes, Tama."

"Before he goes to school?" she looked up in surprise. "But they are so expensive."

"I don't care," he returned. "Get them."

She did not answer, but he could see in the way she hushed Jiro's exclamations of joy that she did not approve of this. And then he caught sight of the maid crossing the room toward the kitchen with Ganjiro asleep on her back. And he, knowing Tama would think him only more unreasonable, went on.

"And why is the baby strapped like that to the maid's back when he can walk? His legs will be as short and crooked as Bunji's."

Here she was indignant.

"I-wan, I beg you—not in the presence of Jiro. And it is a good way to care for a little child. He is warm and safe while he sleeps. The even temperature of her body keeps him from catching cold."

"Put him in his bed—I won't have him strapped like that," he insisted.

He saw in her eyes that he was indeed being unreasonable. She sighed and then smiled.

"Of course, you are very tired," she said gently. "A whole night on the train! Jiro, go away until I call you."

"I am not tired," I-wan retorted.

Nevertheless he said no more. Perhaps he was unreasonable.

Certainly it astonished him to find in himself a feeling that today it would be a pleasure to be able to quarrel with Tama. But it was impossible to quarrel with her. She would not answer him. She went quietly about to placate him, and then she went away for a few minutes as though to give him time to recover himself. He could almost imagine that she withdrew to remember what she had been taught to do when a man, her husband, is irritable. In the past when she had so considered him, invariably she came back with a flower or a sweetmeat or a pot of freshly brewed tea, to make him feel her especial attention. He had always been ashamed of his rare moods of ill-temper. But today he felt irritated with this very seeming pliability of hers, which made allowance for everything he did, and yet, he knew, yielded nothing to any change.

He ate his meal in silence, full of such thoughts, yet hating himself, too. For Tama was not changed. She was what she had always been, the same fresh, naïve, happy creature, the same compound of childishness and sophistication, the same confusion of old and new. And her only fault was that she always did faithfully what she had been taught to do. It occurred to him suddenly that this was true of every Japanese—each one did as he was told to do. But whose was the final command? The spirit of the people, fostered by—what? The Emperor? He had often seen the pictures of the Emperor and Empress. They were in the sacred shrines of every schoolhouse and public building—two doll-like immobile creatures. No, they too did only as they were told. It now seemed to him that the whole nation was trained in the same mold. And into this mold would go also his own two sons!

He rose abruptly. He must get to his office. Then he could not find his hat. And Tama had left the room a moment before.

"Where is my hat?" he demanded of the maid, who came in with tea.

The baby was no longer on her back. At his voice she looked frightened as though she did not know what to expect.

"Hah!" she breathed distractedly, and began running about hunting for the hat in absurd places. He grew impatient.

"My hat, Tama!" he shouted. She came in quickly, Ganjiro in her arms, crying.

"Ah, your hat!" she cried. "Where can it be?"

Behind her came Jiro, strutting along, the hat on his head. Tama snatched it.

"Oh, bad boy!" she cried. "To take your father's good hat!"

"Leave him alone," I-wan ordered, putting the hat on his head. "I am glad if he shows a little independence."

Tama did not answer. She gave the crying child to the maid and motioned her away, and followed I-wan to the door, a smile on her lips. I-wan thought, "She has been taught to present a smiling face to her husband when he leaves home," and hated himself.

"Good-by, Tama," he said, more kindly. And he hated himself more when her eyes grew bright with relief. "I'll be back a little late, perhaps," he added.

"Yes, of course," she agreed. She stood, her smile fixed, as long as he could see her.

What happened when he was gone? He had never thought before to ask himself. Did she take the smile from her face and put it away until he returned? Probably Ganjiro was already again strapped to the maid's back! For the first time it occurred to him that he really knew nothing at all of what went on in his own house.

Long after Tama was asleep that night he lay awake, his head still throbbing. For an hour she had massaged it delicately and

275

firmly, her fingers seeming scarcely to touch his skin, and yet he could feel their tips, manipulating the nerves.

"You know everything, I think," he said after a long silence.

"Are you better?" she asked.

"Yes," he said.

In a little while the pain was back again, exactly as it had been. But he did not tell her. She had done what she could. It was not her fault that the pain was deeper than she could reach. It had its roots somewhere down in his soul, he thought. He had not thought about his soul for a long time. Tama had made his body wonderfully comfortable. Long ago he had accepted everything from her of such comfort. Even tonight, before she put her neck into the hollowed curve of her wooden pillow, she made sure, in her own delicate fashion, that he wanted nothing more of her.

"You are tired?" she bent over him so closely that he caught her body's fragrance.

"Too tired for anything but sleep," he answered.

She touched his cheeks with the palms of her hands and then stretched herself out beside him so quietly he hardly felt her there.

Did she, he wondered, really have no will of her own? But as a girl she had had, he thought. And what was that deep steady persistence in her except the solidity of will? And yet, as he pondered it, he perceived it was less her own will, her individual will, than it was something else—not tradition, because she was not slavish to tradition—her education in a girls' school had broken that. No, it was something else. He felt it in them all— in her parents and in Bunji and in Shio. And in Akio it had driven him to his death, and it had made as simple a creature as Sumie willing to die. It was some solidarity of instinct which he did not understand because he had never seen it until he came here. Certainly it was not in his own family or in his people.

Even in that youthful band which En-lan had led the solidarity had been based upon recognized intellectual convictions, rather than upon any natural instincts. Did his sons have it? He brought before his mind Jiro's small compact round face. Impossible to know! But why should he think it was not there? Tama would give with her blood that which was also indestructible in her own being.

This meant, then, that what was most indestructible in his sons' souls was Japanese, even as Tama was Japanese. He felt suddenly as far from this woman sleeping at his side as though he had never seen her. She lay as she always did, asleep in perfect silence. He could not hear her so much as breathe. He turned and tossed and flung himself about in sleep. But Tama's body never moved. When in the morning she rose even her hair was not disturbed. So she had been taught to control herself, awake or asleep.

They were all controlled. From that strange immobile center of their being there went out this complete command over the whole. Nothing could break it down. He remembered the earthquake. No one had been afraid. No one had complained. And yet an eye far less sensitive than his could perceive their intense inner suffering. . . . Yet had not Bunji lost control? That was what happened. If the control broke, they turned into beasts—even Bunji, the best of them. Bunji was still the best of them, because he hated and feared what he had done and hid it even from himself, so that even to himself he could never be quite the same again.

And Tama, if she broke . . . ? By the light of the small night light he looked at her placid sleeping face. Ganjiro slept on the other side of her, as all Japanese babies slept with their mothers. She had been horrified when he said, "Why not let him sleep with the maid?"

"But how can a maid know if anything is wrong with him?" she had exclaimed.

And it was true that through her blood she seemed able to feel the slightest change in the child, so that if he were to fall ill, she knew it days before, and tended him.

He forced himself to lie still, though every muscle longed to twitch and move. But her quiet compelled him to control, since in its completeness the slightest noise or movement was magnified. And at last he seemed to feel something emanate from her still body into his, as though only through quiet could he perceive her. His restlessness subsided and he lay more easily. And after a while over his mind sleep crept like a comforting warmth. The stir in his brain drowsed until only the unsleeping inner centers were awake, and then his thoughts moved in the deep slow circles of the body.

Why should he upset his life again? He had built it carefully, alone. Alone he had been cast out of his country and alone he had found Tama and with her built his home. His whole being clung tenaciously to this which he had made for himself. Whatever happened elsewhere, this must be kept. No one must take everything away from him again!

He put out his hand and touched Tama's face.

"Tama!" he whispered. He wanted to hear her voice.

She woke instantly, as she always did, awake and alert.

"Yes—what is it?" she asked quickly.

"Nothing—only speak to me," he begged her. "I have been lying awake too long, thinking."

She reached out her arms and put them about him.

"Don't think so much!" she begged him.

"No, I don't want to think any more," he answered.

They clung to each other in silence. And he, putting away

thought, murmured into the sweet stifling warmth of her bosom. Whatever happened outside of this had nothing to do with him.

So peace returned. It was a month of unusual coolness and much sunshine, and each day, as soon as I-wan came home from his work, Tama and the maidservant met him at the foot of the hill with the children and they mounted a bus and went to a beach, or if it were a near one, they took rickshas and rode, and when they had played in the sea until they were tired, then they bought their supper at a small restaurant or from a passing vendor, and ate. Ganjiro lay in a hollow in the warm sand when he grew sleepy, and the maidservant watched over him. And if I-wan saw sometimes that on the way home in the darkness she still carried him on her back, he said nothing, because he knew she hoped never to do it in his sight, and this meant that Tama was trying to have no quarrel, and so he tried too, by silence at least.

Very often, more often than ever before, they all went to the Muraki house and took their evening meal in the garden. Mr. Muraki urged them to it.

"It is Jiro," Tama said proudly. "He wants Jiro with him all the time. My mother says he thinks Jiro is far more clever than Shio's two boys."

It was true that Jiro was a child of greater beauty than was to be seen anywhere. He was taller than other children and he held his head proudly, and he had inherited not Tama's blunt little hands and feet, but I-wan's own, long and narrow and almost too delicate for a boy. Jiro's mind, also, was full of humor and childish wit. And Mr. Muraki delighted to take his hand and walk with him alone through the garden, after they had eaten. I-wan always watched the two, the old fragile man in his soft gray robes, and the vivid upright boy springing along at his side.

279

When Mr. Muraki came back, his lips were always twitching and his eyes shining so that he could hardly wait until Jiro had skipped away to say, "There never was made such a boy as this. I-wan, it is proof of what I have always said—together Japanese and Chinese can make the greatest people in the world. We must unite!"

He laughed his dry old laugh, and everyone laughed and I-wan forgave him anything because of his pride in Jiro. Yes, it was a good time. Even Bunji was more as he had been to I-wan that summer. Setsu was right for him. He had begun his old rough joking again.

"Do you remember, I-wan, I always said I would marry an ugly girl? I recommend it! It makes me feel I am not so bad, and it keeps her humble. Setsu, perfect Japanese wife!"

And Setsu, blushing, laughed happily at everything Bunji said and never retorted. But they were all growing fond of Setsu, who had learned to read only with the greatest difficulty and had no higher dreams than to make her husband and his parents comfortable. Almost immediately her figure swelled with pregnancy and she entered placidly upon the long course of her life as the mother of many children.

And yet, when later I-wan looked back upon that peace, he wondered that he could have dreamed it secure. It ended in a single moment.

It was Mr. Muraki's seventieth birthday and therefore a day to be specially observed. Shio had come from Yokohama with his wife and two sons, and there had been a great feast in the middle of the day at a hotel. There the merchants of the city had gathered to speak in praise of Mr. Muraki and to present to him a gift of a silver plate with all their names upon it, mounted on wood and set in velvet. Mr. Muraki had been pleased enough, but he was very tired too, since he seldom went out of his own home, and he had been compelled to get up and bow a great many times, and also to make a speech of thanks in return.

In the afternoon at his own house, therefore, there were no guests, and since it was very hot, as though a storm were coming, Bunji had told the servants to draw back all the screens, so that though they sat under the roof, on all sides except one the great room was open to the garden, now full of a soft late sunshine. The children played together in the brook that ran near the house, and their elders sat and watched them quietly. Mr. Muraki smoked his pipe, and Shio sat smoothing his piece of jade, and Madame Muraki simply knelt in the still motionless way she did when nothing was wanted. Only Bunji came and went, bustling to see to a servant or to shout to a child.

I-wan, sitting beside Tama, was silent too, enjoying the hour and thinking of Mr. Muraki's life, which had been in a fashion spread before him in this day—a good and honorable life, spent in its own unchanging ways. He looked at the old man and wondered if now at seventy he was satisfied with what he had had. It was hard to believe that Mr. Muraki had ever wanted anything else.

It was exactly at the moment when Ganjiro slipped and fell into the water and burst into a loud cry that the noise in the street began. I-wan remembered that, for in the confusion of rushing to lift Ganjiro out of the water, it seemed that the child was making all the noise. But in a second Ganjiro's crying was lost in the shouting from outside the gate, and Bunji was roaring, "What is the matter—what is the matter?" And Shio was shrieking, "Is it an earthquake? Has anyone felt anything?" And Tama had come running out to I-wan and the children, and they all stood there together, waiting to feel the earth move beneath their feet.

But the earth did not move. Around them in the garden everything was as it had been, the water sliding over the rocks, the sun sinking, its long shadowy rays underneath the trees upon the moss-green ground. Then they saw the old gardener running to them, in his hand a newspaper, the great black letters scarcely dry upon it. Bunji seized it from his hand and they crowded around it. It was easy enough to read. In a moment they knew what had happened.

Three hundred Japanese—men, women, and children—had been killed by Chinese soldiers in a little town near Peking. . . . In revenge, the great headlines shouted, in barbarous revenge for the peaceful policing of Peking by Japanese soldiers!

No one spoke. No one looked at I-wan. They stood just as they had been standing when they were waiting for the earthquake. Even the children, catching the knowledge of disaster, were silent. In the silence the noise of the street seemed louder than it was, for a telephone began ringing in the house without stopping a second, and they could hear that. And in another moment a maidservant came to Bunji and bowed and said, "Sir, you are wanted. It is General Seki's office."

Bunji turned away without a word and went in and Setsu pattered after him. And then there was the stifled sound of a woman crying. It was Tama's little maid, sobbing into her sleeve.

"What is it, Miya?" Tama said to her sharply.

And the little maid blurted out, "My brother—he must be dead, too. He had a little meat shop there in China—where they have all been killed. But business was so bad here—there are so many shops like his—so, when the government said they would help him to have a shop in China, where he could get rich, my father told him to go."

She sobbed aloud, and Ganjiro, seeing her weep, howled in terror. I-wan took him in his arms. But he was too dazed to comfort the child. What did this mean? He had taken the paper from Bunji's hand and he read on. A colony of peaceful people massacred by Chinese trained and paid by Japanese to keep the peace!

"Give me the child," Tama said. "He is still crying."

He felt her take Ganjiro firmly away from him. And now Bunji was coming back, his face grave and cold. He did not look at I-wan. He came to his father, bowed, and said simply, "I am ordered at once to report for military duty."

He turned and went again into the house.

No one spoke. If Mr. Muraki would only speak, or Shio, then, I-wan thought, he could say what he must somehow say, "Surely there was a reason. We Chinese do not kill people for nothing."

We Chinese! A few moments ago he had been so closely knit into this family that he had not doubted he was one of them. But now, this silence—

"We must go home," Tama said in a strange voice.

And then they all began to move, to bow, to say farewell—only to say farewell. There was not a word of anything else. So, therefore, how could he begin to say, "We Chinese—"

He could only follow Tama and go with his sons and the red-eyed sniffling little maid, home through the twilighted streets. Everything was quiet again. People knew what had happened. They walked along talking of it, their faces grim, their voices low. Now and again there was a short rush of noise as a bus stopped, opened its door, and let out its crowds coming home from beaches and parks, those who had not heard.

I-wan, too, did not speak. He felt people's eyes picking him out from among all the others, noting him different, but he walked stolidly on, as though he saw nothing. Inwardly he was a confusion of shame and anger, but anger was the stronger. Now he wanted to cry out to them all, "Why do you play such injury and innocence? I tell you, we don't kill people for play!"

283

But he could not simply begin to shout this in the street to people who said nothing to him and who looked away when he stared back at them.

He strode along, therefore, filling the silence with his own angry thoughts, remembering all the wrongs which Japan had done. En-lan knew them all. It was En-lan who had told them to him, over and over. Even in those days they had not seemed real to him as they did to En-lan. That was because he had never lived in the north where En-lan was, and where the Japanese had pressed the hardest, and because, too, in his father's house he heard nothing. But now he remembered En-lan's passionate voice, saying again and again, "They want to swallow us up as they have Korea. Sooner or later we'll have to fight them." The Twenty-one Demands—how angry En-lan could get over them! And it was the Japanese, he always said, who brought in opium and made it cheap so that poor people could buy it. Every now and then En-lan used to work hard at boycotts against Japanese, and then shops would be ransacked and great bonfires piled up of Japanese goods in Shanghai streets. And sometimes En-lan had been half beside himself with rage because some cowering small shopkeeper tore the labels from his Japanese merchandise and swore it to be Chinese. But somehow, mysteriously, all boycotts came to an end. And at last everything had been lost in the greater rush of the oncoming revolution. And yet even then, I-wan remembered now, as one day he climbed the stone steps to a classroom, En-lan had kept saying in his ear, "Sooner or later, after the revolution, we must rid ourselves of the Japanese."

He wanted at least to tell Tama—to explain to Tama, indeed, above all—but she was very busy.

"Miya, you are to go home at once to your parents," she told the little maid. "I will do everything. Don't come tomorrow. Comfort your parents for a day or two."

284

And while the little maid went away, weeping gratefully, Tama hurried at undressing the children and bathing and feeding them and putting them to bed. And when I-wan would have helped she pushed him away, though gently.

"No, I-wan, go to your study and rest yourself. I can do this quite easily."

He heard her everywhere about the house as he sat in the darkness of his study. The light was no use to him when he wanted only to think, to argue the whole list of Japan's wrongs to his country. Tonight, when Tama would say to him, as she must once the house was quiet and they were alone together, "I-wan, tell me how such a thing could happen"—when she said this, he would say to her—

But she said nothing. She came in after a while and touched the button by the door so that the light poured on him.

"I-wan, why are you in the dark? Come, supper is ready."

She took his hand gently and led him away, and then all during the meal she talked, quickly and softly, not of that but only of her father and what she could remember of him when she was small and how good he was and wise.

"Even when he wanted you to marry old Seki?" I-wan put in, and wished he had not.

For she answered steadily, "Even that he did because he thought it was right."

She met his eyes and he thought, "What is the use of speech, if they make wrong right?"

No use—no use, he told himself, and kept his own silence, too.

He could not be sure whether people were the same or not. He watched everywhere for looks flung at him secretly, for coldnesses. But it was impossible to be sure, because of this long argument he was now continually making inside himself with no one and yet somehow with everyone—that is, with Japan. In his house he came and went as usual. He knew now that Tama would never speak. Whatever she thought—but after a few days he decided that she was not thinking, even. Well, then, he argued, was this, too, sincere, or had she simply determined not to think?

He saw Bunji no more. Bunji had gone that same night. I-wan waited to be told to take his place as he had before, but no message came from Shio or Mr. Muraki. Bunji's office remained empty, and in his own office I-wan worked exactly as he had. But there was now a great deal more work. The shipments of goods had increased again enormously. But most of them were not unpacked now in Nagasaki. They were shipped straight on to Shio in Yokohama and I-wan knew of it only because of Shio's reports and descriptions which had to be checked and filed and catalogued. Peking, he read again and again, goods from Peking. Loot, he thought grimly, what else but loot which Mr. Muraki was buying and selling?

And yet there was nothing but the same silence about him. He could not be sure that there was any other change. The two girls on the other side of the partition were as courteous and quick to answer his call, and if he bought something the clerks in the shops were as submissive and eager as ever. No, but there was a change. People did not speak to him as easily as they used to speak in greeting or in the small talk of everyday. He felt stifled and smothered in silence, as though he were surrounded by darkness. Or was this his imagination, too, and was it simply that people were grave with their fears, and talked less gaily to each other?

He could not tell. And yet in this silence all his life faded into unreality. The tangible things which he had made for himself, his home and his marriage, his children and his place in the world, escaped him. The only reality now became this long constant argument in himself with Japan. For when he argued he seemed to see opposing him not Tama or Bunji or any Japanese, but a vague unknown Japan. He could not connect with that Japan this pretty city in which he lived, or these green hills and the islanded sea whose beauty he endlessly enjoyed.

And in his house Tama was more careful than ever for his comfort. Without planning it so, they now went out no more. One day he said, "Shall we take the children to the park?"

She shook her head. "They are quite happy at home," she replied. "Why should we trouble to take them?"

She smiled at him. But after she had left the room it occurred to him, "Does she suffer among her own people because she is married to me?"

He could not ask her. If she did so suffer, if he knew it, then the very rock under his life would be shaken.

Outside his window he heard Jiro's high sweet voice demanding, "Why does Miya cry, Mother? When you don't see her, she is always crying and crying."

He heard Tama's quiet voice. "Her brother has been killed, Jiro."

"Who killed him, Mother?" Jiro's voice was lively with fresh interest.

"Chinese soldiers, in China," Tama replied.

"Then they are bad!" Jiro's voice came full of indignation.

And hearing it, I-wan was angry with Tama. Why could she not have said simply, "The man is dead!"? He leaned from his window and saw her watering plants in the garden and beside her was Jiro with his own small watering pot.

"Tama!" he said severely. "How can the child understand!"

At his voice she looked up, and he felt her look, long and sorrowful, fixed upon him. Instantly she became real for him. He wanted to explain to her— But now Jiro was watching a yellow

287

and brown butterfly hovering over the wet flowers. The child had forgotten.

He sat down again to his book. But he must explain to Tama tonight—only, explain what? Three hundred innocent people dead—that she knew and would not forget. To anything he said she would, in silence, hold that answer. He sat, not reading, his book in his hand. In Shanghai, he remembered, there used to be a great many Japanese. No one paid any heed to them—there were all sorts of people in Shanghai, people of every nation. And yet somehow it seemed to him that he remembered the Japanese now more clearly than any others because they were so wholly themselves. They remained as they had come, Japanese. And wherever they lived, the houses they made and the gardens they made became bits of Japan, as though they so loved their own country that wherever they were they must still be there. . . . And yet, he knew his own people. They did not kill for play. The Japanese had done something—something new, to make them so angry. This he must tell Tama. He sat, thinking how to tell her.

And then she called to him to come into the garden, and he went out. The children were in bed and Miya had gone home. They were quite alone and together they walked up and down the sanded path which Mr. Muraki had put at the edge of the garden toward the sea. They looked out over the night-dark sea. This now was the time when he must speak. He must speak, but first he must break down her silence—by something, by anything.

"Were the children good today?" he asked her.

"Very good," she replied tranquilly.

"I hope you understand why I spoke as I did about Jiro," he went on.

"Oh yes," she said quickly, and added, "but children don't remember."

Was there more in these words than she meant him to know? He tried to see her face, but all its outlines were lost in the dusk. He saw only a whiteness under her black hair. He must go on, then.

"You know, Tama, I feel so strongly—we must wait until we have the whole truth. I have written to my father, and I, myself, feel I will not decide until his letter comes."

"Decide?" Her white face turned to him quickly.

"I mean, judge," he said.

She turned her face toward the sea again without answering.

"You know this, Tama," he insisted. And when still she did not answer he grew angry.

"Tama!" he cried.

Then at last she spoke.

"What has it to do with us?" she said.

No, but she was evading him. Inside herself she was thinking, feeling, he was sure of it—perhaps against him. He must reach her.

"I must feel you think there may have been cause," he maintained.

And now she replied instantly, as though this answer had long been ready.

"What does it matter what I think when I am your wife?"

No, but this was what any Japanese wife might say. It was retreat—retreat from him, what else?

"Don't be a—a Japanese woman!" he shouted.

Her voice came through the darkness.

"But I *am* a Japanese woman!"

Her voice was gentle with all its usual sweetness, and yet he felt her there at his side as unyielding and as inexorable, as impenetrable as the very night itself.

"The truth is you have already made up your mind," he said

289

roughly. He must beat against her somehow—somehow break her to pieces! "You believe, without any reason, that my people could simply massacre like savages—you don't know us. If you think that, you have no understanding of me. We have suffered for years while you Japanese have been stealing our land, our trade—" He was being unjust enough himself, making her stand for Japan. But, having begun to talk aloud at last, he could not stop. "No, I know what happened. Our soldiers, when they saw Peking captured—and under an enemy flag—they could not bear it after everything else. We've held ourselves back all these years—"

She flew at him. She was shaking his arm.

"And who," she demanded, "killed Japanese in Nanking on March the twenty-seventh, in nineteen hundred and twenty-seven, and who killed Japanese in Shanghai in nineteen hundred and thirty-two?"

"You have held it all these years—against me!" he cried.

But she shook her head.

"No—but against your people!"

"But I am they—to you!" He was angry enough to kill her, he thought—and then he remembered that a moment ago he had made her stand for Japan. Her voice reached toward him sadly.

"Am I to you—one of those—who ought to be killed?"

There was nothing of the Japanese about her now. They were two people speaking across the infinite difference of race. And then suddenly he felt her rush into his arms. Her arms were about his neck and she was sobbing on his shoulder. She was broken, at last. But he felt no triumph. She had broken without yielding.

"Hush—you will waken the children," he whispered. In the stillness of the garden her weeping was loud, and Jiro woke easily. And how could they explain to him this weeping, he thought sadly. In himself he felt weak and tired, now that anger had flown. He smoothed her head.

"You are right," he said. "The truth—whatever it is—has nothing to do with us."

He clung to her and felt her cling to him, closer and more close, in fierce determined love.

. . . And yet, though each desired above all this union, in the midst of their passion in the night before they slept, his desire died. He wanted her—and then could not take her. She waited a moment. Then she whispered, "What is it?"

He could not answer because he did not know. He lay, himself surprised, and said nothing at all, his arms still about her. He was helpless and ashamed—but speechless. And after a little while, without pressing him, she withdrew herself and straightened her garments and arranged herself for sleep.

Did she sleep? He could not tell, since she was able to lie so still, sleeping or awake. He lay, touching her shoulder and thigh and foot. They were so close. Were they not close here in their own house? She moved toward him a little and he felt her hands take his hand and hold it to her bosom. And with her touch he knew. Her flesh, her sweet and intimate flesh, was changed to him. No, it was he who had changed. Tenderness poured into him, but there was no final desire. And in the very way she held his hand, so tenderly, too tenderly, he knew that she too had felt the same death strike across her heart. She too now wanted no more children. Out of the past something long dead had reached out, the will of their ancestors, and had pulled them apart.

"Ganjiro has a cold," Tama said to him next day. "I had better stay by him tonight."

She was moving her sleeping things out of his room into the room where Ganjiro now slept with his older brother. Tonight, she said—but he knew she meant every night. There could be no more passion between them.

But he only said, "Is he feverish?"

"A little," Tama replied.

He took her wooden pillow into the other room and her mirror and the tiny chest of drawers which held the combs and pins for her hairdressing. He would never be angry again with her, he knew. All day long she had been so pitifully kind, so tender that his heart ached. For he knew that such tenderness was a chasm between them. There was no way to bridge it, to find each other's real being. Whatever happened now, their tenderness would not fail. They were caught and held in it as in an amber.

He grew, as days went on, increasingly lonely. Sometimes he imagined that even Jiro and the little one drew away from him as though they disliked him. Then he told himself this could not be. It was simply that he was too solemn. But indeed his life he found more difficult every day. There had been not one letter from his father or from I-ko. Impossible to believe that I-ko at least had not written! He did not want to read the newspapers because he did not believe them. And yet if he did not read them he heard nothing.

One morning when he went to work he had been sent for to Bunji's office and there at Bunji's desk sat a young man whom instantly he knew he hated.

"I am Mr. Hideyoshi," the young man announced briskly. "I am promoted from submanager in the Yokohama office to this post." He grinned. "Unfortunately my eyes are bad, or I should be fighting for my country in China. . . . Sit down."

He motioned to a chair and I-wan bowed slightly and sat down. Last time Bunji went away it was he who had been manager. But Shio had sent this man to work here—perhaps to watch him.

"Have you seen the paper this morning?" Mr. Hideyoshi burst into loud laughter.

"No, I have not," I-wan said quietly. He was already full of hatred against this man.

"Read it, then!" The man flung the paper toward him. "It is really too funny."

I-wan looked at the front page. There was a great deal about—why, about Shanghai! He had not looked at the papers for several days. No, but what were the Japanese doing now in Shanghai? He read hastily down the column. What was this? Laughter, laughter because of a mistake—

"The Chinese Help Japan!" he read. "Chinese Aviator Bombs Shanghai!" Laughter—laughter—down the page he followed hideous laughter! A young Chinese aviator had mistaken his aim upon a Japanese target and had dropped his bombs into a crowded street. "Hundreds of People Killed—"

No, but this was some Japanese trick! He read racing on—no, it was true—incredible, shameful, true. Here were the details, too true to be disbelieved. He knew the street. He had been upon it more times than he could count, and it was always full of people surging about the shops, buying, or simply staring at the show. . . . Here was the picture of it now, badly printed on the cheap Japanese paper, but still to be recognized, though the walls were fallen into twisted steel and crushed concrete, and bodies hung where they were caught.

He looked up to see Hideyoshi's laughing face.

"Hah, you are reading about it! Terrible—but still very funny!" He laughed again. "To drop bombs on their own people—it's funny, is it not?"

I-wan choked.

"It's not true," he muttered. "Some mistake—"

"No mistake," Hideyoshi said briskly. "Every paper has the

same story. Everybody is laughing. It is as good as a Japanese victory. Now the English and Americans will see how foolish the Chinese are. The Chinese are so kind—they help their enemies and kill their own people!"

"Then you admit the Japanese are killing the Chinese?" I-wan demanded.

"We can no longer endure their insults," Mr. Hideyoshi replied, pursing his lips. "You must know that we have been very patient. Boycotts, prejudices, attacks from mobs, assassinations unpunished—we have endured all these for years at the hands of the Chinese. Now our Emperor is determined to put an end to Chinese animosity. We shall fight until all anti-Japanese feeling is stamped out and the Chinese are ready to co-operate with us."

I-wan stared at him, not believing what he heard.

"You mean," he repeated, "you will kill us and bomb our cities—and—and—rape our women—until we learn to love you?"

Now it was he who burst into loud laughter. He could not control his laughter.

"I am to love you, you say! Mr. Hideyoshi, I must love you, because you—you—"

Mr. Hideyoshi looked bewildered. "Not you as an individual," he broke in. "Besides, we look upon you as a Japanese. You have been here so long and you are married to a Japanese lady—"

I-wan's laughter stopped as though it had been chopped off.

"What's the matter?" Mr. Hideyoshi asked, seeing his face.

"Nothing," I-wan answered. "I see—all in a moment—there's nothing to laugh at." He bowed quickly and went back to his own office and sat down. He felt choked again and his head began to throb with the old pain. He pulled out a drawer and drew forth some folders and pretended to begin work. But he could do nothing.

"We look upon you as a Japanese," Mr. Hideyoshi had said. Once En-lan had written down, in the way he had of writing down everything, a history of what Japan had done in China. It was a long list, reaching back, I-wan now remembered, into his grandfather's time. There were forced concessions of land and trade, there were loans made to bandit warlords in the name of government for securities of valuable mines, there was the seizure of Kiaochow and the Twenty-one Demands. He had been a little boy when he himself could first remember, but his nurse had taken him out to see the parades then made against Japan. The flags, he remembered, were beautiful, but he had been frightened at a great poster showing a large cruel Japanese swallowing many small and helpless Chinese, and he had cried so that his nurse took him home again. But for a night or two he had had bad dreams and had screamed himself awake, so that they had let Peony move a little bamboo bed into his room and sleep near him. How therefore could he be a Japanese now? Tama had not touched really that inner self which was he. . . . No, Tama and everyone else now remained outside of him.

Two days later there was fresh news in the papers. Mr. Hideyoshi put his head in the door of I-wan's office.

"We are doing our own bombing in Shanghai now," he remarked, all his teeth glistening in a grin. "Did you see the *Osaka Mainichi* today?"

I-wan stared at him steadily without answering. He wanted to kill this man. This man he wanted to smash, to crush, as one crushed a beetle! Mr. Hideyoshi, seeing his look, shut the door hastily.

And yet it was not hatred which brought I-wan at last to that moment when suddenly, as clearly and simply as though he had been told, he knew what he had to do. It was something deeper in him than hatred could ever be.

295

Seven days after this was a day when a ship came in from China, and it was I-wan's duty to meet it and receive into the customs warehouse on the jetty the merchandise it brought for the house of Muraki. It was a strange sight he saw as he stood watching the unloading of that ship. The carefully packed crates of goods marked Muraki were as nothing compared to other goods being set down upon the docks. These were not curios and fine things, but the common things which people use every day. They were, for the most part, unpacked, as though they had been put hastily upon the ship, and if there was now and then a heavy old desk or a carved chair, there were to be seen far more often beds and tables and stoves of foreign metals and shapes, pianos and pictures and bedding and electric refrigerators, music boxes and carpets and cushions and velvet curtains and all such things as well-to-do Chinese delighted to have in their homes in Shanghai, such things, indeed, as might easily have come out of his own father's house. He looked at the stuff, half expecting to see something he knew, but he did not. And for everything there was someone to expect it and claim it.

"Now I know there is real war," he thought grimly. "This is loot and nothing else. These things have been in people's homes."

And yet in the midst of his rising fury he was stopped. For there was something else on this ship, too. When all else had been unloaded, and he stayed in his anger to see it all, he saw many small wooden boxes begin to be brought off. Each had a name written in letters upon its top. And these, too, were expected. A man stood to call each name, and as he called, a little group of persons came forward and received a box and all of these people were in deepest mourning. And instantly I-wan knew that the boxes held the ashes of those who had been killed in battle.

He had somehow thought only of Chinese being killed. Now

he knew how foolish he was. These people, too, must suffer. He stood, watching and silent, as each small box was received preciously and carried away. There was no sound of loud weeping. People even smiled as they received their dead. They had been taught to smile when those they loved died in battle. But down their faces their tears streamed.

He stood, forgetting who he was, pressing nearer and nearer, until now he became aware that he was so close that the eyes of many fell upon him as they wept. They must have known him for what he was, a Chinese, and yet their looks were not of hatred but only of pure sorrow. And he fell back a little when he saw this. It could not have been so in his own country, he thought unwillingly. No, his people were not so disciplined to sorrow as these. Their sorrow would have overflowed into wailing and cursing.

He moved back again, half ashamed, and knocked against an old man standing alone, a box wrapped in his arms as though it were his child. And I-wan, looking inadvertently into his eyes, saw such patient sorrow that he could not but stammer something about his wonder that there was such patience and no sign of hatred. And to this the old man answered gently, "Why should we hate you? You had nothing to do with this. And besides, our people are taught to suffer gladly for our country." The tears burst from his eyes as he said this, but he only clutched the box more firmly and said, his old voice shaking, "Yes—I rejoice— my only son—"

And this old man uttering these words brought light to I-wan. The dusk, the silence, in which he had been living broke and was gone. He was at that instant recalled to his old self. Yes, to that old self which had been he in the days when he dreamed of his country and lived to make her what he dreamed. How these people loved their country! The love of country which he saw shining in this old man's face—it was the most beautiful love in the world. How small and selfish was the love of one creature for another! There was a love infinitely larger, a love into which he wanted to throw his whole self. Had he not known such love?

. . . "I-wan, you are like a priest," Peony had said. . . . He longed suddenly to lose himself and all his doubts in great sacrifice. He had never been so happy, he now thought, as he had been in those old days with En-lan—no, not even with Tama, and with all her ministering to him. He was one who was happiest when he ministered. This was his nature, only he had not known it. It had taken the suffering of other people to show it to him. In his own country how many suffered now!

He turned, and the old man went away. But I-wan did not need him any more. He had done his work. Fate, that strange fate in which Tama always believed, had used him for the necessary moment, and had then dismissed him. I-wan, without thinking of him again, went back to the goods in the customs house. But all the time while he listened to the demands of the customs officers, while he watched clerks open the crates, and while he checked one paper after another, his mind and his heart were asking:

"How shall I tell Tama?"

At first, on his way home, he thought that he would simply go without telling her. He would write it all down in a letter for her to read when he was gone. Then he could explain to her in his own language, the written language which was hers also.

He had almost persuaded himself to this when he stepped into his house. Usually she was there waiting for him in the garden or at the door. But tonight she was delayed. He was already inside, taking off his shoes, when she came running out of the kitchen, pushing back her hair as she came.

"Oh, I am so late!" she cried. "Well, I was making something you like, and it took me such a long time."

When she came running up to him, her wide eyes frank and her face rosy, he knew he could never go away without telling her. And yet if he waited his heart would fail him. In the rush of the moment he seized her shoulders and began to speak.

"Tama, I must go home—I am needed there."

He said it very quietly, so that he would not startle her, but her body grew still and stiff under his hands and the blood fled from her face. She did not say, "Let me go, too." No, she knew now that he meant he must go alone.

He hurried on. "I have been miserable all these days. I haven't known what to do."

"I knew what you were thinking," she said. Her voice was so small he could scarcely hear it.

"But you didn't tell me," he retorted. "I thought you didn't know."

"I didn't want—I was so afraid—you might think it your—duty—to leave us," she faltered. Her lips were trembling and he could not bear to see it. He pressed her face to his breast and laid his cheek on her hair.

"I didn't know what I ought to do until tonight," he said. "An old man holding a little box of ashes made me see how sweet and—right—it is to die for one's country." He was using old words. She had never heard them, but Miss Maitland had once made them memorize those words. En-lan had argued with her, saying, "One ought not to die for one's country, if the country is wrong. It is better to die for a cause."

And then Miss Maitland had seemed quite angry. She told them about a young Englishman who so loved England that he had said his dust would be forever England. En-lan had said no more, only smiled, unchanging.

But now, holding Tama in his arms, I-wan knew that Miss Maitland was right and En-lan was wrong. It made no difference whether one's country was right or wrong. He would never have believed he could go back and take a place under Chiang Kai-shek. But he could.

She nodded, and took up her wide sleeve and wiped her eyes.

"Of course you must go," she said simply, "if you think your country needs you."

She swallowed once or twice and wiped her eyes again. "As a Japanese, I understand that," she said.

He could feel her heart beating against him, denying the calmness of her words.

"You know—I am the same to you," he whispered.

She drew away from him.

"Oh yes," she said, "I know. This has nothing to do with us. We'll have to plan."

He could see her practical mind begin to work. But at the kitchen door Miya now appeared, in distress.

"Oku-san, now what shall I do?" she called. "It's boiling!"

"Oh!" Tama exclaimed. "We'll talk later," she told him. "After all, there's no use in letting the fish spoil."

She flew toward the kitchen door.

They talked long into the night, sitting with the screens drawn aside so that the garden lay before them and beyond it the sea. All the time Tama gazed out toward the sea. The night was not moon-lit. When their eyes grew used to the darkness, they could scarcely see even the outlines of the garden, though they had put out all the lights because of the summer moths. He could not see her face except to know it was turned away from him.

They sat on the mats, and he held her hand. It was warm and strong in his. She did not weep or protest anything. She had, he now perceived, been thinking for a long time about this, waiting for whatever must come. When he asked, "What do you think you and the children had better do?" she was quite ready.

"Of course we can always return to my own father's house. He is so fond of the children," she answered.

He had not thought of this. He had imagined their staying here until—but until when? Who knew the end of this war?

"It is doubtless the best thing," he agreed unwillingly. Jiro and Ganjiro growing up in Mr. Muraki's house! They would forget this little house he had built for them, where they had lived with him, their Chinese father.

"You will help them—to remember me?" he asked her.

He felt the hold of her hand strengthen.

"Shall I be an undutiful wife because misfortune has caught us?" she replied. She went on in a rush of energy. "Am I to blame you? You are not forsaking us. I shall tell them, 'Honor your brave father, who fights for his country!'—I-wan, may we spend a little money and have a big picture of you? I want a picture of you as you are now, before you go. Then I'll put it where the children will see it every day, and we'll keep flowers by it—" Her voice broke and she stopped and coughed.

"We will do it tomorrow," he promised.

He thought he felt her trembling, but then after a moment she said, her voice quite calm, "Shall you need a new bag, or is the one we have good enough?"

"I shall take very little," he said. "I shall be wearing uniform in a few days."

Now indeed she was trembling, but he knew her well enough, too, to know that she would thank him most if he said nothing to break her down. So he sat smoothing her hand a little and talking on and on.

"I suppose I had better take the next boat," he said quietly. "There is one in four days. That will give us time for everything. I must tell your father."

"Let me," she said in a smothered small voice. "Let us tell no one. I want these four days—as though you weren't going. After you have gone, I'll go and tell him."

He pondered this a moment. "It might seem ungrateful of me, Tama," he said.

"No," she repeated. "No, I will tell them. Let me have my way. He will understand—the one thing he will always understand in you is what you do now."

"He is very kind—" I-wan began, but Tama interrupted him.

"Any Japanese would understand it," she said proudly.

He would not pack his own bag until an hour before he had to go to the ship. The few days, each so long in passing, seemed nothing now that they were gone together. He had let them pass exactly as Tama wished, crossing her in nothing. Each day except the last he had worked as usual, saying nothing, but putting everything in order for the unknown who was to take his place. He had never loved this work of merchandising, and he did not mind leaving it. And yet it had bought him security and a place of his own. If he had wished, he could have stayed safely here always—if he had been able in himself to do it. But he was not able.

On the last day, because he knew Tama wished it, he went with her to pray at the Shinto temple on the hill. He had gone with her there sometimes before, but he would never enter the shrine with her.

"I cannot pray without belief," he always said, "and I do not believe."

So she had always gone in with the children alone. It had troubled him that she took the children in, but he had let it pass, remembering that when he was small he too had gone to temples with his own mother. But when he grew older he had followed his father, who believed in no gods.

"Gods are for women and ignorant people," his father always said. . . . And in the revolution En-lan had fought bitterly against priests and temples. He had not understood even then why En-lan was so bitter against a thing which to him mattered little.

"Religion enslaves men," En-lan said many times in a loud voice.

Well, I-wan had remembered this each time he waited for Tama outside the shrine, and he had wondered because here not only women and laboring people, but sober, wise-looking men in rich garments went into the shrine to pray. And at little wayside shrines men even stopped their motor cars and descended to bow and say their prayers. But still he could not believe in gods.

Yet to please Tama on this last day he stepped into the temple and stood before the inner shrine with her and the children and stood with them while they prayed. Even little Ganjiro knew how to pray, he saw, and was astonished. His two sons—would they grow up worshiping their mother's gods? And yet, how could he prevent this now?

"Let them," he thought suddenly, "if it makes them as good as she is."

For himself, he felt nothing even now except the precious closeness of Jiro's hand in his, and Ganjiro's arm hugging his leg.

And then was the end of the last day, and the next morning came, and then the last hour. He began to put a few clothes into the bag, his extra business suit, his sleeping garments, and some books, and then Tama came in with something in her arms, something silk and blue. He did not know what it was. She shook it out and he saw it was a Chinese robe he had once worn.

"You had this on the first time I saw you," she said, smiling so sadly he could not bear to see such smiling.

"I haven't worn it for years," he said.

"Now you may want it again," she replied.

She folded it carefully, sleeve to sleeve, and put it in his bag.

He felt her, as he had felt her all these four days, as close to him as his own body. He knew continually what she thought and what she wanted and how near she was at every moment to weeping. But he knew that she had set for herself the goal of not weeping until he was gone. She would smile at him while he was here and until he could see her face no more. And he helped her, for he knew if she failed in this she would be ashamed and suffer for it always, thinking she had not achieved the perfection of self-control she should for his sake. They had gone through the hours so close together, and yet they had not touched more than each the other's hand.

So it came to the last moment of all. In the harbor the ship's funnel was beginning to smoke. Its engines were being fired. The ship was to sail at noon.

"I must go now, Tama," he said quietly.

They had agreed three days ago that he would go alone and that the children were not to know. Only Tama knew. They went together, hand in hand, to the garden where the little boys played. They were making a dam of small stones across the narrow brook, and they did not look up. He could hear their voices, Jiro's commanding as it always did and Ganjiro's answering with questions.

For one moment he felt that he could not do what he had planned.

"I shall send for you and the children," he said to Tama. "As soon as I can do it, you shall all come."

But Tama shook her head.

"When shall we be wanted?" she said.

Her words, her voice, her quiet fatal eyes, recalled him and swept him out of this moment again into the vaster hour where their individual lives were now lost.

"I must go," he said quickly.

He seized her in his arms, pressed his cheek against hers, looked at her once, and in her face saw eternity between them.

He stepped upon the ship's deck and at the same instant the gangplank began to move upward.

"Another minute and you'd have been left, my fine feller," a rough American voice said, but he did not answer. He walked toward the stern of the ship where the second class was and found the number of his cabin. The small room was empty, but his cabinmate's luggage was already there, spread upon the lower berth. He flung his own bag into the upper berth and then went out. Doors were open along the corridor and everywhere he heard the unfamiliar sounds of his own tongue.

But he went up the stairs to the deck again and stood watching the hills. Now the ship was moving steadily away from the dock. In a few moments they would be leaving the harbor. He searched the slope of the hill nearest the sea. Yes, there it was, his little house—and the square of green softer than the surrounding green was the garden. And now he could see the spot of color that was Tama. He could not see her face, and yet he could feel her eyes straining to see him. A tiny spot of bright orange moved across the green to stand beside her. That was Jiro—his son.

And then suddenly, if he could have done it, I-wan would have leaped into the sea to rush back to them. That little house—there, it seemed to him at this moment, there was his true home where Tama stood. Why had he left her? What if he followed again what he had once followed before, a mirage which he had thought was his country? She would be weeping, now—he felt his throat thicken with tears.

"Hello," an American voice said.

He started a little and looked down into a square, pleasant, ugly face at his shoulder. It was not an American, but a Chinese, wearing, it is true, an American suit of dark blue striped with white. It was too big for him and he looked up cheerfully out of a bluish-white celluloid collar much too big.

"I'm in the laundry business in Seattle," the man said with a bright American smile. "I guess I'm your cabinmate—Cantonese, named Lim—Jackie—born in U. S. A. though—third generation —though my old granddad went back to Canton when he was sixty. I can't speak my own language. But I figure I can fight without talking. I'm going home to fight the Japs."

"So am I," I-wan said quickly.

The man held out his hand.

"Put it there," he said heartily. And I-wan felt a firm dexterous small hand seize his.

The mists of longing cleared from his brain. When he looked at the hillside again, he could see nothing. The ship had turned and was headed for the open sea.

PART THREE

III

H<small>E KNEW</small> the moment his feet felt the ground beneath them that this was not at all the country he had left. Still less was this the country which he and En-lan had dreamed of making in those days.

The Bund was crowded with distracted people rushing toward boats and docks. Rickshas rolled past him, piled high with cheap furniture and bedding. Men and women clutched their crying children and shouted at the sweating pullers as they ran. Motor cars loaded with trunks and lacquered boxes and fine carved furniture and satin-garbed people, silent and white-faced, rushed by. Farther away, toward the north of the city, there was a dark mass of something which was not cloud.

"Is there a fire?" he asked I-ko immediately, pointing to this mass.

He had sent a radio from the ship telling of his coming, and here was I-ko to meet him. He was glad I-ko was alone and that the German was not with him. I-ko stepped out of his father's great American car and was now standing very handsome in a new uniform of dark blue cloth. He turned to speak to the White Russian chauffeur, who answered with a sharp salute.

Then he answered I-wan's question. "You must grow used to that. There is a fire every hour somewhere," he said.

On the dock I-wan's cabinmate stood diffidently to one side. He had come out very cheerfully to tell I-wan good-by, since he went on to Hong Kong. I-wan had taken a great liking to this

309

strange little American-Chinese. But Jackie Lim, seeing I-ko in his magnificence, was now abashed. He seemed to shrink still further inside his garments.

"I-ko, this is Mr. Lim, from America, who is come back to fight," I-wan said.

Lim put his hand out at once. But I-ko, bowing slightly, pretended not to see it, and Jackie Lim put his hand in his pocket and giggled. Upon his flat nose a sweat broke out.

"Write to me, Lim," I-wan said, throwing an angry look at I-ko. "Tell me how you find your grandfather and let me know what regiment you join."

"Sure," Jackie said, grinning. "I'm not much of a hand at writing, but I guess I can do that."

They shook hands, and Jackie went back on board, and I-wan, stepping into the car, saw him staring earnestly at the shore, his face solemn.

"A good man," he told I-ko. "He's going home for the first time to see his old grandfather in Canton. Then he will enlist as a soldier, simply to fight."

I-ko must understand the heroic quality in this foolish-looking fellow. But I-ko only said impatiently, "There are plenty like him —too many! Fools, full of enthusiasm and nothing else! They have almost ruined us, I-wan—well-meaning fools! They've dropped bombs on our own men, and yesterday they bombed an American ship—oh, by accident, of course, thinking it was Japanese—as if we hadn't trouble enough, without having to read and answer American protests and paying thousands of dollars out in indemnities! I tell you, I haven't found any reason to be proud of being a Chinese since I came home!"

I-ko's handsome profile stared coldly ahead. Had his German wife, I-wan thought, helped to make him ashamed? I-ko leaned over and shut the glass partition behind the chauffeur, and went on. "The truth is, I-wan, the Japanese have beaten us on every point. In the air we can't cope with them. Our air force is nothing —rotten to the heart—and a woman at the head of it!" He gave a snort of laughter. "It's ridiculous! What other country has a woman at the head of the national air force? I don't care if it is the great Madame Chiang! What does she know about aviation? I'm glad to go to Canton."

"Are you going to Canton?" I-wan asked. There was, he perceived, a great deal that he did not know.

"Yes, we're all going, except Father. Frieda went three weeks ago. She disliked living here. Foreign women," I-ko said complacently, "are very sensitive." I-wan wanted to laugh. That woman sensitive! But he was glad he need not see her, at least. "As for me," I-ko was saying, "I am to take a post in Canton under General Pai—Chiang's orders. And it is not safe here any more for the old ones. I take them with me tonight, though of course they will not live with us. Frieda finds them difficult— as they are. I agree with her entirely."

The car stopped to let a stream of rickshas pass.

"I suppose these people are all running away," I-wan remarked. . . . If I-ko agreed with her there must have been trouble in his father's house. But he would not ask of that.

"No use staying to be bombed by both sides," I-ko returned.

They did not speak while the car swerved in and out among the crowded streets. I-ko asked him nothing, either, and I-wan had, he felt, nothing to tell I-ko. He sat in silence, thinking, and looking out of the window. This was much worse than he had imagined. They were passing through streets of charred and roofless buildings. He forgot the German woman.

"Tell me exactly what is happening," he said to I-ko.

I-ko shrugged his epaulets slightly. What sort of uniform

311

was this he wore, I-wan wondered. Not a common soldier's, certainly!

"Exactly what you see," I-ko said contemptuously. "People are running hither and thither and everything is going to ruin. There is no organization anywhere. Nothing is ready. Chiang sits up there in the capital at Nanking like a spider in the middle of a net. Only he catches no flies!" I-ko laughed harshly at his own words.

"But surely he plans something," I-wan said anxiously.

"I have seen no plans," I-ko replied. "When I left Germany I thought of course I was returning to an organized national army. What do I find? Hordes of untrained men, each separate horde obeying its own little head—no national conception of any kind! Obey? They don't even obey their own generals! There is no discipline. A band of men rush out on their own impulse to attack the Japanese army when it is not the time to attack, when nothing is ready at the rear to support such an attack, when it is a foolish waste of men and ammunition—then everybody gets excited and calls them heroes!"

I-ko's clear pale face grew suddenly flushed with pink.

"It seems strange to hear you speak of discipline," I-wan remarked.

"I've learned what it means," I-ko said shortly. He went on after a moment. "Of course the Japanese army's efficiency is simply because of its discipline. They learned from the Germans, too." And then after another moment he added again, "We'll not only never win—we've lost already."

I-wan said nothing. He knew perfectly what I-ko meant. He knew these people of his! It was true that they never believed the worst would happen. And if it did, they believed then that nothing could avert it. They had not prepared for this, he knew. But he would not believe they could lose.

312

Above them three planes suddenly appeared. I-ko shouted to the chauffeur through the speaking tube. The chauffeur drew up to the curb and waited. The planes began to swerve downward, roaring. And then I-wan saw for the first time bombs dropping. They shone long and silver in the sunshine as they drifted downward into the Chinese city. It was impossible to be afraid of them. And yet after each disappeared there was a second of silence, then explosion and a cloud of smoke and dust rose in the distance. The planes mounted again and flew west.

"Go on now," I-ko commanded the chauffeur.

They went on. Neither he nor I-ko spoke. How many people had been killed in these few minutes? Suddenly, before he could think, they were at the door he remembered so well. He went up the steps at I-ko's side feeling strange but somehow not afraid. He would have to see people dead, perhaps, before he could be afraid of bombs.

"Everything is in confusion," I-ko told him brusquely. He rang the bell. "The old lady is so nearly dead I doubt she lasts the trip," he added impatiently.

Then the door opened. And immediately I-wan smelled the old sickish sweetness of his grandmother's opium, and with it all memory rushed over him again. A maid stood at her open door, stirring the stuff in a small bowl with a tiny silver spoon. She stared at I-wan. She was not in the least like Peony, whose place she had taken, this high-cheeked, coarse-faced country girl. Peony! He had not thought of her even in coming home. But now it seemed she must be here with all else.

"Was anything ever heard of Peony?" he asked I-ko.

I-ko was taking off his jacket.

"No," he answered sneeringly. "That was gratitude, wasn't it? Treated like a daughter, almost, for all those years!"

"She earned what she had," I-wan said abruptly, remembering. He turned aside to his grandmother's room. "I'll go in here first," he said.

"She won't know you," I-ko answered, half-way upstairs. But I-wan went on.

No, his grandmother was long past knowing anything now. She lay in the bed, a shriveled nut of a human creature, her flesh brown wrinkled leather on her skeleton as small as a child's. She was blind, he saw. Her eyes were gray with cataracts. He called to her loudly.

"Grandmother, it is I—I-wan—come home again!"

But she could not hear him. He put out his hand and touched hers. It was cold and dry as a bird's claw. When she felt his touch she opened her blue lips and whined a wailing cry. He dropped her hand quickly, half frightened. Could human beings become this in their uselessness? And then he heard a footstep behind him and there was his father come to find him. He had grown stouter, I-wan saw instantly; his look was quieter and his hair almost white, but his face looked the same.

"Father!" he said.

"My son!" his father replied and grasped him by the elbows. "The best thing that could have happened! Only why have you not answered my letters these last months!"

"I had no letters!" I-wan exclaimed. "And I did write!"

His father stared at him and shook his head. "I do not understand Muraki anymore," he said. Then he let him go. "Well, you are here," he went on. "We shall need no more letters."

It was hard to find something to say to his father. There was so much to say.

"Your grandfather is waiting for you in his room," his father told him.

"Grandmother doesn't know me," I-wan replied. He wondered if his grandfather, too—

314

"You'll find him much as he was," his father said. "He is feeble, of course. But he is sitting there dressed in his best uniform and all his medals, ready to go six hours hence. He is full of advice on the subject of the Japanese." He stopped to laugh. "The last time I went to confer with Chiang Kai-shek in Nanking he sent a long plan of his, showing how in three months we could rid ourselves not only of the Japanese but of all foreigners!"

His father laughed again and then sighed, and they turned. The old woman began wailing as they left and Mr. Wu spoke to the servant sharply.

"Give her the stuff—get her quiet!"

"Yes—yes, sir," the girl stuttered, hurrying.

"There is nothing to be done with the old who are like that," his father said. They were going upstairs. "Waste—waste—" he muttered.

I-wan did not answer. He felt a change in his father. He was gentler and yet somehow stronger.

"How is my mother?" he asked.

"She is just getting up," his father replied. "She overslept herself—the bombing last night kept her awake. She is terrified when that begins." He stopped, his hand on the door of the old man's room. "By the way," he told I-wan, "when she says you are to go with her to Canton, do not say you will go. You are not to go. You are to stay here. Chiang Kai-shek has plans for you."

He listened to this, watching his father's face. Chiang Kai-shek, the man whom he had once to escape, who had perhaps killed En-lan! But everything was changed, so why not this?

"Very well," he told his father steadily, and they went in.

The old general sat by the window, the sun falling across his glittering breast.

315

"Ah, you've come!" he said to I-wan, exactly as though I-wan had left only yesterday.

"Yes, Grandfather," I-wan answered, smiling.

The old man trembled now with a slight palsy, so that all his medals jangled faintly. But he was as lordly as ever.

"Sit down, both of you," he ordered, and they sat down. The old man reached to a table and took up a small scroll which he unrolled.

"Now, as soon as I reach Canton," he went on pontifically, "I shall present my plans in person to Pai. The nut of the idea is this—let the Japanese have their way. They tell me ten thousand people have been killed in Shanghai. But I say there are millions of people here. So we have plenty left. Let the Japanese exhaust themselves. When they are exhausted, then we will invite them to return to their own country, not all at once, but so many each year. And, so that they will not lose face—for it is well to be courteous with the enemy—we will request the persons of other nations to return also, and since we will not be exhausted by fighting, we can, having saved all our resources, then use force if necessary!"

The old man gazed at them proudly. I-wan looked at his father. But he was looking at the old man with eyes tolerant and benign.

"What do you think of it, I-wan?" the old man demanded.

"It is perhaps a little hard on the people now being killed," I-wan said cautiously. How was it possible for generations to recede from each other to such distances!

"Nonsense!" his grandfather said loudly. "In the first place, they are already used to famine and to wars, though on a smaller scale. In the second place, even if every Japanese moved into our country we would only feel it as we might some extra flies. Our country is too vast to be conquered, especially by such a small one. And besides, our people can grow used to anything."

His voice was definite, as though he expected no answer. So I-wan gave him none.

The old man suddenly thought of something else.

"I've lost one of my medals," he said to his son. His voice was now wholly different. It was childishly complaining.

"Which one?" Mr. Wu inquired. He went to the velvet-lined case where the old general kept his medals hung upon hooks and opened it.

"It was the one I had made in gold plate," the old man said, "after the one the Italian ambassador wore—don't you remember? Why, it was less than ten years ago I had it made—it was one of my new ones! A servant has stolen it. He must be found and dismissed."

Mr. Wu did not answer. He thrust two fingers behind the velvet.

"Here it is," he said. "I feel it, but I can't get it."

"Let me," I-wan said. He rose and thrust his fingers down, which, being longer, could just catch the ribbon of the medal and bring it up.

"That's it—that's it!" the old man crowed. "Give it to me. This is its place—here by the one with the eagle. I was going to show it especially to Pai when I went south. It would be well if he copied it for his officers."

They left him, laughing, and then out in the hall a door opened, and here was I-wan's mother. She cried out when she saw him.

"I-wan, you are come!"

"Yes, Mother," he answered. He saw she had changed very much, being now very fat. Her small pretty features were almost entirely lost in her face. But she seized his hands and smelled them as she used to do when he was a child, and he thought of her as she had seemed to him then, beautiful and wise and far stronger than he. He used to run to her then and hide in her bosom. Now she was even a little repulsive to him. He had grown so far beyond her that he saw her from the terrible distance of his own maturity and knew that there was neither wisdom nor refuge in her any longer for him. It made him sad. Would Jiro some day feel so to him? . . . Only her voice was unchanged, sweet and rushing.

"Now, I-wan," she was saying, "do not unpack your trunks. You are to come on with us tonight to Canton. It is fearful here. We are bombed every day and every night. Your father will not come. I've cried and cried—but when did he ever hear me? So you are to come and be with me. I-ko—oh, I-ko is lost to me. Oh, that woman! But I must have someone. I can't take care of these two old things alone."

"You are taking all the servants except two," Mr. Wu reminded her.

"But servants must be looked after!" Madame Wu cried.

"I cannot go, Mother," I-wan said plainly. Much better to speak plainly and at once! "I came home to fight, Mother."

Her small underlip, still as red as a girl's, trembled.

"You are just like your father," she said, "so stubborn!"

She was about to weep, but at that moment a servant came out with her arms full of furs.

"Shall we take these, Mistress, or shall we leave them?"

"Surely we will be back by winter—leave them," Madame Wu said.

"Take them," Mr. Wu said.

"I haven't enough boxes," Madame Wu wailed.

"Buy what you need," Mr. Wu said.

"Oh—it's such worry," Madame Wu said distractedly. She turned back into her room, forgetting everything else.

I-wan turned to his father. "I think I will go to my own room now and refresh myself."

He wanted suddenly to be alone. His father nodded and he went on to his own door. And I-wan opened the door to the old familiar place.

It seemed at first as though Peony must be there. It had been strange not to see her anywhere about the rooms, and not to see her here was strangest of all. But there was no touch of her, anywhere. The windows stretched tall and bare, and there were no flowers in them. And on his table there was no pot of hot tea. Everything was clean enough, except for a surface of light dust. No one had come here this morning as Peony would have done to make all fresh before his coming. The bed, the books, the cushions on the chairs, everything had the still and unused look of a room long empty. It would be difficult, he felt, to make this room his own again—he had been so young when last he left it. He had thought once that he would leave it to be destroyed in the revolution. But it was still here—perhaps to be destroyed finally by a Japanese bomb! Who knew the end of such things? Not he, at least.

Then he remembered something else. Long ago En-lan had written his own story for him to read, and he had thrust it far into the back of this drawer, behind his copy books. He opened the drawer quickly and thrust in his hand. It was not there now. No one had touched the books or this drawer and it was full of dust. But the sheets of folded paper were gone. Someone had taken them. Was it in that way that they—the band—were discovered? He felt sweat begin to break out on his forehead. Had his father somehow—but his father never came into this room. And Peony only took care of his things. Surely it could not have been Peony—he sat down, feeling a little sick. Surely it could not have been Peony who had betrayed them all—Peony, whom he had told! He could not rid himself of this fear, once it had come to him. It kept him sleepless half the night though he told himself over and over again that whatever had happened was now finished.

In the evening it had rained, and all the way to the ship his mother had kept saying, "I prayed for rain. I paid the gods well for this rain!"

Yes, his father was changed. He had said nothing when she spoke of gods, though once he would have been impatient with her. They had all gone together to the boat and Mr. Wu had given tickets and money to I-ko. The house was very silent when they entered it again, and his father looked too tired to talk.

"We will have a quiet night since the clouds hide the moon," he told I-wan. "There will be no raids tonight—let us sleep while we can." He had gone to his room and I-wan to his.

But even after he was in the comfort of his own bed, I-wan had kept thinking of Peony—weighing and questioning what she could have done. If Peony had betrayed them, then he would be guilty of En-lan's death. And yet even now he could not but trust her, though no one knew her, not even he. But he had not forgotten her. Somehow he had kept her in his memory, though he had not thought of her, either, in all his years with Tama. . . . Yes, he had thought of her once. On his wedding night he had thought of Peony long enough to be glad that he had never loved her or allowed himself to receive her love. But this he could not tell Tama, and so to Tama he had never even mentioned Peony's name. And yet Peony was something to him, too—he did not know what—perhaps only the memory of a fragrance and nothing more. Nevertheless she was enough so that he wanted to know that she could not have betrayed En-lan.

At their breakfast he put it to his father, therefore, trying to speak calmly as though it were no great matter:

"I have often wondered how it was you found out about our band, years ago. It is so long gone that now I can ask."

"Chiang Kai-shek told me," his father replied.

"Chiang Kai-shek!" I-wan repeated, half stupefied. "How did he know?"

"He knows everything," his father said drily. "We had had much talk together in private during those days and in return for his promised rule of law and order and expulsion of the communists, I promised loans, as he should need them, of sums we agreed upon. Then one day he sent for me in great urgency. I went and he saw me alone. He showed me your name on a list of communists to be executed. I did not believe it—I swore it was a mistake—and he sent for a classmate of yours who, for a sum of money set as a trap, had given in a list of names—and yours was one."

"Was he named Peng Liu?" I-wan demanded eagerly.

"I don't know," his father said. He looked disgusted as he remembered. "He was a cringing yellow-faced boy who said his father kept a small shop."

"That was Peng Liu!" I-wan broke in. "So it was he! Where is he now?"

Then it was not Peony! It was not his fault now if En-lan were dead—

"Dead," his father said calmly. "He was given his money and then executed."

"But why executed if—" I-wan began.

"Chiang despises traitors," his father replied.

"How could he offer a bribe and then blame the man who takes it?" I-wan asked indignantly.

"He can," his father replied. "You have to understand that.

321

He is a hard man, but a true one. He uses everyone, and sweeps away those whom he cannot trust enough to use again."

"An opportunist!" I-wan retorted.

"All wise men are opportunists," his father replied. "It is only fools who will not change when times change. But within himself the man never changes."

His father leaned forward and tapped the table between them with his long fingernails.

"I-wan, I tell you he is the only one who will save us now from the Japanese. I tell you he will do it. He has made up his mind since he came back from Sian, and he will never cease until he has succeeded. See how he has driven back the communists! They are hidden in the farthest corner of the northwest. Year after year he drove them back, determined to bring the country under one rule."

"His own!" I-wan said scornfully.

"One rule," his father repeated sternly. "It was far better than to allow such a civil war as would have ruined us and left the country empty for the Japanese to come into and take."

"Do you mean," I-wan said slowly, "that as long ago as that—ten years ago—he foresaw this day and began to unite the country for it?"

He had forgotten all about Peony now. He was thinking only of this man whom he had hated with such sobbing passionate bitterness on that day, the man whom he had always in his heart called traitor because he betrayed the revolution. But now, what if indeed he had seen more than any of them?

His father was nodding his head.

"I believe he sees everything," he said, "and that he can do anything. He is a very great man."

But he could not somehow so easily accept what his father

said. He remembered certain things which he had read in Japanese newspapers.

"His opportunism led him in evil ways sometimes," he said.

"That was before he was what he is now," his father retorted. "The test of a man's greatness is in whether he can see the evil in his own ways and change."

"He would be really nothing but a warlord in other times," I-wan broke in. "He has the mind and the ways of a warlord. He always settles everything by force."

"He settles it, though," his father said equably.

"And then all his wives—" I-wan began.

He looked up from his bowl to feel his father's eyes on him somewhat coldly.

"I shall not discuss that with you," he said with dignity. "What woman a man chooses is his own business. When your brother came home with—Frieda—your mother cried until I had to call in doctors. She moaned that we should have married I-ko by force before he went away. I told her the principle we chose was right. That our son is a fool has nothing to do with it."

He paused, frowning. I-wan saw him tolerating grimly the white woman in his house. His father looked up and caught his eyes.

"How is it with your Japanese wife?" he asked kindly. "I have said nothing of her. Japanese women make excellent wives. They know their place. I did not mind when you married her. And this war really has nothing to do with such things. Only stupid and ignorant persons would confuse a human relationship with a matter of state."

He was so grateful for his father's kindness that he wanted to tell him everything about Tama.

"She is so good," he said. "I never saw such a good woman—

323

careful in everything she does. I can't think of her as Japanese —to me she is only herself, the mother of my sons."

"Yes—yes," his father mused, as though he were thinking about something else. "Well now, how shall you write to each other? It will be difficult if it is known you receive Japanese letters. But at my office, naturally it will not be noticed. Tell her to address them to me. And you send your letters to me and I will send them on to her. In these times when the young are suspicious and easily angered, you might be assassinated if it were thought you sent and received such letters."

He had not thought of this. "Thank you, Father," he said. "But is it dangerous for you?"

"Oh, they all know me. I'm safe enough," his father said. "Besides, no one dares to kill me. Chiang would make trouble. And everybody is afraid of him."

They were back to this man again.

"Marriage—" his father was saying positively, "well, his old wives were no use to him so he took a new one who could be of use. Not all have the courage for it!" He laughed silently and drank what was left of his tea and drew a letter from his inner pocket. "Let me see," he said, scanning it, "two days from now you are to meet him. These are his orders."

His father said these words, "his orders," with such pleasure that rebellion stirred once more in I-wan.

"You are surely very changed," he said with a little malice. "Have I not heard that Chiang believes in a god—the Christian God? If he is sincere in it, how can you trust him?"

A slow smile spread upon his father's square face.

"Oh, he is always sincere," he said.

And then I-wan, for the first time in his life, heard his father make a joke.

"He is doubtless using the Christians' God, too," he said. "He is such a man!"

He stood for the first time before this man who had once cut off his life and had exiled him, in a fashion, to another world. Yet it was he who now called him back again.

He had never been in any presence so potent, not even in En-lan's. Had he lived, En-lan might one day have been as strong, as controlled, as full of disciplined power as this man now was. But in I-wan's memory he lived as a hot-hearted boy.

"Sit down," Chiang Kai-shek said.

He sat down upon one of the three straight-backed chairs in the room and waited. She had told him—this man's beautiful, foreign-looking wife, who had been the one to meet him first— that he spoke no other language than his own.

"Be prepared, please," she told him, her voice so much softer than her handsome face, "do not use any English words. There are many young men who find their own language not enough and they put in English words and it makes him very angry. He always says, 'What—isn't Chinese enough for them?'" She had smiled a very little.

"I will be careful" he had answered.

How, he thought now, waiting, did this man feel toward his wife? She wore Chinese dress and her black hair was brushed smoothly back into an old-fashioned knot. But even in the few moments she had talked, I-wan had perceived that in a hundred ways she was not Chinese. Her big black eyes shone and sparkled, her soft voice was frank, and all her movements, though graceful and controlled, were free. She was a woman who would do as she liked. I-ko had laughed because she was the head of the nation's air force. But she could be the head of anything— except, perhaps, of this man!

325

Chiang Kai-shek lifted his eyes and stared at I-wan. He had been reading a long document, which he had then signed and sealed. When his eyes were downcast, one said his mouth was the strength of his face, a mouth beautiful by nature and stern by will. But when one saw the eyes one forgot the mouth. This straight black gaze commanded attention.

"Your father is my friend," Chiang said. I-wan bowed a little and met these eyes fully and waited. They did not waver. "I have this letter," Chiang went on, his voice very quiet and somewhat cold. "It is of the greatest importance. This must be delivered to a certain officer in the communist army in the Northwest and from his hand into the hand of the other two generals in command of that army."

"I understand that," I-wan replied. But then he understood nothing else. Why should Chiang be sending documents to the men he had been pursuing so bitterly that many of them were dead because of him and the others driven into that corner of the Northwest? There was no time to wonder. He must listen. This man would never repeat, never explain, never say one word too much. Therefore not one word was to be lost.

"I choose you because your father promises me you are to be trusted. But if you are not, you will suffer as any other traitor does. He understands that. So must you. A plane is ready for you. You are to leave at once."

"One moment, Excellency," I-wan said. "Am I to bring back an answer?"

"The plane will wait to bring you back," Chiang replied. He struck a bell on the desk. The door opened at the sound.

I-wan rose and as by instinct saluted, the old stiff salute his German tutor had given him.

"You've had military training?" Chiang asked sharply. "I thought only your brother had been abroad."

"I have been only in Japan," I-wan said.

"Military training there?" Chiang asked again.

"No—it was before that," I-wan replied.

Chiang banged the bell with the flat of his hand and the door shut again. I-wan remained standing before him.

"They tell me Japan is on the edge of a collapse," he said abruptly. "Is it true?"

"No," I-wan replied. "It is not true."

"Business is good?" Chiang asked sharply.

"Yes," I-wan replied, remembering the busy Japanese streets.

"I am told the people do not want war—is that true?" Chiang prodded him with his brilliant eyes.

I-wan replied steadily, "The people want whatever they are told to want."

"They are loyal to their government?"

"Completely."

"Do they still worship their Emperor?"

"Yes."

Chiang stirred and sighed and for the first time moved his eyes from I-wan's. He picked up his jade seal and looked at it.

"Then they've been lying to me—the people around me," he remarked. "It will be a long war."

"It must be a long war," I-wan replied. And then remembering Hideyoshi, he added, "It will be our strength if we realize it from the first and plan for it. The enemy"—that was Hideyoshi—not Tama and his little sons, who belonged to him alone—"the enemy think it will be a short war."

Chiang's eyes shot at him again.

"Do they? How long?"

"They said at first three months—now, a year," I-wan replied. "But I think it will be many years," he added. Outside he heard the drone of an airplane's engine. But Chiang still held him.

327

"That means—we must plan our war after theirs is finished," he said. He was looking at the seal again. I-wan did not answer. "That means let them spend while we save. That means save what is essential to our national life—not cities, not people. We have those to spare."

I-wan, waiting, caught these words, "Not cities, not people." These were not to be saved. There was something else. Was there, then, a way to fight a war and seeming to lose, yet win?

The door opened and Madame Chiang was there.

"The plane is waiting," she told her husband. "Had he not better go now so that the landing will not be in darkness?"

"Yes—go," Chiang commanded him. And whatever he meant was left unsaid.

Flying over the handful of islands which was Japan had been nothing like this. He felt proudly that such a country as this was security against any victory. Hour after hour they drove across the sky over the solid mainland of China. Here was a country! They sank to follow a thousand miles of broad yellow river flowing through green lands and pallid deserts, they rose to scale ranges of mountains whose crests were barren in cold. Impassable country! Once he had been ashamed when he read in a Japanese newspaper that there were no good roads beyond the seacoast in China—"a backward country," it said, "which the Chinese have done nothing to develop." Yes, so backward that there were no roads now by which an enemy could enter! There was only the sky that was open. Through the sky alone was the passage to be had. And yet, how could even bombs from the sky destroy a country as vast as this!

He remembered something. In the two days before he left for Nanking he had gone with his father over the whole city of Shanghai to see what had befallen it. Devastation enough, he

328

had thought. In increasing silence and desperation they had gone from one place to another, seeing ruins everywhere. But on the edge of the city they found a farmer planting green cabbages, squatting calmly on his heels as he worked. His house was gone. A shed of mats rudely put together told that. They had stopped a moment to watch him, and then because something needed to be said in greeting, his father said, "It is too bad that your house is gone, too."

The farmer looked up and grinned and wiped his face with the blue cotton scarf across his shoulders. He pointed his chin toward a deep hole at the edge of the field. It was full of water. "That's where it was," he told them cheerfully. "A good house my great-grandfather built! But never mind—none of us were killed. We were all out working. And as I told my wife when we saw the water coming up into it, 'Well, we always wanted a pond and now we have it!' "

He roared out a laugh, and they had laughed too, and had gone home somehow cheered. Ruins had lost their meaning. He thought of it again and again.

All day the plane roared across the sky. The pilot was a young American, with whom I-wan had had no chance to talk. Madame Chiang had introduced them quickly, as the plane was ready to take off. "This is Denny MacGurk, Mr. Wu."

"Pleased to meet you," the American had said and had swung into his seat. And then Madame Chiang had handed them each a little bag.

"Your noon meal," she told them.

He had not thought of its being noon until he saw Denny MacGurk eating with one hand while he steered. Then he opened the bag. Ham between layers of foreign bread, a brown creamy foreign sweet, and an apple—he had never eaten this food, but high up in the cold clear air it was good. MacGurk turned and nodded at him and shouted something which the wind tore to pieces before he could catch it, but he nodded as though he had heard. Why, he wondered, should this American boy be here, driving a plane for a Chinese general? But he had heard it said often enough in the Muraki business that none could understand Americans.

And so he sat through the long afternoon until dusk, when the plane drifted down an aisle of cloud into a valley and dropped into a shaven field outside a village. Instantly it was surrounded by soldiers and then by a staring, pushing crowd of children and villagers. MacGurk leaped out, and I-wan, behind him, clambered out of his seat.

"We'll sleep here and start at dawn and finish the trip after noon," MacGurk said. Then he said in the pleasantest voice, "Say, tell these tin soldiers it's their high monkey-monk's plane, will you, and that I'll lick the guts out of any of 'em that touches it? Tell 'em to watch the kids." He locked up as much as he could, and I-wan, translating, told the soldiers, "It is the Generalissimo's plane on official business, and it rests on your bodies tonight."

"Yes!" they shouted, saluting, and as he followed MacGurk he heard them roaring at the awed crowd, "Put your fingers on it and see what falls upon you, you children of turtles! Your mother! Breathe on it even, and see what happens!"

"I guess it's safe," MacGurk said, grinning. "Gosh, but I'm stiff! And there'll be only a board to sleep on tonight," he grumbled, "and nothing but noodles to eat. Oh hell, if there aren't too many lice, I guess I can sleep on anything!"

I-wan did not answer. He tried to smile, but it seemed somehow his fault that there was nothing but a country inn here.

"Ever been in the U. S. A.?" MacGurk asked abruptly as they

330

walked along, side by side. Under their feet clouds of dust rose and spread, dry and alkaline, into their nostrils.

"No, I never have," I-wan said, and added diffidently, "It must be a very pleasant country."

"God's own," MacGurk said fervently, and then gave I-wan a great grin. "Why in the heck I can't stay in it, I don't know. But every time I go home I hanker to get away from it. I'm the damnedest—"

They laughed and marched through the deep cool gate of the earthen wall around the village. At their heels followed a procession of staring children and idle people. But MacGurk seemed used to them. He strode on into the doorway of an inn and then into a courtyard. The innkeeper rushed out to meet him, chattering with pleasure, and, seizing his hand, shook it up and down.

"Hello, you old son-of-a-gun," MacGurk greeted him, and turned to I-wan. "I don't understand a word he jabbers at me every time, but I've taught him to shake hands like a white man. It kind of makes me feel at home when I drop in here to spend the night."

But to I-wan the innkeeper was bowing again and again.

"Come in, my lord, come in and drink tea, and wash yourselves and rest."

He looked at I-wan and seemed ashamed.

"This white man," he told I-wan a moment later, when he himself brought tea and MacGurk was in the next room, "he is of course a little—" he tapped his head and sighed. "But I humor him—I always humor him!"

"A good heart," I-wan replied, not wanting to laugh.

"Oh yes, he has a very good heart," the innkeeper agreed. And seeing the size of the coin I-wan laid in his hand, he grew instantly zealous and rushed at the crowd standing at the door, staring in to see what was going on.

"Be gone—be gone!" he shouted. "Isn't this a man? Have you never seen a human being before?"

The crowd fell back and he slammed and barred the door made of rough planks.

"You must excuse them, my lord," he told I-wan. "They like to see foreigners. What country do you come from, sir?"

"But I am Chinese," I-wan said in surprise.

"Are you, sir?" the old man exclaimed. His wrinkled face was lively with his wonder. "Now I wouldn't have known it—your clothes—"

"Many Chinese wear western clothes," I-wan said. He felt somehow a little hurt.

"But your speech—" the old man began.

"It's Chinese, isn't it?" I-wan demanded.

"Well, I understand what you mean, but each word you say is not quite right," the old man replied. Then lest he offend a good customer, he added quickly, "But I've heard there are many Chinese—and some are tall and some are short—that I know, being an innkeeper here for forty years. And now, do you eat meat or not, sir? I have good vegetable dishes, otherwise."

"I eat meat," I-wan replied shortly. He was still a little angry.

And he stayed a little angry, if for nothing else than that he could not complain. "We Chinese—" the old innkeeper kept saying, as he served them, "we Chinese are not so particular as the white men. It let my heart down, I do assure you, sir, when you said you were Chinese. Now this white man"—he tapped his head again over MacGurk's red head—"he roars when his meat is tough, so I must chop it fine for him, like a baby, and put an extra quilt on his bed, and such a noise if it has a little small insect or two in it, such as we Chinese know must live, too. Do not insects also have their life, I ask him? But he never understands a word I say."

It was true the meat was tough and the bed of boards stretched upon two heaps of dried clay was very hard, and in the night I-wan felt something creeping over his skin. He leaped up and shook himself and was about to shout out. Then he lit the small oil lamp and lay down again.

"We Chinese—" the old innkeeper had said.

But the night was over at last and they were up in the air again and MacGurk's stubby profile was set toward the Northwest. They were going over mountains now, long reaches of barren clay-colored mountains. The roads were deep ruts across the land and ahead lay a mirage. I-wan had not known the trees and waters he seemed to see were a mirage until hour passed into hour and they came to no trees and no lakes. Their noon meal today was cold steamed-bread rolls filled with garlic which they had bought at the inn and stuffed into their pockets —different enough from the white foreign bread wrapped in clean white paper which Madame Chiang had given them. This bread was gray and solid and the garlic was strong. But it stayed hunger.

And then in the middle of the afternoon MacGurk suddenly shut off the engine and the plane began drifting slantwise to the earth.

"There it is!" he shouted.

And looking down, I-wan saw a square-walled village set like a block upon the plain. Outside were fields and inside the courts of houses there were trees growing thick and low. Down the plane drifted. And from the fields blue-clad figures shouted and dropped their hoes and came running to meet it.

"You're in the heart of the Reds!" MacGurk shouted at him

333

and then grinned. "They're just like anybody else," he remarked. The plane bumped gently along the earth. "Fact is, I kinda like 'em. This one you're goin' to see is a swell guy. The madame said I was to lead you straight to him. C'm on!"

They climbed out and again he was following MacGurk.

He had so completely believed that En-lan must be dead. He had always thought of him as dead. So then, how could he believe what he now saw? They had come into the village gate and just inside was a gateway into a court, full of laughing men. This they had crossed and then they entered this plain mud-walled earth-floored room. There was a man sitting at the un-painted table. He looked up. It was En-lan. They stared at each other, doubting. Ten years lay between them—ten years of time and all else. But it was En-lan. I-wan knew him instantly.

"This fellow Wu's got a letter from my chief," MacGurk was saying. "I don't mind telling you now I'm here, I'm glad I am. I didn't tell you, Wu, but I have these"— he drew out two pistols from his pockets—"and orders to shoot if anybody bothered us. But I picked our place last night. I know that old son-of-a-gun."

But they were not listening to him. They were staring at each other.

"It is not you, I-wan," En-lan said slowly.

"It is I," I-wan replied, "but how can I believe it is you?"

They drew nearer. Now they were feeling each other's shoulders and arms, now they were clasping hands—yes, this was En-lan's hand, but it was bigger, harder, stronger than it had once been.

"Where did you go?" En-lan demanded. "I never heard a word of you. Peony came running to our meeting place, but where were you? We waited until the last moment, every second ex-pecting you."

"Say, you two know each other, I guess," MacGurk broke in. "I guess I'll just go and get to work on the plane. It'll need some cleaning and fixing if we're to start back in the morning."

They did not see or hear him.

"Peony!" I-wan repeated, stupefied. "Is that where she went?"

"She's here," En-lan said. "Sit down. How can we ever get everything told between us?"

He clapped his hands and a young boy in khaki uniform came to the door.

"Call the inner one to come here," he ordered.

"Is Peony—are you—" I-wan stammered.

"Married?" En-lan said. "For ten years!"

"For ten years—you two have been together! But why didn't you write me?"

"We did—and signed false names, hoping you would know who we were."

"But I never had letters!" I-wan exclaimed.

"They were sent to your home," En-lan replied.

"I suppose my father was afraid to send them on," I-wan said when he had thought a moment. Yes, his father would be clever enough to know them dangerous letters!

"And you—why should you not write?" En-lan asked.

"I believed you dead," I-wan answered. "And how could I know where Peony was?"

They looked at each other again, measuring, examining, trying to see behind the men they now were, the boys they had been. I-wan thought, "Can I tell him about Tama?"

"And you—what about you?" En-lan demanded. "You are married—you have sons?"

"Yes," I-wan said. He longed to tell En-lan everything, how clever Jiro was and how Ganjiro—but no, it was better not to tell about Tama, better to keep her secret and safe.

"Yes, I have two sons," he said simply.

And then suddenly he heard a quick running step he knew and there was Peony rushing in. But Peony? This slender woman in a boy's uniform, a soldier's cap on her short hair, no rouge on her lips, no powder on her brown skin, no jasmine scent—and her hand, seizing his, so hard and firm, this was not Peony's hand that used to tremble like a bird!

"I-wan—I-wan—I-wan," she was crying. She pushed off her cap and it fell to the floor and he saw this was Peony. But she was no longer the pretty, melancholy, willful girl he had known. This Peony was En-lan's wife. I-wan sat down.

"My legs are trembling," he confessed. "I can't understand everything at once."

He had been like a man asleep, he now perceived. All these years, while he had been making a life with Tama, that old life of his which he had thought cut off and ended had been going on like this!

"How did this come about?" he demanded. "How could you pretend to me, Peony, that you despised the revolutionists?"

"I didn't despise him!" Peony thrust her pretty chin toward En-lan. Her large apricot-shaped eyes grew shy. Now that he looked at them I-wan saw her eyes were not changed at all.

"But you didn't know him!" I-wan exclaimed. "You had only seen him once!"

En-lan suddenly began to roar with laughter, and Peony's face turned pink. "I knew him a little—before I saw him," she confessed.

"Go on," En-lan commanded her. "Tell all your wickedness!"

"Well, I was cleaning your table drawers one day—" Peony went on very slowly.

"I missed something the other day from that table drawer," I-wan said, and he began to laugh, too.

336

"She found my story, that I had written—you remember, I-wan?" En-lan cried. "She stole it and read it—and made up her mind then and there."

Peony sat down on the edge of a chair. She was biting the edge of her red lip.

"It was my business to keep your table drawers neat, I-wan." Her eyes were full of demure hidden laughter.

"Oh yes, of course," I-wan agreed.

They laughed together. It seemed to I-wan he had never had better and more happy laughter. Then suddenly he remembered why he was here at all. He exclaimed to En-lan. "This Chiang who separated us has brought us together again! I am sent with this. You are to give it into the hands of the ones who are with you."

And he pulled the sealed letter from his inner pocket and gave it to En-lan.

"I have been expecting this—but not you," En-lan replied. "And I must not delay it. They are waiting for it. But wait for me here."

He took the letter and went away.

And I-wan, left alone with Peony, looked at her and she looked at him, and then in a moment she began to ask of his parents and his grandparents and he told her and he put in as though it were simply family news that now I-ko was married too, but he did not say to a white woman, for why need he tell that? And still his instinct kept him back from telling about Tama.

She listened to it all and while she listened he saw her face grow more what he remembered it, though still the ten years lay more heavily upon her than they did upon En-lan.

And then in a little while En-lan came back. His whole look was grave and yet alive and he said to Peony, in a solemn voice, "What I said would come to pass has come. Chiang wants union!"

337

She gave a cry of joy and I-wan saw there was more between these two than love.

"Ai, I told you, Peony, he's a great man—yes, he's right!" En-lan said. "Well, now, somehow I have to make my soldiers see it—they won't want to do it at once. Each of us is to talk to his own division. There'll have to be a meeting. I'll make them see it."

He was looking at Peony, asking for her agreement, for her approval. She nodded.

"Shall I go and tell them to strike the gong for meeting?" she asked.

"Yes, tell them," En-lan commanded. "No, wait—say in half an hour. I-wan must refresh himself. And I must be alone for a while."

"He still writes everything down before he speaks it," Peony explained.

He sat upon the dry baked earth of the drill ground. Beside him sat Peony. And helter-skelter, anyhow, and as they liked, sat men and women, but all young, around them. The hard and brilliant northern sunlight fell upon brown burned faces. It was difficult to know which were men and which women. But all these faces were upturned to hear En-lan, who stood so near that he could put out his hand and touch him. He felt strangely carried back into his boyhood. But then, in those days, En-lan had spoken to twenty or so, and now there were these hundreds. How had he done this? Somehow, while he had been thinking him dead, En-lan had been building this—this country; somehow, in spite of endless fighting he was here, strong and alive, and with him all these. En-lan's voice, clear and carrying through the still air, was saying:

"You know what we did. Six years ago we declared war upon

Japan. They laughed at us. Then three years afterwards we made our Long March. Our feet were torn and we were starved and many of us died. But we knew even then who was the real enemy. Though Chiang Kai-shek had pressed us and driven us backward over thousands of miles, we knew there was an enemy greater than he." He raised his voice. "Our enemy was Japan, who even then was attacking our people!"

He paused, and a low roar went up from the people. He put up his hand in an old gesture which pulled at I-wan's heart, he remembered it so well.

"What I tell you, you know. Not many months ago Chiang Kai-shek was kidnaped in Sian. We held him there—in our hand."

En-lan held out his strong rough hand, cupped.

"We might have closed it—thus." He closed his hand. "Then Chiang Kai-shek would have been no more. He who fought us so bitterly, for so many years, was here in our hand." He opened his hand again and stared into it. Over the whole multitude there was not a sound. Breathless they gazed at En-lan. He looked up, over his hand. "There were those of you who said, 'Kill him—kill him!' If your leaders had heeded you"—En-lan's thumb went down—"he would have been dead in an hour. You blamed us then, because we did not move. You blamed us bitterly because he lived and returned safely to his home. Some of you still are angry because today he is still alive."

He dropped his hands now and held them lightly clasped. It was En-lan's strength that without movement, merely by the power of his voice and his words, he held men silent and subdued to him. I-wan felt it, all the old power, but infinitely deeper and more perfected.

"But we remembered who the real enemy is. It is not he. We said to you then, 'If he could so relentlessly pursue us year after year, he can thus pursue our enemy.' We said to him, 'Will you fight Japan?' He said, 'Until I die.' So we let him go."

Now they could feel what was coming. Now they knew this mounting rising terrible power coming out of En-lan meant he would demand sacrifice from them. His eyes began to burn, his voice grew deep, he held himself higher. Their eyes were fixed upon him.

"Today he is the only one who can lead us on to war. There is no other."

But now they stirred. "You! You! You!" This word began to break from the crowd here and there. But En-lan caught it and tossed it away.

"No, not I! I am a communist. This nation will not follow any communist! And Japan would use us still more as an excuse for war—'China is communist,' they say already! No, we must serve our own country, not the enemy."

They fell silent. What he said was true. What would he say next?

"There is only one who can save us all," he said. "He who has seemed to be our enemy. If we come under his flag—not he under ours, but we under his—what can our enemies say? Before the whole world we shall be a united people, fighting together!"

I-wan, staring at En-lan, was sobbing within himself. This fellow, this magnificent man—demanding of his people this supreme self-denial—telling them they must subdue themselves now to one who had so persecuted them—who but En-lan could have made so huge a demand!

"Forget yourselves!" he commanded them. "Remember only that you are Chinese!"

Not a sound, not a word! Peony at his side was smoothing

340

with her fingers the dust upon the ground and writing two characters—"China."

"Those who will, let them raise the right hand!" En-lan commanded.

Up came their right hands—hundreds of hands.

"Those who are not willing!" En-lan demanded again. His blazing eyes dared them.

Not a hand dared. He dropped his head and turned away, and slowly, as though from dreaming, the people began to struggle up, some to walk away, some to stand talking.

But it was over. They had done what En-lan wanted them to do. I-wan saw him stride across the court to his own room. And Peony rose quickly to follow him.

"He is always tired for a little while after such a thing," she whispered. "Something goes out of him." She hurried toward the court.

And I-wan, after a moment, went out toward the field, where MacGurk was oiling the plane. The daze of the past hour was still upon him, as bright as a dream. When he stood again before Chiang, he would say, "Let me go back." Yes, he must come back. Somehow En-lan made this his country, even as he had done in those other days.

"When shall we go?" he asked MacGurk.

"Four o'clock in the morning," MacGurk answered. He nodded toward the dispersing crowd. "Get what he wanted?"

"Yes," I-wan said.

"Great fellow," MacGurk remarked. "Almost as great as the big chief—not quite, though. So I stick by the biggest one."

"I'll be here at four, then," I-wan said at last, not knowing what other answer to make to this. Well, he would say to Chiang, "That is where I can serve you best." And there was no

341

reason for delay. He could be back within five days, if Chiang were willing.

"O-kay," MacGurk replied, and began to whistle through his teeth while he polished the wings.

Sometimes everything except this life he now lived seemed an imagination, years which he had dreamed in his sleep. Days and weeks went by when he did not think once of Tama or the children, when indeed it seemed as though he and En-lan had always worked together like this, as though they were two hands, driven by the same brain. Day upon day they talked of nothing but of the plan of war which they were now following. This army was a flexible, tireless machine. They drove it night and day, a little council of men at its heart. With him En-lan had two others, men whose stories I-wan never knew whole, but whose brains he came to know as he knew his own.

They had to make war with nothing. Chiang Kai-shek had told them there was nothing. When he could give them money he would. But his own armies were only a little more than half-equipped. And he must keep always enough money ready to buy loyalty from the warlords and their armies. There were only a few whom he could be sure of without money.

"I must be able always to pay more than the Japanese." He had told I-wan this calmly, while I-wan felt his own heart angry in his breast.

"Are there truly Chinese who even now can be bought?" he had cried. He did not believe it.

But Chiang Kai-shek had said, "I know them. They cannot be changed, and I must use them as they are."

Yes, I-wan thought grudgingly, perhaps MacGurk was right. En-lan was not so great as Chiang Kai-shek. Nevertheless he belonged with En-lan and so he had gone back to him.

342

"We do not need money," En-lan said, and then corrected himself. "Well, we do need it, but we can do without it. We have fought a war for years without it, and we will go on as we have been."

And this, I-wan soon found, was by the old hide-and-seek of the guerillas. There was not one of these soldiers of En-lan's who did not know how to fight with anything he had in his hand. If they had only twenty machine guns, they seemed to have a hundred. If they had no guns, they fought with old-fashioned spears and knives or they threw javelins or even slung stones from ambush. They did not scorn the single death of even the least of the enemy, although they could kill a hundred so swiftly that it seemed nothing. And all this they did, not massed together in the solid marching regiments the enemy had, but in small scattered handfuls of men here and there and everywhere, hidden in trees and ambushed in caves and working among the farming people with hoes in their hands and pistols and knives under their blue cotton shirts.

For the first thing En-lan had decreed was that they should leave the village where they were and approach the enemy lines. They were to go not as an army but simply as farming people, some one day, some another, to return to their lands despoiled by the enemy.

"Those lands," En-lan told I-wan grimly one night, as they sat over maps in En-lan's room, "I know them well." He put his finger on a certain spot. "Do you remember what I used to tell you about my village?"

"Yes," I-wan replied, "I do remember."

"Here it is," En-lan said and stared down at it. "Its name is still here. But it is gone. Not a soul is alive in it. The walls of its houses are ruined and its streets are scorched earth. I have one

343

brother alive, perhaps—I don't know. But a Japanese garrison fell upon them in revenge after Tungchow."

He was silent a moment, and I-wan did not speak either. What could be said?

"I used to think I would surely go back some day and start a school," En-lan said slowly. And after a while he said again, "I never repaid them while they lived for what they gave me. But I will repay them now, when they are dead."

Peony had been sitting upon a bench mending an old uniform of En-lan's. Now she put down her sewing and rose and came over to En-lan and took the map from his hand.

"It is time for you to go to bed," she said. "You know you need your early sleep, because the dawn awakes you."

His mood changed at once. "I'll always be a farmer boy," he told I-wan, smiling a little. "Any cock can rouse me."

And I-wan, seeing the deep passion between these two, felt his own longing creep over him like a mist. For weeks he lived as though this were the only life he had ever had, and then suddenly, as if his name were called by her voice, he longed for Tama. Over and over again at such times he wanted to tell En-lan and Peony about her. But he could not. He could not be sure that they would understand. En-lan was as implacable as ever. The old calmness with which he once had told I-wan that he ought no longer to own his father, was in him still. He was ruthless in his simplicity. "How," he would ask I-wan, "can you love a Japanese?" And yet I-wan knew that he loved Tama and would always love her and she belonged to no country, but only to him.

Once he thought he might tell Peony alone. He had had that day a letter from Tama, sent as all his letters from her were sent, under an official seal from his father. This day Tama's letter had been long and full of what the children said and did. Jiro was

344

beginning school. She had bought him a brown cloth school-bag for his books and a little uniform and a cap, such as the other boys wore. "But at home," she wrote, "I teach him, too. We put flowers before your picture every day, and every day I explain to them how brave you are and how beautiful a country China is and how we belong to China—do I not belong to you, and they to us?"

Yes, since he was gone, she had written so ". . . we belong to China—"

On the day he had this letter he had been eaten up with loneliness for them. It was a day of unusual quietness. En-lan had commanded rest for them all, for the enemy were changing their position on a certain sector which he wished to attack. And I-wan found Peony sitting with her constant sewing on the sunny side of the farmhouse where they were quartered. And suddenly he wanted to tell her about Tama. Still some caution held him back. So he began, "Did you never have a son, Peony?"

She looked up at him. In the sharp sunlight he saw how her delicate skin was beginning to crack in small fine wrinkles, and her hair, which once she kept so smooth with fragrant oils, now looked brown and dried with the wind. But she was still pretty and still young. Peony, he thought, could not be more than thirty.

"I had two children," she said. She dropped her eyes to her sewing. "I was very ill with the last—I seem never to have any more now." She went on sewing. Then she said. "And why should I not tell you? You are my brother. The first—my son— I lost by a dysentery. It is not a good life for a small child—our life. We have been driven so much. And his food and water changed too often. He was five, though—I kept him as long as that. And then suddenly he died in a day. And we buried him on a hillside in Kiangsi. It is so far south from here I shall never

345

see his grave again, I think." She shook her head but she did not weep. "And the little one," she went on, "that was a girl. It was so long before she came I thought there would never be another. But En-lan doesn't believe in gods, you know, so I had nothing to pray to for a child. And then on the Long March, I conceived."

She paused, bit her thread, and went on. "Well, I hoped the Long March would be ended before she was born. But no—we kept climbing over those high mountains and down the rocky roads and over the deserts. I wasn't sick, but I had to walk all the time or ride a horse. That was worse. The roads were so bad— and sometimes there were no roads. Ah, I was glad then your father wouldn't let my feet be bound! Well, so the child was born very small and thin—and a girl. But we were still marching, so what could we do with her? I gave her to a good farmer's wife and left some money for her and I told her I would come back."

Peony bent her head down close to her sewing. "But that was three years ago. . . . Sometimes I can't be sure if I remember the place, or how the woman looked. And her name was only Wang. . . ."

"Did En-lan let this happen?" I-wan exclaimed.

She looked up at him. "You know him," she said simply.

He could say nothing. He knew En-lan. He would demand everything of Peony, too. It came to him for the first time that perhaps Peony would have liked a home, a little house like Tama's, set upon a hill, and a garden.

"Are you sorry you followed him that day?" he asked.

She shook her head.

"Without him, what would I have been?" she asked. Then she looked at the sun. "It's late," she exclaimed. She put her needle into a bit of cloth securely and folded it up and buttoned it into the pocket of her uniform.

346

"Needles are very precious now. I wish I had all the ones I used to lose so carelessly." She rose as she spoke. "I must go and get his supper," she said cheerfully.

He watched her walk away. She was very graceful still, but so thin. She would not live to be old in this life. But if it were En-lan's life she wanted it. No, he decided, he would not tell her about Tama. She would tell En-lan anything if she thought he ought to know. She would think only of En-lan. He could not entrust Tama to her now.

Each fought in this war as he was able. Elsewhere in the country there were armies uniformed and manned and trained by foreign officers. But here where I-wan had chosen to make his present life there was no such thing. These men could not have borne it. They drew near to the enemy, so near that less than a day's easy walking would bring them into lost territory. There were no headquarters, seemingly, and no head to these scattering men. En-lan lived in a village, looking like any farmer. And around him were other farmers and petty tradesmen and fuel cutters and men who hired themselves out to other men and all that multitude of small people who have nothing to do with war in any country and who care for nothing except to feed themselves and their children. Then from nowhere a band of dark fierce banditry swept by night into a town held by the enemy and killed the garrison to the last man and the next day a foray of angry Japanese searched the countryside in revenge. But these small folk knew nothing and had seen nothing. With the innocent eyes of eternal children they gazed at their enemies and laughed.

"Why should we be those who killed you?" they cried, one and another. "We don't care who rules us, only let us tend our fields and do our business. We hate our rulers. They are all evil and we are eaten up with their taxes. Why should we fight for them? If you will rule us better than they, why, welcome!"

Then Japanese looked at Japanese and wagged their heads and went away, believing, and wrote long reports to their upper officers that the country folk welcomed their coming and thanked them and wanted their rule. In Tama's letters I-wan read that the papers told this and she was glad because surely that meant the war would soon be over and she could come to him with the children.

He could not tell her the truth, that the innocent-seeming country men were En-lan's soldiers and some of them his own men whom he taught and who taught him. For in this strange army there was no high and no low. If a man had something he knew, he taught those who did not know. They ate what they needed of the same food and wore the same kind of garments and no one had more money than another. It was the sort of life his father could never have lived. But that was neither for nor against his father. For I-wan was not now the boy he had been when he weighed in such pain whether or not he must give his father up. He was a man now and he knew that not all men can live the same life. For some poverty is sweet because it is full of freedom. But there are men who hate such freedom and his father was one of these.

And even for himself I-wan no longer felt this way of En-lan's was the only way. En-lan would choose it until he died. He would never have a home of his own, goods he owned, or children to inherit. He was one to make a war somehow if there were not war already at hand. There would always be something wrong he had sworn himself to right. But I-wan now discovered that he himself was not so. When he had been a boy in his father's house the imagination of such freedom had seemed the best life he could live. But though he would never have been satisfied

348

if for a while he had not lived it as he did now, yet he became sure as the days went on that it was not enough for the making of a whole nation. These men did now the work for which they were made. But what would they be when the war was over? They would hate any rule as much as they hated their enemy today.

He argued long with En-lan over this.

"What will they be when the war is over?" En-lan repeated. "Why, what they are now—simple honest brave men, and I had rather they ruled over me and made my laws than any other men."

"Well enough for you," I-wan retorted. "But you are one of them."

"Are you not?" En-lan broke in.

"Yes, I am now, too," I-wan argued, a little impatiently— En-lan saw slowly sometimes!—"But you and I do not make up a nation. A nation today is not a simple society of simple men. It is a great machine and men must know many things to make it perform its service to the people."

"We do well enough, don't we?" En-lan exclaimed. "We are fed, we are clothed, justice is done to all. And we are free. These are what men require."

"But not all they require—" These words were on I-wan's tongue, but he did not say them. He saw that En-lan was as he was made and that he was one who saw no further than what he himself believed. In his youth En-lan had taken for this belief certain dreams and ideas and then he had not changed. His whole life until now had been spent in making them actual. He had made for himself a sort of world, a kind of nation such as he believed was right. All his life until he died would be spent in this struggle to perfect the same dream.

But I-wan's dream had changed. The more he lived among

349

these men, the more he lived with En-lan, the more he perceived that what was changed in him was the dream, the perception of what he wanted his country to be. He knew now he did not want to be ruled by these men, honest though they were. Their simplicities were not enough. Honesty and simplicity, surely, were not essential companions! If they were, then honesty was not wide enough. It must be made wider.

He began to ponder very much on these matters. Who, after this war, would make his country and how must its laws be made and what must these laws be? He saw now that En-lan could never be a ruler over that which he could not understand. Enlightenment and knowledge, order and grace, these were things life must have, too, but En-lan would never know it. . . . And it came into I-wan's mind that Tama had somehow changed him. She had taught him to love order and right behavior and grace in everyday acts. He had the ten years with her forever in his being. Yes, and though it was bitter to know it, he had the ten years of his life in Japan in his being, too. He was too honest within himself not to see that the people there were more secure than the people were here in his own country. They lived more secure because they lived in order. He dared not say to En-lan that there was anything good in the enemy, for En-lan would not have believed he could be loyal to his own and yet find good in his enemy. But I-wan knew himself and knew that he loved his own country none the less when he saw that its people were too poor and that the freedom they loved had ceased to be freedom when because of it they went in bondage to hunger and flood and fear of robbers and of wars between mischievous and lawless men. He pondered much on what the moment was when freedom and security came nearest to being the same.

And that he thought of such things showed him what he had become as a man. He knew now he could never follow En-lan to the end as once he could have done. To the end of each day, yes, and to the end of this war, yes. But beyond that there must be a new world again. What it would be he did not know now, and then he gave over thinking so far and he thought no farther than to the time when he could bring his wife and children home.

In the days of that long winter when they waited for spring to come and the maize and the kaoliang to grow high enough for ambush by day, he would dream how when the war was over he would bring Tama and the children across the sea and how they would find their home. Where would it be? He considered his vast country. Well, the sunshine of the north, the cool summers and bright cold winters—these were full of health. But there was the rich and fertile beauty of the mid-country, and the fruits and flowers of the south. Tama would love the flowers. It was not easy to choose from such a country where his sons could best grow into their manhood. He thought of all the fine cities where they might live, Hangchow and Soochow, Nanking and Hankow.

And then the enemy began to take those cities, one by one. In the late autumn Shanghai had been yielded. His father wrote him of desperate, useless fighting, of wounded men who were too many to be tended. And Soochow was lost and in early winter Hangchow was no longer theirs—the heavenly city of Hangchow, where when he was a child he had gone with his father and mother for holidays in spring and autumn.

Somehow all this time while the enemy marched inland he had not believed that Nanking could be seized because Chiang Kai-shek was there. He smiled at his own superstition concerning this man. He was as bad as his father, who would believe in no gods, but believed in Chiang as though he were a god! And then they heard Nanking, too, was lost. For a day the men could do nothing but sit and mourn and wonder if now were not the time for them to withdraw to themselves as they were

351

before, and only by holding a great feast and gathering them all together to hear him speak to them could En-lan make them bold again against the enemy.

"What are cities to us?" he shouted to them when they were full of meat and wine. "What is Nanking to us? We have had nothing from Nanking—we shall not know it is lost! And if we withdraw now and the enemy win, must we not fight them alone later? And if we stay by and win, and we shall win, will not the country then be ours?"

With all the old magic of his brilliant eyes and deep voice and simple speech always to be understood by any man, En-lan drew them back once more and they fought on. And I-wan could not deny that magic, but he knew that when the war was over and men needed not so much to be led to battle as to the daily building of a great new nation, the magic would not hold. No, in that day En-lan himself perhaps would grow weary of patience and work and go away to be his old self somewhere and start another revolution. But now he had his use.

And under his magic after this, each time a city fell to the enemy and with it the region where it was, the men went more firmly to their hidden vicious warfare. They made no great battles, there was no open victory nor vanquishment, but the drain upon the enemy was like the bleeding of a secret wound. Nothing was told, no one knew, and newspapers printed nothing, but one night a hundred men were swept clean from an enemy post in a country town and another night a bridge fell and the river swallowed up half a regiment, or a train was wrecked, or mines were hidden in the dust of a country road and exploded beneath the wheels of an enemy truck, or a strange fire broke out in an enemy camp, or a shipment of rifles was taken or a gun captured from the Japanese who were left dead where it had stood, or a dike was broken and a flood seized the enemy.

This was the sort of warfare they knew how to make, these men of En-lan's. And it was the wisest way to fight, I-wan became sure. For when he read in his father's letters how in the south the Chinese armies fell, he grew sick while he read. They would do anything they were told to do, they were so brave, his father wrote. When they were told to march in the open in ranks against the enemy, then they marched, though only to fall before the machine guns of the enemy like wheat beneath the scythe. The more he thought of this the more I-wan could not bear it, and he wished that Chiang would give over trying to fight as the foreigners fight and go back to these old ways of their own which En-lan had learned so well to use.

One day his father wrote for the first time as though he were fearful of the end. "Our men have nothing but courage. They go into battle as good as empty-handed, with little popping hand guns to stand before machines. All our best young men are already gone. We cannot train them fast enough for such massacre."

He went to En-lan with his father's letter and showed it to him and asked him, "Will you go to Chiang and explain our way of fighting and persuade him to it?"

They talked for a long while. En-lan was not willing at first, for he suspected there might still be those who wanted to kill him.

"Why do you not go for me?" he asked I-wan. "You are always safe, being your father's son!"

"Chiang would not listen to me," I-wan replied quietly, ignoring En-lan's hidden taunt against his father, "but he knows what a foe you are!"

En-lan laughed and gave in then, and I-wan telegraphed his father, who arranged it that MacGurk came to fetch En-lan. They had one moment of laughter together, when suddenly En-lan, who had never feared anything in his life, was now afraid to go up in the air, but I-wan's laughter drove him and he was gone. I-wan watched the plane rise and lose itself in the sky. Those two meeting thus, he thought to himself—what a thing it would be to see!

And I-wan was right. When En-lan had been back a few days —and he came back without delay, shouting that he could not endure that city for another hour—Chiang announced everywhere that hereafter the Chinese armies would fight not after the western ways they did not know, but after their own ancient ways. When the enemy advanced, they would retreat. When the enemy retreated, they would advance. When the enemy did not expect it, they would attack. They would never again meet the enemy in pitched battle as western armies did.

When this pronouncement was made it seemed as though every Chinese took heart again. If this war could be fought as they knew how to fight, they would win. And I-wan took his own private comfort in the knowledge that fewer would die uselessly now. In the future, he thought grimly, they must make armies to match any in the world, armies and navies and thousands of airplanes of every sort. But now they must make shift as they could to save themselves.

For in their way of fighting he and En-lan lost almost no men. It was counted as a fault if a man lost his life, that is, a clumsiness somewhere that ought not to have been. But steadily they counted the lives of their enemies taken day after day.

Now peace between En-lan and I-wan grew to be an uncertain thing, and more and more as time went on, especially as the maize and kaoliang grew high enough for ambush and the men went out every day for warfare. When they killed their enemy I-wan said nothing, but they brought back prisoners—and upon this En-lan and I-wan could not agree. In his own way in this, too, I-wan had grown beyond En-lan, who must always remain something of what he was born. It seemed En-lan could never forget his poor childhood and the famines which he had seen and the hardships he had suffered. He held mankind responsible for all he had suffered, and though he loved his own loyally, he hated all who were not like him and therefore not his own. If a man were not poor he hated him and was ready to kill him. And to him every Japanese was something less than man.

But I-wan had been gently reared and he had no great bitterness to remember. All the things he had once thought bitter now seemed small. In his childhood he had hated his grandmother. Yet when she died in the second month of this year and her body had been encoffined and put in a temple to wait for peace, since these were no times for the display of a great funeral, I-wan wondered then that he had grown so bitter over the smell of her opium and had not remembered rather that she loved him most tenderly and steadfastly and had always coaxed him when he was sullen.

So this was another difference between him and En-lan, now that they lived together day upon day in such closeness. It was about the killing of the prisoners they took. Sometimes it came almost to open quarrel, and then Peony must come between them to scold them and explain them to each other.

"You, En-lan, are too stubborn in your own mind! You are stubborn like an ox. And I-wan, you are stubborn too, but you are stubborn as a swift willful horse who has been fed too daintily and never known anything but a golden bridle. Now, ox, do not ask horse to become ox, and, horse, remember he is ox!"

But about this one thing not even Peony could make them laugh or agree.

It had been a habit of En-lan's men, when I-wan came, to kill

355

all the men they captured except a few—some who, they thought, looked the strangest or who were young and troublesome and did not yield, or those for whom, for one reason or another, it seemed quick death was too easy. Very often they brought these back with them and then by slow merry ways they made them die. First they locked them in cages or chained them to a tree and let any who liked come and see them and spit upon them or prod them with pitchforks or hold blazing torches to their fingers and toes, or any such things as amuse common folk who have an enemy at their mercy.

At last one day I-wan went in a mighty rage to find En-lan.

"Do you allow this?" he demanded.

"What?" En-lan replied. He was sitting in a room examining upon a map a certain road where that night they planned to make attack.

"Look out of the door!" I-wan cried. And En-lan rose and came to the open door and looked out.

"What is it?" he asked.

"Do you see nothing?" I-wan asked him fiercely.

"No, I see nothing," En-lan said deliberately, "unless you mean the men at play."

"Do you call it play?" En-lan shouted.

At that moment a buffoon had come out of the laughing crowd and had dug his thumb into the chained man's eye and his eye burst and streamed out. The man screamed once. Then he bit his lip and was silent. But in the bright air sweat ran shining down his face.

"You can't deny these men everything," En-lan said coldly as he watched. "Think what other soldiers have if they are victorious—extra food, money, wine to drink, loot! But our men throw their lives away every day, and yet they eat the same poor

356

food and we have no money to give them and there is no loot. They are simple men—they must have something."

"Not such degrading play as this!" I-wan retorted. "This is the play of savages!"

"Well, so they are savages," En-lan replied in a reasonable voice. His brilliant eyes hardened a little now as he looked at I-wan. "Are you still the dreamer, I-wan? Do you still believe the poor will be better than the rich? I hate the rich, but the poor are not gods. They are only children. And at least what they do is done openly."

I-wan groaned and came into the room and leaned his arm against the wall and hid his face. He felt sick.

"You are too squeamish," En-lan told him after a moment and kindly enough. "You should have been hardened as I was. I killed pigs when I was a small child and in a famine I helped my father kill our ox for food, and I saw my mother kill a girl she bore. And I grew up on bandits and what they did. I saw men's noses slit and their eyes gouged and their ears gone and their backs flayed, and as long as I can remember a dead man was nothing. Why should I care for a Japanese?"

I-wan straightened himself, wiped his face, and sat down. "It is not only that a Japanese is a man also," he said. "It is that I am ashamed to see Chinese do such things."

"Do you forget what the Japanese did at Nanking?" En-lan asked angrily. "Nothing we can do will be enough revenge!"

"I know. I don't excuse them," I-wan replied doggedly. "But I say, 'If the Japanese are like that, it is not my business—but it is my business if my own people also . . .'"

"Oh, the patriot!" En-lan broke in. "Oh, what a patriot! I-wan, you are a fool. I say it plainly. When you have been through what I have—"

357

"The more I see of it, the more I shall hate it!" I-wan said violently.

"Then you had better go somewhere else, where it is not to be seen," En-lan declared. "Perhaps you would like to join the benevolent work of the Japanese and become one of the puppet governors—"

When I-wan heard En-lan say this, he suddenly felt an anger rise in him that lifted him from his feet. Upon its power he leaped forward and fell upon En-lan and En-lan, not being prepared, fell under him upon the beaten ground of the floor, and they struggled together as though they were two boys instead of men. Each held the other with both hands by the hair of his crown and shook as hard as he could, and thus Peony found them at this moment. She had been asleep in the other room and their voices had awakened her and now she came at them shrieking and pulling and scolding.

"Oh shameful! Oh, I-wan, how can you—En-lan, you foolish—" And then she opened her mouth and bit one hand and then another until they let go. They scrambled to their feet and wrung their hands with pain.

"I'm bleeding," En-lan accused her.

"So you should bleed," Peony answered him.

I-wan drew out his handkerchief and wrapped his own bleeding hand and said nothing.

"Now, what is your quarrel?" Peony demanded.

En-lan laughed suddenly.

"I called him a patriot and he fell on me!"

"No, now, truly, En-lan!" she exclaimed. "I-wan is not so foolish."

"It was about the prisoners," I-wan said suddenly.

"What prisoners?" Peony asked.

358

They looked, but while they had been quarreling the man had been taken away.

"He is dead," I-wan said abruptly.

"Then why quarrel over him?" Peony coaxed them.

"There will be more tomorrow," I-wan said.

"I-wan wants them all gently killed," En-lan broke in. "And I say the men must have some pleasure out of their hard lives."

"And I say," I-wan retorted, "that we ought to teach them something better."

He looked at Peony. "En-lan says I am soft," he said. "But you were a child in my father's house, too. Am I right or wrong?"

He would not care what she said, he thought. He knew he was right.

"But Peony was a slave," En-lan said sharply. "A slave in a rich man's house has to suffer—"

"Yes, but still I-wan is right," Peony said slowly. "It is not good for our men, En-lan. I know what he means. Sometimes when his grandmother used to—to burn me with her pipe"—she glanced at I-wan and flushed a little and went on quietly—"I remember I used to say to her in my heart, 'But it is you who are cruel and wicked and mean—it is not I. I have only a bit of aching flesh on my arm, but you have become wicked!' "

"Did she do that?" I-wan asked in a low voice. She pulled up her sleeve and he saw on her thin upper arm deep round scars, many scars running in together.

"You never told me," he whispered.

"I couldn't tell—anyone," she said mournfully. "I don't know why—except it seemed to make me a real slave and so I hid it."

"You should have told me," I-wan said. He wanted suddenly to weep with anger. "I hate every torture!"

"I also," Peony said simply. She drew down her sleeve and turned to En-lan. "I-wan is right," she told him.

"Perhaps he is," En-lan agreed. It was impossible to tell from his face how much he had inwardly yielded.

But from that day on I-wan at least saw no more torture.

It was soon after this that I-wan began to perfect a plan which for a long time he had been musing upon in his mind. It had begun many months before, when it had occurred to him to imagine what he would do if some day when he led his men in a secret attack, one of those whom he must kill or see killed should happen to be Bunji? He put the thought away as soon as it came. There was so little chance that this would happen that he could think of it as no chance.

And yet there was enough chance left so that he never looked from ambush at Japanese upon a road where he was hidden or through an open door suddenly upon men surprised without taking his first quick look to see that none of the faces was Bunji's face. No, and he never killed a man from behind, lest the man be Bunji, and if a man tried to make his escape and he had not seen his face, he let him go. . . . Yet he had heard nothing of Bunji. Tama never told him where he was, if indeed she knew herself. She only wrote that he was still alive and well, and that his little son was walking now, and that Setsu longed to have her second child. But who knew when that would be? This war was endless in spite of all the times set for it to end. . . . And as long as he knew Bunji was alive, I-wan was afraid.

He knew, of course, what he would do if Bunji were among the ones they captured. He would help him to escape. That he had decided long ago when first he had thought of it, so that if it happened he would be ready. But first he would talk with Bunji and explain to him the evil of this war which his people made upon I-wan's people. For I-wan had talked to many prisoners and he now knew that they were not told why they had to leave their homes and families and die in such hundreds and thousands. And he found very often the letters and writings in the pockets of those dead, and he read them that he might know what they thought and felt before they died. And always they said the same thing, that this was a righteous and necessary war which they fought to save their own homes and their own country. And I-wan longed to say to them, "We do not want your country and you have nothing you need to save yourselves from with us, so why have you died?" But they were dead.

And then he thought of how the men used to bring back many living prisoners until En-lan put a stop to it for mercy's sake after Peony had showed them her burns, and he thought, "Why should we not teach these prisoners the truth and treat them kindly and send them back to their own army, to spread knowledge of the truth among their fellows?"

He went to En-lan with this plan, not being sure at all what En-lan would think of it, and if he would not say again that he was too soft. But En-lan, when he had heard it, seized it at once as a good clever plan.

"It makes a man's arm slack if he does not believe in what he does," he said. "And if we can spread doubt among them and make them distrust their leaders, it is a clever thing to do."

The more En-lan thought of it, the more he liked it. He clapped his hand against I-wan's and laughed and cried, "It's as good as capturing a trainload of guns—well, I will say that skull of yours has something in it, I-wan!"

Somewhere or other, I-wan knew, his idea and En-lan's idea of the same thing did not quite hit together. But he let it go. If the thing were accomplished, the end was served. And the men, when En-lan explained it to them, were pleased with what they thought was such clever trickiness, and so the thing was done. And thereafter a certain number of prisoners were taken alive and fed and

361

given courtesy and kindness and "educated," as En-lan said, for a week or two, and set free again, looking, every man thus freed, so bewildered at what had happened to him that he was wholly dumb and did not know what came next.

But for Bunji it was no use after all. In the autumn I-wan had a letter from Tama and in it she was all grief and mourning. Bunji had been killed in the fighting at Taierhchwang. I-wan, after he had read and burned her letter as he must all her letters, sat awhile in his own room in great sorrow, remembering Bunji as he had known him when first he went to the Muraki house. How warm a heart had been his, and how merry! If there had been no war, how long and happy a life would have been his desert! But war had soon spoiled him. He was too simple for the strain and cruelty of war, and it had broken him. . . . And so all I-wan's fears of meeting him were useless. And all Setsu's hopes were useless, too. She would never have a second son.

One day in the autumn I-wan received a telegram from Chiang Kai-shek, commanding him to come to him, and saying that MacGurk would be there to fetch him the next day if the storm then raging had abated. I-wan took this message to En-lan and they looked at it together and put their two minds on it and could imagine nothing for a cause. At last they decided it could, at least, have nothing to do with the state, since if there had been an official reason, the message would not have come to him alone.

"Unless, of course," En-lan said, "he is displeased with something and wants you for a messenger."

But this seemed not true, either, for only a few days before this they had all rejoiced because without expecting it, they had received from Chiang a present of money and enough to buy winter clothes for the men who were most ragged. It must be, I-wan thought in himself, something of his own private self.

His mind flew always to Tama. It might be that Chiang wanted to test him concerning his Japanese wife. For one moment I-wan thought, "What if he demands that I give her up?"

Well, he would not, he knew. What he could do or what he would say beyond that, the moment must tell him when it came. At least that he had come back to his country and was here fighting should count for the truth of anything he said. But what was between him and Tama belonged to the past and to the future. The present he had given to his country. But to none would he promise that future which none could know.

Thus encouraging himself he tied up his extra clothes in a piece of square cloth as farmers do, and was ready on the landing field when MacGurk came for him.

"You ready?" MacGurk bawled at him over the side of the plane.

"Quite ready," I-wan replied.

"Well, we'll hop off again then in about twenty minutes," Mac-Gurk said, and leaped out of the plane. He took off his cap and beat the dust out of it. "Gosh, it's a trick making this run now—nothing like as easy as it was when the chief was in Nanking! The air from Hankow here is full of holes and I fell in every one of 'em." They were walking toward the farmhouses which were En-lan's camp. "I'll take a swallow of tea and a cigarette and then we'll be off. Lots of daylight yet," MacGurk went on.

They sat down at an outdoor table of the village teashop and the old woman whose husband kept the place came and wiped off the table with a black rag and then blew into the teacups to rid them of dust and prepared to wipe them also. But MacGurk stopped her with a roar.

"Here, lay off that cleaning, will you?" He turned on I-wan. "Tell her I want 'em dirty! Sa-ay! I can do my hop-skip-and-jump between bullets all right, but germs is something else again!"

He stared at the old woman in mock anger while I-wan told

her to leave the bowls, and when he saw her cower before his gaze he broke into a grin. "Never mind, old lady," he told her. "I wash 'em myself anyway." And he poured some of the boiling tea into the bowls, threw the tea on the ground, and then filling his bowl and I-wan's, he blew the hot tea loudly and supped it.

"Will you never learn any of our language so that you can make your own complaints?" I-wan asked him in good humor.

"Naw—don't need it," MacGurk replied. "If I yell loud enough and say it over a coupla times and stare at 'em hard they see what I mean pretty quick. I don't have much time, anyway."

In a little while they were back in the plane and now I-wan saw still more of his country than he had ever seen. Mountains rolled their curling length beneath, and clouds coiled and covered them or left them bare. But I-wan could not put his mind to enjoyment of beauty. He was eaten up with wondering why he was called to this meeting.

He had never been in Hankow before. Time and again when he was a child his father used to say that some time soon they must return to Hunan to visit the ancient lands of the family, from which they still received rents, and I-wan knew that the city of Hankow on one side of the Yangtse River and the city of Wuchang on the other were like pillars to the gate which opened to the vast territories of the inner provinces. Somewhere within them lay his family's inherited lands which even his grandfather had never seen, planted and harvested by generations of farmers who rented the fields from father to son, and who sent their rent moneys as they might have sent tribute to an unknown emperor. But who they were I-wan did not know. And indeed he had never thought of them except when his father said, "The rents are good this year." Or he said, "The lands have paid us nothing these two years, what with a flood last year and the bandits very bad this year still." But everything was the same in his father's house whatever the year was.

Nevertheless, as he rode through the streets of Hankow to be taken to the house where Chiang Kai-shek was, he looked at all the people and listened to their language. He could understand what they said, but it was different in its cadence from En-lan's language, and altogether different from his own Shanghai speech. Yet they were all one people and he was one with them. He thought very often and deeply of these differences among his own people. Tama's people were close to each other in every thought. But his were not. When this war was over which now united them for the first time in all their history, then what could they find still to unite them? He asked himself this question very often, thinking, too, somewhat of himself and En-lan. This war held them together still. But after it was over, what would there be, unless memory held? But human memory never held. There must be something else, as strong as war, as necessary as defense against an enemy.

He was lost in his pondering on the future as he was so often now, when suddenly the car in which he was sitting stopped with a jerk before a common brick house and the driver motioned with his thumb that they had reached their place. I-wan got out alone, since MacGurk had stayed to mend a fault in his engine, and he rang a bell at the door. It was opened by a servant in a white gown, and the servant expected him, for he bowed and took I-wan into a small side room and asked him to sit down for a few minutes. He went away and I-wan sat waiting. There was nothing in this room to hold his interest, since the furniture was plain and usual, and so he was about to fall to his thinking again when the door opened and his father came in. I-wan stood up at once, greatly astonished.

"Sit down," his father said.

They sat down and then I-wan saw his father looked very tired and much thinner than he was when I-wan saw him last year.

"Are you not well, Father?" he asked. The more he looked at his father, the more anxious he felt. He had never seen his father like this. All of his old energy and stubbornness seemed gone. He sat there as though it would be an effort to rise again.

"I am as well as any can be now," his father replied. And then he said, "This war is killing us all in one way or another. I have just had letters from Nanking." He paused, and then went on, "In my way I had helped to make that new city. We made great loans there for the capital. I was proud of it. Well, it is gone."

"You mean—completely destroyed?" I-wan asked in a low voice. He remembered that before he went to see Chiang there his father had told him to look at this great new building and that one, and to see the fine new streets which had been made from the winding narrow streets of the ancient city. And they were beautiful. Everyone was proud to see them there.

"What is not ruined belongs to the enemy," his father said. Then he leaned forward and put his hands on his knees and whispered to I-wan, "But what sickens me and makes me afraid is not men dead and houses in ruins, but this—that on every street opium is for sale openly! They want to ruin those who are still alive, too."

And to I-wan's horror he saw tears come into his father's eyes and begin to roll down his cheeks, and his father did not wipe them away but he let them roll down. And I-wan could not bear to see it, and yet he did not know what to say, so he looked down and said nothing. . . . He had heard of this opium. Nothing else so angered En-lan as the opium they found ready for sale when they took back a town from the enemy.

"I weep for much," his father said at last, half in apology, and then he took the ends of his long sleeves and wiped his eyes, one and then the other. And then he said, pleadingly, "I-wan, can you

366

take a few days from your life and go with me to see the lands? Some day they will be yours and your sons'. I shall never live there, but it may be you will live there with your children."

Looking back upon this later, I-wan remembered that even then he thought it strange his father said nothing of I-ko, but only, "The lands will be yours."

"I should like to go," he said.

"It may be the only China left will be in these inner provinces," his father went on. "Who can tell? But something must come from what is happening to us—the people who have fled here from the lost coastal provinces—the schools moved here. Last week I gave my name to a loan of many thousands of dollars for an iron works to be moved from Hankow inland."

"Is Chiang not to defend Hankow?" he asked.

His father shook his head.

"Canton was abandoned yesterday. In a few days Hankow, too, will fall," he said. "Well, I hope Chiang is right—" His father sighed. "If he is not right, then we are lost indeed."

He sat silent for a moment, and I-wan wondered if it could be that he did not believe so perfectly as he had in Chiang? Canton gone, and then Hankow . . . ? And at that moment the door opened and there was Chiang Kai-shek's wife. They rose and she nodded a little to them and said in her quiet soft voice, "The Generalissimo is ready for you," and she led them across a room and into the room where Chiang sat.

He rose when they entered. I-wan had not seen him stand before. He looked taller now than he was, being straight and very thin. He did not speak and they sat down together and his wife felt of the teapot and then poured tea into their bowls. Everything she did was done with such a smoothness and grace that eyes could not but follow her to see the curve of her neck and the turn of her head and the swift accurate gestures of her hands. She looked at her husband and he looked at her and nodded, and then she went away and shut the door quietly.

Now they were alone with him and I-wan lifted his eyes to him to inquire of him what he wanted.

"I have sent for you for two reasons," Chiang Kai-shek said without any greeting or beginning. "The first reason is to tell you of the death of your elder brother."

This he said in an even strong voice and when he had said it, he waited a moment for I-wan to comprehend it. . . . He could not comprehend it, indeed. I-ko dead! He felt his blood leave his head and then rush back into it, burning hot. He looked at his father. But he was sitting there in his seat, his head drooped and his eyes looking downward.

"You knew this, Father?" he said in a thick voice.

His father nodded. "Yesterday," he whispered.

"You will want to know how he died," Chiang Kai-shek said abruptly. He took up a letter from the desk and gave it to I-wan. It was badly written upon a dirty piece of paper, and it was in penciled English. There was no name upon it but what it said was plain enough. It gave a list of names of men, five men, who had been seen in secret meeting with certain of the enemy. And I-ko's name was third.

I-wan looked up to Chiang's eyes again.

"But why should my brother—" he was not able to go beyond this.

"There was a plot," Chiang said harshly, and yet no more harshly than he said anything, "and the enemy promised your brother a high place in the government they will set up." He nodded toward the letter, which I-wan put back upon the desk before him. "I had that by messenger fourteen days ago. It was not the first news I had had. But I sent for this man who did not write his name here, but who gave it by mouth to the man who, on foot and by any way he could, came to me with it. I sent for him. When he came he said his name was Lim and that he knew you and your brother. He hated your brother for some cause or other." Chiang paused. "Well, I use men's hate." He paused again, and then went on. "This gave me proof that your brother was a traitor. I ordered him executed with the others."

These words I-wan listened to one by one, knowing the end while he listened, and fearing it, too. But he sat on, looking at Chiang's face.

"How could that—how could that—that man—" he began to stammer in a hoarse voice. It seemed horrible to him that Jackie Lim, to whom he had been kind, should be the one to spy out I-ko.

But Chiang said quickly, "Do not blame him. He is an honest man. But he is very simple. It made him angry to hear what was gossiped everywhere among the common soldiers, that some of their officers took bribes, and, being simple, when he heard it he examined into it and he was brave enough to report it to me direct. He has lived in America where, he said, men do not fear those who rule them."

"Where is he now?" I-wan demanded.

"I sent him back to fight," Chiang replied. "I don't know what became of him."

There was nothing then to be said. His father sat without moving. I-wan breathed one deep breath and straightened his shoulders. He tried not to see all the pictures of I-ko that his memory now brought before his eyes—I-ko playing with him in the garden when they were very small and he thought his elder brother beautiful and strong, I-ko willful at being denied something and flinging himself to the ground to weep and kick his legs, I-ko a handsome young man. . . . How did I-ko meet his death? Was he brave and silent, or was the spoiled child the real I-ko to the last? Impossible to know—he did not want to know.

369

"It was his foreign wife—I shall send her back to her own country," his father now said slowly. "It was she who was always making him despise his own people. From the very first moment she came, nothing was good enough for her. She did not like the food or the way we lived. Nothing we have was so good as what she had in her own country. And she laughed at our soldiers and she always said to I-ko that the Japanese were better, until he began to believe there was no use trying to fight them. So—I suppose"—his father's voice dropped—"he thought since Canton was doomed to fall, he might as well—" He looked up at Chiang haggardly. "I don't defend him," he said in a whisper.

Chiang had let him speak on, and while he spoke his grave face took on a sort of stern kindness. Now he said, "We have understood each other."

I-wan saw his father nod. And at that moment he knew he loved his father as he never had before. . . .

"Go out now," Chiang was saying to his father. "Rest yourself a little while. I want to talk to your son."

His father rose and bowed, and they waited while he went out. Then when they were alone suddenly Chiang changed. All the mildness in his face was gone. He turned on I-wan his full stern black gaze.

"You I have used," he said. "I had planned to use you again." He paused. "But you are married to a Japanese," he added sharply.

I-wan jumped a little in spite of himself. This man knew everything. But he was ready.

"Yes, I am," he answered.

"If you are your father's son, you are also brother to a traitor," Chiang said. His voice was harsh enough now and there was not a hint of kindness in his face. "How do I know what you are?"

"There is no way for me to tell you," I-wan retorted. He could be afraid of this man, but he would not be.

"Will you give up your Japanese wife?" Chiang demanded.

"At your command?" I-wan asked.

Chiang did not answer, but he did not move his eyes from I-wan's face.

"No," I-wan said quietly. And then after a moment he said, "I left my wife and my children to come back and fight. I am fighting. When peace comes, I shall bring them here. My sons are Chinese. And—she—their mother—is loyal to me."

"It will be a long time before peace comes," Chiang said.

"I know that," I-wan said.

"This city will be in ruins, too," Chiang said. He looked about the room and then out of the window, where roof touched roof in the crowded city. "This city and many others, perhaps. When peace comes there may be no cities left."

"There will be land," I-wan replied. . . . Now he understood why his father had said, 'The lands will be yours and your sons'."

"Yes, there will be land," Chiang repeated. And then with one of those vivid changes which I-wan had now learned to expect of him, he said, "What sort of woman is your wife?"

For answer I-wan took from his pocket Tama's last two letters, which he had not destroyed because they had come just before he left and he wanted to read them again. He opened them and spread them before Chiang.

They were simple letters, written in Tama's fine clear handwriting. She had not returned to her father's house because when I-wan was gone she found she could not. So now these letters were full of small things such as how a certain tree had grown in the garden and how the chrysanthemums they had planted together were in bloom again and how a storm from the sea had torn the paper in the lattice to the west, and she and Jiro had mended it, and how big the boys grew and how she told them their father was a hero and that he fought for his country, which was theirs

371

too, and that he must think of them as waiting for the future when they would all be united again. They were, indeed, nothing but the letters which any wife would write to her husband whom she loved and who was at the front in any war.

He watched Chiang's face while he read them. But he could tell nothing from it, and he waited while Chiang folded the letters and put them into the envelopes, slowly as though he were thinking of something. Then he handed them back to I-wan.

"And now—is there anything you wish?" he demanded.

"Only to have a few days with my father," I-wan replied quickly. "We will visit our ancestral lands together, which we have never seen."

"And then?" Chiang demanded again.

"To return to my place in the army," I-wan replied.

"Granted!" Chiang exclaimed. He turned away and struck the bell on his desk and the door opened and his wife came in and I-wan knew himself dismissed. He rose and bowed, but Chiang was not looking at him.

"Where is that map of the new road to Burma?" he was asking her as though she had not been away from him. "I had my hand on it a moment ago."

"Here it is," she said, laughing at him a little, "here under your hand!"

And I-wan went out with these words in his ears. The new road to Burma! Was that finished already? He had heard it was being made—thousands of men and women were making it. Well, it was a strange way to fight a war, perhaps, to make a great road westward while the enemy bombed the east! But it was their way. What if the real country his sons would know was this new inner China, looking not seaward but across the mountains to India? Who knew? But who knew anything?

And he went to find his father.